# Tempted

# Also From Lexi Blake

ROMANTIC SUSPENSE

**Masters and Mercenaries**
The Dom Who Loved Me
The Men With The Golden Cuffs
A Dom is Forever
On Her Master's Secret Service
Sanctum: A Masters and Mercenaries Novella
Love and Let Die
Unconditional: A Masters and Mercenaries Novella
Dungeon Royale
Dungeon Games: A Masters and Mercenaries Novella
A View to a Thrill
Cherished: A Masters and Mercenaries Novella
You Only Love Twice
Luscious: Masters and Mercenaries~Topped
Adored: A Masters and Mercenaries Novella
Master No
Just One Taste: Masters and Mercenaries~Topped 2
From Sanctum with Love
Devoted: A Masters and Mercenaries Novella
Dominance Never Dies
Submission is Not Enough
Master Bits and Mercenary Bites~The Secret Recipes of Topped
Perfectly Paired: Masters and Mercenaries~Topped 3
For His Eyes Only
Arranged: A Masters and Mercenaries Novella
Love Another Day
At Your Service: Masters and Mercenaries~Topped 4
Master Bits and Mercenary Bites~Girls Night
Nobody Does It Better
Close Cover
Protected: A Masters and Mercenaries Novella
Enchanted: A Masters and Mercenaries Novella
Charmed: A Masters and Mercenaries Novella
Treasured: A Masters and Mercenaries Novella

Delighted: A Masters and Mercenaries Novella
Tempted: A Masters and Mercenaries Novella

### Masters and Mercenaries: The Forgotten
Lost Hearts (Memento Mori)
Lost and Found
Lost in You
Long Lost
No Love Lost

### Masters and Mercenaries: Reloaded
Submission Impossible
The Dom Identity
The Man from Sanctum
No Time to Lie
The Dom Who Came in from the Cold

### Masters and Mercenaries: New Recruits
Love the Way You Spy, Coming September 19, 2023

### Park Avenue Promise
Start Us Up, Coming August 8, 2023

### Butterfly Bayou
Butterfly Bayou
Bayou Baby
Bayou Dreaming
Bayou Beauty
Bayou Sweetheart
Bayou Beloved

### Lawless
Ruthless
Satisfaction
Revenge

### Courting Justice
Order of Protection
Evidence of Desire

**Masters Of Ménage** (by Shayla Black and Lexi Blake)
Their Virgin Captive
Their Virgin's Secret
Their Virgin Concubine
Their Virgin Princess
Their Virgin Hostage
Their Virgin Secretary
Their Virgin Mistress

**The Perfect Gentlemen** (by Shayla Black and Lexi Blake)
Scandal Never Sleeps
Seduction in Session
Big Easy Temptation
Smoke and Sin
At the Pleasure of the President

URBAN FANTASY

**Thieves**
Steal the Light
Steal the Day
Steal the Moon
Steal the Sun
Steal the Night
Ripper
Addict
Sleeper
Outcast
Stealing Summer
The Rebel Queen
The Rebel Guardian

LEXI BLAKE WRITING AS SOPHIE OAK

**Texas Sirens**
Small Town Siren
Siren in the City
Siren Enslaved

Siren Beloved
Siren in Waiting
Siren in Bloom
Siren Unleashed
Siren Reborn

**Nights in Bliss, Colorado**
Three to Ride
Two to Love
One to Keep
Lost in Bliss
Found in Bliss
Pure Bliss
Chasing Bliss
Once Upon a Time in Bliss
Back in Bliss
Sirens in Bliss
Happily Ever After in Bliss
Far from Bliss
Unexpected Bliss

**A Faery Story**
Bound
Beast
Beauty

**Standalone**
Away From Me
Snowed In

# Tempted
A Masters and Mercenaries Novella
## By Lexi Blake

1001 DARK NIGHTS
PRESS

Tempted
A Masters and Mercenaries Novella
By Lexi Blake

1001 Dark Nights

Copyright 2023 DLZ Entertainment, LLC
ISBN: 979-8-88542-019-8

Masters and Mercenaries ® is registered in the U.S. Patent and Trademark Office.

Foreword: Copyright 2014 M. J. Rose

Published by 1001 Dark Nights Press, an imprint of Evil Eye Concepts, Incorporated

All rights reserved. No part of this book may be reproduced, scanned, or distributed in any printed or electronic form without permission. Please do not participate in or encourage piracy of copyrighted materials in violation of the author's rights.

This is a work of fiction. Names, places, characters and incidents are the product of the author's imagination and are fictitious. Any resemblance to actual persons, living or dead, events or establishments is solely coincidental.

# Acknowledgments from the Author

Thanks to the amazing team at Evil Eye Concepts. I was in the first group of 1001 Dark Nights authors and have been thrilled to see the company grow. Here's to many more years of amazing books!

# One Thousand and One Dark Nights

*Once upon a time, in the future…*

*I was a student fascinated with stories and learning. I studied philosophy, poetry, history, the occult, and the art and science of love and magic. I had a vast library at my father's home and collected thousands of volumes of fantastic tales.*

*I learned all about ancient races and bygone times. About myths and legends and dreams of all people through the millennium. And the more I read the stronger my imagination grew until I discovered that I was able to travel into the stories... to actually become part of them.*

*I wish I could say that I listened to my teacher and respected my gift, as I ought to have. If I had, I would not be telling you this tale now. But I was foolhardy and confused, showing off with bravery.*

*One afternoon, curious about the myth of the Arabian Nights, I traveled back to ancient Persia to see for myself if it was true that every day Shahryar (Persian: شهریار, "king") married a new virgin, and then sent yesterday's wife to be beheaded. It was written and I had read that by the time he met Scheherazade, the vizier's daughter, he'd killed one thousand women.*

*Something went wrong with my efforts. I arrived in the midst of the story and somehow exchanged places with Scheherazade – a phenomena that had never occurred before and that still to this day, I cannot explain.*

*Now I am trapped in that ancient past. I have taken on Scheherazade's life and the only way I can protect myself and stay alive is to do what she did to protect herself and stay alive.*

*Every night the King calls for me and listens as I spin tales. And when the evening ends and dawn breaks, I stop at a point that leaves him breathless and yearning for more. And so the King spares my life for one more day, so that he might hear the rest of my dark tale.*

*As soon as I finish a story... I begin a new one... like the one that you, dear reader, have before you now.*

# Prologue

Ally Pearson looked over the glittering lights of Los Angeles and wondered how long it would be before she saw this view again. She loved her Los Feliz home on the hillside. When the realtor had brought her here, she'd known in an instant she would buy it. It wasn't nearly as luxurious as her parents' place in Santa Monica. That was a mansion. This was a really nice house, but it felt like home. When she'd stepped over the threshold, it had felt like a new beginning.

It had felt like she was leaving the past behind and concentrating on her real work, her real self.

The past, it seemed, wasn't finished with her.

"Hey. I brought you some tea." Her mother stepped onto the terrace. It was attached to the primary bedroom and overlooked the pool and the hillside.

Some mornings she sat out here and drank coffee and thought about how good it was to have a safe place.

It wasn't safe anymore.

She took the tea from her mom. "Thanks."

Her mother was silent for a moment. It was how Ally knew she was steeling herself for a talk. They always cut those long moments out of the reality TV show they'd starred in for years. When her mom had one of her mom talks with her, they would cut away from that long moment before she began. The producers wanted her to look more assertive, but there was something intimate about that moment. Her mom rarely had a filter. She said what was on her mind and didn't care what anyone thought. Except when she paused like this, Ally knew it was serious. Whatever her mother said next meant something.

She was glad they did those cutaways because this moment was meant for her and her sister and her stepdad. Not for the fans of *Match Made in*

*Hollywood*. She'd loved the show and sharing it with her mom and stepdad, but it had been a relief to shut down the day-to-day production. She'd bought this place when she'd moved out of their mansion in Gillette Regent Square. Los Feliz had been her new start, and she loved it because it was full of accomplished people and up-and-comers. She fit in here better than her parents' old-money neighborhood.

But she had the feeling she wasn't staying here for long.

"Your stepfather and I have been talking," her mom began. "Sweetheart, this can't go on. Do you know what could have happened tonight?"

She took a deep breath and then turned her mother's way. "I think murder could have happened. At least that's what the cops think. Maybe if the guy had cut my head off they would do something about him."

She strode back into the bedroom, stubborn will settling in even though she knew she would give in eventually. But damn it, she should be safe in her own home.

Her mom walked right behind. "Don't talk like that. Allyson, this is the third time we know that he's been close to you physically. It's one thing to troll you on social media. It's another thing to follow you to events. This is getting serious. He's escalating."

Ally kept walking because if she didn't involve her stepdad, she would have to have this talk twice, and she didn't want to. "I'll get a dog. I'll get a big mean dog who loves me and no one else, and if this guy shows up again, puppy will eat him and I'll bury the bones in the garden."

She made it to her kitchen, which rarely was used to do more than heat up the meals she had delivered once a week.

"A dog is not going to solve the problem." There was her stepdad. Gavin Jacks had been a journeyman actor for forty years. At sixty, he could still play leading men with actresses in their twenties. Ally's contemporaries.

It was gross, and she was happy when he'd told his agent he wouldn't act in any production where his character's romantic partner was younger than forty.

"I put in the security system. I'm careful about coming and going. I have a gun, and I know how to use it." She kind of wished her stalker had still been in the house when she'd come home. Then the problem might be over.

"You need round-the-clock security," her stepdad said gravely. He was more casual than normal, but that was probably because he'd been pulled out of bed at one in the morning when the cops called him.

He had friends in the LAPD because he'd played law enforcement characters so often. Those friends did not care about her privacy. She could have handled the situation, but no, her parents had come flying in to save the day.

Could she handle the situation? Damn, but she was tired.

When she'd seen what he'd done to her living room, she'd stood there for a moment, and it hadn't been fear that had risen up inside her. It hadn't been anger at her safe place being violated.

It had been genuine confusion. She'd stood there and looked at the dead birds he'd lain out on her living room floor like some offering and wondered what she'd done to deserve this. All she'd ever wanted was to do what she loved and make a living. She'd wanted to entertain people.

She'd wondered where he'd gotten the birds from and if they'd suffered and why he'd needed to use them to spell out the word *WHORE* on her coffee table. She'd wondered why he couldn't have sent her a note instead.

All those poor birds dead because one man hated her.

A man who didn't even know her.

Then she'd heard a car screeching down the street and realized it was probably him, and that was when the anger hit.

"He got around the security system," her stepdad pointed out. "I don't know how, but I'm going to find out. I'm hiring a security team to go over everything. Until then, your mother and I think you should spend the week with us in Santa Monica, and you should think about pulling out of the project you start next Monday."

Oh, that was not happening. "Absolutely not. Do you have any idea how hard I had to fight for this chance? I've starred in every rom com that's come my way because I've tried to build some kind of a box office record that erases my reality star past."

"That show is the reason you have this house." Her mother always got defensive about the show. Probably because it had been her idea. She was a momager of the highest order and had been since Ally's sister starred in her first commercial as a kid.

Her sister, Brynn, was out of the business, but this was Ally's dream. "I know. I wouldn't take it back, Mom. It opened a lot of doors for me, but it's closed some, too. This is a great part. It's a dramatic part, and with a director who has three Oscars under his belt. I'm not walking away because some asshole left dead birds all over the place. Besides, it takes me out of LA for three whole months."

"I think he followed you to New York," her stepdad reminded her.

"That was a press tour. I'll be on set most of the time." She'd been dreading the three months on set in Dallas where she knew no one and would likely be an outsider in the cast, but now it seemed like a haven.

And she would show all those snobs that she had talent, too.

"And when you're not?" her mother asked. "When you're in a hotel room alone at night?"

"I won't be alone. I'll call Greg." Greg had been her driver for the last couple of years. She'd met him in small-town Louisiana where he'd started his own golf cart limo business he called Guber. She was his only client, and her being driven around LA in a tricked-out golf cart had been one of the fans' favorite things about the show.

"His daughter had a baby," her mom reminded her. "That's why he moved back in the first place."

Tears pierced her eyes. She hated crying, hated how open and vulnerable it felt. "I worked so hard for this part."

Her mom hugged her. "I know, baby. I know."

"How do I just give it up?"

Her stepfather sighed. "You don't. You'll come to Santa Monica with us tonight. I'm hiring the security firm my friend Jared and his wife recommended. McKay something. I have a conference call with the owners in the morning. As luck would have it, they're based in Dallas and also offer personal security."

A deep sense of relief spilled over her. This didn't have to be over. "A bodyguard?"

"I know you said you didn't want…" her mother began.

She shook her head. She knew when being stubborn had crossed the line into too stupid to live. "I'll take it. I'll be a good girl and do whatever the bodyguard says."

Her mother frowned. "No, you won't."

She probably wouldn't. She was something of a free spirit. "How about I'll tone it down and try to follow the rules."

"You do that," her father said. "Now get some clothes, and we'll try to have all of this sorted out by the time you finish the shoot and come home."

Ally set the tea down, feeling better than she had before.

This would all work out. They would figure out who was trying to scare her, and she would hang with her bodyguard in Dallas. Her parents would be happy she was being watched over. Yes, it would work out for everyone.

Except the birds…

\* \* \* \*

West Rycroft looked down at the file on his desk and then up at his brother because he had to be kidding. "No."

Wade Rycroft rolled dark eyes and sat back in his chair. He occupied the only actual office on this floor, the one the rest of the company called the "Man Cave," despite the fact that there were several women who worked as bodyguards, too. Beyond being his brother, Wade was also his boss. "Is there any particular reason you're telling me no to this assignment?"

"Come on, man. I just came off entitled-princess duty." He'd glanced through the file on his potential client, and it hadn't taken long to determine what kind of gig this would be. "I had to spend three weeks with an actual princess, and I now know why the French Revolution happened. I am one peasant who is sick of putting up with their shit."

Princess Amelia of the small European country whose name he'd already forgotten had been the worst. She'd tried to ditch him three times. He'd caught her with a pharmacy of drugs she didn't need. And she liked to shoplift. He'd had enough of celebrities to last a lifetime.

And she'd treated him like he was her beck-and-call boy. He'd had to firmly explain to her that servicing her sexual needs wasn't part of his job. She'd had eight hands, that one.

"You do know that you're a personal bodyguard, right?" His brother was looking at him like he was the biggest dumbass in the world. "You signed up for this gig. *Please, Wade, I don't want to punch cows for the rest of my life. I want to see the world.* Well, this is seeing the world, buddy. I'm sorry we don't have a bunch of blue-collar workers who need bodyguard services. We're kind of stuck with the wealthy and famous."

That was where his brother was wrong. He actually liked his job. It was simply one class of clientele he had a problem with. "I don't mind businesspeople. I can handle most of them. There was that writer fellow. He was nice. He only got mean when someone tried to tell him lingonberries were the same as cranberries. He was serious about his juice. I could work for him again. I learned a whole bunch about history."

But Ally Pearson would be a handful, and he needed some peace in his life. Three months of following after one of the most overprivileged and undertalented people in Hollywood was too much to bear.

Ally Pearson had been handed everything in life. Beauty, fame, money, a place in society.

It was a long assignment and would keep him away from his friends and brothers. The idea of giving up so much time for a woman who would treat him like a servant at best held little appeal.

Besides, he'd been starting to wonder if there wasn't something else out there for him. He'd had specific goals when he'd joined McKay-Taggart, and he'd reached them.

He was getting restless again.

"I'm afraid Ms. Pearson is the client we have," Wade replied. "If you actually read her folder, you would know she needs a bodyguard. She's got an active threat to her life."

He'd seen her show a couple of times. He'd had a girlfriend back in Broken Bend who'd been obsessed with *Match Made in Hollywood*. She'd even tried to dress like Ally Pearson and had ridden around in a golf cart stolen from the country club like a jackass. "Given how annoying she is, it doesn't surprise me."

"Fine." Wade frowned at him. "If you're going into the job and you don't care if the client lives or dies, you're not the man for this."

He sighed. "I didn't say that. I said I don't want to deal with another Princess Amelia with the octopus hands. She's not the only one. I hate it when the client is awful to the people around them. They act like the rest of the world is nothing but staff, and the staff is so far beneath them they aren't human."

"I get it." His brother's expression had turned sympathetic. "We all want to be treated with some dignity. If you'd told me about the princess, I would have reassigned you. I would have put Tessa on her, and if she comes back, that's what I'll do. No one at this company wants to set you up for sexual harassment."

He shrugged. "I didn't want to complain."

"But you complain so well and so often," his brother countered, a ghost of a smile on his face. "Come on, West. This isn't a terrible assignment. She'll probably ignore you most of the time. She's here to work. She's going to be rehearsing for a week or two, and then they're shooting around the city. I think they've got a lot of time in a studio here, too. You can sit there and read or play on your tablet when she's working. You would be her twenty-four seven guard for most of the week, and I'll rotate in two other guards to make sure you have time off. If that's too much, I'll think about splitting it further."

Whoa. Twenty-four seven for three months? It was insane because none of the married agents could do it. Most of the singles wouldn't want the assignment either. He would get maybe two days a week off, and he would be on all the rest of the time. "How much?"

McKay-Taggart paid overtime for anything beyond forty hours, and they also had hefty per diems.

A brow rose over his brother's eyes. "You really didn't read it?"

He had to explain this away because now he saw the upside. "Look, you remember when I was going out with Rhonda?"

"The one who kept trying to get you to propose and take her away to the big city?" Wade snorted slightly. "She thought the big city was Harlingen."

"Oh, she wanted to move to LA so she could be like her girl crush." West pointed to the folder. "Ally Pearson. Have you ever had to watch that show? It's mind-numbingly boring, and those people are so full of themselves. All they do is party and spend money like it's water. I had this whole family thrown at me for a year and a half."

"You could have walked away," Wade pointed out.

He didn't understand how hard the dating scene was in Broken Bend. There wasn't a lot to do but work and hang out. "I liked her otherwise. But that show put all kinds of notions in her head. She wanted to be an actress, thought I was holding her back when I didn't support her dreams. It got to be too much."

"I find it ironic that you're here in Dallas while she's back in Broken Bend," Wade pointed out.

"She went to LA for a while. She came back with an infant and not much else." It was a sad story because it was one that happened a lot to people in Broken Bend. "She's living with her momma again and working at the diner."

Where she would probably be for the rest of her life.

"You do know that's not Ally Pearson's fault, right?" Wade asked. "She didn't make Rhonda's choices for her. She's an actress playing a part."

The part was her life. Reality TV blurred a lot of lines, but he did believe in personal responsibility. "I just wished Rhonda had been obsessed with someone else."

"Well, now someone else *is* obsessed with Ally Pearson, and not in a fangirl way." Wade tapped the folder. "Read it if you want to consider the assignment because she has a serious stalker. And the job estimate is over a hundred thousand. Her parents are paying the bill. Your part of that would easily be fifty K."

Fifty thousand dollars. Between that and what he had saved up, he could get his own place. It was past time for him to move out of the condo he and his twin had bought when they'd come to Dallas. "All right. I'll do it."

It was probably a mistake, but it would be a mistake that paid.

# Chapter One

"Ms. Pearson, am I boring you?"

She forced herself to look up from her phone and directly at the big guy who seemed to be the boss of this particular company. He was big and broad and totally gorgeous. "Oh, yes."

The hot guy at the end of the table snorted and started to laugh but quickly covered it up when the hot dude beside him sent him a death stare. It was a good death stare, as those went. She believed it.

They looked a little like brothers. Brothers or really close friends, though one of them seemed significantly older, so she was betting on a familial relationship.

A brow rose over the big boss's icy eyes. "Well, don't let me keep you then."

"So you don't need me?" She stood up. If she could go, there were a million things to do before the table read.

"Allyson, sit down." Her stepdad had flown out with her and seemed determined that she take things seriously, hence she was at McKay-Taggart sitting in a conference room going over things she'd already lived through.

She sighed and sat back. "Fine, but I already know all these things. And everyone has a folder about the case. You know this is the part of the movie I never understand. The scene is obviously only there to inform the audience about the facts of the case. Wouldn't a smart writer find another way?"

"I don't know the facts." The ridiculously hot guy at the end of the table held up a hand. He had sandy blonde hair and all-American good looks. His accent was slightly twangier than the rest of the people in the room. She would bet he hadn't grown up here in Dallas. Most of the people she met from Texas cities had light accents. "I mean, I know some of them."

"That's great, West." Sarcasm dripped from the big hot guy's mouth. "Since she's your client."

That was interesting. The minute she'd entered the conference room, she'd noticed the guy at the end of the table. He was big, too, though not as massive as the truly scary dude. Lucky for her, she'd learned how to handle scary dudes. You ignored their scariness and plowed right through.

"Sweetie, this is not a movie," her stepdad pointed out. "They need to be able to ask you questions, and that means going over the case with you."

"But they have the reports." She wasn't sure why she would have to go over it again. She mostly wanted to forget those episodes of her life.

"Sometimes there's more nuance to a situation than what shows up in a report." The big guy's wife was gorgeous, and she seemed to be something of a fan.

The morning had started okay. She'd been greeted by a bevy of women. Charlotte Taggart had introduced her friends as Genny Rycroft and Yasmin Tahan. She'd signed some autographs and answered some of their questions. They seemed to be the kind of fans who understood that reality TV wasn't a hundred percent real. Charlotte had offered her some truly excellent coffee, and they'd all talked while they waited for the exposition…conference thingy to start.

She liked those women. They were cool. And there was a teenaged girl hanging around who looked like she wanted to murder someone. Ally already liked her.

"I think I can get what I need from the reports," the hot bodyguard guy said. He was seriously gorgeous and had a smile that lit up a room. There was no smile on his face now, though. "I doubt she'll add anything to the discussion."

Oh, he was not a fan. She wasn't sure if it was because he knew who she was or he simply didn't enjoy the company of fun, charming, successful women. It could be either.

"I have questions, and I have procedures," the big boss explained. "If you don't want to follow them…"

He let the threat dangle, and Ally sat up a little. Now she was interested because this dude knew how to make a few regular words into a threat that had everyone at the table straightening their shoulders like they were soldiers and the general wasn't happy. Even her stepdad. This dude had some serious mojo, and she could work with that.

She'd played an ex-military character before. She'd done training with a group of soldiers who took her through an abbreviated BUD/S program. It wasn't like the infamous *Saving Private Ryan* training, but she'd done her time in the field. She'd eaten MREs and learned how to survive in a forest and the desert.

Mr. Taggart could be excellent inspiration if she ever had to do it again. Not that the character had to be military. She could use it for Delia Crowne. She had a monologue that she knew the director wanted her to shout her way through, but now she wondered if she shouldn't go quiet. It might be far more impactful.

"I'm sorry, sir," Hot Guy Who Didn't Like Her said. "I only got the assignment last night. I'm happy to be brought up to speed."

"Ms. Pearson, this is West Rycroft." Taggart sat back, using the pen he held in his hand to point West's way. "He's going to be your main bodyguard and will be coordinating all of your security. You'll spend most of your time with him, but he'll have two other guards who fill in when he needs time off or if he thinks you need more than one set of eyes."

Oh, wouldn't her life be easier if she only had one set of eyes on her.

Nope. She wasn't pulling the poor little rich and famous girl routine. She was not falling into that trap. Her life was good, and she was working to make it even better, and she wasn't going to apologize or whine and cry about it. "Excellent. I promise I'm here in Dallas to work. I'll film for ten to twelve hours a day, and I'll be in my trailer most of the rest of the time. I have a couple of social events, but they aren't high risk."

"Social events?" West had picked up his pen and looked down at the blank legal pad in front of him, but not before she'd caught that hint of disdain in his eyes.

She was so sick of men. They came in two types, it seemed—the ones who thought she was a sex toy to be passed around and the ones who decided she was an airhead with no thoughts in her head past her next shopping trip. She twirled her hair in one hand and gave her best blank look. "You know. Parties. Chilling with some of the hot people here in Dallas. Gotta get in my socials, you know."

Charlotte Taggart's gaze narrowed, and she could practically hear the woman calling bullshit, but West simply put his pen down.

"You'll have to run anyone you're…chilling…with by me," he said, clearly taking on the disapproving authority role.

"She's not going to be partying." Her stepfather sent her a death stare of his own. "Believe it or not, she's not a partier."

"I just play one on TV," she quipped.

"I think you'll find the social events she has scheduled are all charity gatherings." Her stepdad pulled out his phone. Unlike a lot of the older people she knew, her stepdad was a whiz with tech. Gavin Jacks wasn't letting the world pass him by. "I sent your boss her schedule for while she's here. She's resisted getting a personal assistant, or her assistant could help you. Ally won't tell you this, but when things get hard for her during this shoot, take her someplace out in nature when she has a day off. She looks like a city girl, but she enjoys hiking and being by herself. This is going to be hard on her. She's used to a lot of alone time."

"Not according to her actual socials she's not," West argued. "Look, Mr. Jacks, I am a huge fan of yours, and I respect the fact that Ms. Pearson is your stepdaughter, but you need to understand that I'm her bodyguard, not her nanny. I do not need feed and caring instructions."

"Damn straight." It was good to see someone stand up to her stepdad. He was good to her mom and had always watched out for them, but he was also a leading man in Hollywood, so he could play the massive dick card when he wanted to.

Her stepdad frowned her way. "You are not helping."

"How about we discuss the reasons why Ally needs security?" Charlotte seemed determined to turn this whole thing around.

Exposition it was then. "A couple of years ago, I picked up a stalker."

"Since the beginning of her career, she's picked up four of what I would call credible threats," her stepdad interjected. "Everyone who works in show business at our level has to deal with overzealous fans. These four went beyond that."

"We disagree on that," she countered, not wanting to overestimate the threat. "One of them was a mom who lost her daughter, and I look like her. She fixated on me. That was all."

"She found your house," her stepdad argued.

They weren't going to have this fight in front of people they didn't know. "And I handled her. The other two the police caught, and they haven't bothered me again. That we know. Honestly, it could be one of those two men."

"I'm sorry. The math isn't adding up." West had a pen in his hand again, so she figured she was talking about something he was actually interested in now. "You said four stalkers?"

"Mrs. Jackson wasn't a stalker. She was a woman dealing with grief, and she's getting help." She wasn't going to tell them that she personally was paying for the woman's therapy. "Brian Hudson is in jail. Not for breaking into my place. He attacked a model."

"Yes, and you were lucky it wasn't you," her stepdad said.

She ignored him. Nagging was one of his love languages, which was great because it was her mom's primary language. "The other known stalker is a man who goes by JK Harris. He was a set designer, but he hasn't worked in the last two years. I met him on a set a few years ago. It was my second film."

"*Ready for Love?*" Charlotte asked.

It was nice to have one person in the room who liked her. "Yeah. I was the gloomy best friend. It was actually a fun part. Anyway, I talked to the guy. When you're on set, unless you're some kind of huge star or some assholey method actor, you end up spending a lot of time with the crew. You get to be friends. Well, JK took it too far. He got drunk at one of the crew parties and got super handsy. I called him out, and he got fired. So I became the bitch who ruined his career."

"Of course." Charlotte's eyes rolled. "I've heard that accusation a couple of times myself."

"Oh, baby, you did not. You never ruined a career. You blew heads off." Taggart winked his wife's way. "No one complains after that. Have you thought about doing that, Ms. Pearson?"

Oh, they were a fun couple, and she wanted that story. "Every day. Did you do it up close or from a distance?"

Charlotte's elegant shoulder shrugged. "It all depended on the job. I will tell you it's far less messy from a distance."

"Do we know where this JK Harris is? Also, who is the fourth stalker?" West seemed excellent at ignoring his elders, too.

"He disappeared a while back," she admitted. "And that's where things get interesting. The police think Harris is the one causing trouble, but I don't think so. Harris's letters were all full of threats, and he sent them through the mail. He liked to stand outside red-carpet events shouting about what a whore I was until he was escorted off the grounds. He didn't send elaborate, horrifying art projects."

"He could be escalating," West offered.

"Or he could be someone new, hence the fourth stalker, who might or might not exist." It was what she was afraid of. Like she needed another person who wanted to take her down a peg, who blamed her for their problems.

"West, if you were running the investigation portion of this case, where would you go from here?" Taggart asked. "You're not, of course. Think of this as an academic exercise."

Oh, she knew a teaching hospital when she saw one. Was she getting the newbie? That could be fun.

"I would ask Eve McKay for her opinion," West replied. "I would request that Eve study the case reports and give me her thoughts on whether this is the same JK Harris or if she thinks we're looking for another person."

"Unsub." See, this part was interesting. Or it would be if it also wasn't horrifying because she was living through it. There was a reason she preferred fiction to real life. "We're looking for an unsub. I once got through four rounds of auditions to play an FBI special agent who hunted serial killers. I did a ton of research and even wore a boring suit and everything, but they went with the brunette."

"I told you to dye your hair," her stepdad said.

He'd been right about that. Apparently, blondes made better victims than feds, according to the completely dickish casting director who'd offered to let her play a dead body. Naked, of course.

"Excellent. That is exactly what I'm going to do." Taggart pushed back and stood, straightening up that big muscular body of his. "I'll leave you and West alone to work out your schedule. As for the investigation, I'll be the lead on that."

"I appreciate you taking care of this personally, Mr. Taggart." Her stepdad stood.

"Jared is a friend of the family," the big boss replied, shaking his hand. "Why don't we go to my office and settle up the accounts? You're not staying in town, right?"

"No. I have to get back to LA. I start my own shoot in a couple of days," her stepdad said as they started out of the conference room.

The last man standing was the one she was almost certain was West's brother. Or cousin. Or stunt double. "Can you handle this on your own or should I stay to referee?"

West gave him a steady smile that held only the slightest hint of dismay. "We'll be fine."

She was glad one of them was optimistic.

\* \* \* \*

She was pretty much every bit as bad as he'd imagined. Ally Pearson was bratty and privileged and didn't care one bit about anyone but herself. He wasn't buying the whole "she's a sensitive soul and needs nature time." Parents could have rose-colored glasses on when it came to their kids. She was snobby and generally everything he tried to stay away from.

But damn she was pretty. He'd seen pictures of her with all different colors of hair. She seemed to change the color as often as the wind blew, but the warm brown she had now seemed to suit her spectacularly. It caressed her shoulders in waves that framed her face. She'd walked in wearing sunglasses that probably cost more than he made in a week and deceptively plain jeans and a T-shirt. On most other women they would be everyday, ordinary clothes, but somehow her graceful curves transformed them into something deeply sexy. When she'd taken off the sunglasses, he'd been struck by how pretty her eyes were. They almost matched her hair color.

Pretty much everything physical about the woman called to him, but then it was probably that way with every man she met.

The good news was he wasn't led around by his dick. He'd grown past his "girl pretty, follow her" phase of life. It wasn't that he didn't want to find a woman to spend time with. It was just that he was of an age where he wanted to spend long periods of times with a woman. Like the rest of his life. He wasn't about to dick around with some Hollywood hot chick who couldn't be bothered to remember how many stalkers she had.

"So was that like your brother or something?" Her eyes were on the door Wade had walked through.

He was going to stop that in its tracks. "Yes, he's my brother, and he's also married. Happily married with a kid."

Her eyes went wide. "Why would… Oh, if I asked about him I must be interested in him sexually. We're going to go right there, are we? No fucking around."

He wasn't going to go into her reputation as a maneater. All it had taken was a quick Internet search to figure out she'd been linked to most of the men in young Hollywood at one point or another. And a couple of her married directors. Well, those had been rumors, but most rumors had a hint of truth. "Just putting the truth out there. Wade is my brother, and he's married to Ian's admin."

"He's Genny's husband?" Her nose wrinkled. "He doesn't have an ex-military look. If I had to guess, I would say he grew up on a ranch. He has small town turned big city vibes. And I would bet they were high school sweethearts but something went wrong and they didn't reconnect until they were older. I got that because when she references her son, she refers to her husband as Wade, but when she talks about her daughter, he's Dad."

That was a fairly dead-on representation of Wade and Genny's love relationship.

She flushed a little, giving her cheeks a pretty pink color. "Sorry. I'm nosy, but it's because I study people. Especially the interesting ones. This office is filled with them. When I meet someone interesting, I try to figure them out. It's kind of my job."

"I thought your job was letting cameras follow you around while you shop." At least that was what he'd gotten from the research he'd done.

He watched as any relaxation in her body fled, and she shifted into a brittle stance. "You've made it plain how you feel about me. Now could you please go over the schedule? Or do you think that will be too much for my womanly brain?"

That wasn't fair. "I did not say that."

"No?" She looked at him, her head cocked slightly in a challenging way. "Okay, so you're not a misogynist. It's just me you hate."

She would try to make this dramatic. He needed to remember that she was the client. Or rather her stepdad was. No matter how distasteful he found her, he had to be professional, and up until now he hadn't been. "I'm sorry I gave you that impression."

"Because you would rather keep that impression to yourself?"

"I would rather we have a professional relationship."

"Well, Mr. Rycroft, I'm not the one insulting the other part of this professional relationship, so if that's what you want, you'll have to find a way to make it work. Why don't you give me the schedule and then I think you'll find we don't have to talk. I like my bodyguards like I like my men. Pretty and silent."

Oh, she wanted to play that way? West started to open his mouth and stopped. Hadn't he started this nasty little bit of conversation? She'd asked about his brother, and he'd gone to the worst possible place. If he wanted a respectful relationship with her, he should probably try to start over. He'd promised his brother there wouldn't be trouble, and here he was causing it ten minutes into getting into a room with her. "I'm sorry I wasn't respectful, ma'am."

She snorted. "Ma'am? I'm younger than you, and I don't give a shit about respectful. Respect is something you earn, and you don't know me. What you weren't was kind, and that does mean something to me.

However, I'm not going to be picky about it. It's either you or some asshole who thinks he can hit on me and have a story to tell his friends. At least you're the kind of guy who obviously keeps his hands perfectly to himself around whores."

He didn't like the flush of shame that went through him. He hadn't been nice, but he certainly hadn't called her names. "And I didn't say that either."

"No?" She stood up, settling her designer bag over her shoulder. "You assumed because I asked about your brother that I wanted to hit on him. You want to know something sad? The only guy here I thought was my type was you. And then you fixed the problem by opening your mouth. So we're all good. Anything else we need to discuss? Otherwise I need to go find my stepdad."

He should have known this was going to happen. The minute she figured out he wasn't going to fall all over her, he became useless. He should have played this another way. "So you can get him to fire me?"

She stopped, frowning his way. "Why would I do that?"

He was confused. And he had to stop himself from getting to his feet and into her space. "I think it's clear you don't find me acceptable."

"Are you talking about that fight we just had?"

"I wouldn't call it a fight." He needed to lower the temperature in the room. "I would call it a misunderstanding."

"I didn't misunderstand, West. You need to understand that you can't gaslight me."

"Gaslight?" The accusations kept coming.

"The fact that you call what happened a misunderstanding is the very definition of gaslighting. We both know what you meant. Own it. If you feel bad about it, apologize, but don't try to make me think I didn't understand what was going on."

She was rude and prickly, and he had to admit to himself that she was also right. How many times had he had a girlfriend tell him nothing was wrong when it obviously was? No matter what she'd done, he was also in the wrong. "Fine. I'm sorry, Allyson. I shouldn't have said those things to you, and I shouldn't have tried to twist it around so I didn't have to feel bad."

She stared at him for a moment and then seemed to come to some decision. "Okay."

Things still didn't feel settled. "We should talk about working together since this didn't seem to go well."

She shook her head, the chestnut strands caressing her shoulders. "We'll be fine. I already told you I'm not picky. You don't like me. I get it. Join half the world, man. I was the brat princess on a reality show. Everyone either hates me or they want to be me, which means deep down they hate me just a little."

He definitely did not understand this woman the way he'd thought he would. Maybe she simply didn't comprehend the stakes. She'd been a bit casual when talking about men who wanted to kill her. "You would trust me with your life?"

"No, West," she said with a weary sigh. "That's why it works. I don't trust you at all, but then I don't trust anyone with my life. You're here because my parents need to know they've done everything they could to protect me, but I learned at a young age that I can count on no one but myself. I won't rely on you in any way. Don't get me wrong. I'll stick to your schedule. I'm not going to run off and do something stupid. But I also won't expect you to lift a finger to help me because in the end, you won't find me worthy of saving. So I'll save myself."

She started for the conference door.

Now he did what his instincts told him to do. He stood up and blocked her way, looming over her because she didn't cede a centimeter of space to him. She simply turned that gorgeous face of hers up, one brow rising in obvious challenge.

"I need to make something clear to you." He was so stinking close to her, and the camera did not lie. She was even more beautiful in person. "I'm in charge while you're here in Dallas, and I'm not in charge because your parents are paying me. I'm in charge because I am the man who will step in front of a bullet for you. I am the man who will take whatever is coming your way. We can not enjoy each other's company and I'll still protect you. I take my job seriously, and I will not put anyone's life above yours for as long as we're together. And that includes mine. Do I make myself clear, Allyson?"

She stared at him for a second, and a deep sense of satisfaction went through him. He now knew how to shut her up. Get into her space and challenge her. He would bet no one ever challenged her. She was a woman in control of the world around her, the queen of all she surveyed. It would do her some good to be around people who didn't worship the ground she walked on.

He didn't want to acknowledge that the air around them seemed to have come alive and was crackling with tension. Sexual tension.

The first woman he'd ever had real chemistry with and she was the one he was never going to touch.

"Perfectly clear." She took a step back. "I'm going to wait on my stepdad. I'm taking him to the airport."

"*I'm* taking him to the airport," West corrected. "The job starts now. We have three guards, though I'll be with you most of the time. When I'm off, it'll be Tessa or Matt. I'm working out a schedule with them, but for the first day or two, it's me twenty-four seven. I need to evaluate the situation and assess threats. When do we need to leave the office?"

"About an hour." She didn't look happy about it, but at least she wasn't arguing with him.

"I'll meet you and your stepdad in an hour then. Tess will meet us at your hotel and make sure it's secure. I need an hour to pack and make sure everything at my place is handled, but then I'll be with you for the night."

She turned and walked away.

And West knew the real battle had just begun.

# Chapter Two

West Rycroft was an asshole.

It wasn't like she wasn't used to dealing with assholes, but she'd kind of hoped for some older lady who might view her as a daughter type. She could hang with older people. When she'd been young, her mom had been preoccupied running her sister, Brynn's career, and she'd been left hanging around movie and TV sets. There had been a couple of older women who had taken her under their wing. The woman who'd run the costume shop on Brynn's long-running TV show had taught her how to knit.

Which was what she did now as she sat in the small break room waiting for her stepdad to finish up with the Taggarts.

She pulled out her knitting needles and cast on, starting with a garter stitch. It was the easiest stitch, but she wasn't really trying to make something. This was self-soothing.

*Do I make myself clear, Allyson?*

He'd loomed over her, every inch of him masculine and commanding. Those stark green eyes of his had stared down at her, and she'd had the most ridiculous impulse to turn her face up. To see if she could tempt him into kissing her.

She was such a stupid girl.

"Aren't you that person on TV?"

She glanced up, and the goth kid was standing there. Maybe not goth, exactly. The girl wore ripped jeans and combat boots, a concert T-shirt with her hair in a high ponytail. She looked an awful lot like Charlotte Taggart now that Ally really studied her. "I am. Shouldn't you be in school?" There was probably a reason, and sympathy welled hard and fast. "Yikes. Suspended?"

The girl shrugged. "I'm always in some kind of trouble, but not this time. In this case, it's a teacher in-service day and I'm grounded, so I have to be up here. I might have snuck out to see a friend a couple of months ago. At night. In the middle of the city. It also might have gone really wrong. Anyway, I'm stuck here for all vacation days. Fun. I'm Kala Taggart. The big scary guy is my dad, and my mom's one of the owners of the company. What are you in for?"

Ally's hands moved out of long habit, the rhythm of knitting soothing her. "Asshole guy killed a bunch of birds and presented them to me as a message that he wants to kill me."

The girl's face wrinkled up in distaste. "He killed birds?"

It was good to know that was worse than the death threats to this girl. Ally approved. She tended to like animals more than humans as well. "Yeah. I thought that was awful, too. At least my sister's dogs weren't around. I would have hunted that fucker down if he'd laid a hand on them."

"Duke and Dolly are the best." The girl sat back, seeming to relax a little.

Ally would bet this young woman didn't reach out to many strangers. Her sister had gotten married and left show business behind, but she still visited, and for years, that had meant being on *Match Made in Hollywood*. Her husband, Major, hated it, but Duke and Dolly had become canine stars. "They are. I love them. When my life gets a little more settled, I'm going to get a couple of my own. It doesn't seem fair to leave them in crates while I'm working. Are you in high school?"

"I'm a freshman. You are not what I expected. You're really cool on the show. My sisters love it. Actually, everyone loves your show. The girls at my school freaked out over the Christmas special."

Her mom had gotten them all together for a series of specials in the last couple of years. Her mom claimed she wanted to keep the brand going. Ally wanted to level with this girl, though. "You know it's not all real, right?"

"You didn't break up with Kellan?"

She shrugged. "Oh, I did. He was a total dickhead who only dated me because of the show." That had hurt more than she'd thought it would. "I'm talking about the big argument with my mom. They exaggerated that. We're cool, me and my mom."

"So you're not as much of a bitch as you seem?" Kala asked, and immediately her cheeks went red. "Sorry. My mom says I have no filter."

Ally didn't mind. "I rarely bother with one. Why should I? I mean, I try not to go around insulting people, but isn't honesty better? As to your question, well, it's all in the editing, isn't it? I mean, did I do and say all those things on the show? Sure. Did they always show my motivations? They showed whatever made the best TV. It's okay. It's a good question to ask."

"If it helps, I actually think you're pretty cool," Kala said quietly. "Like you're not fake. A lot of the shows my sisters watch are about fake people. You seem more real. And it's funny how you take down the fake people. Your sister seems a lot like mine."

Ally wrinkled her nose, feeling a kinship with the kid. "Yours perfect, too?"

"Yeah, but I have two of them. And one of them is my twin."

Ally whistled. "That's rough. It's hard to be the one who always gets into trouble. I can't imagine having to go to the same school as my sister."

"It's not easy. She gets along with everyone. She's probably going to be in the spring court," Kala said.

"Spring court?" Ally hadn't gone to a regular school. Her mom hadn't wanted to be tied to some school's schedule, so she'd done distance learning.

"Yeah, our high school has this thing called spring formal, and Kenzie is all freaked about it, and even my best friend wants to go," Kala said with a sullen look. "She's a couple of years younger than me, but she's in the same grade because she's super smart."

"Sounds like fun," Ally said. "Do you not want to go?"

A slim shoulder shrugged. "There's a stupid dress code. There's always a stupid dress code. I don't wear ball gowns."

Something about the way she said the words made Ally think she was putting on a front. "I love wearing them. Not all the time, of course, but it's fun to step out of your normal self sometimes."

"I think people would freak if I showed up in some poofy dress," Kala insisted.

Oh, she knew this girl. She'd been this girl. "You know I have this thing I like to do every now and then. I'll do something completely out of character and throw off my haters. It's got to be something I want to do. Something for me. Kala, do you think you would enjoy going to the dance?"

"There's this guy," she said. "I thought it would be cool to see him there, but I don't think he would want to see me. I think he feels comfortable that I won't be there so like his friends don't see him with me. His friends don't like me."

Poor baby. "What might be cool is putting on a dress that will blow his socks off and dancing the night away with someone else."

"Yeah, I thought about that. But like this is my look. This is who I am."

This was her armor. Ally understood the importance of armor, but she'd learned a few things over the years. "You can be anyone you want, Kala. Even if only for a little while. It can be fun to see yourself in a different way."

"Like playing a part?" She seemed to think about the idea.

"Sort of, but even when you're playing a part, you're always in there. You can learn a lot about yourself when you try new things."

"You don't think people will make fun of me?"

"Sweetie, I know they will. People suck. What I've learned is they only really win if you let them control your life," Ally explained.

"I wouldn't let them…" Kala sighed. "I kind of want to wear a pretty dress, and I'm letting the idea that they might laugh stop me."

"The clothes you wear, they're cool. You look good in them. But they're also a kind of armor. They're your costume. But even if you put on a different costume, that doesn't make you less you. You are whoever you say you are, and screw anyone who tells you differently."

She nodded, a look of determination coming on her youthful face. "Screw 'em."

"There you are." Charlotte Taggart stood in the doorway.

"Yep. I'm still here. Haven't been kidnapped or anything." Kala stood with a long-suffering sigh. "I'll go back to my desk and do something boring."

Charlotte's eyes closed as though she was counting mentally as her daughter stormed past. When she opened them, a businesslike smile crossed her face. "Are you all right? Can I get you anything?"

"I'm good. Just waiting on my stepdad. She seems like a great kid."

Charlotte looked to the doorway as though trying to figure out if there had been another kid in the room. "Really? I was worried she would say something to upset you."

"Not much upsets me. She actually reminds me a lot of me. It's hard to have perfect siblings."

"Kenzie isn't perfect." Charlotte took a deep breath and sat down in the seat her daughter had occupied. "Tasha is, though. I will admit Kenzie is easier to deal with. Kenzie is every bit as stubborn as Kala, but she somehow seems easier."

She knew this scenario. "She probably says all the right things and then goes and does what she wants. It's what my sister did. We often did the same things. I was honest. She placated everyone around her. Because she was more pleasant, I often got worse punishments."

"Well, Kenzie never snuck out of the house and got herself kidnapped by a rogue agent," Charlotte said, her jaw firming.

So Kala was totally interesting. "Yeah, Brynn never did that, either. Kala seems cool. We all have issues. Hers are laid out for all to see, and that can be hard."

Charlotte seemed to think about that for a moment. "I never thought about it that way. I'll consider it. Now how did things go with West? He's not usually so serious. I thought he would be the best person for the job because he's normally fun to be around."

That didn't surprise her. "Oh, I bring out the bad side in many men."

"Bad side?"

"Let's just say he's made it plain that he's not a fan." Before Charlotte could say anything, Ally shook her head. "It's fine. It's better, honestly. We can both do our jobs and not worry about anything else. It makes things easier."

She wouldn't have to worry about falling into bed with him. She wouldn't have to think about how good his hands would feel on her skin or how long it had been since she'd been so wickedly attracted to a man.

"Are you sure? I can talk to the other two guards. Tessa can't take the lead on this one, but I might be able to convince Wade to approve of Matt. That would cut down on the time you would have to spend with West. I'm really surprised. He's usually quite charming."

This was a conversation she'd had many times before. "Trust me. It's me, not him. You bring my sister in and he would be sweet as pie to her. I irritate all the little boys. I kind of got the feeling I irritated your husband. It was cool how he did that lower his voice and the world suddenly seemed cold thing."

"He's got that down, and everything irritates Ian. Don't worry about that. I think if he spent time with you, he'd likely find your honesty refreshing. He's a lot like Kala. Oh, here's one of the people I wanted you to meet. Matt, come and meet Ally Pearson. You'll be working with her for a couple of months. Ally, this is one of our newest employees, Matt Edwards."

A man who looked to be in his late twenties/early thirties stepped into the break room. He was handsome, with dark hair and blue eyes that would probably catch the attention of most women.

He looked far smoother than West, and for some reason, that turned her off.

"Ms. Pearson, it's a pleasure to meet you." He reached a hand out.

She put her knitting down to shake his hand. Instead of shaking it, he placed his other hand over hers, surrounding it. It irritated her because it was far too much intimacy, too fast.

Although she wondered if she would think the same thing if West had been the one to do it.

"You, too." He was slightly shorter than West, but she would bet he was more muscular. West's strength seemed to be all lean while Matt barely fit into the tight dress shirt he wore. "I hope this is a totally boring assignment for you."

"I doubt it." He gave her a ready smile. "I doubt anything about your life is boring. I'm ready for some adventure."

"There will be no adventure," a deep voice said.

Well, her hidey-hole was getting full. West Rycroft walked in, staring down at her hand between Matt's.

She pulled her hand away, not liking the weird sense that went through her. Like she was betraying someone. Which was stupid since it wasn't even like West considered her a decent person. "It's nice to meet you, too, Matt."

"I bet it was," West said under his breath. "Ally, it's time to head out." He frowned. "Are you going to kill someone with those?"

It took her a second to realize he was talking about her knitting needles. "Are you offering?"

"I was just wondering what you were doing with them."

"Knitting, asshole." She stood, packing them and her yarn away. "I'm sure that it will come as a surprise to you that I can manage to do anything beyond order my next latte. Speaking of, we'll need to stop somewhere to get a latte. I need my fix."

She wasn't going to win with this guy, and she wasn't a masochist, so she wouldn't even try.

It wouldn't be the first shitty relationship she'd had with someone she was working with.

"West?" Charlotte's eyes had gone wide. Likely because she'd never seen him act this way.

Ally simply walked out because it was nothing new to her.

It was time to ship her stepdad out and then she could concentrate on the movie.

And utterly ignore West.

* * * *

"What was she like? Does she have the most perfect skin or is that all a filter they use?" Martin Rehn sat at the bar in the two-bedroom condo West shared with his twin, Rand, in Lower Greenville.

Soon it would be Martin's condo because once West had enough cash, he was buying his own place.

After all, Martin and Rand would be newlyweds soon, and they deserved to start their lives off right.

His brother had felt like he'd had to hide who he was for most of his adult life. It was good he didn't have to hide here.

Rand grinned as he entered the kitchen and winked his fiancé's way. "Are we talking about Ally Pearson?"

"Of course. Your brother is now a bodyguard to the stars. I'm star adjacent," Martin announced. "It's all very exciting. Especially for me."

He liked the hell out of Martin. Martin was the reason they'd moved to Dallas. Not that they'd known it at the time. They'd moved because Rand couldn't handle their small town a second longer. There were some small towns that would have accepted Rand for exactly who he was, but Broken Bend was not one of them. It was still the town that had turned a blind eye to years of abuse suffered by Genny before Wade had finally come home and brought her back with him. When Rand had come out as bisexual, watching the way people they'd grown up with cut his twin out of their lives had been heartbreaking. They'd moved to Dallas for the possibilities it offered, and one of those possibilities had been Martin.

"Well, I wish you were the one packing up to spend most of the next three months with this woman." He grabbed a box of protein bars since he had no idea if they would be taking meal breaks. He was on Ally Pearson's schedule now. It was better to be prepared. "I spent the afternoon with her, and we managed to say maybe three words. I don't think she likes to talk to the help."

Rand leaned against the counter, his arms crossing over his chest as he considered West. "Really? She seems like she would be talkative."

"You've watched her show?" He was surprised. His brother generally preferred sports and action films.

"I made him watch the whole thing with me in anticipation of this year's Christmas special. I might be a little obsessed with it," Martin admitted. "Diane Pearson is iconic. If she'd been my mom, I would be the dancer I always thought I should be. And you have to admit Gavin Jacks still has it. I was surprised he wasn't gay, though."

"You think every hot guy in the world is gay," Rand pointed out, an indulgent look on his face. "Though I have to admit, I find them both very attractive."

"That's the bi guy in you," Martin retorted. "But the real star of the show is Ally. She's like April Ludgate got dropped in the middle of Hollywood. I love her so much. I hate to hear she's snobby. On the show, she takes down everyone. Rich, poor, in the middle. She treats everyone with the same brutal and painful honesty. Oh, I just realized she's my grandmother but in a young, hot body."

She'd definitely been hot. And she'd obviously found someone she liked far more than him. She'd been holding Matt's hand, looking up at him. She hadn't even noticed when he'd walked in the room.

Matt was a good guy, but he was something of a player. He wouldn't care that she was rude and looked down on everyone who wasn't from her lofty world. He would hop right in bed with her and enjoy the good time.

Rand was frowning his way. "What are you not saying? Was she mean to you? Did she throw her cell phone at your face or something?"

"She's not a thrower," Martin corrected. "She slays with words."

"I wouldn't say she slayed anything." It wasn't like she'd insulted anyone. She'd been off-putting. "She has zero focus. We're there talking about her situation and she's zoned out. When Big Tag asked her if we were boring her, she said yes."

Martin laughed, slapping a hand on the bar. "Now that sounds like the Ally we know and love."

"I wish I'd been there to see how she handled Big Tag," Rand admitted.

She'd barely looked Big Tag's way. Most women he'd ever met stared at the big guy and did whatever he asked of them. Or they argued with him and told him what an ass he was. Either way, most women were interested in getting the boss's attention.

*The only guy here I thought was my type was you.*

He wasn't going to think about that, but he did need to figure out if there was a way to repair the relationship. Despite what she'd said, he still half expected her to fire him.

"He told her she could leave if she was bored, and she tried to," he admitted. "It was actually kind of fun to see someone who was in no way intimidated by Big Tag."

"So you liked her?" Martin asked the question with an anticipatory air.

"I did not say that." He was shutting that shit down now.

"But you didn't not say that," Martin countered.

He wasn't even sure he could follow that line of thought. "I didn't like her. She was rude and obnoxious, and she's way too sensitive for her own good."

Rand snorted. "No, she's not. I mean, say what you like about her, but the girl can take a hit and get back up. Do you have any idea how many auditions she went on? That woman spent years getting rejected, and every minute of it was filmed. I'll be honest, I would have quit if I'd gone through what she did."

"I'm sure it's terrible to not get a role and have to go back and hang out at your parents' mansion." He wasn't buying that she was some pillar of strength. The worst thing that happened to the girl in a day was she chipped a nail.

Or had people break into her house to terrify her.

Rand had that look on his face, the twin-sensors-going-off look. "What is going on in your head? Because you don't judge people this quickly…unless…shit. You're attracted to her."

Martin sat up, his hands clapping together. "I knew it. This could be my every fantasy come true. It's a little like watching you with a Hollywood star because he's your twin, but I don't have to share you. If they get married, can we have a double wedding?"

"You don't even know how she feels about same-sex marriage," West pointed out.

Both of the other men stared at him like he'd said something stupid.

"So she's cool with it?" They obviously knew something he didn't.

"Half the charities she works with are LGBTQIA." Rand said the words with a shake of his head, and it took everything West had not to point out that up until a couple of years ago, Rand himself wouldn't have known what all those letters stood for.

"That's good to know, and I'm not attracted to her."

"You're not attracted to one of the most beautiful women on the planet?" Rand asked, skepticism obvious.

"Honey, I'm attracted to her, and I'm gay," Martin added with a shake of his head.

"Fine, she's pretty, but it's not going to go anywhere because I'm not playing stud to some reality star," he explained.

Rand snapped his fingers like he'd just figured something out. "Oh, this is about the princess person."

Some of it, maybe. But Ally Pearson had her own set of issues. "She wasn't as bad as Princess Amelia, though she was rude. But all of that said, I was not as professional as I could have been, and maybe that was about the princess assignment. Maybe I was a little too aggressive."

"What did you say to her?" Martin asked.

They were treating her like she was their friend or something. "I might have pointed out that she was being rude." It was worse than that. She probably would have shrugged that off and agreed with him. "I might have also accused her of trying to hit on Wade."

"What did she do to Wade?" Rand's eyes had gone wide. "Does Genny know?"

"She didn't actually do anything. She asked about him."

Rand raised a brow. "She asked if Wade was single?"

Yep, this was the part where he was the asshole, and he needed to slow his roll because now he was worried Rand was right and he was being affected by something she hadn't done. "She asked if he was my brother."

"Oh, she was doing that thing where she tries to guess everyone's story," Martin said like it was a perfectly normal thing to do. "It's one of the best parts of the show. It's a segment called Ally Reads the Room. She makes up a story about new people she's met. Some of them are just funny, but she's right a surprising amount of the time."

She'd mentioned that, and he'd doubled down. He sighed. "I was kind of an ass… I was a total dick, and she hates me. I'm serious about not getting involved with her…not that I think I could. What I'm saying is there's no potential romantic connection between us, but it would be nice if she didn't hate me. I think she really liked Matt. It would suck to get replaced as lead by Matt."

He and Matt got along fine. They were buddies who grabbed a beer after work often, but he'd been surprised at the nasty feeling that had taken root in his gut when he'd seen Ally's hand in his. It made zero sense since he should be thrilled. He hadn't wanted the job anyway. He was doing it for the money and to please his older brother, but there were other ways to accomplish both. And the idea of Matt taking over pissed him off.

"Matt?" Rand exchanged a glance with his fiancé.

Not a good one. "What's wrong?"

Martin shrugged a single shoulder. "I don't like that man. And he doesn't like us. He's not the same when you're not around."

West looked to his twin. Even when they were dumbass kids, Rand had always been honest with him. West had known about his sexuality almost from the minute Rand had the revelation. He didn't like the thought of his twin keeping something from him. "What did he do? Did he say something to you or Martin?"

"Oh, I love it when one of you gets all protective. You bulk up. I mean it. It's like you grow extra sets of muscles," Martin said with a happy sigh. "Sometimes I wonder if we should go to that town in Colorado."

Where threesomes were a thing. West couldn't help but laugh. "I don't think Rand and I would be good at sharing."

"I don't think you would be good at the man sex thing," Rand said with a grin. It faded, and he got serious again. "As to Matt, no, he's never said anything specific. It's more a feeling. An instinct. He doesn't like us, and it's not about our sparkling personalities. I've also seen him try some fairly skeevy lines on women. Watch out for him. As for Ally, did you apologize?"

"Yeah, but I don't know that I meant it at the time. I don't know that she would believe me even if I did again," he admitted.

"Bring her Flamin' Hot Cheetos," Martin suggested. "She loves them, but she won't buy them for herself because she says the camera adds five pounds and she's always got at least four cameras on her at all times. That's how to win her heart."

He didn't want to win her heart, but some peace between them might be worth it.

Two hours later, he stepped into the big suite Ally was staying in at one of Dallas's luxury hotels. Tessa Santiago-Hawthorne grabbed her jacket and met him in the entryway.

"All's good here. We had a quiet dinner, and she worked on her lines." Tessa glanced down at the bag in his hands. "You planning on snacking all night, Rycroft? By the way, she thinks you're an asshole."

Well, of course she'd made herself plain. "I bet she didn't think the same thing about Matt."

Damn it. Why had he said that?

Tessa's lips curled up like a cat who'd found the cream. "Oh, that's interesting. She actually did ask me about Matt."

"Good for her. She's a girl who goes after what she wants."

"She's a woman," Tessa corrected. "And she asked if Matt was a perv. She thought he held her hand too long. She didn't like him."

That weirdly did something for him. "Well, she hates me, too, so hopefully you're the bright spot for her."

Tessa seemed to think about what she wanted to say next. "I don't know about that. There's dislike and then there's pulling your armor around you because you know you're going to get hurt. If I was a betting person, I'd lay money on the latter when it comes to you. All right. I'm off. See you the day after tomorrow. She's got her first read-through this week, and no matter what she says, she's anxious about it. Go easy on her. She's not a bad kid."

"She's not a kid."

Tessa chuckled. "I swear all twenty-somethings look like kids to me. I'm heading out. I've got a professor to meet."

Tessa left, and West locked the door behind her.

He took a deep breath and forced himself to walk into the main room. She was probably watching herself on TV or doom scrolling on her phone.

Soft music was playing. It was folksy but modern. Not at all what he would expect. And she wasn't in front of the TV. She sat at the dining table which was covered in... Were those puzzle pieces?

"Hey," he said. "I'm here for the rest of the night and through tomorrow. Was Tessa okay?"

Her head came up, and she damn near took his breath away. She was in pajama bottoms and a tank top, her face scrubbed free and hair piled on top of her head. She was every bit as gorgeous this way. "She was great. I liked her a lot."

"But you didn't like Matt?"

Her lips turned down. "Well, now I like Tessa less."

He set down his duffel on one of the chairs and set the grocery bag on the table away from the numerous puzzle pieces. She'd started working on the edges, and it looked like she was a sorter. "Don't. It's literally my job to make sure you're okay. She's going to give me any information I need."

"Did she tell you I thought you were an asshole?"

For some reason, that made him smile. "She did. And I was. And if Matt does anything at all to make you uncomfortable, I expect you to tell me. Ally, I had a job go weird a couple of weeks ago. I know men are supposed to want any pretty woman who comes their way..."

She sat up, her expression turning distinctly sympathetic. "Someone tried to sex you up when you didn't want to?"

That was one way of putting it. "She was very aggressive, and it bothered me more than I realized. I think I took a little of that out on you today, and for that, I am truly sorry."

"Did she look like me or something?"

"Not even close," he said with a huff. "Like she wasn't as… No, she didn't look like you. But she was something of a celebrity. She was a European royal."

"Please tell me it was Kate." Her eyes had gone super wide like this would be the best gift ever.

She would so get along with his brother and Martin. "It was not. She's a minor royal but a major pain in my ass. I'm sorry. I hope you'll give me a second chance."

She stared for a moment as though assessing the situation. "Are those Flamin' Hot Cheetos?"

"My brother's fiancé swears you like them. His name is Martin, and he's a big fan."

Her shoulders relaxed, and he would have sworn that girl…woman…glowed. "That's so nice. If he has any time, he could come up to the set and have lunch with us. And he's right. Gimme. I love them, but the camera adds five pounds and…"

"You always have four cameras on you." He handed her the chips and sat down. It would be a much quieter night than he'd counted on, but he kind of liked that.

She opened them and had one of those suckers in her mouth very quickly. She sighed, obviously content. "Not now I don't. All right, Rycroft, we start again. And Matt's probably fine. You'll know he's done something wrong if he has to go to the hospital because I kicked him in the balls. Pass me that blue piece. I think it goes here."

He handed her the piece, and they got on with their first night.

# Chapter Three

Ally stood outside the studio and mentally went over everything she needed. The script and her notes were in her bag. She had a list of questions for the director, and she'd made a point to spend some time on IMDB getting to know her costars' work. She was reasonably sure she could speak to them on an intellectual level.

"You okay?" West was right behind her.

But then he had been for the last couple of days. He was her near-constant shadow. It was weird.

It was unnerving because she was getting very, very used to having him around.

After that initial terrible first day, they'd settled into a nice routine. He accompanied her to the gym every morning and worked out beside her. While he watched sports reports on the overhead TVs, she caught up with social media on her phone during cardio. Then they had a quiet breakfast up in the suite, and she spent the rest of the day teleconferencing with her mom, who acted as her agent and manager, or her publicist, or the woman who ran her socials and complained that Ally wasn't doing anything interesting.

"I just need a minute." She hadn't sent her social media manager the usual flurry of photos of what she was doing because every single thing she did was with West. Or was boring stuff she actually liked to do. No one wanted pictures of her latest knitting project or the 2000-piece puzzle she was working on.

"I had Matt do a walk-through of the building if that's what you're worried about. It's big, and there are a lot of ways in and out, but I'm going to be close. I'm more worried about when you shoot on location. Shouldn't you have done this table thing in LA?"

"Usually, but the movie's set here in Dallas. The director is known for his method work. Usually that's an acting term, but it works for this guy."

"Method?"

Sometimes she forgot that not everyone had been raised in Hollywood. "It's a reference to Stanislavski. He was an acting coach back in olden times. Like way old. Marlon Brando old. Anyway, there's a school of thought that the best performances come from truly inhabiting the character. Some of them never break character even when they're not filming."

"And you do this?"

"No. Eww. They call it acting for a reason. Those people are pretentious douchebags. You know they never play like nice people. It would be one thing if some asshole actor was suddenly being nice twenty-four seven because he was playing Jesus or something, but no. They're always playing some mega jerk, and the rest of us have to put up with him playing out his megalomaniacal fantasies. Jared Leto decided to live inside the Joker twenty-four seven. How do you think that worked out for his castmates?" She'd never had it that bad, but she could imagine.

"That seems like a bad idea from what I know from the comic books." West was looking particularly all-American hero this morning in his black jeans and T-shirt. He had a jacket on, but she couldn't forget about the shoulder holster and guns under it. "How does a director do this method thing?"

"Like having the table read here when we could have done it back in LA." It was cool out but not cold, the sun shining down and making West's eyes look a little like emeralds. It was a good thing she preferred diamonds. "This movie is about a family in Dallas who fought over the millions left behind by the grandfather. It's based on a true story. My character is the youngest daughter, and the brother played all these pranks on her to make her look like she was going insane. For a while she feared the house was haunted and fell out a window running from 'the ghost,' who was actually her brother. Broke her neck, but she learned to walk again. In a psychiatric ward, where she spent the rest of her life. It's not a really happy story."

But it was fascinating to her. Playing Delia Crowne was going to open doors for her. No more low-budget rom coms or playing the hot girl all the teen boys wanted to bang. Or the mean girl. She got that role a lot.

"Is that why we're touring some old mansion tomorrow morning?" West sat on the bench beside her.

Poor West. He was going to have to do so many things he would likely find boring as hell over the next couple of months. "Yes, and I'm going to the psychiatric hospital where she died only a couple of years ago." She noticed a limo pulling up, and then a familiar man was stepping out.

Bryce Jericho. He was playing her father. He had three Oscar nominations but no wins yet. He was a mover and shaker in the artistic film world.

He gave her a big smile as he walked toward her. "You must be Ally. I would know that face anywhere. My girls adore you."

He gave her a hug. She wasn't much of a hugger, but she'd learned at a young age that there were some things one put up with, and forced intimacy was one of them.

"It's so nice to meet you, Mr. Jericho. I'm a huge fan. I've enjoyed your work for years," she said.

He pulled back, his handsome face the amalgamation of great genes and excellent plastic surgery. "That's nice to hear. And it's Bryce, Ally." He gave her a very unfatherly look up and down and then a grin. "We'll be working together for months, and I'd like to get to know you better. Maybe we can have dinner tonight."

"She can't," West said in a blunt tone. He put a hand on her shoulder. "I'm afraid Ms. Pearson's social calendar is full."

Bryce looked over and took another step back, hands coming up as though to apologize. "Sorry. Just trying to be friendly. Well, see you inside, dear."

She stared at West. "You let him think you're my boyfriend."

"I never said that." His eyes were steely again, like they'd been the first day they met.

She thought about it and realized she was actually grateful. "Thanks for that. He was...eww...he's my stepdad's age. I think they're friends. And he's married. He was totally hitting on me. Right? I'm not making that up in my head."

"He was an old man skeeving on a young girl," West agreed. "And without an ounce of subtlety."

"Thanks." She straightened her skirt. "But I'll let everyone know you're my bodyguard. You don't want the rumor to get out that I have a new boyfriend. The reporters can be vicious. It's nice here because I haven't seen more than a few."

West moved in close. "Hey, I'm your bodyguard, and I can also be the bad guy. Anything you don't want to do, let them know your nasty old guard is overprotective. And, Ally, you're ready for this. You can do this."

She needed this pep talk. Usually it was her mom who did it. She didn't have an assistant because she'd seen how often that went wrong. She liked doing it on her own.

But damn it felt good to have West with her. "I can. I got this part by auditioning twelve times. I got it because I'm the right person for this role. I can do this."

West nodded. "You can do this. Now let's get you settled in. I was told I'm not allowed in the room, but I'll be right outside."

Yes, that totally made her point. "See, method. Jay Clarke is totally method. He's reading all the directions himself, so we don't have any production assistants with us. It's cast only." She glanced down and realized she'd let the time go. "And I'm late."

She pushed through the studio doors and was waved through by one of the aforementioned assistants, who pointed her to the room. She was about to round the corner when she heard something that made her stop.

"She's pretty, but there's not a brain in her head," a familiar voice said.

Channing Lloyd. She was a gorgeous forty-four-year-old. Two decades before she'd been Hollywood's it girl, and she'd had an amazing career. Three Oscar wins. She was Ally's idol. Ally had been thrilled she was playing her daughter.

"I remember her as Bria Knight's wannabe little sister," another voice said. Reid Wilson. He was playing her brother. The one who tormented her. "Does she count as a nepo baby if it's her sister who was in the business?"

"Oh, I assure you it wasn't her sister who got her this job," Bryce said with a lofty chuckle. "This reeks of her stepfather. Gavin is giving in to Diane, I'm sure. That woman's soul died a little when the older one walked away. She's just got to have a kid in the business. She lives for it."

"Ally," West said quietly.

She was not going to cry. They didn't get a second of her tears. Did they think she hadn't heard every word of that before?

She'd hoped to be accepted. The humiliation she felt was absolutely real, but she couldn't let herself wallow in it. Not now.

She had to do this, and she had to do it alone. She forced a smile on her face. "Thanks for escorting me, West. You can wait out here. I'll be done in a couple of hours."

His expression went blank, and she wondered if she'd hurt him. She hadn't meant to, but she needed every inch of her armor now. She pulled it around her like a warm cloak even though she knew it was cold and steely and kept even the warmth in her life out.

But that was acting. Head high, she turned the corner. "Hello, fellow Crownes. I'm so happy to be here."

The fake goodwill game was on.

\* \* \* \*

It had taken everything West had to not go into that room and deal with the situation. Even two hours later, he was still shocked at what he'd heard.

But then he remembered the look on Ally's face as she'd told him to wait here like a good employee and walked in like nothing had happened. He could hear them talking and laughing and acting like no one had insulted and belittled her and they were all one big family.

Did she even care that those people had been talking shit on her? He'd felt humiliated for her, but she'd simply shrugged it off and gone about her day.

It would be good to remember who she was. The last couple of days had brought a nice peace between them. He'd actually enjoyed the time they'd spent together, and he'd started to wonder if maybe they shouldn't explore the chemistry between them.

She might be pleasant to be around when she wanted to be, but it was good to be reminded that all she cared about was her career, and it didn't matter what mud she had to slog through for it.

The doors came open, and Ally walked out surrounded by her "friends."

A handsome, familiar-looking young man gave her a wink as he walked by. "I'll see you later, sis. Maybe we can grab dinner or something next week."

Ally smiled. "I would love that. I'll have to bring my bodyguard, though."

West was absolutely certain he'd seen the guy on some TV show, but he couldn't remember his name.

The actor gave him a once-over that let West know he didn't find him impressive. "Well, I'm sure he can hang out somewhere close by. Hopefully you'll be able to dump him soon. I'm sure the police will catch this…is it a stalker?"

Ally's smile didn't waver. "He's merely a nice layer of security."

"Of course. I'm sure he's good for the press, too. I always like to have an entourage. Makes one look important," the asshole said, and then strode away.

"Yes, we all love a bodyguard." Channing Lloyd was a name he did know. The legendary actress looked chic in her silk blouse, slacks, and stilettos that made her tower over Allyson. "Such a nice accessory, and this one is quite attractive."

"He's good at his job," Ally replied. "I haven't even gotten killed yet. I'll see you in a couple of days. Can't wait to get to work." She turned his way. "I'm going to run to the bathroom and then I'll be ready to go."

She walked by him, resettling her bag on her shoulder.

Channing looked him up and down like he was a treat she might be able to order. "If you ever want a serious client, give me a call."

Yeah, he bet he knew what she would be serious about.

He said nothing as the woman walked away.

"Wow, if I needed a steely-gazed cop, I would cast you immediately."

The hallway had cleared out, and only a curly-haired man in a T-shirt and jeans was left. He wore glasses and had a messenger bag over his slender shoulders. He held out a hand. "I'm Jay Clarke. I'm Ally's director. You must be the head of her security."

West reached out and shook the man's hand. He seemed young for a director of his stature. "West Rycroft and yes. I'm in charge of her security, but there will be three of us in rotation. I've informed security in the building and your production team. My question for you is should I expect everyone to view my client's situation as a joke?"

Jay nodded as though in complete agreement. "Yes, you have the intimidation thing down, and I'm sorry about that. I'm afraid the rest of the cast doesn't see what I see in Ally, but they'll come around. She's a good actress, and she's serious about her craft. Unfortunately, her past is coloring their vision when it comes to her. I'm afraid actors can be a bit on the pretentious side."

"I don't care if they don't like working with her. What I care about is that your cast and crew take this threat seriously." If Ally wasn't worried about her tender feelings, he wouldn't be either, but he was concerned that the cast seemed to think he was around for photo ops. "I need to know that one of these people won't think it's funny to prank her and let her supposed stalker into her trailer."

"Oh, they would never do that." Jay stepped back, his hand coming up. "I know some of the cast isn't happy about working with Ally, but they are professionals. And I think that once they see how good she is, they'll come around. I believe in her. All she needs is a little push here and there. I think she'll find working with my method will unleash her talent." This man was interested in her. It was clear in the way he talked about her, how he looked back to see if she was coming out of the bathroom. "I think we should do some one-on-one work. I've got a brown belt in…"

"No." He wasn't about to leave her alone with a dude who looked like he weighed a hundred pounds soaking wet. He wasn't sure Ally wasn't bigger than this guy. Of course he also wouldn't leave her alone with a fully-trained bodyguard who wasn't on his team. She was his responsibility.

"No?" The director's brow rose. He was not a man who was used to having his authority challenged. "Are you telling me you're going to stop me from working with an actress on my own set?"

"Not at all. You said you wanted to get her alone and then you attempted to explain that you could protect her. I don't care if you're ex-military who specialized in personal protection. I won't leave Ally alone with anyone as long as I'm on the job."

"Maybe you won't be on the job for long," Jay replied, his tone losing its "let's be friends, dude" vibe. The director was in the house. "I know her stepfather. I could call and ask him to replace you with a guard who is willing to work with me. This is for her own good, after all. If she can't do what I need her to do, then she's not a lot of use to me, is she?"

"West, are you okay with being outside the room while we work?" Ally had somehow snuck up on them.

She was pale in the early afternoon light, clutching her script to her chest like if she let it go, she would lose everything.

Now she showed some emotion. Her career was being threatened, and it didn't matter that she could be killed. Still, he had a job to do. He didn't stop doing it because the client cared more about a movie part than her life. "As long as I've checked out the room and all the entries and exits, yes."

She turned to her director. "Then we'll be able to talk freely because he won't be in the room. If you refuse to have him in the building, then I worry that what you want isn't a rehearsal. If that's the case, then I should head back to LA and let you find someone else."

Jay put his hands on her shoulders. "No. That is not what I want at all, and I promise you this is all about the work. You know I have a method. I've had these sessions with all the other actors. I'm having another one with Bryce this afternoon. I don't know how other directors have treated you, but you're an important part of this project. Of course your bodyguard is welcome to sit outside. I'll find a space for us that will work for him. I want you safe. But you also know I'm going to want to talk about what's happening to you."

She nodded. "I know. I can use it as fuel for the character."

"Your experiences are one of the reasons I think you're the right person to bring Delia to life. You have a lot in common, and being able to tap into those life experiences will help unlock your performance."

"I'm willing to go to all my dark places. Hey, at least I've gotten something out of all that terror," she said with a jaunty smile. "Let me know when you want to have a session."

Jay nodded and stepped back. "Perfect. You relax the rest of the day. We'll be getting down to business soon. The reading went well. I like the direction you're going in with Delia, but we need to go deeper."

"Absolutely," she promised, stepping back. She looked West's way. "I'm ready to go back to the hotel."

They said good-bye to the director, and he walked her out of the building in complete silence.

Uncomfortable silence.

But he wasn't going to break it. He unlocked his SUV and made sure she was settled in. That was when he noticed that while her face was perfectly placid, her hand was red from holding on to the strap of her purse so tightly.

"Are you okay?"

Her head turned his way. "I'm fine. You heard Jay. The session went well."

Had he misread her? A whole lot of his training had been about learning to read body language, and hers was completely disconnected. Her face was set in her normal "I don't care about the world" expression, but her body was stiff.

He was still viewing her through the lens of her celebrity. What if there was a real woman underneath all that bravado? What had she told him the first day they'd met? That she couldn't count on anyone to protect her.

Her stepdad had told him something too that day.

She kept her sneakers in her bag, and he had his gym bag in the back.

"Hey, I've been cooped up for too long. I was thinking about going hiking," he offered. "There are some great trails only twenty minutes away. We could spend the afternoon hiking, and you would still be back for dinner. Or I could call Tessa and have her watch you for a while."

He wanted to give her options. He couldn't be completely sure that her anxiety only came from what had happened. It could be exacerbated by the fact that he'd witnessed it, and then some time apart might help her.

"I could use the exercise. I have some yoga pants in my bag and a T-shirt and cap." The hand she held her strap with relaxed slightly. "That would be good if you don't mind the company. I promise, I can keep up, and we don't have to talk."

Damn but he'd done a number on her. "Or we can if you want to. Whatever you want."

She turned, eyes finding his. "Are you doing this for me? Because of what happened? Because of what Gavin told you?"

"I think we could both use some peace and quiet and to be outside for a while. I spent the first twenty-five years of my life living on a ranch. I love the city. I really do. I love how many doors it's opened for me, and I definitely love how good it's been for my brother. But sometimes I just need to breathe."

That answer seemed to satisfy her as she nodded and turned back to look out the front window. "Okay. We should pick up some water and sandwiches."

He could do that.

He closed her door and moved around to the driver's side. He was pulling out of the parking lot when he heard her speak again. She was almost so quiet he missed it.

"Thank you, West."

He nodded and realized that a thoughtful, vulnerable Ally might be the most dangerous kind.

# Chapter Four

Ally leaned against the big rock they'd been using as an impromptu dining table and let the warmth of the sun kiss her skin. Despite the fact that it was early spring, it was a sunny, warm day here in North Texas. She closed her eyes, letting the weight of the day roll off her.

They'd walked for over an hour before West had found this big boulder and declared it the perfect place to take a break and eat the sandwiches they'd bought at a Starbucks as they'd left Dallas proper. They'd bought sandwiches and waters and some trail mix.

This was what she'd needed. Peace. Calm. Quiet.

Out here with her hair in a ponytail and sunglasses on, no one noticed her. She was simply another girl enjoying the afternoon.

Out here, no one called her a nepo baby and complained about having to share space with a talentless hack like her.

"You want to head back or go a little farther?" West glanced down at his watch. "We've got plenty of time."

"Can we sit for a while? It's nice here." They were at the top of the biggest hill for miles around. From this vantage, she could see the rest of the nature preserve and the Dallas skyline in the distance.

"Of course." West leaned back beside her, his gaze on the blanket of trees below them. "We can stay as long as we like. It's a little early for snakes, and the biggest predator out here is a coyote or a bobcat. Whichever one of us can run the fastest will live."

She snorted. "I thought you were supposed to throw your body in front of anything that might come my way."

"That was human predators," he corrected. "Some nasty critter comes after you and you're on your own. You should have checked your contract.

I'm a people guard."

She wished she didn't like him so much. The kindness he'd shown her today hadn't lessened the attraction, and she loved his snarky side. Over the last couple of days, they'd found a peaceful coexistence. They hadn't really talked a lot, but he'd helped her work her puzzle, and he would turn on a basketball game while she studied her lines. It would probably be better to keep it there, but she couldn't resist the temptation to learn more about him. "I thought you grew up on a ranch."

His lips curled slightly. He'd changed into his gym clothes and settled a ball cap on his head. He didn't look like a rancher. He looked like he could model. Or act. The fact that he wanted to do neither was part of his attraction. "That's how I know to stay away from coyotes and bobcats. But honestly, the snakes freak me out way more. I hate snakes. When I was a kid, we would sometimes camp out, and I mean real camping. No tents. Just my brothers and the stars overhead and a sleeping bag. And one time a snake crawled in with me. I woke up, and there that sucker was, curled up right beside me."

She shuddered. "I would have died. I'm now very glad my mom wasn't into camping. I slept on a lot of couches, though. When my sister was working on her TV show, I would sleep on the couch in her dressing room when they worked late. Not a lot of snakes there. Well, not the slithering kind."

"Were there other kinds?"

"There's always some asshole who wants to take advantage of a young woman," she explained. "I learned to lock the door if I was taking a nap." She was misrepresenting the situation. Or not giving him a full view. Suddenly it seemed important that he didn't think her mom had been terrible. "It wasn't all bad. I got to see a whole lot of the world at a young age."

"And I didn't see anything outside of rural Southern Texas until I was eighteen," West admitted.

"Really? Your family didn't take vacations?"

"You don't understand ranching families. You see when you run a ranch, the ranch is all that matters. The ranch is the sun, and everyone in the family revolves around it. My father basically worked himself to death. He had a heart attack when I was just a kid. My twin and I were the babies of the family. We were a big surprise to our parents. They thought they were done. They had four boys before us. Clint, Heath, Clay, and Wade, and then ten years later, oops. I don't have a lot of memories of my father.

My oldest brother had been planning on going to college, but when my dad died, he took over the ranch, and we all held on and tried to survive." West huffed and turned her way. "I'm sorry. This is supposed to be your quiet time, and I'm giving you my life story."

"The hour-long hike was good enough for me. I'm enjoying the talk. I know we started rough, but we actually have a lot in common."

"We do?" The question was asked as though he didn't believe he would like her answer.

But she was totally right about this. "Oh, yes. We both came from similar families. Your family revolved around the ranch. It was how you survived. Mine revolved around my sister's career. My dad died when I was a baby. My mom was left with a substantial amount of debt. She'd been a model, but she was past her prime in that world and couldn't get work."

"So she put her kid to work?"

There was a ton of judgment to that question. "You didn't work the ranch?"

He stopped, seeming to think the comparison through. "Okay, I can see where that might be similar. I missed school many times because my brother needed help with something. Money was tight, and losing the ranch wasn't an option. I don't like to think about everything Clint and Mom did to save the ranch."

It was good he could make the connections. Too many people only saw her upbringing as privileged, but there had been so much uncertainty. "The only thing my mom had when my dad died was two young children and her connections. It was the only world she knew. When I was younger, I resented her for how much time she spent on Brynn's career, but I wonder if I wouldn't have resented her if she'd been a doctor or a lawyer."

"I resented the hell out of my dad for a long time. I didn't even know the man." Though West said the words with an even tone, she thought she could detect a sorrow beneath them. "Every picture I have of him has something to do with work."

"Is that why you left?"

"I left because my brother needed to get out." West kept his eyes on the horizon. There was the faintest hint of a five-o'clock shadow breaking over the hard line of his jaw. "Broken Bend is a small town, and it's stuck in an era where they don't like their town heroes coming out as bi. Rand was the high school quarterback. He won a couple of championships. We came up here to Dallas for college. By that point, the ranch was profitable because we found natural gas on the property. A lot of it. Otherwise Rand

and I would likely be right there fighting to keep a piece of land that sucked the soul out of our dad."

She kept quiet when he did, not wanting to give him a reason to move on to another subject. She wanted to know about him, the hows and whys about him coming here. If he longed to go back. If he missed someone from his town.

"Anyway," West continued, "when we were up here in Dallas, that was when my brother finally was able to be honest with himself and me about his sexuality. When we went back home, he thought he could be open about it, but him dating a guy was apparently one step too far. It's not like they threw shit at him or hassled him physically."

She knew exactly what they'd done. "Being shunned can be every bit as hurtful. Especially when they do it and when you call them on it, they swear they're not. Please tell me your family accepted him."

He nodded. "Yes. Clint is my oldest brother. He's married with a couple of kids, and they all love their Uncle Rand. But Clint also understood when Rand decided to take a job up here in Dallas. He thought I should stay, though. I told him I had to come with Rand to make sure he was okay, but I wouldn't have stayed. The only thing there for me was to live my father's life. So I took my part of the gas money and moved up here. I finished my degree. I thought about going into some kind of law enforcement and then realized that was not for me. Wade then offered for me to go through training to work for McKay-Taggart. They usually only hire ex-military or ex-law enforcement for bodyguard positions."

"What kind of training did you do?"

He huffed out a laugh. "What kind didn't I do? I trained on weapons, self-defense, situational awareness. At one point, I was left out in the wilderness, and I had to find my way back. I'm going to be honest, I wasn't sure that wasn't some weird hunt thing. I think if I hadn't made it out, Big Tag might have had my head on his wall."

She didn't like the thought of that. "That sounds terrible."

A hint of a smile hit his face. "It was at the time, but it was also kind of fun. It was challenging, and these are some of the best people I've ever met. They come from all walks of life, and they get along because they all have one purpose. They want to do their jobs and have happy lives, and they work for it. There was also a lot of therapy involved. It was part of the training. Rand ended up working at McKay-Taggart's sister company. They specialize in missing persons. He works on their logistical team. He had therapy, too. And now he's engaged to a guy I think is perfect for him."

She loved that story. "I'm happy for him. For them. How about you? Is there a woman in your life? I never even asked if you were married."

"No. I've dated a little since we moved up here, but nothing serious," he admitted. "I had a serious girlfriend back home for a while, but that was over when she started asking me if Rand could maybe tone it down around her. My brother doesn't need to tone down anything."

"No, he doesn't." She was glad they'd found someplace they felt comfortable. She wasn't sure if she'd wanted that particular answer to her question. A married West would be less dangerous.

He let a moment pass before he turned her way. "Are we going to talk about it?"

She took a long breath and decided to not pretend with him. "It wouldn't do any good to."

"At first I thought it didn't bother you. I thought you didn't care what they thought."

She was curious. His answer would tell her a lot about whether she could somewhat trust this man. "And did you think I was strong for that? Or did the words cold-hearted bitch run through your head?"

"Unfortunately, it was the latter." He pulled his sunglasses off and held her gaze with those emerald eyes of his. "I'm sorry about that. I realize now that you're excellent at hiding your pain, but you absolutely feel it. They were assholes. You didn't deserve that."

Of all the things he could have said, *you didn't deserve that* hit her right in her chest. Everyone—even the people who were sympathetic to her—believed she deserved some of it. Even her mom told her it was part of the job. "I don't know. I've got a certain reputation."

He straightened up, putting his hands on her shoulders and looking her dead in the eyes. "You do not deserve that kind of treatment, Ally Pearson. Your reputation is bullshit. I've been with you for days, and you're not the person they portray on TV. You work your ass off, and they shouldn't make judgments. Especially where they know damn well you could have heard them. They knew you were on your way in. They wanted you to hear."

He wasn't saying anything she hadn't already thought, but it all came back in an awful rush.

"Baby, you can't shove this down and go about your business. Talk about it. Let it out so it doesn't poison your whole experience here." He grimaced. "I'm sorry. I called you baby, and that wasn't…"

She went on her toes and kissed him, planting her lips right over his.

What the hell? He'd flat-out told her he'd been through a terrible experience, and she'd put him through another.

She backed off, and she couldn't do anything to stop the tears now. "West, I'm so sorry. I… Please forgive me. I was emotional, and you were being so nice to me, and I think you're really beautiful. I should never have put you in that position."

She half expected him to walk away from her, but his expression softened, and he reached out and gently pulled her close. He wrapped his big arms around her, and the world seemed to close off.

"It's not the same, Ally." He whispered the words in her ear as he held her tight. "It's not the same at all. Go ahead. You hold on for however long you need to. Just hold on."

The awfulness of the day washed over her again, and she realized the hikes were all about avoiding this. She pushed her body so she didn't have to deal with her soul. She didn't like to cry, to feel so vulnerable, but she did now. She sobbed into West's strong shoulder while he stroked a hand down her back.

A weird peace hit her after a couple of moments. When the tears dried up, she felt calm and in control again, as though she'd purged some toxin that had been sitting inside her.

She tilted her head up. "Thank you. I think I'm okay now."

He was so gorgeous as he stared down at her. "You sure?"

She nodded.

"Good. Because I'm going to kiss you now. Then we will have both kissed each other, and we'll be on the same level, and we can decide where to go from there."

"Is this a pity kiss?"

"Nope. It's a balance kiss. I would hate for you to go around thinking I have something over you because you kissed me. This puts us right back on the same footing. Now, hush. I've got to make it good."

She had to look terrible. "Maybe we should…"

Then his mouth was on hers and there were no maybes. There was only warmth and comfort and a wild arousal that she'd never felt before.

After a long moment, he pulled away and grinned down at her. "See. Now we're even, and you don't have to be embarrassed that you totally kissed me first and told me how beautiful I am." He was stunningly gorgeous when he smiled like he did now. He stepped back and grabbed his backpack. "I know, by the way. How pretty I am."

"I've created a monster." Oh, she could fall so hard for this guy, and she wasn't sure she could stop herself at this point.

"Come on. There's a pretty spot about a half a mile down, and then we can make our way back," he said, holding out a hand. "Maybe we can order pizza for dinner since we have burned some calories."

She should put them back on a proper footing. She could save this. He was right. They were even, and they didn't have to go further.

Her hand went right into his, and she knew she was fucked when it came to this one.

"That sounds perfect." She let him lead her down the trail, consigning all her good sense straight to hell.

* * * *

"You know the director is into you, right?" West asked the question tentatively as he turned on the road that led back to the hotel. Dusk had fallen, and a chill was in the air now, but they were safe and warm in the SUV, and it was time to talk about serious things again.

He needed to know she was aware of a possible problem. Although it might not be a problem. After what happened a couple of hours ago, he kind of hoped it would be a problem. He wished he could avoid the question. The last thing he wanted to do was wreck the peace they'd found this afternoon.

It was more than peace. It was possibility. Somewhere while they walked through the nature preserve together, a possibility had come to life, fragile and new.

And he wasn't sure if it would be smart to pursue it, but damn it had felt right to draw her close and hold her while she let out all her tension.

Now he couldn't stop thinking about how much better it would be if they were naked and in bed and he was releasing all her tension in a different way.

"He's attracted to me, but I can handle it. I don't flirt with him. I actually don't flirt a lot. I can keep a careful distance between us," she promised. "Also, how do you know? Is it because you're into me?"

There was the hint of bitch. It had been off-putting at first, but now he kind of liked it. It was Ally's spirit. It seemed brittle, but her strength was quite robust. She protected her softness like a Valkyrie warrior. How many people had seen this woman break down and cry? How many were allowed to see the real Ally Pearson? "Maybe."

"I thought you would fight me on that one," she admitted, sitting back with a sigh. "It can't work, you know."

He rather thought she was saying that as much for her sake as his. "I think it could. I have all the parts I need. I'm pretty sure you do. Even if you don't, we can get creative."

The little brat's eyes rolled. "I wasn't talking about sex. I was talking about us. Even if we wanted to, we would have an expiration date. I'm here for three months and then I go back to LA where hopefully I'll find another job."

He knew she was right, but the idea of not pursuing that kiss in any way didn't sit well with him. "Does everything have to be forever?"

"It would be nice if there was a possibility of it working out, but I think you're right. I don't know. I think you could break my heart, Rycroft."

"I know you could break mine," he admitted. And that was probably reason enough to back off. He didn't want to cause her more pain. "Do you want me to have Wade assign someone else?"

"No." The answer came out of her mouth quickly, and then she flushed a pretty pink. "I don't want another bodyguard. I wasn't saying no, West."

She was doing what she did—talking through the situation with brutal honesty. He needed to remember that was all a part of Ally's process. It was one of the reasons people found her off-putting. They didn't get to know her, didn't understand why she did some of the things she did. Ally was honest with herself, and she didn't see the point in hiding it. What other people thought of as rude, she viewed as being realistic, and there was an odd kindness in her process. "We'll play it by ear. I'm going to let you set the pace. Let's be friends for now."

"I think I would like that," she replied quietly. "I don't have a lot of those. And I'm thoroughly aware that Jay has some designs on me. It's nothing you need to worry about. I also know that he sleeps with most of his younger leading ladies. I've learned how to handle it."

He didn't like the thought of leaving her alone with a man who could potentially manipulate her. "You shouldn't have to."

"Every woman in Hollywood has to deal with it, and honestly, a bunch of the men do, too. We're equal opportunity gropers in Hollywood. Every place has its pros and cons. Your old hometown wouldn't accept your brother. Well, he could come out to my hometown and they would accept him without hesitation, and then someone would cop a feel."

He snorted at that. She wasn't wrong. There were always pros and cons. "If you need help with him, I stand ready. I really will be right outside the door."

"We need to get you a Sudoku book or something. Maybe crosswords," she said. "It'll be easier when we're on set. I'm planning on making this the most boring job you've ever had."

He seriously doubted that. He pulled into the round driveway and was surprised to see a familiar face waiting there alongside the valet.

Matt Edwards moved in the minute West stopped the SUV, cutting off the valet who'd been trying to do his job. Matt had Ally's door open in a heartbeat and was holding a hand out to help her down. "Welcome back, Ms. Pearson. West, I'm supposed to take the night shift. Wade wants to talk to you. In the office."

Shit. He felt his gut clench, and his first thought was about Clint. He'd talked about the ranch all afternoon. Had it claimed another one of them? What if something happened to the boys? "What's going on? Is everyone okay?"

Matt shrugged. "Not sure, but Wade looked damn upset. Big Tag showed up, and they were in his office for a good thirty minutes. When they came out, they told me to haul my ass over here and be ready to spend the night."

"I could come to the office with you." Ally looked concerned, her bottom lip disappearing behind her teeth. "I don't mind waiting in the lobby."

"No one wants to inconvenience you, Ms. Pearson," Matt assured her. "Whatever is happening at the office is nothing for you to worry about. I'm here to ensure a smooth transfer. I'm not sure what's happened, but it won't affect you at all."

"Yes, it will." She turned away from Matt. "Can I come with you, West?"

"Ba…" He had to stop that. It was already too easy to slide into intimacy with her. Maybe a couple of hours apart would do them some good. Then there was the possibility that something really bad had happened. "I'm not sure what's happening. It could be one of my brothers."

She held up a hand. "Go. Go and do what you need to. Please call me and let me know you're okay."

He had the wildest urge to change his mind and ask her to get back in the SUV. He ignored it. It was better for her to not get too involved. She had her own troubles. "I will. Matt, I'll be back to work the rest of my shift.

Tessa's supposed to take over for a couple of hours tomorrow."

Matt put a hand on her elbow, and West kind of wanted to growl.

Ally stepped away and started to walk inside the hotel.

She could handle it. But if Matt got handsy with her, he would take the fucker apart.

"I think you should worry about yourself, brother. I don't think anyone's hurt. They were pissed, and it's something you did. Good luck with that. I'll take care of our client." Matt slammed the door and hurried to catch up with Ally.

West took a long breath and started back for the office.

Twenty minutes later, he was walking in as everyone else was walking out. Wade must have been upset with him because he wasn't answering his phone. All he'd gotten was a text telling him to get his ass in the office.

What the hell was going on? His anxiety was reaching epic proportions, and he was going to have a long fucking talk with his brother.

He strode through the lobby, and his sister-in-law was still sitting at her desk across from Big Tag's office. Genny might be a good source of information. She was Big Tag's assistant, and the man loved to talk. "Is everything okay, Genny?"

She looked up from her computer screen, and a sympathetic look came over her. "We should talk before you go in."

Why wouldn't anyone answer his questions? "Is everyone okay?"

She stood. "Of course. Everyone is fine. Oh, I'm sorry. They are not handling this well, but they won't listen to me. Everyone is fine. Big Tag and Wade were surprised is all."

"Surprised?" Now he was completely confused.

She looked him over. "Is that what you've been wearing all day? We were trying to figure out when it happened, but it looks like it was today."

Before he could answer that surprising question, the door to Big Tag's office came open, and he was confronted by the man himself.

"How long did it take you? Did you set a fucking land speed record for how fast you could get the client into bed?" Big Tag asked in that bad-dad mode he got into with a lot of his employees. "I should have known you couldn't beat Nina Blunt. She fucked her client before she even knew he was a client."

"Then it doesn't count, and he is still in contention for the title." Charlotte sat on the couch beside Wade. "Nina didn't realize who JT was, so there was no informed consent to break your silly rules that everyone always breaks anyway."

"West knows better," his brother said. "This is all a mistake. He was just being kind to her."

"Was his tongue being kind to her throat?" Big Tag asked.

They knew about the kiss? How the fuck would they know he'd kissed Ally? "Do you have someone shadowing me?"

He was out of his probationary period. Was his brother sending someone senior to check up on him? Was it because he was the only one who hadn't been in the military? He'd thought they accepted that he could do his damn job.

Big Tag reached for the tablet on his desk, unlocking it and turning it toward West. "No, but someone sure as hell was, and the fact that you didn't catch it makes me wonder if you're right for this job."

West felt his eyes go wide and his blood pressure tick up as he realized what he was looking at. It was a picture of himself and Ally on the hiking trail, her hand in his. Another picture followed, and it was of the passionate kiss they'd shared, the one he'd initiated.

"It's from a gossip website." Charlotte was the only one who didn't seem angry about the situation. "They posted those pictures about an hour ago along with an article that is not flattering to Ally."

He took the tablet from Big Tag. "I didn't see anyone following us. There was no one on that trail who recognized us."

"Her," Big Tag insisted. "They wouldn't care to recognize you."

"Give him a break," Wade said with a sigh.

Big Tag's head shook. "Nope. Language is important, and the fact that he used the word *we* means he's more invested than he's going to try to tell me. *We* and *us* are words you use when you're a couple. She's a client. No one recognized the client."

Big Tag was obviously going to be a pain in his ass about this. "No one recognized the client. I don't think anyone followed her."

"You don't think?" Now Wade was standing by Big Tag.

"I checked, but I didn't see any car following us. I don't know, man. It's a big fucking city." Had he not done his job? Had he been too concerned with Ally that he wasn't properly protecting her?

No.

"Screw this," West said, handing back the tablet. "I did exactly what I was trained to do. No one followed us. I didn't even talk to her on the ride out. I was very aware of everything around me. Those pictures were taken with a telephoto lens. They never got close to us…to the client. I need to figure out if Ally told anyone where we were going. She was texting on the way to the nature preserve. I don't think anyone could have overheard our conversation."

There was another possibility.

"I need someone to check my SUV for a tracker." He hadn't thought about it because the studio had security. "It was parked in the studio's lot. The lot has full time guards, but it could have been someone on set."

"You think someone tipped off the photographers?" Charlotte asked.

"It's the only thing that makes sense. I assure you I would have noticed if assholes with cameras were hanging around…the client." He really was using the *us* and *we* words a lot. "I almost hope there's a tracker and it's someone from the studio who's making some side money. I would hate for it to be someone Ally trusts."

She trusted so few people.

"Jamal is already downstairs checking your truck." Big Tag sighed and stared at him like he was trying to figure out how to deal with him. "I think we should reconsider having you take lead on this project."

"Then I'll quit and she'll hire me privately." Now that he was standing here having to defend himself, all his damn doubts had washed away.

Ally needed him. It might not work out, but who the fuck knew? He would never have said a few years back that he would be living in Dallas getting ready for his brother to marry the man of his dreams. Life threw curveballs, and learning to catch them or avoid them was the measure of how successful a person could be.

Ally was a big old curve ball that could knock him into the dirt. Or she might be the best thing that ever happened to him. All he knew in that moment was that Big Tag and his brother weren't going to make the choice for him.

"I've got a signed contract," Big Tag argued.

Charlotte stayed on the couch, watching the argument like it was the best tennis match she'd ever seen. "That contract is with her stepdad. She is her own actual person and of an age that legally we can't treat her like medieval property. I know. I'm no fun."

"He didn't mean it that way." Wade seemed determined to treat him a lot like the stepdad treated Ally.

They were whole-ass adults who'd been facing adult choices and situations long before they should have been. They weren't dumbass kids who followed their hormones and thought of nothing but pleasure. Ally tied herself up in knots over every decision, and he was a careful planner. "I meant exactly what I said. Ian, I've done nothing wrong on this job. I'll find out who tipped off the gossip rags, and we'll be more careful in the future. Now I should get back to Ally and no, I'm not going to call her the client because it's obvious I like her."

Tag pointed to the tablet. "Yes, your tongue likes her throat. And don't say you haven't done anything wrong. Do you not remember the don't fuck the fucking client clause?"

"No one pays attention to that clause," Charlotte added. "He also tried to put in a no dating anyone from the office rule. Half of us are married to each other. He's just upset because you're excellent bait."

"What is that supposed to mean?"

Tag grunted, but Charlotte continued on. "It hasn't come up yet, but sometimes we need to send in someone to flirt with a target and get information."

"See, then it would be fine if you wanted to hop into bed." Big Tag started to pace.

"I'm not your honey trap, Ian." He was never going to play that way. "Talk to Matt. I'm sure he'll be happy to screw someone over for intel."

There was a knock on the door, and Jamal popped in, holding a familiar item in his hand. "Found it."

"I told you he wouldn't have allowed someone to follow him." Wade nodded Ian's way. "I'll go with Jamal to Hutch's office and see if he can figure out who left this present. West, you need to do a search every time you get in the car."

"I'm still not sure he's employed here," Big Tag argued. "After all, I'm the one who has to deal with her stepdad. The man is going to have questions. And her mom is going to drop a bomb on our heads."

"That's why you get paid the big bucks." He wanted to get back to Ally. "If there's nothing else…"

"West." Big Tag stood with his hands on his hips. "This is a bad idea."

"I'm ready to work however you would like me to, but I'm not leaving her until she tells me to go." Even then, he might end up watching her from afar.

Tag groaned, and there were a bunch of curse words mumbled under his breath.

"Well, I think you'll make a gorgeous couple," Charlotte said with a big grin.

A buzzing sound came over the line. "Ian, I've got Gavin Jacks on the line for you."

Ian's eyes narrowed, and if a man could shoot lasers from the fiery depths of his soul, that man would be Ian Taggart.

It was definitely time to leave.

And hope Ally wasn't angry with him.

"Let me know when you find out who tagged my car." The best way to deal with the beast was to power through. "Thanks for the pep talk, boss."

Ian growled.

And West made his very hasty exit.

# Chapter Five

Ally watched as West drove away and prayed nothing was too wrong.

"So what shall we do with our evening, Ms. Pearson?" Matt Edwards was handsome, but he had absolutely nothing on West. He was charming, but she was good at figuring out who was authentic and who was trying to play her.

West wouldn't know how to play her. It wouldn't even occur to him to try. He hadn't even tried to hide his feelings. When he was annoyed with her, he told her. When he was happy, she knew that, too.

*Is it because you're into me?*

She'd expected him to hedge, to shrug off the question like it was no big deal because he wasn't going to admit he might have feelings for her. That would give her the edge in the game of flirtation.

*Maybe.*

That was when she'd known beyond all doubt, it wasn't a game to him.

"I need to get up to the room. I have work to do." She didn't. She'd planned on asking West if he wanted to watch a movie while they ate their forbidden pizza. She was supposed to be eschewing carbs, but he was right. They'd burned a lot of calories today.

It had been an awful day that she would likely forever remember as one of her favorites. Hiking with West had been peaceful, and she'd never felt so safe.

What if something had happened and she didn't get to see him again? What if he got pulled off the case for some reason, and no one ever told her why?

"I was hoping we could have dinner." Matt followed her to the elevators.

"Sure. You can order whatever you like. I think food is part of the contract." She wasn't about to not feed the guy.

But she would wait to see if West came back. Any hunger she'd had was morphed into anxiety about West. She touched the button to call the elevator as her cell rang.

She glanced down. It was her sister. "Hey, Brynn."

"Hey, what's going on with that hunky guy?" There was a wealth of amusement in Brynn's tone. "He's gorgeous, and you look… I'm not joking, you look amazing. Where were you?"

And just like that, she knew why West had been called in. Someone had taken pictures of them. She hadn't seen a photographer following them, but those fuckers could work miracles with telephoto lenses. "Damn it. Someone followed us? That was fast. I literally got back from the hike a few minutes ago. Which site is it?"

"StarCall.com," her sister said as the doors opened. "Gavin is freaking out. I'm out to lunch with Mom and the whole restaurant could hear him yelling over her phone."

"You look amazing, darling," her mother said in the background. "And honestly, you haven't been seen with anyone in a long time. Your lack of a dating life has been remarked upon. I think the blue-collar lover thing will play so well. Can we get him on the show?"

She covered the phone and looked to Matt. "Can you pull up a website called StarCall.com?"

He nodded and started working on it as she pressed the number for the floor of her suite.

"No. Absolutely not. And no one is going to suggest it to him. This was all a huge mistake." She wasn't putting West on her mother's radar. How bad were the photos? She should have known the day had been too good to be true. "West and I are just friends. He's a nice guy, and I had a rough day. He took me hiking because I had to listen to Channing Lloyd talk about how it's beneath her to work with me and everyone chimed in."

"That bitch." Her mother seemed to have taken her sister's phone. "Does she think no one knows why her ass is suddenly so flat? It's because all that fat's in her face now. How dare she."

Ally sighed. "Mom, you know why she doesn't want to work with me. I have to prove myself. It's fine. I didn't make a scene, but West figured out I was upset and he took me hiking, that's all. It was completely innocent."

"You haven't seen the pictures, have you, darling?" her mother asked.

Matt cleared his throat and turned the screen of his phone her way.

Oh, wow. Nope. She wasn't getting out of this one. Someone had captured the moment when West had wrapped his arms around her and tried to close out the world. There were several photos. The two above the fold were of West leading her down the trail and of him with his big hands framing her face as he kissed her.

They looked hot together. Superhot, and not merely in a sexy way. They looked so into each other. She had an expression on her face she'd never seen before. Trust. Peace. Joy.

She didn't look like the brat princess when she was in West Rycroft's arms. She looked like a woman who was precious to someone.

He was going to be so upset by those pictures.

"Tell Gavin if he tries to get West fired, I'll never speak to him again." That might not be the worst threat. "Forget that. Tell him I'll move back in and never leave. He'll die with me in a room down the hall."

Her mother chuckled. "Don't worry. I think Mr. Taggart can handle your stepfather. Now tell me what's going on. Are you okay, darling?"

She wasn't sure. She was used to having intimate moments plastered on tabloid pages, but it would bother West. She knew she should be more upset, but in her mind, all it did was show the world she liked a guy. She didn't care if they knew. It was part of her life. It wasn't part of his. He was used to his privacy, and he wouldn't get that if he was involved with her even for the short term.

Her heart clenched because this had to be a deal breaker for him.

Even though she'd decided to take it slow, to be careful with him, now the possibility that he would walk away tonight made her infinitely sad.

How much did she have to give up to follow her dreams?

"I'm fine." She had to suck it up. "It was a moment. Now it's over. I'm going to concentrate on the movie. I think the read went well."

"Allyson," her mother began.

"I can't." She couldn't break down in front of this new guy.

"All right, my love." Her mother had always been good about giving her space when she needed it. "I was joking about the show, you know. I hope you can talk to him and work this out. Do you want me to try to get the photos taken down?"

For West's sake she would. "Yes, please. It probably won't work, but it might make him feel better if we try."

"I'm on it. Call me later," her mother said. "And Brynn says good-bye but wants to talk when you're ready. I could come out there if you want company."

Her mom meant well, but she would bring her own problems with her. "I'm fine. It will die down if we don't feed it."

"All right. And I sent you a little care package," her mom said. "It's got the blender you wanted, and the protein shake packs. I love you, Ally."

"You, too, Mom." She hung up as the elevator doors opened.

"So you and West are a thing?" Matt asked as Ally used her key card to open the door to the suite. "No wonder Big Tag was pissed. He's got this famous clause in all of his contracts."

She didn't like the idea that West was going to get in trouble with his boss. "What clause?"

"It's the famous 'no fucking the fucking client,'" Matt explained. "That's the actual name of the clause. It's usually cool, though. I've heard everyone breaks it."

She set her bag down on one of the couches in the sitting area.

"We're not sleeping together." She hadn't even thought about how it would affect West's job. All she'd known was what she wanted in that moment, and it had been him.

Was she as selfish as everyone made her out to be?

"Could I talk to West's boss? The Taggart guy?" She had to make sure the man understood it was her fault.

"I don't know if that's a great idea." Matt grimaced. "The big boss is someone I try to avoid most of the time. Wade's cool. He handles the bodyguard unit. I stay in my lane. I think you should, too. Like I said, everyone breaks that clause. I wouldn't be surprised if Big Tag yells at him, throws him a box of condoms, and sends him back out in the wild. Or he could fire him and then I'll get to spend more time with you."

He said it in that charming way that let her know he would like that, and not merely in a professional way.

"No." She had to play games with Jay. He was directing the film that could break her out. There was a certain level of polite game playing she had to do with him. She didn't with this man. "Just so we're clear, I'm not going to fall into your arms and play out some bodyguard fantasy with you. If you get skeevy with me, I'll have you replaced."

He stopped, his expression going cold. "Well, you didn't seem to have that problem with West."

"You're not West, and I'm not some experience for you to have and brag about with your friends. If I've misinterpreted your actions, then I apologize, and I hope we can have a perfectly professional relationship." It was best to set things on the right footing. She wasn't going to spend days placating this dude's ego.

The slight stain on his cheeks let her know how pissed he was. "You think a lot of yourself, Ms. Pearson. I assure you you're not my type. How about I go and stand outside the door like the good employee you seem to want. Couldn't have you being friendly with the staff, huh?"

He didn't wait for an answer, merely turned and walked out the door.

Proving he was a shitty bodyguard. She could enrage West and he wouldn't have left her. She went back to the foyer of the suite and checked the peephole. Sure enough, he was standing by the door.

Lot of good that would do her if there was someone in the suite.

West always checked the suite when they came back. He checked the closets and under the beds. She stood in the foyer until he gave her the all-clear.

She might have to get used to life without that kind of protection because West could leave on his own. If he didn't get fired. He might realize how hard it would be to be close to her and not want the trouble.

She sighed and moved away. She needed to find the number for McKay-Taggart. The least she could do was try to save his job. She could tell Ian Taggart that it was all her fault and she came on to West. The pictures didn't tell the real story.

The man would believe her. Everyone always believed the worst of her. This might be the first time it worked in her favor.

She found the number, dialed it, and was told Mr. Taggart was busy and would have to call her back.

Was he yelling at West? Or being yelled at by her stepdad?

She paced, anxiety threatening to eat her up.

And she was perfectly pleasant with staff, thank you very much. Despite her reputation, the crew of the reality show adored her. She'd had far friendlier relationships with hair and makeup people than she'd ever had with other actors.

There were two boxes on the small dining table. The staff at the hotel must have brought them up for her. Her mom had said something about a care package. She'd missed her little blender and the organic protein shakes she loved. They didn't have them out here. She'd promised West she'd let him try one.

*Hey, I know I just forced you into the public spotlight, but here's the best blueberry acai protein smoothie you've ever had.*

That would make up for it, right?

She picked the larger of the two boxes and started to peel off the packing tape. If West left, she would probably go into a shame/loss spiral and then all she would be able to stomach were these shakes. She would drop ten pounds of pure sadness weight and someone would tell her she looked great.

Fuckers.

She pulled one side of the box open and then pure horror swept over her as something cold and sticky exploded across her face.

Blood. She was covered in blood.

Ally screamed and jumped back, and all she could remember thinking was how much she wished West was here.

\* \* \* \*

West ran up the hallway, his heart threatening to pound out of his chest.

The minute he'd seen the red and blue lights, he'd known something had gone terribly wrong. As he'd pulled into the hotel's roundabout minutes before, he'd been surrounded by police cars and an ambulance.

He'd known it was about Ally, and he was going to kill Matt if something had happened to her.

"Sir, I'm going to need you to get back to your room." An officer in uniform stood outside the door. "This is an active police investigation."

"This is my room," he insisted. He wasn't about to be pushed aside by the police, and in this case, his boss's name would actually open doors for him. "I'm with McKay-Taggart. We're handling Ms. Pearson's security. I need to see my client."

The officer opened the door and disappeared for a moment, obviously conferring with whoever was inside. It took mere seconds before he was allowing West into the big suite. "You should talk to Lieutenant Ramos. She's taking the lead."

The first person he saw was Matt, who had a cup of coffee in his hand, talking with a pretty dark-haired officer. Matt was chuckling. The lieutenant looked like she was about to punch the asshole.

"What the hell happened?" West practically growled the question. "Where is Ally?"

Matt put the coffee down. "Hey, man, it was nothing more than a practical joke. Lighten up. She's fine. If you ask me, this is a little overkill, but I followed procedure. I've got a call into Wade, but he didn't answer his phone."

Probably because he was dealing with the GPS locator they'd found on his car.

It was a lot to happen in one day.

He looked to the cop. "Is it overkill, Lieutenant?"

The police officer shook her head. "Absolutely not. I came out because I run a special unit that handles stalking cases. That woman's being stalked. That was some straight-up Carrie bullshit, and she has every right to file a police report. I know the men in this room will shrug it off as some kind of prank, but she was scared. I listen when women are scared."

"It wasn't even real blood," Matt argued.

"You're off her protection," West announced. Had Ally had to deal with Matt telling her she was overreacting? He might not be able to fire the fucker, but his brother would get a loud report about his behavior tomorrow. "Go home."

Matt's eyes rolled. "Yeah, it's clear you're going to be able to be professional around her. I'll see what Big Tag has to say. You can't fire me, and I'm not going to let your brother fire me for something that wasn't my fault. She's the one who opened the package."

"The package was spring loaded," the lieutenant explained. "Like those packages that send glitter everywhere. Except instead of glitter, it was a substance intended to mimic blood. I've already had the package taken into evidence. Ms. Pearson was checked by EMTs because some of it got in her eyes. She's showering now. I've got a basic statement, but it's clear that she's shaken up. I'd like to give her some time to calm down before I ask her more questions. Are you watching her tonight? Given what she said about her situation, she should never have been left alone in this room."

"She didn't want me in the room with her," Matt complained. "She told me to stand outside. Otherwise I would never have allowed her to open the package."

He was done with Matt. If she'd asked him to stay outside, it was likely because he'd annoyed her, and they would deal with that later. "Officer, can I take her out of here?"

The officer in charge nodded. "Yes. I think a change of scenery might help her. Is MT looking into this? Or are you strictly protection?"

"Ian Taggart is handling the case himself, so he's going to want an update. I'll call him in a few minutes and let him know what's going on and that you're the one to contact."

The officer whistled. "Damn, I'm about to hit the big time. Well, best get to work then. Tell your boss I'll have an update in the morning, and I hope he'll share information with me. This feels like way more than a prank. There was real malice behind that."

He'd done his job, and now he got to do what he'd wanted to do since the moment he'd driven away from her. He got to find her again. "Ally?"

He moved into the living area.

"West?" Ally's voice floated through the suite.

He made his way to the big bedroom. He'd slept on the couch the nights they'd stayed here. There was a smaller bedroom, but it was too far from the main room. The couch had placed him squarely between her and whatever was coming her way.

Ally's hair was wet and her skin a pale white. She stood there in clean sweats and a T-shirt, her feet bare, and she looked so fucking vulnerable it threatened to break his heart. "Hey, I'm sorry. Someone sent me a package, and I thought it was from my mom, and we should also talk about these pictures that some asshole took."

Why the fuck wasn't she asking for what she needed?

Because she so rarely got it. Because she was always the afterthought.

"My mom is trying to get them off the website," Ally explained, not really looking his way. "I'll put out a press release explaining that we're not seeing each other. Hopefully…"

He didn't let her get the rest of the sentence out. He scooped her up and into his arms. "I'm taking you somewhere safe, baby."

She gasped as he settled her against his chest and started walking out. "But…"

He shook his head. "I'll have Tessa bring you your things. I'm in charge now, Ally. I won't let anything happen to you."

When she laid her head against his chest and allowed him to walk her out the door, he felt more worthy than he'd ever felt before.

# Chapter Six

West heard Ally laughing in the background and was finally able to take a deep breath. She was calm now, and he'd managed to get her to eat something and have a glass of wine.

She was safe.

"She's delightful." His brother walked into the kitchen and reached into the fridge for a beer. "She's way funnier than I thought she would be."

Since he'd driven Ally to his place, she'd been regaling his brother and his fiancé with tales of Hollywood gone wrong. She was being charming and lovely in her droll way, and they were eating it up. He rather thought having an audience that obviously adored her was helping calm her down. She'd been through a lot today. She deserved some adoration, but he could see the anxiety and sorrow hiding behind her smile.

"She's putting on a front, and I have to break through it." He kept his voice down because he didn't want to disrupt her conversation with Martin.

Rand looked back at the two of them. "Yeah, I thought she was handling the whole 'someone sent me a blood bomb' thing pretty well. She's an excellent actress."

"She doesn't get enough credit," he murmured. Rand didn't even know all the crap she'd been through today. "In this case, she's had years and years of experience sucking up every bad thing that happens to her because if she didn't, she might upset her sister's career which would have apparently sent them all into homelessness and ruin."

"Well, we know how that feels." Rand leaned against the counter. "You've nicely summed up our childhood."

He hadn't been able to stop thinking about that. They had far more in common than he would have believed. Once he'd seen that, he'd started to understand her. Then it had been a really quick slide into wanting her more than he wanted his next breath. "She pointed out the similarities."

"You like her."

West went silent. His twin usually knew what he was feeling.

Rand's brows rose. "You really like her."

He stared his brother's way. "Are you the only person in the world who hasn't seen the pictures on the Internet?"

"There are pictures?" Rand leaned over, raising his voice. "Marty, did you see pics on the Internet of my brother?"

"There are pictures?" Martin's eyes lit up, and then he seemed to remember he was sitting next to Ally. "Did the paparazzi follow you two around? That has to be annoying. After all this, I hope they give you some space."

"It's on Star Call," Ally said with a frown and a wave of her hand, giving Marty permission to go look. "You better be fast, though. I'm trying to get them taken down. I never intended to drag West into that part of my life."

Martin sat there, his hand not going for his phone, but there were practically tears in his eyes.

"I don't care about the pictures. You can go look." He needed to start breaking down the walls she was putting up, and that began with making it plain that she hadn't done anything wrong. "Ally, don't bother with the website. If it doesn't bother you, it doesn't bother me. There was nothing in those pictures I'm embarrassed about. I would rather talk about why you had to send Matt out of the suite."

Martin was already on his phone, standing close to Rand, both looking for the pics.

Ally turned her barstool toward him. "I didn't order him out. He started in on the flirty thing, and I explained I wasn't interested. He got butt hurt and decided to station himself outside. Also, I know I shouldn't have opened a package without it going through a guard, but my mom had just told me she'd sent one. I wasn't thinking. I was worried about you. What did you get called in for?"

He moved around the bar and got into her space, bringing his hand up to smooth back her hair. "The boss was upset about the pictures. He wanted to let me know I fucked up when I let a photographer follow us. There was a GPS locator in the wheel well of my SUV. It was placed there either at the studio or the hotel. I have to figure it out. I won't let it happen again."

"It's not your…" she began.

He let his hand find the back of her neck. He wasn't sure if she did it consciously, but her legs shifted open to let him in between. "It is, and my brother and Ian were right to call me out on it. I wish it hadn't happened, but the pictures worry me far less than what happened after."

"You're not upset?"

"That someone sent you a box of blood?"

"No, about the pictures," she corrected. "Those reporters will find your name. They'll figure out you're supposed to be my bodyguard, and they'll make a big deal out of it. They can make a scandal out of me eating a burger and having the tiniest little belly."

"I don't care if they find out my name. I'm sure we're not the first man and woman who started a relationship from a professional connection." Maybe they should have this conversation somewhere private.

His brother and Martin were perfectly silent and still, as though not willing to interrupt the show.

Ally turned her gaze his brother's way, not breaking the physical connection they had. "Are you upset? You are his twin. People might think it's you."

"People might think I'm the one passionately kissing a gorgeous actress in the middle of a sun-kissed nature setting?" his brother asked.

"I'm already planning on covering a wall in framed prints," Martin assured her. "You both look gorgeous."

She sighed. "Guys, it's not as glamorous as it seems."

Martin went serious. "No. It sucks, but West is sturdier than he looks. You're worried he's going to get hurt, but West has a pretty thick skin, and he doesn't scare easily. He moved his whole life to support his brother. He's a solid guy, and a little tabloid press isn't going to make him run away."

"How about the possibility of losing his job?" she countered.

Had she been thinking about this all evening? "Big Tag isn't going to fire me. If he did, I would find another job. I do have a degree, you know. It's in agriculture management, but it's a degree."

There was a knock on the door, and West felt his hand move to the pistol in his shoulder holster.

Martin had moved over to the monitor that the camera over the door fed into. One of the reasons he'd brought her here was the complex was gated, and he had an excellent security system. And there were three of them to watch her. He trusted his brother and Martin.

"It's Tessa," Martin announced, moving to answer the door.

Tessa Hawthorne walked in carrying a big, familiar suitcase. "I packed everything and checked you out of the hotel per your request. Including the other package, which I verified was in fact a blender and protein shake pouches. And your mom sent a nice note. She's very proud of you. So what did you do to Matt to put him in such a shitty mood?"

"Matt is an asshole who hit on the client and didn't like it when she turned him down," West announced, taking the bag from Tessa.

Tessa cleared her throat, another way to point out he might be being a hypocrite.

He was about to explain that she hadn't turned him down, but Ally stepped up.

"It wasn't the same. I was the one who came on to West," Ally said. "I practically threw myself at him. Those pictures don't tell the whole story. They don't show you the part where he kindly turned me down."

Tessa's head tilted slightly. It was a total tell that she didn't believe what someone was saying. Tessa had an excellent bullshit detector. "Really? Because he didn't look like he was turning you down."

"Like I said, pictures don't always tell the truth," she reiterated quietly. "There are angles that make things look worse than they are."

"Then why did he stand in the middle of the office and tell Big Tag he was madly in love with you and leaving for LA, and if Big Tag didn't like it, he could eat a bag of dicks?" Tessa asked.

It was good to know the gossip mill was running hard and fast. "I did not do that. I told him if he tried to replace me as the lead on Ally's case, I would quit and still protect her."

"You did?" She looked up at him like she couldn't believe he would say that.

"I was going to tell you that if you get the big guy a bag of dicks, they better be chocolate." Tessa shrugged it off, proving she was excellent at dealing with workplace drama. "Someone sent him gummy ones once, and it pissed him off. Also, he made me…"

West groaned. "I don't need condoms."

She shrugged again. "And yet you have so many now."

"His office is way cooler than yours, babe," Martin whispered his brother's way.

"I don't know. We have this horny AI who keeps telling all the men their butts look good," Rand whispered back. "Except for Adam. She tells him he's getting pudgy. Not sure what's up with that. I thought he programmed her."

Hutch and Big Tag were still having fun with Adam. He needed to get Ally alone. They had a lot to talk about.

Or not talk about.

She was wound so tightly, and they couldn't go for a hike.

He hoped she hadn't changed her mind about giving them a chance. Even if he had to go slowly.

"Ally has a research tour tomorrow, so I'm going to make sure she gets some rest," he announced.

"Uh huh." Tessa started for the door. "I bet she'll get lots of rest. It's the best clause to break, man. I should know. I married mine."

"I'll set the alarm, and then Marty and I are going to bed," Rand said, locking the door behind Tessa.

Martin's face fell. "But we could…"

"Go to bed so my brother and Ally have some privacy to work out the whole picture thing," Rand corrected. "Good night."

And he was left alone with Ally.

"Thank you for bringing me here. I like your brother and Martin," she began.

He moved in, hating the distance between them. Until Tessa had shown up, that distance hadn't felt so far, but the walls had come up again. "They like you, too. And Martin is right. I'm not some fragile guy who can't handle a little scrutiny. Now before this conversation twists and turns, let's cut to the heart of the matter. Are you planning on throwing yourself on the sacrificial altar of the career I kind of fell into?"

"If me telling your boss it was my fault helps, then yes," she insisted.

"No." He stared down at her, her head tilted up and eyes wide.

"No?"

"No." Damn but she was the single most gorgeous woman he'd ever seen. How had he missed the softness in her eyes? The sweetness that hid behind her exterior? Was it all the sweeter because it was only shown to a few people in her life? "I already told Ian he wasn't going to order me around when it comes to you."

"You told him that?"

"In so many words. He threw that clause in my face, and he can fire me if he wants to. Only one person can tell me to stay out of your bed, and that's you, Ally. You're the only one who can stop me."

"West." His name puffed out of her mouth with a little wonder behind it. Like she couldn't quite believe what was going on.

"Baby, you've had a day, and if you want me to sleep out here on the couch…"

"I don't. I just…you said you didn't need condoms."

He chuckled and let his hands find her hips. "I don't. I have my own, though you should know I'm going to check the expiration date. I haven't dated in a long time. And the boss is big on condoms, but I'm pretty sure he buys the cheapest ones he can find. It's nothing but the top of the line for you."

That was the moment he realized she wasn't touching him. She stood there, looking up at him like she was trying to make a decision.

What if she was trying to decide if he might not handle rejection well? What if she was as nervous about him as she had been about Matt? She could have spent the last few hours deciding he wasn't worth the trouble.

He was about to pull away when she went on her toes and brushed her lips against his.

"I hope you don't regret this," she whispered. "Because I'm pretty sure I will."

He intended to make sure she didn't.

\* \* \* \*

The minute she felt her lips against his, her body started to sing. It was like her skin came to life and anticipation was an actual sensation running through her veins.

It was stupid because it wasn't even like she was crazy about sex. She'd had a couple of boyfriends. She'd had a couple of men who'd tried to initiate her far too young, but she'd managed to save herself from those situations. It was probably why she was so reluctant to throw herself into the physical.

*But this is the right one*, a voice inside her kept whispering. *This is the right man. Even if he doesn't stay. Even if this doesn't last.*

Even if he walked away at the end of this job, she would know what it meant to be with him in every way that mattered.

His arms drew her in as he took over the kiss. She gave over immediately, more than willing to follow his lead. The truth was she usually felt completely awkward during sex. It was one of the reasons she didn't have much of it, but this was different. Her body seemed to move instinctively with his. When his hand found the back of her neck, her chest seemed to swell, flattening against his as he deepened the kiss.

"Do you know how long I've been thinking about this?" He whispered the words against her mouth.

He was so deliciously strong and muscular, his big body looming over hers, surrounding hers. "A couple of days."

He stepped back, but his hand found hers. "Forever. Even if it's only been a couple of days. Come with me. I don't want to sleep on the couch tonight. Let me tell you all the things I'll do if you let me in that bed with you."

Her heart rate had tripled, and if anything else had happened today, she couldn't remember what it was. There had been bad stuff, but it slipped away as she followed West down a short hallway and into his room.

That man was gorgeous. Somehow he looked better in a T-shirt and jeans than all the Hollywood stars she'd seen on the red carpet put together. She stared at him as he closed the door behind her, taking in his sandy hair and the sexy scruff that had made an appearance at some point today. He didn't know it, but she'd watched him shave the other day, standing in front of the bathroom mirror in nothing but his jeans.

"What will you do to me, West?"

There was the distinct sound of a lock clicking closed. "First, I'm going to kiss you again because I cannot get enough of that mouth of yours, Ally. I love how it looks and the snarky words that come out of it. I love the way you smile, and when you bite your bottom lip, I swear I feel it in my cock."

"I thought the words part would be a negative. I've been accused of being hard on a man's ego."

"Only because they had fragile ones. I've learned that you only complain when you need to. You keep calling me out, baby. It won't make me walk away."

Damn it. He was saying all the right things, and she didn't want to cry. She didn't want to get so emotional it ruined this first time between them. "Tell me dirty things, Rycroft. I can't. Not tonight."

He moved in, brushing her hair back. "We'll play this dirty tonight, but I need you to acknowledge that this is more than sex. I'm not going back to friends in the morning."

He was such a frustrating man. Did he know how many men would kill to be able to slip in and out of her bed? And that was why he was the right one. He didn't want to be her living vibrator, didn't want to be here to merely provide stress relief. "You matter to me, West."

He stared at her for a moment, acknowledging the agreement between them. They were together. For now. Then his hand moved to her hair, fingers threading through, and he tightened them, sending a sizzle across her scalp. "I'm in charge here, Ally. Do you understand me? You get to call all the shots. When you want to relax, we'll work on puzzles and watch whatever show you want to, but when that door closes, I'm the boss."

She'd heard the rumors about the company he worked for. There was a series of movies based on books by an author who was married to one of the employees.

Doms. Tops. BDSM. Was he a BDSM person?

She felt her nipples tighten at the thought of being tied up and helpless, at his mercy. She'd never considered the fantasy because she would have told anyone who'd asked that she wouldn't be able to trust any man that much.

Until she'd met him.

"Is this one of those things where we need a contract?" She'd heard of them.

A wicked grin hit his lips. "I don't think we'll get that far, baby, but you should understand I've taken the training class, and if you ever want to visit Sanctum, I'll take you. But this is fun and games to me. It's play. I don't need you to be truly submissive. I don't need to spank you, though I think it would be fun. All I need is for you to let me take the lead most of the time."

"What do you want me to do, West?" She prayed he said take off her clothes because they were starting to feel like they were too small for her.

"Take my shirt off."

That was even better. She reached down and pulled his shirt overhead, revealing that sculpted chest with a light dusting of hair. She tried to remember what she knew. "Can I touch you? Should I call you Sir?"

He caught her hand in his, placing it against his warm skin. "I'm West, and we'll ease into play. I'm pretty sure I will never tell you not to touch me. Unless you have some very specific fantasies. We can play out all of those."

Fantasies. Kinky, dirty fantasies. "I don't think I've had many up until now, but I could see you as a cowboy fresh off the range looking for some fun."

"I can make that happen, but for now, I'm just a bodyguard who's madly attracted to his gorgeous client. Did I mention I intend to kiss you again?"

When he kissed her, she couldn't think, and that seemed like the best idea right now. "I think you should."

He leaned over, lips skimming hers. "Did I tell you all the places I'm going to kiss? Definitely here."

He ran his tongue over her bottom lip, and she felt arousal flood her veins. She'd never gotten so hot so damn fast. She usually took forever to warm up. She let him lead, opening her mouth to allow him inside. He was a dominating presence, his big tongue sliding over hers in a silky glide.

"But as crazy as I am about your mouth, it's not the only thing I'm going to kiss. Give me your shirt, Allyson."

The deep command seemed to roll over her skin, and she found herself dragging her T-shirt over her head and tossing it away. She hadn't bothered with a bra. When the police had told her she could take a shower, all she'd cared about was getting that blood stuff off. She hadn't picked one up.

"Stay with me, gorgeous." He reached out and put a hand on her shoulder. "You're safe. You don't have to think about anything but what we're doing for the next couple of hours, and in the morning, I'll be with you."

He knew how to calm her in a way no one had before. "Where else are you going to kiss me?"

His hand trailed down to her breast. "I think this looks like an excellent place to put my mouth."

He got on his knees in front of her, and she couldn't breathe when he licked her nipple.

"Yeah, this is beautiful and definitely deserves a little attention," he murmured before drawing the nipple into his mouth.

He sucked her, and she felt her pussy go soft and wet for him, every cell in her body longing for what was going to happen next. He palmed her other breast, twisting the nipple lightly before caressing her. The nip of pain was eased with his softness, the two sensations making her head reel.

Before she knew it, his hands were on her sweats, easing them down. He managed to maneuver her to his big bed, settling her on the soft comforter. He pulled off her shoes and tossed them aside and then he made quick work of her pants and undies, and she was naked in front of him.

She had no problems with her body. She worked damn hard for it, but the look in West's eyes made all those protein shakes worth it. Ally watched as he untied the strings at the waist of his sweats. He kicked off his shoes, and then his pants and boxers went wherever her clothes had gone.

The man was a golden god. The scars on his body did nothing to lessen his attractiveness. She merely wanted to know the story of every single one. She wanted to know everything about him.

One thing she knew about him now was he had the prettiest cock. She'd never considered the male member to be a thing of beauty, but like all things West Rycroft, his was different.

He could rip her heart out, and she wouldn't be able to put it back together. Not ever.

Then he was on his knees again, his big hands going around her ankles and pulling her down the bed, and she wasn't thinking about anything but his kiss.

"Now see, this is definitely in need of attention." West spread her legs wide and leaned in. He breathed deeply, and she knew she should likely feel self-conscious, but it wouldn't come. All she felt was sexy as hell. "You smell like heaven, baby. Let's see how you taste."

Her vision went soft when he put his mouth over her pussy. Like everything the man did, he did this with precision and care. His tongue stroked her, mouth sucking her labial lips before diving deep inside. A searing heat spread through her when he fucked her with his tongue.

She squirmed under him, but his hands held her tight. Yeah, that did something for her, too. He wouldn't let her get away, wouldn't let her miss a single second of this exquisite pleasure.

When he licked her clit, she went right over the edge.

She was still panting when he got to his feet.

"Move up on the bed." The command came out of his mouth in a harsh tone, but she did as he'd asked.

He was back in seconds, a goofy grin on that gorgeous face of his as he held up a condom. "Still good, and so much better than what Tag would have sent."

Oh, she was falling in love with this man. "That better be ribbed for my pleasure."

The smile turned distinctly dirty. "Always, baby."

He rolled the condom on his cock and then covered her body with his. She expected him to start thrusting. She was so wet and relaxed she wouldn't mind. If he took five seconds, she would be happy because he'd brought her more pleasure than she'd ever had before.

She felt the hard nudge of his cock at her pussy, but he held himself there, staring down at her. All of his goofiness was gone.

"You matter to me, too, Ally." He kissed her, a soft stroke of his lips over hers. "You matter."

He kissed her again, and she felt him inside. In that moment, she felt him in her soul.

Ally wrapped her body around his, arms around his neck, legs cradling his hips. He thrust inside and dragged his cock back out. Their bodies felt perfectly locked together, fitting in a way she'd never experienced before. This all felt new, and she was overwhelmed, emotion threatening to choke her.

When the orgasm came, she let it carry her along. She rode the wave. It crashed over her, destroying every defense she had. All her walls seemed to come down, and she clutched him, the horrors of the day blending in because she couldn't hold it all back. She cried even as she came.

Because she was safe. Because it was all too much, and he was safe.

She felt him stiffen, his arms holding her so tightly as he went over the edge.

"That's right, baby. You let it out." He whispered the words to her, his forehead against hers. "Let it out. It's okay now. You're going to be okay. I'm going to make sure of it."

He rolled to the side, but not before she could have sworn she saw that his eyes held a watery sheen.

He eased her head down on his chest, cradling her.

Ally cried and let all the toxic moments of the day out because there was no room for them. Not anymore.

He was still holding her when she fell asleep, the world a better place than it had seemed mere hours before.

# Chapter Seven

"I can tell you fucked her. You know that, right?" Big Tag's eyes narrowed as he walked into the apartment bright and early the next day. "I could tell from all the way across the city."

West frowned. "Hey, keep it down. She's determined to take the rap for this, and I'm not going to let you make her uncomfortable. I take it you found something. You know you could have sent Wade over."

He wasn't used to the big boss showing up at his condo early in the morning. He was actually surprised Big Tag knew where he lived.

"I wanted to make sure your place is secure." Big Tag glanced around. "This is nice. What's your brother's boyfriend's name? Martin? He's got good taste."

"He does. When Rand and I first moved in, we had two lounge chairs and used paper plates every night." Now that he thought about it, he was really glad Martin had insisted on "doing" his bedroom, or he would have been forced to leave Ally in a room with a mattress on the floor and a dresser someone had left behind.

She was still snuggled down sleeping. He intended to let her rest until they absolutely had to go. He had her full schedule for the day, but there was nothing that was more important than her health.

Which was precisely why he'd forced himself to get out of bed. If he'd stayed, he would have been on top of her again. That little taste he'd had wasn't even close to enough, and he'd spent much of the morning wondering if even a lifetime would be enough.

He had some serious thinking to do.

His brother's bedroom door came open, and the man they were talking about strode out still wearing his pajama bottoms and a robe that looked like it could have come straight out of the fifties. "Morning, all. Please tell me our Hollywood princess is still here. I want to win her over with my world-famous lemon crêpes."

West snorted because now he knew why Big Tag was here. "I think you better make a lot. This is my…"

"Master Ian." Martin stood up a little taller. "Good morning, Sir. Are you here with an update on our girl? Can I get you some coffee?"

Of course Martin knew Ian. Probably better than West did. Rand and Martin played regularly at Sanctum. Rand was far more invested in the lifestyle than he was.

Though the thought of Ally tied up and naked, waiting for him, did something for him.

"I would appreciate that, Martin. Thank you and, yes, I've got an update." Ian moved to the kitchen table. "And I would not mind a couple of those crêpes. Charlie was busy this morning, so she shoved a box of cereal my way. Luckily, I had this errand to run."

Yes, Big Tag always knew where to get the best lemony treats, and he would work to get them.

"You two sit down, and I will get things started," Martin announced.

Big Tag took a seat at the small dining room table. "I'm looking forward to that wedding. Martin won't disappoint when it comes to dinner. Unlike my nephew. The kid has a celebrated chef for a stepdad and he served corn dogs at his wedding because he thought it would be whimsical. You know what's whimsical? A nice rib eye."

The boss was definitely a carnivore. "I do believe they're talking about a surf and turf menu. Did you get in touch with the lieutenant?"

"I did. She called me last night to go over what she's found out. The package was delivered via courier. It arrived at the hotel around noon, and a bellman delivered it to Ms. Pearson's room. I've already contacted the courier service, and it will not surprise you to know that the delivery was paid for with cash."

Of course it was. "There would still be paperwork."

"And I have a copy." Big Tag slid a file folder his way. "It's all in there, and every bit of information is fake."

It might still tell him something. "I'm going to assume you checked the security cameras around the courier office."

"Yes, and all I've got is a nondescript male in a ball cap who never glances up or takes off his sunglasses. Adam's already looked at it," Big Tag began. "He'll go into more detail today, but he says the person presents as male and appears to be roughly five foot eight and between one hundred and seventy and one ninety. It's hard to tell because of the jacket."

"So it could be JK Harris." That fit the rough description. He stared at the photo for a moment. If it was JK, then the man knew how to hide his distinguishing features. "Where was this?"

"Right here in Dallas," Big Tag said, his voice going grim. "The courier office is three blocks from the studio. And the great news is we lost track of JK Harris. Or rather we never had it. We know he was at his apartment in LA the night Ally's home was vandalized. LAPD contacted him. According to them, his very excellent alibi was he was home alone binging *Game of Thrones* for the third time."

"Do we have any idea when he left? And can we trace his cell?" West asked.

"His cell is in LA. From what we can tell, he is not. The last thing he purchased on his credit card was a burner phone." Big Tag seemed completely devoid of any good news.

"So he's in the wind."

"I'm worried the wind brought him right here." Big Tag sat back.

There was another problem to be dealt with. "Did you find out anything on the tracker someone placed on my car?"

"The GPS was easy to trace back to a large purchase from a mega corporation," Tag said with a grim look on his face.

West could guess what came next. "We have no idea which subsidiary we're talking about, do we?"

"It's got fifty different companies under its umbrella," Tag affirmed. "It's going to take a while to figure out which one we're looking at. The good news is a couple of them have entertainment arms. But this could take weeks not days, and there's no certainty we'll be able to legally tie anyone to that GPS."

So everything was moving at a snail's pace. "All right. Is there anything else you want me to do?"

Big Tag stared at him like he was trying to decide how to handle him. "Look, I know I was hard on you yesterday."

West shook his head. "I let a photographer follow us. I didn't check my vehicle. It won't happen again."

"West, this isn't instinctive for you, and you haven't been doing it long enough that it's engrained. If this gets worse…"

A bit of uncertainty started to creep in. The boss was right. There were guards with far more experience. "Then Tessa can take the lead, but I'm not leaving Ally. I'll stay by her even if you fire me."

"Her stepfather wants me to."

There wasn't a lot he could do about that. He'd thought the scenarios through, and he was comfortable with any decision Big Tag wanted to make. "I screwed up. If it makes your life easier to fire me, you should do it."

Big Tag sighed. "I told Gavin Jacks that if he wanted to do my job, he should start his own company. I offered for him to find another security group, but that wouldn't solve his problem. You would still be right there. If it helps, he called me back this morning and apologized. I suspect you'll get a hearty 'don't hurt my daughter' lecture, but otherwise they seemed to be supporting her."

"I'm glad because she deserves it." At least they had the bad part out of the way. "I think she should be safe here. The building is gated, and you need a security code to get the elevator to work. I've already told the front office to hold any packages any of us receive down in delivery. I'll check each and every one. I have a meeting with the head of studio security, and I'll go over all of this with him."

Big Tag nodded as though this was exactly what he'd expected. "All of this is very by the book."

"Am I missing something?" There was a weird air around his boss. Like he knew something West didn't.

"Yes. You accepted the whole job loss possibility with relative ease."

Had the boss expected him to throw a fit or something? "I know I screwed up."

Big Tag's eyes rolled. "Some of my employees have literally almost caused World War Three and I didn't fire them. All I'm saying is this might not be your passion and time is wasting. I know it seems like life is long but, brother, it goes by in such a flash. You did the right thing. You came to Dallas so your brother wouldn't be alone. He's good now. He likes his job. He's found his other half. It might be time to let go and start looking for what you want."

He kind of wanted to look around for the camera because this had to be leading to a prank of some kind. Big Tag barely noticed him. Right? "I'm perfectly happy here."

"Are you?" Big Tag asked. His demeanor had changed from his perpetual annoyance to something much warmer. "It's okay to not be."

Was he trying to get him to quit? That felt bad. "Do you think I want to go home? Do you think all I'm good at is herding cows?"

"That's not what I said," Big Tag corrected. "There are a lot of people who thrive in small towns and genuinely enjoy rural life. I don't think you're one of them. You're a curious one, West. I'm still trying to figure you out. Rand was easier. He needed the discipline and confidence to allow himself to be who he is. You never had that problem. You adapt to every situation. When you lived on the ranch, you were an excellent cowboy."

He wasn't sure where Ian was going with this, and he had to admit it made him a little wary. "I wouldn't say excellent, but I did the job that needed to be done."

"You went to college and seemed to do well there."

He hadn't loved every class, but he'd enjoyed the experience. Though there had been a lot of pressure on him at the time. "I was very aware at the time that money was being spent. It's easier now. We don't have to worry about the ranch going under."

"And if that gas hadn't been found, I would bet you would still be there working beside your brothers."

There was no question in his mind. "Probably, but I wouldn't be happy. I wasn't cut out for that life. Clint was. Heath and Clay are happiest when they're on the back of a horse."

"Where are you happiest?"

West had to think about that.

Big Tag pointed his way. "And that is what I mean. It can be hard. It can feel wrong to make the decision to figure out what you want to do, what it takes to make you happy. Prioritizing your own needs can feel selfish, but you've done your duty. It's your time."

"He's not wrong about that," a familiar voice said. Rand put a hand on West's shoulder. "You have been the best brother I could have had. You stood beside me even when it was hard, when it cost you friends."

"They weren't my friends if they couldn't accept my brother for his very normal need to love who his heart tells him to love." He was getting emotional.

"I want that for you, too." Rand sat down beside him. "I think what Ian is trying to say is that all of your options should be open. Especially given what happened last night."

Big Tag snapped his fingers. "See. I knew he fucked her."

"I think it was more than that, hence this conversation." Rand shook his head. "Sorry, the big boss struggles with his words sometimes. You are so into this woman."

He wasn't going to argue the point, but there was a problem with it.

"I've only known her for a week."

"I married my Charlie after a week," Big Tag said with a shrug.

West was confused. "I thought you were against this relationship."

Big Tag's lips curled up in a mischievous grin. "Am I? Or do I know how to get a stubborn asshole to speed up his timeline? We'll never know. And despite what I said, you didn't really screw up. I wouldn't have looked for a tag on my wheel well. You were in a gated parking lot at the studio and a secure lot at the hotel. No one should have gotten near your car. When you meet the security head, make him show you all the logs. Let's see if we can connect anyone to JK Harris. He worked in the industry. I'm sure he still has friends."

Martin walked in with two mugs of coffee in his hands. His eyes lit up when he saw Rand. "Hey, babe. Master Ian, here's your coffee. And West." He put the mugs in front of him and Big Tag. "Bacon or sausage?"

"Why choose?" Ian asked.

"Both it is then," Martin agreed and turned back to the kitchen.

"He's a keeper." Ian took a long drink of coffee. "Just think about what I said. Keep your mind open to the possibilities."

A soft gasp from behind had him turning. Ally stood in the hallway, her eyes on Big Tag. She'd pulled on one of his T-shirts and wrapped his bathrobe around her. Both were far too big, but she looked adorable standing there with wide eyes.

A look of determination came over her face, her chin coming up stubbornly, and she started to walk toward the dining room.

He started to stand, but Ian reached out a hand.

"Don't. I want to see what she does," Ian said under his breath.

"Mr. Taggart, if you're here to fire West, you should understand that I'm firing you," Ally announced in her full-on brat reality princess voice.

"Well, that should be interesting since you didn't hire me in the first place." Big Tag looked more amused than annoyed, so West relaxed a bit.

Ally had her hands on her hips, facing off with the scariest man West knew. He'd seen grown-ass military men who wouldn't stand up to Ian Taggart, but his girl simply powered through. "You know what, Mr. Taggart, if you don't want clients to jump your guards, maybe you should hire less attractive ones. Or you know what? You could upcharge for services…"

"Nope." He reached out and grabbed her hand, tugging her until she was sitting on his lap. "Too far."

"Sorry." She started to stiffen up. "I think we should…"

"Hush." There was only one way to deal with Ally. He nuzzled her neck. "He's not here to fire me. He knows we're together now. Stop making it less than it is."

"I wasn't…" She relaxed against him. "Fine, but if he's mean to you, I'll show him I can be mean right back."

"Well, I couldn't have that." Big Tag sat back. "I'm not here to be mean. Just here to sample the crêpes."

She sat up, gasping a little. "There are crêpes?"

Martin stuck his head out of the kitchen. "We are a full-service B&B."

"I love crêpes," she said as she snuggled against him. She reached out and grabbed his coffee mug, bringing it to her lips.

She was a coffee thief. He would have to remember that.

He kissed the top of her head as Big Tag started talking about how movies had been made of his exploits.

West sat with her, his mind going over and over what Ian had said.

The trouble was he was starting to think the only thing he was passionate about was the woman on his lap.

\* \* \* \*

Ally stood on the balcony of West's condo, looking out over the green space and wondering if the press had found her here. There weren't a bunch of people standing around shouting questions, so she thought no. It wouldn't be long, of course.

She liked it here, and it wasn't only because this was the place where she'd figured sex out. Sweaty, emotional sex with a gorgeous ex-cowboy was merely a part of the appeal.

She also liked Rand and Martin and lemon crêpes, and not having to be on every second of the day. For so long, even being with her family involved cameras and crews and playing a part. She wouldn't take that back. The show had set her mom and stepdad up for the rest of their lives and ensured she was taken care of financially. It gave her the freedom to pursue her dreams, but it had come at a cost. Being with West and his family made her realize how long it had been since she'd let her walls down.

It felt good. It had felt so good being with him the night before, and it hadn't all been about sex. Crying in his arms had felt like she'd released a pressure valve she hadn't even known she had.

She heard the sliding glass door open and turned. West was in the shower. They needed to leave in an hour, and she would have to face her castmates. She was eager to get to do some research today while they were on the tour, but she wasn't happy about putting her mask back on.

It wasn't West who walked out. It was Mr. Taggart's big body taking up all the space in the doorway.

"Is it all right if we talk before I head out to the office? I've got a couple of questions Eve wanted the answers to." When he wasn't frowning, he was a spectacularly gorgeous man. Not that he was bad when he frowned.

He reminded her of her stepdad. When he wasn't in authoritative mode, he was quite pleasant to be around.

She stepped to the side and allowed him to join her. "Sure. What does she need to know?" Eve was the profiler who was doing a work-up on her stalker. "Although I can make it easy for her. If she's wondering why JK does what he does, it's because he's an asshole."

Taggart chuckled. "Yeah, I got that. I think she wants to understand why he's an asshole."

She wasn't sure having someone profile her stalker would really do any good. "Does it matter? It's not like I'm going to pay for his therapy. He could use it, though."

Taggart joined her, resting his arms on the balcony railing. "Yeah, we all need that from time to time. How are you this morning? Yesterday seems to have been pretty rough on you."

She was surprised he was being so nice to her. She'd gotten the feeling they hadn't exactly hit it off, but he'd been charming this morning. That could have been all about Martin's breakfast. "I'm okay. It was rough, but good things happened too. I mean, the exploding box thing was awful, but it turned out to not be real blood. I knew it the minute I calmed down enough to smell it. It's a common mixture the FX guys use for blood on movie sets. I know the policewoman said she needed to send it to a lab, but that's what it is."

"So you think he's working with someone? I thought he was in set design not special effects," Taggart said.

He might have been the inspiration for a couple of movies, but it was clear he didn't know how crews worked. "He would know how to make it. Everyone pitches in, especially on small budget sets, and almost everyone starts there. I happen to know JK started out working for the set dresser on a couple of low-budget horror films, so he would have helped the FX guys. He would also know how to spring-load a box."

"But he's never done anything like this before," Taggart mused. "None of his stalking behavior has been physical."

"The LA cops told me they thought he might be escalating. Not that they would do much about it." They hadn't arrested him for the dead birds in her home citing they didn't have enough evidence to get a warrant. "West told me he's probably here in Dallas."

Over breakfast, he'd given her a rundown of all the reasons she needed to be super careful. She rather thought she was about to get another lecture.

"We're looking for him," Taggart assured her. "I've got our sister company actively taking the lead. Despite teasing Adam about his design choices, he's the best in the business. He'll find this guy. Did anything happen around the time he first broke into your home? If I understand correctly, before that he'd never physically accosted you."

"He liked to yell things at me," she admitted. "It sucked, but I didn't feel like I was in real danger. It's not like he cornered me or tried to get me alone. I think it was more like he wanted an audience to air his grievances to. Oh, he was big into trolling me on all the socials."

Taggart's head nodded as though that was the answer he'd expected. "So what changed?"

"I don't know. I've heard he's had trouble getting a job. I don't feel bad about that. He was harassing women. He should have trouble getting a job." Most men she talked to about it hedged in some way. They talked about giving him another chance and him learning his lesson.

"He could have kept his mouth shut, done some training, and been a better human being. Then he would deserve a job. Until then, fuck him."

Okay, she kind of liked West's boss. It gave her the courage she needed to tell him the bad part. She knew West would tell his boss about what had happened with Matt, but she needed to do it herself. "Speaking of, we should talk about Matt."

A brow rose over Taggart's blue eyes. "Why? I don't have an employee named Matt. I had one. He fucked up and could have gotten the client killed. Then his ass argued with me and he said a couple of things I didn't like, and poof, he's gone. It's one of the true joys of being in charge."

"I can bet what he said. I know that I'm seeing West, but…"

"That doesn't mean you hit on Matt," Taggart agreed. "It doesn't mean you flirt with everyone. I'm starting to figure you out, Allyson. At first, I thought you were a typical brat princess, but then my daughter bought a dress for spring formal that does not involve black or leather."

That made her smile. She'd thought a lot about the young woman lately. "Good for Kala."

"I'm pretty sure she did that because someone took the time to tell her she didn't have to wear a costume to be herself."

"I think she'll probably be back in combat boots come Monday, but it's good for her to understand she can be whoever she wants to be. She can be goth girl one day and wear a princess dress the next. She doesn't have to wear her armor all the time. It's freeing when you realize the armor is your bones and skin and soul and it's always with you when you need it."

"You remind me very much of her. I thank you for being kind to her," Taggart said.

"Of course." She took in a deep breath. "You know the world would be a way better place if we felt like being kind was like the norm."

"It would," he agreed. "Now because I like you, I'm going to have a dad talk with you. I know you have a stepfather, but he appears to be a 'protect the women' kind of dad."

"You don't protect the women?"

"Absolutely, but the first protection is learning to protect yourself. If anything like what happened with Matt happens again, you are to call me. You are to lock yourself in somewhere safe and wait for a guard who is interested in keeping his or her job to show up."

She knew what came next. "I promise I also won't open any packages. I will allow West to take the fake blood next time."

He stared at her for a moment. "I'm worried you're not taking this as seriously as you should."

She thought she was taking things pretty seriously. She hadn't been back to her own home in weeks. "What else should I be doing? I've got a guard on me twenty-four seven. I promise I'll follow all the protocols. If this is about the hike…"

"It's not," he countered. "You were with West, and you can't be cooped up inside all the time. As long as you have West or Tessa with you, it's fine. This is about something else, something I want you to think about. It's honestly about instincts and about the fact that you remind me so much of my daughter. She powers her way through things and ignores her instincts. I worry she can't hear them because she's so busy giving the world her middle finger. That part she gets from me."

"I'm not afraid of JK Harris if that's what you're worried about."

"That is exactly what I'm worried about and why we're having this talk," Taggart said. "I want you to be afraid of him. Have you ever heard the phrase fear is a gift?"

"I thought military people weren't ever supposed to be afraid."

He chuckled, but it was easy to see he was serious about whatever he was going to say next. "That's complete bullshit, and I hope Hollywood isn't getting that message out. I want you to be careful, but beyond that, I want you to listen to your fear. The kind of fear I'm talking about isn't something to be overcome. It's something to listen to, to give in to. Don't mistake it for panic. Panic is the real enemy, but fear can save you. Fear is the instinct that someone is watching. If you feel that, do not ignore it. Don't shrug it off as paranoia. Accept it and find safety. The problem with fear is if we're right about it, most of the time, we have nothing to show for being correct. That's why people will tell you you overreacted. Fuck 'em. They don't know what you felt or what could have happened."

A chill went through her. "You think he really wants to hurt me."

"I think he already has," Taggart replied. "I also think there's something more happening here. He escalated from screaming at you and trolling you online to invading your home and sending you pranks that could have genuinely hurt you. He's putting more on the line now. If we're right about who this is. That is what Eve is trying to figure out."

"She thinks it could be someone else? Someone new?" She hated the fact that there was absolutely more than one person out there who wanted to bring her down a rung. "I get a lot of hate mail. Some of them are harmless. Some of them feel… Well, they spark that fear instinct you talked about."

"Is there a reason you didn't send them to me?"

"Because I don't keep them," she admitted. "Like I said, there's a lot of them. I delete the emails and throw away the letters. I don't like having them hanging around. It would be like a weight on me. But my direct messages are still on my social pages."

"Yeah, I checked those out. You get a lot of hate online."

She wondered if those assholes would soon find West's socials and give him a big dose, too.

Did she have any right to drag him into her world?

"I think that's all part of being a celebrity online," she explained. "Everyone gets it. Some people don't see us as real living human beings. We're characters to them, and that makes it okay to put all their hate and anxiety on us. To others, they feel like they know us so well we're best friends. When you don't acknowledge that relationship, they get offended. It's a tightrope."

Taggart sighed. "It sounds like hell to me."

"That part is, but I also get to do something I love, something I've wanted all of my life." As long as she could remember, being in front of that camera, bringing characters to life, had been her passion. It had been hard to be the one who wanted it while her sister had it.

"Your sister got out of the business."

"It wasn't really her passion. It might have been if she'd come into it when she was older. Brynn is a very artistic person, and she was a good actress, but her childhood was a lot of work. I resented her a little when I was younger, but by the time we were teenagers, I wanted to take some of the burden from her. I was her assistant for a long time. I think it's why I don't have one. I know how hard that job can be. Even if you've got a great boss, you can feel invisible."

"Some people prefer to be behind the scenes," Taggart pointed out. "They usually pair well with partners who like to be the center of attention."

He'd been so nice to her that she wanted some advice. "What do I do if my haters find West online?"

Taggart's lips tugged up. "Can they find him? I don't think West has a bunch of social media pages."

"What?"

The door opened, and West looked out, a brow rising. "Am I missing a meeting?"

Big Tag held both hands up as if to declare himself perfectly harmless. "Not at all. I was just updating our client on the fact that she's going to be handled by you and Tessa only for a little while. I'll work Jamal into the mix when he finishes up his current job."

"What happened to Matt? I was going to talk to you about him today." West joined them on the balcony. "What he did last night was unacceptable."

"Precisely why I fired his ass," Taggart replied. "Now Ally here is worried her legions of haters are going to find your Instagram and overload it with criticism your tender feelings won't be able to handle."

West's expression went confused. "What is Instagram?"

Ally rolled her eyes. "That's bullshit."

He grinned, a heart-stoppingly adorable expression. "I know what it is but baby, I don't have one of those. I am not the kind of guy who spends all his time taking pics of his food and posting it online. I do not see the point."

She stared at him for a moment, wondering what century he was living in. "You don't have a single social media page?"

West seemed to search his memory. "I think I had a Vine for a couple of months."

She shuddered. "I don't understand."

He leaned over and kissed the top of her head. "You don't have to. You have enough social media for all of us. The point, though, is that first of all, I don't have a bunch of tender feelings. I leave that to the big boss."

Taggart nodded. "I'm known for my delicate emotional state."

Sarcasm was big with these people. She liked that, but she wanted things to be clear. "So they won't be able to scare you off by trolling you?"

"The best way to avoid a troll is to not go over any bridges," West said. "Some dude in a bar told me that. Of course, he also claimed to be a werewolf, but I did think it was relatable advice. I don't have bridges for them to set up shop on, so we're good. And if you're worried about how I'll deal with photographers who show up, you'll find I'm cool under pressure."

She needed to find a way to make him understand. "They sometimes say bad shit about me, but you can't let that get to you."

"It's your career on the line. I won't let them get to me. I'm not going to hurt your career by trying to defend you with my fists. But I will try to get you out of there as quickly as possible. We need to decide how we're playing this now."

"Playing this?"

"He wants to know if he can hold your hand in public," Big Tag translated. "Did he wear a condom?"

"Yes," she shot back. "But one of his own because yours are trash. You know you should really think about this. You claim to provide a premium service, but those are like bulk condoms."

Taggart's laugh boomed through the yard, and he shook his head. "I like this one, West. Keep her alive."

He walked away, and she was left with West.

And his question. "I don't want to hide you. I don't want to pretend like you're just my bodyguard, but I also want to look…"

She thought about what she'd been about to say. Professional. She'd been perfectly professional, and these people didn't care. They only cared about her past. Why was she trying to placate them?

"You want to look…?" West asked expectantly.

What had she told Kala? That she got to decide who she was. No one else. West was the first man she'd had real feelings for in a long time, and she didn't want to hide that. She went on her toes and kissed those ridiculously sensual lips of his. "I want to look like the person I actually am. I think I'm going to save the acting for the set this time around if that's okay with you. But you should know the paparazzi will find us."

His hands found her waist. "Let them."

She leaned her head against his chest and let herself breathe. The bad parts might not be so bad if she had this man to hold her hand.

# Chapter Eight

West studied the grand living room, utterly fascinated by the transformation. Just a few days ago, it had been a blank slate, a soundstage with nothing but equipment, and now it looked like the inside of a luxurious mansion.

Just a few weeks into this assignment and he was finding a world that never bored him. He'd thought he would absolutely hate the times when Ally was working and he was at loose ends, but once the crew figured out he didn't mind helping, they'd started to put him to work. He'd learned a lot about lighting and special effects when he was sure Ally was in a safe space. The acting part didn't do anything for him at all, but there was something magical about using lights to make an actress practically glow.

Of course he didn't need lights to make Ally glow. All he needed to do was kiss her until she couldn't think.

He was rapidly falling in love with a woman who would leave in two months. They had an expiration date, but he didn't like to think about that.

Ally sat on one of the ornate couches, watching as her "mother" gave a speech about keeping the family together in the face of the tragedy they were going through.

This he'd been told was "blocking."

Over the last few weeks, Ally had done an enormous amount of research. Her days were filled with working out, doing publicity stuff that he didn't understand, and then she got down to the actual work. Sometimes she fell asleep in the car and he had to carry her up to the condo.

He wasn't sure how she managed it all, but at least JK Harris had been perfectly quiet. They had to deal with the paparazzi, but he'd found a fun way to get around them when he wanted to.

Sometimes having an identical twin came in handy.

"Mr. Rycroft?"

West turned, and the director was walking his way. He hadn't talked to the director much. He didn't seem to be around the set a lot, which confused West. Jay Clarke seemed to spend most of his time in one-on-one sessions with the cast. "Hello, sir. You can call me West. Shouldn't you be in there? Aren't you the director?"

Jay looked like he'd just walked in. He hadn't set his messenger bag down yet, but the cast had been working for over an hour. "I don't handle this part of the production. That's what second units are for. I have two second ADs I trust. I oversee things. When we actually film this scene, I'll be on set, but this is more for the actors to get the blocking down and to test the light and make sure everything will run properly."

So the director had better things to do than grunt work. "Understood. I'll be honest, I thought this would be far more boring than it actually is."

"That's odd because most people are eager to get a behind-the-scenes look and then realize how complex the whole thing is and they lose their fascination," Jay replied. "If you have any questions, feel free to ask. Most of this crew loves to explain what they do. Actors aren't the only ones in Hollywood who love attention. Speaking of attention, I heard a rumor that Ally's stalker has followed her to Dallas. Is that possible?"

"Did it finally make the news?" He'd been surprised the press hadn't picked up on it until now. DPD had kept the whole thing quiet, but it was inevitable that it would get out. Now the reporters would really be looking for them.

Jay frowned. "It came across a gossip site. Someone sent her a box of blood? Tell me it wasn't real."

He'd been meaning to have this conversation for days but hadn't been able to pin Jay down. He was also a little surprised security hadn't gossiped. The head of the studio security unit had all the reports and had agreed to implement new protocols now that they were going to start spending most of their time here. "The police haven't sent me a toxicology report yet, but Ally claims it's absolutely fake blood. She seemed to think it was something a special effects department would use. Can I ask you if you've ever worked with a man named JK Harris?"

A brow rose over Jay's intellectual-looking glasses. "Can't say I remember the name, but it's a small world. It's possible. How is she? She must have been terrified."

He wouldn't ever forget the look on her face when he'd come to pick her up. "She's handling it as well as she can."

"Yes, she seems to be handling it phenomenally. She hasn't mentioned anything about it in our sessions. You think it's from this JK guy?" Jay seemed to consider the idea for a moment. "You know, now I think I do recall hearing his name, but it was connected to Ally. Is he the set decorator she accused of harassment?"

West didn't like how the director framed the situation. "He's the asshole who harassed her, so yes."

"Hey, not trying to offend. It's hard to know what's the truth sometimes. If Ally says he did it, then I believe her. I believe women. But the trouble is sometimes perfect politeness isn't good for artistic environments. Not in that case, I'm sure, but in some cases, we have to be tolerant."

He wondered how many times someone asked Ally to put up with shit to keep some bigwig comfortable. He wasn't going to argue with this man, though. He'd promised Ally he would behave. "Anyway, yes, that's the man LAPD has been looking at. Someone broke into Ally's house before filming started."

"And you think he's the same person who sent her the box?" Jay looked out over the set.

"My boss is not entirely sure." Eve had finished her basic report, and one of her scenarios was that this was not JK Harris, but another person with a more sinister purpose than revenge.

"She has another stalker? Because it would seem to me that this guy has a reason to hate her," Jay pointed out. "I bet he's having a hard time finding a job."

Ian and Eve seemed unsure at this point. He trusted his boss's instincts. "I'm sure he is. I think the investigators are simply trying to keep an open mind. I hope you'll understand the new safety protocols I asked security to put in place."

It involved more patrols, more security camera coverage, better vetting of visitors.

"I want her to feel safe here," Jay said. "But I would bet this is going to be a hardship on the rest of the crew. Hopefully our insurance doesn't go up. But the important thing is Ally is safe."

Yes, that was all West cared about.

"Jay." A familiar face walked toward them.

West had seen several of Bryce Jericho's films. He usually played the stalwart hero. Now he looked like he'd been cast as Annoyed Man.

"I'm late because I was forced to show ID to get on set. What the hell is going on?" Bryce completely ignored everyone but the director. "Like the security team doesn't know who the hell I am? What kind of a second-rate production are you running here?"

He was loud enough that the rehearsal had stopped, and the actors were now staring, trying to figure out what was going on.

He saw Ally standing with her arms crossed over her chest, her expression blank.

"Hey, we've had some trouble," Jay started to say.

Bryce shook his head. "No, we haven't had trouble. She's had trouble. That ridiculous bit of fluff you've brought in is the only person here who has trouble."

Ally barked out a laugh. And then shook her head. "Sorry. I've never been called fluff before."

That was his girl. "Mr. Jericho, I made that call. As the head of Ally's security…"

"Seriously? The head of her security?" Bryce shot back. "We all saw the pictures. The whole Internet is loaded with shots of the two of you acting like teenaged lovers. It's not enough that she's apparently bringing her stalkers along. She has to cause a scandal in the tabloids, too?"

"I'm not sure how it's a scandal." It was obvious Mr. Jericho was going to play out this drama. West intended to at least point out the flaws in his logic. "Neither Ally nor I are involved with anyone else. We're two consenting adults who've started a relationship. How is that scandalous?"

"See? I knew she was fucking him," Channing said under her breath.

Ally's eyes rolled, and the brat was in the building. There was a tipping point with Ally, and she'd reached it. "Oh, you're just jealous. He was never going to do you, lady. And Bryce, it is the twenty-first century. Me falling for my superhot and awesomely amazing bodyguard is not a scandal. Do you know what is? You fucking your trainer behind your wife's back."

A gasp went through the room.

Ally shrugged. "Well, we all know it. Do you know why no one talks about it? Because you guys are happy to throw me to the wolves so they're fed and don't try to eat you. You think I don't know that? I know I'm incredibly pretty, but there is a brain under all this, too. I'd like to know which one of you put a tracker on my boyfriend's car."

The actor West had been told was playing Ally's brother shook his head. Reid something. "Why would we do that?"

"Again, to throw off the scent," Ally explained. "You guys know the paps are going to show up, and you want all eyes focused on me so they don't see what you're doing. Which in your case, Reid, is a shit ton of cocaine."

The actor's face turned red, and West was worried he would have to intervene.

When his baby decided she was through playing, she got mean. Though it was nothing less than they deserved.

"You little bitch," Reid said between clenched teeth.

West started for the stairs. It looked like he might be guarding her body today.

"See, that's way more apropos than calling me a bit of fluff." Ally pointed Reid's way. "Cocaine Bear understands."

Channing snorted. "Well, she's got you there. All that scruff. You should shave, son."

"How dare you accuse me of using drugs." Reid stared up at Ally. "Do you think I haven't heard what you say about me behind my back?"

"Said behind your back?" Ally asked. "Dude, I will always insult you to your front. That's the great thing about me. And I know one of you tipped off the paparazzi."

Bryce threw his hands up. "This is ridiculous. I don't know why I should have to put up with a sniveling little no talent like you at all. I think I won't for now."

He turned and walked away.

"What was that about?" Ally asked as he joined her. Her hand found his, and despite the bravado, he could suddenly tell she wasn't enjoying the confrontation.

Jay held up a hand, addressing the cast and crew. "I'm going to find out. Allyson, I'd like to have a word with you in my office in half an hour. And no, I am not firing her if that's what you're thinking. I want to talk to each of you. This is getting out of hand. I happen to know that there's going to be a story in *Vanity Fair* about chaos on this set. I won't have it."

Jay stalked off after Bryce.

"You should quit. You're the one causing all this chaos, and I bet no one put a tracker on his car," Reid said, venom dripping. "I bet you called the paparazzi yourself, you attention-seeking whore."

Oh, he was not going to be able to keep that promise he'd made. West felt his fists clench.

Ally simply squeezed his hand. "He's not worth it. Reid, you should go to the bathroom. You missed a spot right under your nose. Can't get messy with the drugs now."

She was going to kill him.

Reid stormed off.

Channing sighed and smoothed back her hair. "Oh, honey. I utterly underestimated you. I shouldn't have given your mother's reputation. Cocaine Bear, indeed. That's very amusing. Well, this is a complete mess. I don't think we're finishing this today, so it feels like wine o'clock. I'll be in my dressing room if you want to talk. I've got an excellent Pinot if you're interested."

Ally frowned. "I thought you hated me."

Channing shrugged one elegant shoulder. "I suppose I'm jealous of what you can get away with, but I came up in a different time. I'm being a bit hypocritical because you're beautiful and young and have that pretty stallion to ride."

"Excuse me," West began.

Ally put a hand on his chest. "You know she's right. Hush. I think this is going to be an incredible monologue."

Channing did seem to be gearing up. She put a hand over her heart. "It's hard getting old in this business. Especially since they think you're old at thirty-five. When I was coming up, I had to hold my tongue about everything. I fought, though. I brought down a producer who viewed actresses as stress relief. He was incredibly powerful, and I had to risk my career to do it. At first I thought who is this mouthy kid? You know what? You can say the things you say because women like me and your mother fought and won. So you go, kid. You're not a half bad actress, and you only tell the truth, which this industry needs more of. And Reid really should shave. That beard made him look like he was recently shipwrecked."

"And it's a catchall for the coke that doesn't make it into his nose," Ally said.

Channing nodded. "I'll go talk to Bryce and Jay. Mr. Bodyguard..."

"It's West. Or Mr. Rycroft," he corrected.

Channing shook her head. "No. I don't remember names unless they have some sort of production attached to them. You are Mr. Bodyguard or Ally's Hot Piece. Your choice."

Channing seemed to have learned a thing or two from those men she'd claimed to bring down. "Mr. Bodyguard it is then."

"Excellent. Can we allow security to identify Bryce from his very familiar face? The old boy needs the affirmation," she explained. "He'll be much more amenable to the rules if he knows they've been bent for him.

Can we all agree that Bryce Jericho isn't a stalker?"

Ally looked up at him. "It's so not Bryce."

He sighed, giving in. He didn't see the imposition, but apparently, allowances must be made. "Fine, but he does have to check in."

"Well, of course. How else would he get the fawning attention he needs?" Channing asked. "He would be disappointed if they didn't acknowledge his godlike presence. And Ally, let me know if you get contacted by actual reporters. I'm not worried about the tabloids. They'll take a grain of truth and turn it into a massive conspiracy. Every set has chaos. Honestly, it's publicity, and that never hurts. But if *Vanity Fair* or some other industry publication is starting to write about it, that could be bad. I wouldn't want you to get a reputation for being difficult to work with."

"Pretty sure I already have that," she admitted.

"Well, it's not earned. I've found you very amusing to work with," Channing admitted. "And it's not all about the pretty landscape you bring with you. Let me know if you need help."

West frowned. "Did she call me landscape?"

Ally leaned into him. "Shhh. You know you are the prettiest of all landscapes."

She sniffled, and he totally forgot about being objectified. He kissed the top of her head. "Want to go sit somewhere for a while?"

"Yeah. I think this might be a cowboy, take me away moment."

He swept her up and carried her back to her dressing room, closing out the rest of the world.

For now.

* * * *

Ally felt somewhat better an hour later as she sat down in Jay's big trailer. It had been delivered mere days before, taking up a whole row of parking spots. Hers was being hooked up tomorrow in preparation for the weeks they would be filming on the sound stages. Four weeks of studio work and then a couple of location shoots and they would be back in LA.

And West wouldn't be there. Unless he agreed to stay on as her bodyguard.

They were floating through, not talking about what came next because she kind of dreaded what came next. West had a job and a family here, and her life was pretty much on the road at this time.

She didn't see how they could work, but she also couldn't imagine her life without him. There were moments and events that changed a person so thoroughly there was a before and after. She would forever view this time as After Meeting West. AMW. She was a changed person, softer than before, more capable of being hurt.

"Cocaine Bear? Was that necessary?" Jay looked at her like she was a naughty ten-year-old.

"He annoyed me. And honestly, he's been awful to me this whole time." She was halfway getting along with Channing and Bryce—or had been—but Reid was a complete dick weed. "He walks away when I try to talk to him. He's beyond rude."

"Have you considered that it's part of his process and you should honor it?"

"Process?" She tried to tamp down her annoyance. Jay had been trying to teach her his method for weeks now. His "method" was to be miserable all the time, to find the pain the character went through and allow herself to be traumatized. He'd wanted her to check herself into a mental hospital for a couple of days to experience the horror.

Her character was only shown in the mental hospital once, and she figured she could scream without forcing herself to endure something terrible.

"Yes. Reid is taking this production seriously," Jay said, adjusting his glasses. "His character hates his sister, so he hates you."

It took all she had to not roll her eyes. "I think that has to do with more than the character." This would get her nowhere.

She'd come into the production planning to do anything she had to do. So why had she ignored what Jay wanted?

West freaking Rycroft, of course.

When Jay asked if she wanted to spend time in an asylum, she'd thought about how she would explain that to West, and it sounded so ridiculous she'd said no.

Before Meeting West, she would have gone all wide-eyed and thanked him for teaching her to be a better actress.

After Meeting West, she knew she had a process, too, and it wasn't to act like a jackhole because of a character she was playing.

Her mom and stepdad had been in the business too long. She didn't spend enough time with her sister and brother-in-law, so being around West, his brother and Martin, and all their friends had been a revelation.

If she'd never met West, she wouldn't be sitting here on the cusp of being fired. She would be a sheep following this guy's every word, but she would have a career.

"I know not everybody gets along." Jay sat back, seeming to relax. "That's a good thing, in my opinion. I think there's a lot of drama to be found in real-life conflict."

"You mentioned something about the press picking up some stories about conflict on the set. Shouldn't we be worried about that?" She couldn't help but think about what Channing had said. The tabloids were one thing. Industry news was another, and Ally was absolutely the one with the most to lose.

She'd meant everything she'd said earlier. They did hide behind her. She was the chum they threw into the water to distract the sharks while they swam away to the next project.

If it got out that she was the reason for production problems, there might not be another project for her.

Jay waved that off. "You know all publicity is good publicity. If it gets people talking about the movie, I don't mind it."

"It's not good publicity for me," she pointed out.

"I disagree, but I think we should talk about how it affects the production. You have to deal with the tabloids on your own. I can't do anything about it. Now while I think you should be a bit kinder to Reid, I don't entirely hate the vibe you two have. The friction between the two of you actually works. I've watched your rehearsals, and I think you and Reid have an odd chemistry that's going to pop on screen. That's not the part of your performance I'm worried about."

Ally's gut tightened. How close was she to losing this job?

The last couple of weeks seemed like a dream. Beyond a couple of nasty DMs online, it appeared her stalker had gotten a life or something. All had been quiet on that front, and she'd been able to sink into the relationship with West. She'd felt more like herself than she had in years. Even the paparazzi didn't bother her. If they wanted pics of her and her superhot boyfriend, have at it. Though she'd had to warn Martin that they would never go away if he kept bringing them coffee and cookies. They would have a whole pack of stray photogs to feed soon.

Except Martin wouldn't be in LA with her.

She forced herself to focus. "What part of my performance are you worried about?"

His fingers tapped on the notepad he held on his lap. "I think you understand Delia's isolation. You have her compassion down. What you are missing is her fear. I thought you held back in rehearsals. This is where actually experiencing what she went through would be helpful."

Yes, traumatizing herself for art sounded so fun. It was supposed to be acting. She held her tongue on that part. It wouldn't help her. Instead, she chose to defend her portrayal based on historical evidence. "All of the accounts I've read claim Delia was afraid, but she was also calm and tried to use reason to explain what was happening to her. That's what makes it so tragic. Her brother was trying to make her look insane, and when she would question him, he gaslighted her."

Jay shook his head. "That's not going to work for my vision. I'm making a statement here, Allyson, and your portrayal is the centerpiece. Of all the Crownes, Delia's story is the most tragic. The audience needs to feel the horror of what is being done to her. Your restrained performance in rehearsals is not what I'm looking for. I don't understand it. Is it that you don't trust me enough to open yourself?"

"I'm trying to be true to the Delia I've come to know." She took a deep breath and realized she was going to have to compromise. "I'll rehearse it with more horror energy, I promise. But I would like a couple of takes where I get to experiment."

He would use the take he wanted to anyway. He was the kind of director who said he listened to actors and brought them into a collaborative process, but he really just moved them around like chess pieces.

"Sure. But I also want to talk to you about some experiences that will allow you to draw on your own feelings," he explained. "I'd like to set you up with a therapist who can maybe walk you through some of your recent events."

"Why?"

"Ally, you've had some scary situations happen to you recently, and you're not using them as fuel. What good is anything if an artist can't use it?"

Well, it was called life, and not every second of it had to be picked apart and stuck on screen for all to see.

Some things were private. Some moments were only for her and her family.

She never used to think this way. Fucking West.

Life might have been easier BMW.

"I also think you should talk about your experiences," Jay was saying. "I was surprised you didn't. No one even knew about what was happening to you until today."

"Security knew," she pointed out.

"But your castmates didn't. Your fans didn't. These are the most important people in an actor's life, and you're cutting them out."

That felt like an accusation. "I think I put enough of my life out there. Besides, one of the things my security professionals have told me is this guy is hungry for attention. He would love it if I was on the news nightly talking about him. I'm not going to allow him that much space in my life."

A brow rose over his eyes. "Your security professionals? Or your boyfriend?"

"He's both."

"Yes, and he's had a huge impact on you. That's quite clear. You aren't the same actress I hired. You seem much less focused. Honestly, one of the reasons I brought you onto this production was I liked how hungry you were. It was obvious to me you would do anything to be a better actress, to make great art. To leave behind your somewhat unsavory past."

Why was it unsavory? Because she'd made money from a reality show? Why did that make her a lesser species? "I assure you I'm still hungry. Acting is all I ever wanted to do."

"Are you sure it's acting and not simply being famous?" Jay asked. "I thought I knew the answer, but lately I fear it's the latter. You're choosing your personal life over the opportunity of a lifetime. Do you want to be Meryl Streep, or are you satisfied with being Lindsay Lohan? Is your boyfriend going to star in your next reality show?"

West would be horrified at the very notion of being on the show. But if she didn't have a career, wouldn't she need that stupid show again?

Could she coast through life on what she had? Give up on everything she'd wanted because she couldn't quite seem to break through?

"Are you telling me in order to keep this job I have to break up with my boyfriend?"

Jay stared at her, the moment almost becoming awkward before he spoke. "I'm saying you should think about whether having him around is helping you to focus. And you should think about the advice he gives you. He doesn't live in our world. He doesn't understand it, and it's going to cost you and quite frankly the whole production. I simply thought you would be more committed to doing the work."

She was going to lose this job. "I'll consider everything you've said."

Even as she said the words, she kind of hated herself. It felt like capitulation.

"And I'll call in the therapist," Jay said, smiling for the first time. "It's a brand-new part of my method. I'm writing a book about it. I honestly think this is going to be one of those productions that goes down in history as legendary. If you stay with me, you'll be a part of changing the way our industry works. All I need is a little compromise from you and for you to be open to the process."

Wasn't that what she'd always wanted? Jay Clarke was a director on his way up. He could open all doors for her.

But he might close the one to the room she felt most comfortable in.

Was she going to be smart and prioritize herself? Or was she just a stupid girl who liked a boy?

All she wanted was to get somewhere private, somewhere she could cry and try to figure out where the hell it had all gone so wrong.

As she walked out, she wondered if she didn't have a lot in common with her character after all.

# Chapter Nine

West was happy they were heading back to the condo because he knew the route so well. He was pretty sure he wouldn't have been able to navigate a new route because his brain was buzzing.

Something had gone horribly wrong in that private talk with the director, but he couldn't get her to talk about it. Despite the argument the cast had gotten into, Ally hadn't been upset that afternoon. Getting Channing on her side seemed to have energized her, and she'd wanted to spend the time they had making out in her dressing room. She'd walked into the meeting with Jay relaxed and ready to talk about work and come out strained and quiet.

It had taken every bit of restraint he had to not knock down the door and demand to know what Jay had said to her.

But then being Ally Pearson's boyfriend was a constant lesson in restraint. He couldn't beat the shit out of all the people who hurt her. He had to have skin as thick as hers and understand that behaving the way he wanted to would only cause more trouble for her.

He was getting there, but then he had a day like today and he couldn't stand the thought that he hadn't been in there, in that room with her to deflect all the crap the director had likely told her.

He pulled into the parking lot, and sure enough, he had to move through three photographers shoving their cameras at the car.

Ally flipped them the bird.

That was the first time in weeks she'd been so openly bratty. She'd been either ignoring them or smiling and giving them a great pic before moving on.

Oh, she was a roiling ball of emotions, and he had to figure out how to get her to let them out or she would boil over, and that fire would burn them all.

Calm. He had to be an ocean of calm even when he was anxious himself. When Ally was upset, she could say things she didn't mean.

West parked the car. They were past the gate, and management had let the photographers know they would enforce trespassing rules.

"Ally, do you want to take a walk? Or go to the gym?" Sometimes she got rid of her nervous energy that way. He wanted to offer to take her to bed, but she hadn't reached for him when she'd walked out. There had been no hand in his, no hug or tilt of her head to ask for a kiss.

This was about him, and he was suddenly worried this might be a fight he couldn't win.

"I need to work on my lines."

She didn't. She knew that script back and forth.

"Okay." He didn't open the car door. "I wish you would talk to me."

"About what, West? About how the director thinks I'm wasting a great opportunity because I'm too focused on my boyfriend to do my job? That?"

Ah. He was right. This was absolutely about him. "Yes, I definitely think we should talk about that."

She threw the passenger side door open. "I told you I have to work."

He followed her, locking the car and heading into the building. Ally blew past the doorman, who frowned since he was used to her stopping to chat and ask him about his wife and kids.

She was throwing those walls up as fast as she could.

West nodded his way. "Sorry, Frank. Bad day."

He hustled to catch up with her. This was going to get bad if she was behaving like she'd been given villain duties on this particular episode of life. She didn't even hold the door to the elevator for him. He had to jog or she would have gone up without him.

Was she trying to piss him off? "I get that you've had a bad day, but you don't have to take it out on me."

She pushed in the code that would take them to their floor. "Don't you know that's what I do? See, if you'd ever watched the show, you would know that I'm a mean brat who takes her problems out on everyone around her."

He kind of understood how that show had worked. There wasn't a whole lot of reality to a reality show. "I'm sure you were used to create a whole lot of drama, but I do know who you are, and this temper tantrum is not you."

Her eyes widened, and he realized he'd made a mistake. "Temper tantrum? Are you kidding me?"

She wanted to fight.

West took a deep breath, his brain working. He needed to keep calm and understand that whatever was going through her head, she didn't want to hurt him. She was stressed and anxious, and he was the only safe target.

"I'm sorry, baby. That was a poor choice of words. Could you please tell me what upset you? Or if you don't want to talk to me about it, please call your sister. You need to talk to someone."

Her jaw went tight, and she stared straight ahead. "Maybe what I need is to get my life back to normal. I want to move back to the hotel. Nothing's happened in weeks, and I'm tired of playing out this stupid suburban fantasy. Jay is right. This is why I'm fucking up."

That man had gotten into her head. Maybe he was the one who needed to call her sister. He'd learned rapidly that Brynn was the one who saw the world outside of work. He worried if Ally talked to her mom, she would agree with the director.

Or maybe he needed to give her what she asked for. "I'll make the arrangements. I'll try to find a place close to the studio. Do you want me to call Tessa?"

The elevator doors opened, but she stood there, staring ahead like she wasn't sure of what she wanted.

He pushed the button to keep them open. "Ally, if you honestly believe being involved with me is going to cost you your career, I'll step back because you've become the most important thing in the world to me."

Tears shimmered in her eyes. "I think this role is getting to me."

If he could bust down that wall, he might be able to save this because no matter what he was saying in the moment, he had no intention of leaving her. Not for any real amount of time. It might be different if he genuinely believed he wasn't good for her, but he was, damn it. They fit together in a way he'd never imagined he could.

Big Tag had told him to find his passion. Well, his passion might be the woman in front of him, and he couldn't lose her now.

"Okay. So how about I let Tessa take you to the studio. She can be at work with you, and I'll watch you when you're not working." It might take the pressure off her.

She sniffled and then her shoulders fell back, and that gorgeous stubborn expression made another appearance. "What's the point, West?"

She stalked off and strode toward the condo door.

He followed. "The point to what?"

"To any of this? What are we doing? It's not like it's going to work between us. Channing is right. You're a pretty guy I use for stress relief, and in a couple of months, I'll find another one who looks just like you."

His heart hurt. This was all bravado. She had a decision to make and she couldn't, so she was pushing him to make it for her.

That wasn't going to happen.

"I need to tell you a story." He opened the door and was happy that it looked like they had the condo all to themselves.

Her eyes rolled as she slung her bag on the sofa. "And if I don't want to listen?"

"Then I guess you can plug your ears or something, but I'm going to tell you a story, and you're going to realize that what you're doing right now isn't going to work."

"What I'm doing?"

"You are trying to push me away so I'll leave at the precise moment you need me the most. You think it will happen eventually, so you want to take the pain now and it won't be so bad. Everyone treats you like the annoyance they have to deal with. You know that speech you have about the rest of the cast using you to hide behind? Well, your family did some of that, too. When they needed drama for the show, they didn't look to Brynn. They didn't ask Gavin to act like a douchebag. It was you."

She shook her head. "I agreed to it."

"And now we deal with what that means. Baby, I don't care if the rest of the world thinks you're a selfish brat. I know the truth. I know who you are deep down, and I love you."

"Don't you fucking say that." She'd flushed a nice shade of pink, and he knew he had her.

This was the corner he'd needed to put her in to see if she would fight her way out or if she could accept that all she had to do was hold his hand and they could get through anything.

"I'll say it because it's true, and now I'm going to tell you my story. Not mine, really. It's my brother Wade's. You've met his wife."

They'd had dinner at Wade and Genny's a week before and spent the night talking on the back porch.

"Yes," she agreed.

"They were high school sweethearts. You've got to understand that at the time, my father had recently died, and my mother was in a terrible position financially. Wade was going into the Army, and Genny was going to join him after basic training. Then one day she called him and told him she was marrying another man."

"She didn't," Ally said, obviously surprised.

"She did. She was marrying a friend of hers. He was rich and came from a powerful family. My brother decided she'd found a better bet, and he didn't see her again for fifteen years."

Ally shook her head. "What did the other guy do? Who did he threaten to get her to marry him? Why the hell didn't Wade show up at the wedding and stop it?"

"Because he was young and had his pride hurt," he admitted. "It's so much worse. What Wade didn't know was that Genny's first husband had bought the mortgage to our ranch. I was a kid at the time, so I didn't know this until long after Wade did. My mother and oldest brother showed up and begged Genny to save the ranch, and she loved my brother so much she put up with an abusive asshole for as long as she could. She also kept the secret of why she did it. My brother was awful to her. Hell, I was awful to her because I bought the lie that she dumped my brother for cash. Allyson, I will not leave you. I will not put pride or some fucking ranch in front of you. But, baby, you have to meet me halfway. You have your ranch. It's your career. You're willing to sacrifice everything for it. Does that include me?"

The tears were pouring down her cheeks now. "That's not fair."

"Not a lot about your life is fair. I'll step back if you need me to, but I won't stay away forever. You need me. You need me to balance out your life. You need me because I will put you first, because you will always be my priority. I love you, Allyson."

She stood up and shook her head. "I don't want to feel like this. I was untouchable before I fucking met you."

"No, you weren't," he argued. "You just didn't have anyone to share the burden with. You're used to people using you, and you have to wonder if I'm going to do the same. I won't, but you have to trust that I won't, and that's hard for you."

"God, West, please fight with me."

He moved in, brushing back her hair. "No. There's no fight between us. It's all inside you, and I'll be here to help you, but you have to make the choice. Something that asshole said to you made you think you have to choose between me and your career. That's bullshit, but it's something you have to deal with. Do you want me to get a whiteboard out? I'm pretty sure Rand has one around here. We could make a pros and cons list."

Her jaw had actually dropped. "What is wrong with you?"

And then she smiled and shook her head and dropped back down to the couch, her head in her hands.

"The only thing that's wrong with me is my girlfriend is hurting and I feel helpless."

"I told you you're just a walking vibrator to me and you say you love me. Who does that?" she asked.

"A man who loves you, Ally. What would you say if I told you I want to be an actor and I've been using you all along to get access to your contacts?"

She looked up, and even with watery eyes she could roll them. "I would say that's ridiculous."

The tension in the room seemed to ratchet down, and he knew he'd navigated his way through the worst of the storm. "You are doing a fabulous job, and I think that Jay is a massive ass who thought he would have more control over you. You are not missing focus."

She sniffled and then reached for his hand. "He doesn't like how I'm handling this one scene. He says I'm not intense enough, but I don't want the audience to think Delia is some raving madwoman."

He sat down beside her, and she immediately crawled onto his lap, arms winding around him. "So you have a difference of opinion, and he tried to manipulate you into thinking it's not about your instincts as an actress. It's about your boyfriend."

She gasped. "He negged me."

"Baby, I don't know what that means." One day he would catch up on trendy lingo.

"It's like when a guy gives a girl a compliment but it's really cutting her down so he has more power in the relationship," she explained. "Like you would be so pretty if you lost a little weight."

"Someone said that to you?"

"Hello, have you met the press? But yes, some guys swear by it. I do not date those guys. I apparently only date ones who magically know how to deal with me. West, I was going to cut you out of my life. You were right. The whole way over, I was thinking about the fact that you would get sick of dealing with my damage someday, and at least if I took that pain now, I would still have a career."

Jay was pretty good at creating chaos himself. "You will still have a career. How many projects do you have lined up?"

"Three, and two specials for the reality show."

"Do you want to do those?"

She seemed to think about it for a moment. "Maybe, but in a different way. I think I want to be more of me. I think that was scary before because if I'm me, then what they say about me hits differently. But I want to leave this persona behind, West. I want to be the person I think I'm becoming with you."

"I'm very proud of you."

"And I lied." She wiped at her eyes. "I like the suburban stuff. I like sitting down to dinner every night and it's not a damn protein shake. I like hanging out with your family. But West, I really will have to leave. I understand that my life can't revolve solely around my career, but I have to work, and you're going to be here."

She was a woman who needed stable ground. "Or I could be with you."

She stilled, sniffling again. "You would come back to LA with me?"

He'd been thinking about this for days. He knew it was probably too soon to upend his whole life for a woman, but sometimes a man had to follow his instincts. Every single one told him she was the right choice, the right challenge, the one who would fascinate him for the rest of his life. "The boss told me it was time to figure out what I want to do with the rest of my life. What if I worked on film sets for a while? I bet my girlfriend's mom has connections that could get me on whatever sets she's working on. I could try some things out, learn from people who know what they're doing. I could figure out what I want to specialize in. I'm going to be honest, I love working with the lighting units."

Her lips curled up. "So you are with me for my connections."

He held her close. "I'm with you. I'll be with you for however long you'll let me."

Her arms tightened. "I'm afraid that might be forever."

"That is perfectly fine with me." He lowered his lips to hers. They'd made it through, and he was the one who needed some reassurance now. "But I need to know I'm more than a damn stallion you like to ride."

Her hands found his hair, running her fingers through it. She looked at him like he was precious. "You are so much more to me. I wonder if I can think of a way to show you." She brushed her lips over his, and the mood shifted immediately. Her body relaxed, and she kissed along his jaw. "You do such a good job of showing me how you feel. I knew, you know."

"Knew?"

"That you loved me," she whispered. "I knew because of how you take care of me. Do you know, West?"

She took care of him, too. She made his lunch when she made hers.

She made sure he took his vitamins, and despite the fact that he knew she didn't care about sports, she sat with him while he watched games. She was knitting him a sweater. He wasn't sure when he would wear it in LA, but he would love it. "I know, Ally. But I'd like to hear it."

"I love you. I've never loved anyone else." She slid off his lap and to her knees. "I'm going to tell Jay tomorrow that he can find someone else if he thinks I'm not giving him what he needs. I'm not going to let him have control over my personal life. I never had a personal life before, so I'm going to have to get used to this balance thing."

"I'll help you with that." His cock was stirring to life now that he had what he really wanted—her admitting she loved him. He knew. It was good that she'd figured it out, too. "Now why don't you come up here and show me how nicely you can ride this old cowboy."

Her head shook, and she bit her bottom lip. "Not yet. I want to play first."

Her fingers went to the fly of his jeans, and he groaned as she opened them and eased the zipper down. His cock went rock hard, desperate for the touch of her hands…and that mouth. That mouth drove him crazy.

He let his hands find her hair as she licked the tip of his dick.

Heat poured through him.

"You're pretty everywhere, West Rycroft," she said before taking another swipe with her tongue. She traced the ridge around his cockhead. "I need you to remember that you're all mine when the Channing Lloyds of the world decide they want a taste."

He was going to tell her how little a temptation that was to him, but she chose that moment to suck him into her mouth, and all that came out was a low groan.

She was soft and sweet around him.

Her tongue whirled and stroked him, and he watched as her head moved up and down, working to take him deeper and deeper.

If he didn't stop her, he wouldn't get inside her, and he really wanted to get inside her. He needed to be inside her.

"Come up here, baby. Please." He tugged lightly on her hair. "I want to see you. I want you with me."

Always.

She got to her feet and kicked off her shoes. She let that gorgeous hair of hers out of the bun she normally wore, the tresses flowing around her shoulders. She pulled her shirt off and then slipped out of her jeans.

There was a reason she was considered one of the most beautiful women in the world, but for him, her loveliness went so much deeper than what showed up on a picture. Ally was perfect for him because she was a mystery. She showed the world one thing, but the truth was for him.

He was a man who had a twin brother, who had been one of what seemed like endless sons who gave their all to the ranch. She saw him. Only him.

"West, are we in a committed relationship and can we both say neither of us has anything we could pass on to the other?"

"I don't have an STI. I actually hadn't had sex for a couple of months before you." He wasn't a player. Almost all the sex he'd ever had had occurred in relationships. This was the last relationship of his life. But he knew where she was going, and he knew she was on birth control. "Come here, baby. We don't need to dig for a condom if you're comfortable."

Big Tag would yell at him, but he was willing to trust her. And he was also willing to take whatever came their way. He rather thought he would be a pretty good stay-at-home dad. Or follow-his-wife-around-while-she-chased-her-dreams dad.

That didn't sound like such a bad thing. And he knew a good thing when she was standing in front of him completely, beautifully naked.

"I'm comfortable." She climbed on him, straddling his hips. "With any outcome as long as we're together. I'm not going anywhere, Rycroft." She rubbed her pussy right along his dick. "I mean that figuratively, of course. We're going to go to LA."

Fuck, that felt like heaven.

"I'll go wherever as long as you keep doing that to me." He thrust up, filling her pussy with his hard length.

The pure pleasure damn near made his eyes roll to the back of his head.

She leaned back, changing the angle and working his cock. "That feels so good."

She was a freaking goddess riding him, moving her hips and encasing him in her heat. She rode him until she shuddered and moaned out his name. He let himself go, let the orgasm rush through his system. His balls drew up and shot off, a crazy blast of pleasure as he filled her.

"I love you, West Rycroft," she said, lowering her lips to his.

"Oh, god. West, what the hell? You're supposed to leave like a sock on the door," a familiar voice said.

They hadn't noticed the door had come open.

Ally yelped and tried to grab a pillow to cover herself.

"I should never have to see that," Rand complained as he raced around them to get to his bedroom.

"I thought it was beautiful," Marty said with a smile. "You two keep going. Make some pretty babies for Uncle Marty to love."

"We have to move," Ally said, and then she broke into laughter.

"The straights are not all right," Rand shouted.

He rather thought the straights were doing just fine. But they were definitely going to have to move.

# Chapter Ten

West reached for the door to the studio and allowed her to walk through.

She forced herself because she really wanted to be back in bed with him. Today was going to be hard because she was going to tell her boss that he needed to stop being an asshole, and that never went well for her.

What had Channing said the day before? Something about how she'd done the hard work so younger women could feel safer.

Well, it was time for Ally to do some good for the little girls who would someday be in her position, and taking on Jay Clarke was how she planned to begin.

"Hey, baby, it's my boss." West stood in the doorway, holding his cell phone. "I should talk to him."

She nodded. "I'm going to grab some coffee and then I'm due in hair and makeup. I promise I won't leave the building."

He put the phone to his ear. "Hey, Ian. What's going on?"

She doubted Jay was here. He wouldn't show up until everything was in place and they were ready to shoot. She likely had an hour or two before she had to deal with him.

She grabbed her coffee and made her way to the small rooms where the principal cast had hair and makeup done.

And there was the last person she wanted to see. Well, not the last. It was sad that there were so many people she didn't want to see. This one was Reid. She should have studied the call sheet. She would have been better prepared.

He glanced over from his seat, looking up from his phone. "Hey."

At least he hadn't added a bitch in there. That was practically polite for Reid. She set her bag down. It looked like the makeup artists were prepping in the back, leaving her semi alone with the man who was playing her sibling. "Hey."

He turned the phone her way. "The *Vanity Fair* article came out."

She sighed. "I'm sure I'm the bad guy."

"I don't think any of us comes out great," he admitted. "I mean with the exception of our grand leader."

Naturally Jay would be seen as the adult in the room. She sat down in the chair with a huff. "Of course he is. He's Hollywood's golden boy. No one's going to say a bad word about him."

"At least they didn't call me a cocaine bear," Reid said with a sigh.

Maybe it wasn't nice of her to make fun of a dude's drug problem. "I'm sorry. I'll be nicer. Though you should probably lay off it."

He was quiet for a moment. "You're different than I thought you would be. You're not as awful as we all feared."

"I take it you've seen my show then." She should ignore him, but she was making an effort today.

"I don't think you come off all that bad on the show. It can be quite entertaining. I do think you show fairly accurately what it's like to be in this business. I particularly liked when you drove around with that weird guy in the golf cart."

"My Guber. I miss Greg." Greg would like West.

"Anyway, I was hoping we could start over. Reading that article… I don't want to be this guy. It's not how I like to work. This has been one of the hardest shoots of my life, and I've played some nasty characters. I genuinely hate the guy I'm playing."

It was the most he'd talked to her the entire time. Well, at least in a friendly way. Would he understand what she was going through, or would this get her in more trouble? She found she couldn't not respond. Once she started genuinely trying to fit in, she couldn't stop. Damn, West. That man was going to kill her.

Or lead her to an actual happy, balanced life.

"I don't think Jay and I are going to agree on how I should play Delia. He wants me to go full-on lunatic, but that isn't who she was."

"That was the real tragedy of it all. Delia was tormented by this asshole and she survived it, and he still managed to get her committed. She had to live her life in misery, and she was sane when she went in," Reid agreed. "I think that's way worse. But then I don't think Jay would say he's making a true crime drama. He's using a true story to make a point about how capitalistic greed has corrupted the American family or something. At least that's what he said during one of our private sessions." Reid sighed. "I thought those would be cooler. It's mostly the two of us talking about how awful you are."

She didn't like the sound of that. "My character?"

Reid turned her way, his voice going low, and there was an almost apologetic look on his face. "No. You. He thinks I need to hate you in order to play this character. At first, I thought it was some dumb thing I had to get through. It's not the first time I've had a director think he can mold me into what he wants. I'm pretty good at agreeing with everything and still doing what I want. But he brought in this therapist, and I think he's fucking with my head. I don't hate you, Ally. I mean, I don't like you or anything, but you're okay. The therapist told me it was okay to do whatever I needed to get in touch with this character. Jay said the same thing. I hadn't done coke in years."

A chill went through Ally. One of the things Jay wanted her to do was talk with a therapist about getting in touch with the character. By using her own history and background. "Reid, did he supply the coke?"

Reid turned in his seat, sitting back and staring at the mirror again. "He thought it wouldn't be a terrible idea to remind myself how it feels. Look, it's not like I'm sober or anything. I do a lot of weed. I drink. He didn't force me."

"Didn't he?" Was this what Jay had been moving her toward? "Did you feel like you would be able to keep your job? Because yesterday he pretty much told me to dump my boyfriend if I wanted him to consider me a serious actress."

He'd never said the actual words that he would look for someone else, but the implication had been there. It had threatened to send her right over the edge. He'd known exactly how to slide the knife in. If West wasn't so fucking perfect, she'd have pushed him out the door.

"I don't think you should do that. It's obvious he's the reason you're not a raving bitch. I'm not sure what Jay is thinking."

"He's thinking a vulnerable me is someone he can manipulate, someone he can turn into anything he wants." Jay had seen her for who she was. Lonely. Desperate to prove herself. So fucking desperate to mean something in the world.

West had seen the same things, and he'd done what he could to lift her up, to show her she was already meaningful. West had shown her she could be more than a career.

"I don't know if I would be that harsh. I mean, we've all known directors who pushed a little too hard."

"Reid, he encouraged you to do cocaine and then be mean to me. When you think about it, he actually did turn you into a cocaine bear." The dude had ravaged a couple of people. At least he had in the movie. "And now I wonder who is really talking about the chaos on set."

"I thought it was the crew."

A snort came from behind them, and Ally realized one of the makeup artists had joined them. It was the one she'd worked with. Kathy.

"The crew hates working with this asshole." Kathy set her kit on the counter. "And you can quote me on that. There's a reason he only retains the higher-up crew. The second ADs keep holding on because they think he's going to win another Oscar and they'll get their own directing gigs. The rest of us are almost entirely new. I wish someone had told me what a dick he is. Did you know he told me I shouldn't compliment you? We're supposed to tell Reid, Bryce, and Channing how amazing they all look, but we're supposed to not talk to you. At first, I thought that was because you were one of those 'don't look me in the eyes' assholes, but you're fun to be around. He heard me talking to you the other day and threatened to fire me if I didn't ice you out."

She'd never had a chance with this crew. Her director—the man who'd promised her he respected her—had made sure no one else did. She hated the fact that tears pulsed behind her eyes. She'd never cried this much until freaking West softened her up. Well, he would have to do a lot of cuddling and taking care of her because she was about to quit this whole fucking thing.

"Hey, you know we like you, right?" Kathy's tone had softened. "You're a good one, Ally Pearson, and that's why we're not going to follow his rules any longer. And if you ask me, he's the one who's talking to the press. He doesn't think we have ears or anything. Maybe he just doesn't notice us because we're beneath him or something."

The other makeup artist joined in. Kenny was a doll of a man, and she'd so enjoyed listening to his stories while he worked on Reid or Bryce. "Are we talking about what the PAs overheard?"

Kathy nodded and started to unpack her kit. "I got my sister a production assistant job. She hates it, of course. I tried to tell her she would be getting a lot of coffee for people, but she insisted. Anyway, she overheard Jay talking about this million-dollar book deal he would be getting after this project was done. And she's certain he was talking to the *Vanity Fair* reporter."

"I know none of us is talking," Kenny swore. "If we were talking, old Jay wouldn't look like the golden boy who puts up with everyone's shit for the sake of art. I think he's the one causing all the chaos, and he's doing it because he likes it."

He didn't merely like it. He thrived on it. If the cast hated each other, they didn't talk to each other. They didn't find out that the director was playing nasty games to "get them into character."

How far had his games gone?

Mr. Taggart had asked a specific question, and she hadn't been able to answer it. What had changed?

This role. That was the only thing that had changed.

The fucking call just might be coming from inside the house.

She stood up. "I think this is going to have to wait. I'm calling a cast meeting."

Reid turned her way. "We can do that?"

Probably not, but she'd been known to get her way.

\* \* \* \*

West opened the doors as the big boss approached. Ian Taggart was dressed for work in his usual button-down and slacks. He only wore a tie when Charlotte forced one on him, and a jacket was even harder to get him in, but he still managed to ooze authority.

"You talked to him?" West asked.

"Alex is taking him up to the office. We want to get a full statement out of him," Ian replied, walking through the doors.

They'd found JK Harris. It was why he'd called twenty minutes before. They'd tracked him down to a motel just outside of Dallas.

"So did he do this?" It was the question that bothered him on a nightly basis. Who was coming after the woman he loved and how could he stop them?

How much pressure would be off Ally if they caught the man who was trying to torment her?

"He claims he didn't," Ian replied. "According to him, he received a note the night Ally's place got vandalized. It told him all he had to do if he wanted his career back was leave without telling anyone where he was going. He claims he received a call from a director who would be willing to hire him but only if he spent a couple of months at the motel."

It didn't add up for him. "Why would he believe that? Or think we would believe that?"

"Dude, he's from Hollywood. Their scripts don't always make sense." Ian glanced down the hall. "Of course, there is one scenario in which it does make sense. Not for him to do it. That's stupid, but he's not the smartest guy in the world."

"Who would want to send him here for months?" West wasn't sure he was following Ian's reasoning.

"Hey, babe." Ally rounded the corner and reached for his hand. "Mr. Taggart, nice to see you. I think I figured out what's happening. You know that scene in the movie where the detective gets everyone in a room and points to the bad guy? I'm about to do that. Except I'm prettier than the old dude who usually does it. Come on."

He started to follow Ally, but he looked back at the boss. "Shouldn't you be the one doing this? Do you know who it is?"

Taggart strode along behind them, a mischievous light in his eyes. "Oh, I wouldn't take this Benoit Blanc moment from her for all the world. I'd like to see if she's figured it out. If she has it right, I've got some receipts I can show the room. Or is Scooby-Doo closer? He would have gotten away with it if not for those meddling kids."

"I prefer to think of myself as a superhot Angela Lansbury," Ally announced as she opened the door to the soundstage.

Up on the set of the Crownes' living room, it looked like the principal cast was assembled. Channing sat beside Reid, patting his shoulder, as Bryce paced and Jay sat in one of the big wingback chairs, his eyes narrowed.

"Hello, Allyson," Jay said with obvious disappointment. "Would you like to explain why you've demanded we all join you here? You know we have things to do. We're supposed to start shooting soon. If you're still interested in working on this project. I know you have better things to do."

Ally walked right onto the set, her ponytail swinging. "I can do my boyfriend and my job, thank you very much. He can be quick when I need him to be, and he's surprisingly flexible."

Taggart snorted behind him. "I can't believe I didn't like her in the beginning."

"She gets that a lot." He stood outside the lights. The spotlight was for her. He was the man who waited for her to come off stage, to take off the costumes and makeup and be herself again. He was her safe space.

"I bet he is. Hello, Mr. Bodyguard." Channing winked his way. "Who's your friend? He looks nice."

"He's married to a former mafia assassin." He did not want to be the reason America lost Channing Lloyd's talent. "I'm not joking. She really was an assassin, and she can be cranky about women coming on to her husband."

"Well, I didn't say she couldn't join us." Channing huffed.

"Could we be serious for a moment?" Bryce asked. "Our whole production is in chaos. I'm getting calls from my friends back in LA talking about us. We don't look good."

"Jay doesn't care about that." Ally put her hands on her hips. "Do you, Jay? Are you worried about how the press is looking at us? Or are you just happy that they are?"

Jay frowned, seeming to understand that this wasn't going to go the way he thought it would. "I assure you I am concerned, but I also understand the value of publicity."

"Chaos surrounding this film will do nothing but make people interested in the end product, right?" Ally faced down the director. "This is a film about people fighting over money. On the surface, it's not too interesting. Happens all the time. What's more interesting is a chaotic shoot. People were already talking about how the legendary Channing Lloyd would handle being cast as the mother to a nepo baby."

Channing waved a hand. "I handle all things with aplomb. It turns out you're quite amusing."

"She's the problem," Bryce argued.

"Well, that's what Jay seems to want us to think." Reid seemed more serious than usual.

A nasty suspicion hit West. Eve had told them she thought this could be another person. He turned to Ian. "Do you think…"

"I think I want to see how she handles this. You need to be ready in case he gets nasty," Ian advised. "He doesn't have a gun. If he hits her, you can't kill him here. We'll find a quieter way to dispose of the trash."

He wasn't about to let anyone hit her. He moved onto the stage.

"Did you or did you not tell everyone in this cast and crew to treat me like shit?" Ally asked.

How hard had this been on her? All the rejection had weighed her down.

Jay was quiet for a moment, and then it was like the mask came off and the real man was finally here. "Well, dear, you couldn't get it right on your own, so I had to make adjustments."

Fucker.

Tag moved in behind him, putting a hand on his shoulder. "Not here. Not now. This is her stand."

He forced himself to stay back. Tag was right. This was Ally's moment, and unless that asshole raised a hand to her, he was going to let her handle it. She was strong and brave and resourceful, and maybe now she would value herself for something more than her screentime.

"How would you know, Jay?" Bryce had a confused look on his face. "We hadn't even started rehearsals when you told me how I should treat her. I believe you said she'd requested it so she could follow your method."

"Yes, I was told the same thing." Channing was in full costume and looked every inch the grand dame of the manor. "I thought it odd since she didn't seem like a method girl."

"I'm not. I think it's silly." Ally frowned. "Though I'm sure it works for some people."

She could soften her rough edges. He gave her a thumbs-up, and she nodded his way.

"You told the crew to be mean to me, too," Ally continued. "So the question now is how much more were you willing to do to get what you needed out of me? It was more than a performance, wasn't it? You need me to click all the boxes, don't you? You want something more. You want me to be proof that your method works."

Bryce's eyes rolled. "His method? It's ridiculous. He's not even an actor."

"No, but he's an excellent manipulator." Reid stood up, his jaw firming. "I don't think what he's trying to teach is how to act."

"No," Jay agreed. "I don't want to teach acting, per se. I want to teach directors how to get what they need out of actors. Most of you are completely worthless. You're either so full of yourselves you can't collaborate or so pathetic you can't possibly process your own emotions. You, Allyson, are an odd combination of both. You couldn't touch the emotional truth of the character, so I had to find a path to connect you."

"I hate this guy." Ally didn't need another person telling her how she didn't measure up. "He did this to her."

"Yes, he did," Tag whispered.

"So you had someone break into my house and leave a bunch of dead birds," Ally said quietly. "Or did you do it yourself? The funny thing is I didn't get the symbolism. Was Delia supposed to be the dead bird?"

"You don't understand symbolism at all, sweetheart," Jay said with syrupy sarcasm. "However, I certainly wouldn't go to those lengths. That would make me a criminal. I believe you're confusing me with your stalker. How many do you have? You get into so much trouble."

"It wasn't JK Harris. It was you," Ally said with certainty. "And it was you who sent the box to the hotel, and you've been blasting my socials with horrible messages."

Channing stood up, her shoulders going straight and regal. "Is this true, Jay? Have you been tormenting this young woman so you could manipulate her performance?"

"If she would listen to me, I could get her a nomination," Jay snarled.

"He's got a book deal," Ally explained. "I would bet it's scheduled to come out around the time the movie is released. He's done all of this to hype the movie and his method. He makes us all look like we're at each other's throats…"

"Because he told us to be," Reid interjected.

"…and then he releases a magnificent film and everyone holds him up as a master," Ally finished. "He gets his Oscar and takes his place as the next Spielberg."

"Spielberg doesn't terrorize his actors," Bryce said, coming to stand beside Reid. "We're a part of this process, Jay. You know what? I think you're the one who struggles with collaboration."

A smattering of applause broke out, and that seemed to be the moment Jay realized he had more of an audience than he'd thought. The crew stood in the shadows watching the scene playing out in front of them.

Jay's expression cleared. "This is all a misunderstanding. Of course I didn't stalk Ally. I did feel she needed a push from the rest of the cast, but it's obvious she doesn't want to explore her acting skills to their fullest."

"Nope. You did it," Ally insisted. "You did all of it. JK never sent me anything physical, and this trolling feels different from his. He never uses big words, but suddenly I've got twelve accounts trolling me, and they've got spectacular vocabularies."

"Well, Allyson, I don't think you need to worry about that anymore since you're fired." Jay picked up his bag. "Everyone else get back to work or the same thing is going to happen to you."

West saw Ally pale, but she didn't back down. "I know you did this to me."

It was time for him to step up. West moved in beside her. "I'll prove it, Ally. I promise. I won't stop until I can prove what he did to you."

"I'm going to have security escort you out now, Allyson. You can take your boy toy." Jay started to pull his cell out. "Have fun trying to prove anything at all."

"I bet I can prove it."

All eyes shifted to Ian, who leaned casually against the big couch. He grinned Channing's way. "You were fabulous in the Julia Child biopic. I wanted to eat all that food. And my Charlie won't share, but she would love to watch you get nasty with any number of subs at our BDSM club. Very private. Very exclusive. You let me know, and I'll make it happen. I get the feeling you would make a lot of subs happy."

"I would say I would never, but we all know I would," Channing replied with a confidence only a woman with three Oscars could have.

"Channing," Bryce said under his breath. "This is serious."

"Yes, I'm going to need security. We need some trash taken out," Jay was saying into his phone. "And you should send everyone. There's a big guy here who might give you some trouble."

West was a little offended because he was pretty sure Jay wasn't talking about him. And he could actually give security a lot of trouble if he wanted to.

"I've got some trouble for you." Tag stood, holding up the folder he'd been carrying.

"I'm going to have to ask you to leave," Jay said, but he'd really taken a look at the big guy and took a step back. He slid his phone into his pocket.

"I don't think so. Come on, man. This is the fun part," Tag promised. "Well, for me. You see, along with providing Ms. Pearson with bodyguard services…we're not going to talk about the extra benefits…"

"Ian." He wasn't about to let the boss go off on a tangent.

"They were excellent benefits, Mr. Taggart. I would have paid extra." Ally could go off on a tangent of her own.

Tag nodded her way. "I think it's a cash opportunity we're missing out on, but I digress. As I was saying, in addition to ensuring Ms. Pearson stayed alive, my firm conducted a thorough investigation into who is behind these attacks on her."

Jay's eyes rolled. "Attacks? That's a lot. And we all know it was JK Harris. She ruined his career. He hates her."

"He does, but I talked to him earlier today, and he says he's not responsible," Ian assured him. "The good news for him is I have proof."

"What kind of proof do you have?" Jay asked, though some of his arrogance had eroded.

"Funnily enough, receipts. You paid for the courier with cash and managed to create a dead end there," Tag explained. "But the GPS locator you placed on West's vehicle had a serial number."

"I don't know what you're talking about," Jay said.

Bryce huffed. "He's lying. A good actor knows a bad one."

"I certainly didn't purchase a GPS locator, and even if I had I don't see how this proves I set up the pranks someone played on her," Jay replied.

"Pranks?" Ally asked.

West reached out and held her hand. He'd learned it was best to let the bad guy trip over his own feet.

Big Tag obviously had the same philosophy because he plunged ahead. "The GPS serial number led us to a large purchase through a company called the Hearthwright Corporation. That is a mega corporation with fifty different subsidiary companies, so it took us a while to figure out which company purchased the GPS locator. Luckily, I have people with nothing better to do. They discovered the lot was purchased by a company that rents out expensive camera equipment. You see, they provide the equipment for productions like this one, and they don't like not knowing where their hundreds of thousands of dollars' worth of equipment is."

"Like this production?" Ally asked. "Or this actual production?"

"She's a smart one, West. You should keep her," Tag acknowledged. "It was this actual production, and knowing that led me to wonder what I could find from that spring-loaded present you sent Ally. I worked with DPD on this one. Turns out the equipment came from here as well. I think you'll find your props master is down at the station and he's talking. Jay here couldn't build that thing himself, so he brought in one of the crew."

"I believe he likely brought in more than one of the crew," Channing said, her lips pursed as she looked around. "He doesn't do anything himself. So I'm curious as to which of the production assistants he sent to the courier."

Jay shook his head. "This is my crew. Mr. Taggart is bluffing."

"I'm not mad at the crew." Ally joined Channing after letting go of his hand. "You were doing your job, and I understand that. You probably had zero idea what you were doing. The props master likely didn't either. Even if he did, I know how it feels to have one man hold your future in his hands, and you know he has no mercy. I know our boats are more luxurious, but we're all capable of capsizing, and he's the wave. I don't know if you know what he's been doing to the cast, but it was pretty much torture. I think he wanted to drive me a little insane."

"I wanted to make you a star, but your skull is too thick for it," Jay shot back.

"It was me." A young man who couldn't be past twenty-five stepped up. "I was the one who went to the courier. I didn't know what it was, but I knew it was weird because he gave me cash and told me not to let the cameras catch my face. I also am the one who put the birds in your house, Ms. Pearson. He promised that I would get a promotion and also that this was nothing that could hurt you. I'm very sorry."

"I don't know what you expect will come from this, Ally," Jay said with a shake of his head. "I played a few pranks on you and used a method to enhance your performance. All you're going to be able to do is get a couple of low-level employees in trouble and set back my production a few days while I find another actress. Then we'll be right back on schedule, and you'll be a sad footnote in Hollywood history. I assure you no one is going to employ you after this."

"I will," Channing declared. "I'm making my directorial debut next year, and I think Ally would be perfect in the role of my daughter. But also, do you think I'm staying quiet after everything you've done not only to us but to our crew? You put them in harm's way. You manipulated each and every one of them. I will not stand for that, Jay. I'll be calling the head of the production company and explaining that I will no longer be working with you."

"I won't either." Bryce's shoulders straightened. "We have to stick together. For some of us, we're the only family we have."

"I'll talk, too." Reid seemed to find his strength. "He put me through hell."

They rallied around Ally, these people who'd looked down on her before. She'd been stalwart and true and proven herself.

Damn, he loved that woman.

"I think we need a new director," Ally said.

"Yes, I think we do," Channing agreed.

"Good luck with that," Jay said, sarcasm dripping.

"Mr. Clarke, I believe you'll find the Dallas Police Department would like to have a word," Tag announced. "And the security guards here won't be kicking me out. I trained them all. Do you need a ride down to the precinct or shall I let the police escort you?"

He was going to let the boss handle Jay. He seemed to be having fun with it. West had better things to do.

"Don't worry, dear," Channing was saying. "I think I can handle this. I believe the production studio will decide Mr. Clarke made this a hostile work environment and will find a replacement. They've got too much invested. I think I might know the perfect person to take this project over. He's a friend of mine who's been trying his hand at directing. I'll float his name by the money boys. We'll be back to work soon, and Bryce and I will take care of the crew."

"Now wait," Bryce began and then seemed to read the room. "Of course we will. Be happy to."

West started to walk toward Ally, but she raced to him first, wrapping her arms around him.

"Can we have some cowboy take me away time? I need you," she whispered.

He picked her up. That was a request he would never refuse.

# Epilogue

*Eighteen months later*
*Santa Monica, California*

"Hey, I need a hiding place."

"It's a big tree, man. We can both hide here."

Ally couldn't help but smile because the guys were getting along spectacularly. They'd bonded over surviving the whole Hollywood experience. Brynn's husband, Major, had welcomed West into the family with grateful and open arms. Honestly, they had a bromance going that would look adorable on camera. If they didn't hide from it constantly.

"They're so cute when they're trying to hide. And they look awfully festive." Brynn looked festive, too. She was wearing an adorable Christmas sweater that did nothing to hide her pregnant belly.

Ally was getting a nephew in two months, and she couldn't wait to be the best fun aunt ever.

And one day she would be a mom. Some day. In the future. Right now, she and West had all they could handle between her busy shooting schedule and his classes. He was pursuing a career in cinematography. He was taking some classes, but the majority of his learning was hands-on. He'd gotten his first job working on Channing Lloyd's directorial debut. He'd pretty much been the lighting department's PA, but he'd soaked it all up. The genuine excitement that man got over the right lighting was probably something she would never understand, but damn she loved it.

"You're sure you don't want to film the birth?" Their mom joined them. No ugly Christmas sweaters for her. She was in an elegant twin set, the green color the only real concession to the season. She'd been unhappy at the idea of not dressing to the nines for this annual Christmas photo, but she and Brynn had put up a united front.

No tuxes and evening gowns. They were going for a little reality this year.

Though West would look excellent in a tux. She knew it because he'd been his brother's best man, and he'd been so hot, she'd tackled him the minute they'd gotten back to their hotel room.

He was going to look hot in a tux again when they walked the red carpet this awards season. *Crowne of Thorns* was ready for release in a couple of weeks, and there was crazy buzz about it. Channing and Bryce were almost sure locks for nominations, and there had even been talk about her role.

Whatever happened, she would be forever grateful she'd gotten to work with the new director Channing had brought in. Joshua Hunt was more known for being one of the biggest box office draws in the world, but the man could direct, too. He'd taught her so much, and the cast and crew had adored him. His wife was pretty awesome, too.

"We are not filming the birth, Mother," Brynn said with a shake of her head. "And honestly, Major and I decided we don't want our baby on screen."

Her mom took a long breath and then ran a hand over Brynn's hair. "I think that's an excellent idea, my love. This can be our last special. Between you starting a family and our Ally's film career, it's time to leave the show behind. I want this one last special to show how truly wonderful Ally is."

They'd been filming for days, and Ally had expected all the normal parties and shopping days. West had sat with her for a few interviews, talking about how they met.

And then her mom had sat down and talked about how the business had affected Ally and Brynn. She'd been open and honest about her successes and failures, and her mother had asked for forgiveness.

She wasn't the villain anymore. She was just Ally.

"Well, for the record, I'm good with it, too." Gavin put an arm around her mom, leaning in to kiss her cheek. "I knew the show was over when this one eloped. I thought for sure we would have a massive special if she ever got married."

She hadn't even thought about it. She'd been the one to suggest they fly to a beach in Bali and make their vows together there with only their immediate family around them.

She didn't need photographers for validation anymore. All she needed was her family.

Which was getting bigger because of her. She was sure Brynn had gotten pregnant at the wedding. She kept trying to get her sister to name her son Bali.

Major apparently thought it would be better to name the kid after his beloved father or something.

While they'd been in Bali, the news had come out that Jay Clarke's book deal had been canceled and a bunch of the crew was suing him.

Good times.

"I liked my wedding. And I'm glad this is the last year we're filming this, but I think we should definitely keep up the Christmas cards," Ally said, sipping on mulled wine.

"I would like that," her mother said and then shook her head. "Oh, I'm going to be a grandmother."

Gavin grinned down. "We'll be the sexiest grandparents the world has ever seen."

"Eww, those words do not go together," Brynn announced.

Ally thought her mom could pull it off.

A big mutt raced through the crowded space, romping around like the puppy he was. He leapt over camera equipment and nearly tripped the photographer in his desperate need to get to her.

Ally dropped to one knee, welcoming the baby she and West had agreed was their only one for now. "Hey, Taggart. How are you, you gorgeous buddy, you."

"He's going to kill me when he finds out you named a rescue mutt after him," West said with a grin, reaching down to give the dog a pat. "Although he does look a little like him."

"He's protective and nice, and he's very large. I think it fits." She had fond memories of all the people at MT.

And she was glad she didn't need them now. Since she'd married West, things had calmed down, and while her socials weren't hopping anymore, she still had plenty of people who followed her for the right reasons.

Brynn and Major's dogs, Duke and Dolly, joined Taggart, each pup in its own Christmas sweater.

"Can I get everyone around the tree?" the photographer asked. "And by around, I really mean in front of. Gentlemen, you cannot hide from me."

Major groaned but joined them.

They all lined up, and Ally had the craziest rush of emotion.

This was her family, and she finally felt like she was a real part of it.

"Hey, you okay?" West whispered.

She was better than okay. She turned to him and kissed him while Taggart tried to climb up her body to get his kiss, too. "I'm perfect."

"Well, I'm in a heavy sweater in LA in the middle of October, and there's a Christmas tree in your mom's house," West replied.

"Welcome to Hollywood." She turned back and gave the camera her brightest smile.

It wasn't hard. She didn't have to act anymore except onscreen.

She'd found her happy ending.

* * * *

Also from 1001 Dark Nights and Lexi Blake, discover Delighted, Treasured, Charmed, Enchanted, Protected, Close Cover, Arranged, Devoted, Adored, and Dungeon Games.

Sign up for the 1001 Dark Nights Newsletter
and be entered to win a Tiffany Key necklace.

There's a contest every month!

Go to www.1001DarkNights.com to subscribe.

**As a bonus, all subscribers can download
FIVE FREE exclusive books!**

# Discover 1001 Dark Nights Collection Ten

DRAGON LOVER by Donna Grant
A Dragon Kings Novella

KEEPING YOU by Aurora Rose Reynolds
An Until Him/Her Novella

HAPPILY EVER NEVER by Carrie Ann Ryan
A Montgomery Ink Legacy Novella

DESTINED FOR ME by Corinne Michaels
A Come Back for Me/Say You'll Stay Crossover

MADAM ALANA by Audrey Carlan
A Marriage Auction Novella

DIRTY FILTHY BILLIONAIRE by Laurelin Paige
A Dirty Universe Novella

HIDE AND SEEK by Laura Kaye
A Blasphemy Novella

TANGLED WITH YOU by J. Kenner
A Stark Security Novella

TEMPTED by Lexi Blake
A Masters and Mercenaries Novella

THE DANDELION DIARY by Devney Perry
A Maysen Jar Novella

CHERRY LANE by Kristen Proby
A Huckleberry Bay Novella

THE GRAVE ROBBER by Darynda Jones
A Charley Davidson Novella

CRY OF THE BANSHEE by Heather Graham
A Krewe of Hunters Novella

DARKEST NEED by Rachel Van Dyken
A Dark Ones Novella

CHRISTMAS IN CAPE MAY by Jennifer Probst
A Sunshine Sisters Novella

A VAMPIRE'S MATE by Rebecca Zanetti
A Dark Protectors/Rebels Novella

WHERE IT BEGINS by Helena Hunting
A Pucked Novella

*Also from Blue Box Press*

THE MARRIAGE AUCTION by Audrey Carlan
Season One, Volume One
Season One, Volume Two
Season One, Volume Three
Season One, Volume Four

THE JEWELER OF STOLEN DREAMS by M.J. Rose

SAPPHIRE STORM by Christopher Rice writing as C. Travis Rice
A Sapphire Cove Novel

ATLAS: THE STORY OF PA SALT by Lucinda Riley and Harry Whittaker

LOVE ON THE BYLINE by Xio Axelrod
A Plays and Players Novel

A SOUL OF ASH AND BLOOD by Jennifer L. Armentrout
A Blood and Ash Novel

START US UP by Lexi Blake
A Park Avenue Promise Novel

FIGHTING THE PULL by Kristen Ashley
A River Rain Novel

A FIRE IN THE FLESH by Jennifer L. Armentrout
A Flesh and Fire Novel

# Start Us Up
A Park Avenue Promise Novel
By Lexi Blake
Coming August 8, 2023

From *New York Times* bestselling author Lexi Blake, discover The Park Avenue Promise Series...

*Three young women make a pact in high school—to always be friends and to one day make it big in Manhattan.*

*She's a high-tech boss who lost it all...*

Ivy Jensen was the darling of the tech world, right up until her company fell apart completely after she trusted the wrong person. Her reputation in tatters, she finds herself back in the tiny apartment she grew up in, living with her mom. When a group of angel investors offer her a meeting, she knows she has to come up with the new big idea or her career is over.

*He's an up and coming coder...*

Heath Marino has always been fascinated with writing code. He's worked on a dozen games and apps and is considered one of the industry's more eccentric talents. But now he's back in New York to spend time with his grandmother. She was known as one of the city's greatest matchmakers, and he wants to know why. Surely there's some kind of code in his grandmother's methods, and he's going to find them.

When Ivy meets Heath it's instant attraction, but she's got a career to get back to and he just might be her on-ramp. It could be a perfect partnership or absolute heartbreak.

\* \* \* \*

"You need funding." Didn't we all, but this explains why he was so interested in having me be the one to help out. He probably knows twenty coders who could help him out. But he didn't know anyone who could navigate investor-filled waters the way I can.

The words seem to fluster him, and I feel a brief sympathy for him. That first move into the big bad business world can be hard. It's obvious he's been splashing around in the kiddie pool.

"Yeah. If I want to keep working on this, I need some funding. I'm going to be honest."

"That's always helpful."

He plunges on, completely ignoring my sarcasm. It's a point in his favor if we're going to work together, and that's where this seems like this thing is going. "I could use your help on the interface, but more than that I need advice on how to proceed. I've never done anything like this before. It requires more resources than I know how to get myself."

"He can't ask his Nonna for a couple hundred bucks for this one." Darnell is the only one who doesn't seem to feel the weird tension in the room. Or he doesn't care.

"What is your endgame? And buddy, it can't be helping people. I can't get you funding for helping people."

"I don't see why not. It's what Jensen Medical did," Heath points out.

He fundamentally misunderstands our business. How to explain to him? "I got the funding for Jensen Medical Solutions not because it helped sick people fill out less forms and streamlined their ability to gain access to services. That was a side effect. A bug not a feature. The feature was allowing hospitals to run more efficiently, which meant they could cut back on everything from storing paperwork to employees who dealt with that paperwork. I know it sucks, but that's what investors will care about, so you need to show me how you plan to make money off this. You need to be able to talk to investors about why backing you will make them even more money than they already have."

He sits back, and I can see he doesn't like what I've said. I hate to disillusion him, but I've said nothing but the truth.

"So I can't get funding." He takes a steadying breath. "I'll look for grant money."

"That's not what she's saying, man." At least Darnell is keeping up. "She's saying you gotta be sneaky about it."

"I wouldn't use that word. I would say he's got to be smart about it," I correct.

"But my purpose is to help people," he insists.

"Can't you help people and make money?" I'm not sure what the problem is. And then I kind of do.

He'd said something about a nurse. When he'd walked in he'd been talking to his grandmother and said he wanted an update.

Oh, I figure out what I'm dealing with. His grandmother is sick. He loves his grandma. He's working on something close to her heart.

"I didn't start this project thinking I would become some millionaire," he says.

"Good, because you probably won't, but if you want it to work, you're going to have to find a way to focus on it. Unfortunately, that means having the money, and in order to get the money, you're going to have to bring people in, and that means working with them." And then I spring my trap. I don't know why this is suddenly so important, but I want this. I want to work with him. I want to see where this thing he's built can go and how far I can take it. "Of course if you wanted me to, I could handle that part for you."

Darnell whistles. "That's some Faustian shit right there. I think you should do it."

"What do you mean?" Heath asks.

"I think she means she'll get you the money and deal with all the scary shark people and all you have to do is give her a little tiny piece of your soul." Darnell proves he's probably a pretty good writer.

"I don't care about your soul," I admit. "But I would need a piece of whatever comes out of this. Say sixty percent."

I go high so we don't negotiate too low. I think I've figured this guy out a little and he'll want to be fair, but he'll still want to feel like he talked me down.

"Twenty," he replies, and that magnificent Captain America jaw of his has gone steely.

Now I have him. "Fifty."

"Forty."

I hold out my hand. "Done."

# Discover More Lexi Blake

### Delighted: A Masters and Mercenaries Novella

Brian "Boomer" Ward believes in sheltering strays. After all, the men and women of McKay-Taggart made him family when he had none. So when the kid next door needs help one night, he thinks nothing of protecting her until her mom gets home. But when he meets Daphne Carlton, the thoughts hit him hard. She's stunning and hardworking and obviously in need of someone to put her first. It doesn't hurt that she's as sweet as the cupcakes she bakes.

Daphne Carlton's life revolves around two things—her kid and her business. Daphne's Delights is her dream—to take the recipes of her childhood and share them with the world. Her daughter, Lula, is the best kid she could have hoped for. Lula's got a genius-level intelligence and a heart of gold. But she also has two grandparents who control her access to private school and the fortune her father left behind. They're impossible to please, and Daphne worries that one wrong move on her part could cost her daughter the life she deserves.

As Daphne and Boomer find themselves getting closer, outside forces put pressure on the new couple. But if they make it through the storm, love will just be the icing on the cake because family is the real prize.

\* \* \* \*

### Treasured: A Masters and Mercenaries Novella

David Hawthorne has a great life. His job as a professor at a prestigious Dallas college is everything he hoped for. Now that his brother is back from the Navy, life seems to be settling down. All he needs to do is finish the book he's working on and his tenure will be assured. When he gets invited to interview a reclusive expert, he knows he's gotten lucky. But being the stepson of Sean Taggart comes with its drawbacks, including an overprotective mom who sends a security detail to keep him safe. He doesn't need a bodyguard, but when Tessa Santiago shows up on his doorstep, the idea of her giving him close cover doesn't seem so bad.

Tessa has always excelled at most anything she tried, except romance.

The whole relationship thing just didn't work out for her. She's not looking for love, and she's certainly not looking for it with an academic who happens to be connected to her boss's family. The last thing she wants is to escort an overly pampered pretentious man-child around South America to ensure he doesn't get into trouble. Still, there's something about David that calls to her. In addition to watching his back, she will have to avoid falling into the trap of soulful eyes and a deep voice that gets her heart racing.

But when the seemingly simple mission turns into a treacherous race for a hidden artifact, David and Tess know this assignment could cost them far more than their jobs. If they can overcome the odds, the lost treasure might not be their most valuable reward.

\* \* \* \*

**Charmed: A Masters and Mercenaries Novella**

JT Malone is lucky, and he knows it. He is the heir to a billion-dollar petroleum empire, and he has a loving family. Between his good looks and his charm, he can have almost any woman he wants. The world is his oyster, and he really likes oysters. So why does it all feel so empty?

Nina Blunt is pretty sure she's cursed. She worked her way up through the ranks at Interpol, fighting for every step with hard work and discipline. Then she lost it all because she loved the wrong person. Rebuilding her career with McKay-Taggart, she can't help but feel lonely. It seems everyone around her is finding love and starting families. But she knows that isn't for her. She has vowed never to make the mistake of falling in love again.

JT comes to McKay-Taggart for assistance rooting out a corporate spy, and Nina signs on to the job. Their working relationship becomes tricky, however, as their personal chemistry flares like a wildfire. Completing the assignment without giving in to the attraction that threatens to overwhelm them seems like it might be the most difficult part of the job. When danger strikes, will they be able to count on each other when the bullets are flying? If not, JT's charmed life might just come to an end.

\* \* \* \*

## Enchanted: A Masters and Mercenaries Novella

*A snarky submissive princess*
Sarah Steven's life is pretty sweet. By day, she's a dedicated trauma nurse and by night, a fun-loving club sub. She adores her job, has a group of friends who have her back, and is a member of the hottest club in Dallas. So why does it all feel hollow? Could it be because she fell for her dream man and can't forgive him for walking away from her? Nope. She's not going there again. No matter how much she wants to.

*A prince of the silver screen*
Jared Johns might be one of the most popular actors in Hollywood, but he lost more than a fan when he walked away from Sarah. He lost the only woman he's ever loved. He's been trying to get her back, but she won't return his calls. A trip to Dallas to visit his brother might be exactly what he needs to jump-start his quest to claim the woman who holds his heart.

*A masquerade to remember*
For Charlotte Taggart's birthday, Sanctum becomes a fantasyland of kinky fun and games. Every unattached sub gets a new Dom for the festivities. The twist? The Doms must conceal their identities until the stroke of midnight at the end of the party. It's exactly what Sarah needs to forget the fact that Jared is pursuing her. She can't give in to him, and the mysterious Master D is making her rethink her position when it comes to signing a contract. Jared knows he was born to play this role, dashing suitor by day and dirty Dom at night.

When the masks come off, will she be able to forgive the man who loves her, or will she leave him forever?

\* \* \* \*

## Protected: A Masters and Mercenaries Novella

*A second chance at first love*
Years before, Wade Rycroft fell in love with Geneva Harris, the smartest girl in his class. The rodeo star and the shy academic made for an odd pair but their chemistry was undeniable. They made plans to get married after high school but when Genny left him standing in the rain, he

joined the Army and vowed to leave that life behind. Genny married the town's golden boy, and Wade knew that he couldn't go home again.

*Could become the promise of a lifetime*

Fifteen years later, Wade returns to his Texas hometown for his brother's wedding and walks into a storm of scandal. Genny's marriage has dissolved and the town has turned against her. But when someone tries to kill his old love, Wade can't refuse to help her. In his years after the Army, he's found his place in the world. His job at McKay-Taggart keeps him happy and busy but something is missing. When he takes the job watching over Genny, he realizes what it is.

As danger presses in, Wade must decide if he can forgive past sins or let the woman of his dreams walk into a nightmare...

\* \* \* \*

**Close Cover: A Masters and Mercenaries Novel**

Remy Guidry doesn't do relationships. He tried the marriage thing once, back in Louisiana, and learned the hard way that all he really needs in life is a cold beer, some good friends, and the occasional hookup. His job as a bodyguard with McKay-Taggart gives him purpose and lovely perks, like access to Sanctum. The last thing he needs in his life is a woman with stars in her eyes and babies in her future.

Lisa Daley's life is going in the right direction. She has graduated from college after years of putting herself through school. She's got a new job at an accounting firm and she's finished her Sanctum training. Finally on her own and having fun, her life seems pretty perfect. Except she's lonely and the one man she wants won't give her a second look.

There is one other little glitch. Apparently, her new firm is really a front for the mob and now they want her dead. Assassins can really ruin a fun girls' night out. Suddenly strapped to the very same six-foot-five-inch hunk of a bodyguard who makes her heart pound, Lisa can't decide if this situation is a blessing or a curse.

As the mob closes in, Remy takes his tempting new charge back to the safest place he knows—his home in the bayou. Surrounded by his past, he can't help wondering if Lisa is his future. To answer that question, he just has to keep her alive.

* * * *

## Arranged: A Masters and Mercenaries Novella

Kash Kamdar is the king of a peaceful but powerful island nation. As Loa Mali's sovereign, he is always in control, the final authority. Until his mother uses an ancient law to force her son into marriage. His prospective queen is a buttoned-up intellectual, nothing like Kash's usual party girl. Still, from the moment of their forced engagement, he can't stop thinking about her.

Dayita Samar comes from one of Loa Mali's most respected families. The Oxford-educated scientist has dedicated her life to her country's future. But under her staid and calm exterior, Day hides a few sexy secrets of her own. She is willing to marry her king, but also agrees that they can circumvent the law. Just because they're married doesn't mean they have to change their lives. It certainly doesn't mean they have to fall in love.

After one wild weekend in Dallas, Kash discovers his bride-to-be is more than she seems. Engulfed in a changing world, Kash finds exciting new possibilities for himself. Could Day help him find respite from the crushing responsibility he's carried all his life? This fairy tale could have a happy ending, if only they can escape Kash's past…

* * * *

## Devoted: A Masters and Mercenaries Novella

*A woman's work*

Amy Slaten has devoted her life to Slaten Industries. After ousting her corrupt father and taking over the CEO role, she thought she could relax and enjoy taking her company to the next level. But an old business rivalry rears its ugly head. The only thing that can possibly take her mind off business is the training class at Sanctum…and her training partner, the gorgeous and funny Flynn Adler. If she can just manage to best her mysterious business rival, life might be perfect.

*A man's commitment*

Flynn Adler never thought he would fall for the enemy. Business is war, or so his father always claimed. He was raised to be ruthless when it came to the family company, and now he's raising his brother to one day work with him. The first order of business? The hostile takeover of Slaten Industries. It's a stressful job so when his brother offers him a spot in Sanctum's training program, Flynn jumps at the chance.

*A lifetime of devotion....*

When Flynn realizes the woman he's falling for is none other than the CEO of the firm he needs to take down, he has to make a choice. Does he take care of the woman he's falling in love with or the business he's worked a lifetime to build? And when Amy finally understands the man she's come to trust is none other than the enemy, will she walk away from him or fight for the love she's come to depend on?

* * * *

## Adored: A Masters and Mercenaries Novella

*A man who gave up on love*

Mitch Bradford is an intimidating man. In his professional life, he has a reputation for demolishing his opponents in the courtroom. At the exclusive BDSM club Sanctum, he prefers disciplining pretty submissives with no strings attached. In his line of work, there's no time for a healthy relationship. After a few failed attempts, he knows he's not good for any woman—especially not his best friend's sister.

*A woman who always gets what she wants*

Laurel Daley knows what she wants, and her sights are set on Mitch. He's smart and sexy, and it doesn't matter that he's a few years older and has a couple of bitter ex-wives. Watching him in action at work and at play, she knows he just needs a little polish to make some woman the perfect lover. She intends to be that woman, but first she has to show him how good it could be.

*A killer lurking in the shadows*

When an unexpected turn of events throws the two together, Mitch and Laurel are confronted with the perfect opportunity to explore their mutual desire. Night after night of being close breaks down Mitch's defenses. The more he sees of Laurel, the more he knows he wants her. Unfortunately, someone else has their eyes on Laurel and they have murder in mind.

\* \* \* \*

## Dungeon Games: A Masters and Mercenaries Novella

*Obsessed*

Derek Brighton has become one of Dallas's finest detectives through a combination of discipline and obsession. Once he has a target in his sights, nothing can stop him. When he isn't solving homicides, he applies the same intensity to his playtime at Sanctum, a secretive BDSM club. Unfortunately, no amount of beautiful submissives can fill the hole that one woman left in his heart.

*Unhinged*

Karina Mills has a reputation for being reckless, and her clients appreciate her results. As a private investigator, she pursues her cases with nothing holding her back. In her personal life, Karina yearns for something different. Playing at Sanctum has been a safe way to find peace, but the one Dom who could truly master her heart is out of reach.

*Enflamed*

On the hunt for a killer, Derek enters a shadowy underworld only to find the woman he aches for is working the same case. Karina is searching for a missing girl and won't stop until she finds her. To get close to their prime suspect, they need to pose as a couple. But as their operation goes under the covers, unlikely partners become passionate lovers while the killer prepares to strike.

# Love the Way You Spy
Masters and Mercenaries: New Recruits
By Lexi Blake
Coming September 19, 2023

Tasha Taggart isn't a spy. That's her sisters' job. Tasha's support role is all about keeping them alive, playing referee when they fight amongst themselves, and soothing the toughest boss in the world. Working for the CIA isn't as glamorous as she imagined, and she's more than a little lonely. So when she meets a charming man in a bar the night before they start their latest op, she decides to give in to temptation. The night was perfect until she discovers she's just slept with the target of their new investigation. Her sisters will never let her hear the end of this. Even worse, she has to explain the situation to her overprotective father, who also happens to be their boss.

Dare Nash knew exactly how his week in Sydney was going to go—attending boring conferences to represent his family's business interests and eating hotel food alone. Until he falls under the spell of a stunning and mysterious American woman. Something in Tasha's eyes raises his body temperature every time she looks at him. She's captivating, and he's committed to spending every minute he can with her on this trip, even if her two friends seem awfully intense. His father will be arriving in town soon, and he's excited to introduce him to a woman he could imagine spending the rest of his life with.

When Dare discovers Tash isn't who she seems, the dream turns into a nightmare. She isn't the only one who deceived him, and now he's in the crosshairs of adversaries way out of his league. He can't trust her, but it might take Tasha and her family to save his life and uncover the truth.

# About Lexi Blake

*New York Times* bestselling author Lexi Blake lives in North Texas with her husband and three kids. Since starting her publishing journey in 2010, she's sold over three million copies of her books. She began writing at a young age, concentrating on plays and journalism. It wasn't until she started writing romance that she found success. She likes to find humor in the strangest places and believes in happy endings.

Connect with Lexi online:

Facebook: Lexi Blake
Twitter: authorlexiblake
Website: www.LexiBlake.net
Instagram: www.instagram.com

# Discover 1001 Dark Nights

### COLLECTION ONE

FOREVER WICKED by Shayla Black ~ CRIMSON TWILIGHT by Heather Graham ~ CAPTURED IN SURRENDER by Liliana Hart ~ SILENT BITE: A SCANGUARDS WEDDING by Tina Folsom ~ DUNGEON GAMES by Lexi Blake ~ AZAGOTH by Larissa Ione ~ NEED YOU NOW by Lisa Renee Jones ~ SHOW ME, BABY by Cherise Sinclair~ ROPED IN by Lorelei James ~ TEMPTED BY MIDNIGHT by Lara Adrian ~ THE FLAME by Christopher Rice ~ CARESS OF DARKNESS by Julie Kenner

### COLLECTION TWO

WICKED WOLF by Carrie Ann Ryan ~ WHEN IRISH EYES ARE HAUNTING by Heather Graham ~ EASY WITH YOU by Kristen Proby ~ MASTER OF FREEDOM by Cherise Sinclair ~ CARESS OF PLEASURE by Julie Kenner ~ ADORED by Lexi Blake ~ HADES by Larissa Ione ~ RAVAGED by Elisabeth Naughton ~ DREAM OF YOU by Jennifer L. Armentrout ~ STRIPPED DOWN by Lorelei James ~ RAGE/KILLIAN by Alexandra Ivy/Laura Wright ~ DRAGON KING by Donna Grant ~ PURE WICKED by Shayla Black ~ HARD AS STEEL by Laura Kaye ~ STROKE OF MIDNIGHT by Lara Adrian ~ ALL HALLOWS EVE by Heather Graham ~ KISS THE FLAME by Christopher Rice~ DARING HER LOVE by Melissa Foster ~ TEASED by Rebecca Zanetti ~ THE PROMISE OF SURRENDER by Liliana Hart

### COLLECTION THREE

HIDDEN INK by Carrie Ann Ryan ~ BLOOD ON THE BAYOU by Heather Graham ~ SEARCHING FOR MINE by Jennifer Probst ~ DANCE OF DESIRE by Christopher Rice ~ ROUGH RHYTHM by Tessa Bailey ~ DEVOTED by Lexi Blake ~ Z by Larissa Ione ~ FALLING UNDER YOU by Laurelin Paige ~ EASY FOR KEEPS by Kristen Proby ~ UNCHAINED by Elisabeth Naughton ~ HARD TO SERVE by Laura Kaye ~ DRAGON FEVER by Donna Grant ~ KAYDEN/SIMON by Alexandra Ivy/Laura Wright ~ STRUNG UP by Lorelei James ~ MIDNIGHT UNTAMED by Lara Adrian ~ TRICKED by Rebecca Zanetti ~ DIRTY WICKED by Shayla Black ~ THE ONLY ONE by Lauren Blakely ~ SWEET SURRENDER by Liliana Hart

COLLECTION FOUR
ROCK CHICK REAWAKENING by Kristen Ashley ~ ADORING INK by Carrie Ann Ryan ~ SWEET RIVALRY by K. Bromberg ~ SHADE'S LADY by Joanna Wylde ~ RAZR by Larissa Ione ~ ARRANGED by Lexi Blake ~ TANGLED by Rebecca Zanetti ~ HOLD ME by J. Kenner ~ SOMEHOW, SOME WAY by Jennifer Probst ~ TOO CLOSE TO CALL by Tessa Bailey ~ HUNTED by Elisabeth Naughton ~ EYES ON YOU by Laura Kaye ~ BLADE by Alexandra Ivy/Laura Wright ~ DRAGON BURN by Donna Grant ~ TRIPPED OUT by Lorelei James ~ STUD FINDER by Lauren Blakely ~ MIDNIGHT UNLEASHED by Lara Adrian ~ HALLOW BE THE HAUNT by Heather Graham ~ DIRTY FILTHY FIX by Laurelin Paige ~ THE BED MATE by Kendall Ryan ~ NIGHT GAMES by CD Reiss ~ NO RESERVATIONS by Kristen Proby ~ DAWN OF SURRENDER by Liliana Hart

COLLECTION FIVE
BLAZE ERUPTING by Rebecca Zanetti ~ ROUGH RIDE by Kristen Ashley ~ HAWKYN by Larissa Ione ~ RIDE DIRTY by Laura Kaye ~ ROME'S CHANCE by Joanna Wylde ~ THE MARRIAGE ARRANGEMENT by Jennifer Probst ~ SURRENDER by Elisabeth Naughton ~ INKED NIGHTS by Carrie Ann Ryan ~ ENVY by Rachel Van Dyken ~ PROTECTED by Lexi Blake ~ THE PRINCE by Jennifer L. Armentrout ~ PLEASE ME by J. Kenner ~ WOUND TIGHT by Lorelei James ~ STRONG by Kylie Scott ~ DRAGON NIGHT by Donna Grant ~ TEMPTING BROOKE by Kristen Proby ~ HAUNTED BE THE HOLIDAYS by Heather Graham ~ CONTROL by K. Bromberg ~ HUNKY HEARTBREAKER by Kendall Ryan ~ THE DARKEST CAPTIVE by Gena Showalter

COLLECTION SIX
DRAGON CLAIMED by Donna Grant ~ ASHES TO INK by Carrie Ann Ryan ~ ENSNARED by Elisabeth Naughton ~ EVERMORE by Corinne Michaels ~ VENGEANCE by Rebecca Zanetti ~ ELI'S TRIUMPH by Joanna Wylde ~ CIPHER by Larissa Ione ~ RESCUING MACIE by Susan Stoker ~ ENCHANTED by Lexi Blake ~ TAKE THE BRIDE by Carly Phillips ~ INDULGE ME by J. Kenner ~ THE KING by Jennifer L. Armentrout ~ QUIET MAN by Kristen Ashley ~ ABANDON by Rachel Van Dyken ~ THE OPEN DOOR by Laurelin Paige ~ CLOSER by Kylie Scott ~ SOMETHING JUST LIKE THIS by

Jennifer Probst ~ BLOOD NIGHT by Heather Graham ~ TWIST OF FATE by Jill Shalvis ~ MORE THAN PLEASURE YOU by Shayla Black ~ WONDER WITH ME by Kristen Proby ~ THE DARKEST ASSASSIN by Gena Showalter

COLLECTION SEVEN
THE BISHOP by Skye Warren ~ TAKEN WITH YOU by Carrie Ann Ryan ~ DRAGON LOST by Donna Grant ~ SEXY LOVE by Carly Phillips ~ PROVOKE by Rachel Van Dyken ~ RAFE by Sawyer Bennett ~ THE NAUGHTY PRINCESS by Claire Contreras ~ THE GRAVEYARD SHIFT by Darynda Jones ~ CHARMED by Lexi Blake ~ SACRIFICE OF DARKNESS by Alexandra Ivy ~ THE QUEEN by Jen Armentrout ~ BEGIN AGAIN by Jennifer Probst ~ VIXEN by Rebecca Zanetti ~ SLASH by Laurelin Paige ~ THE DEAD HEAT OF SUMMER by Heather Graham ~ WILD FIRE by Kristen Ashley ~ MORE THAN PROTECT YOU by Shayla Black ~ LOVE SONG by Kylie Scott ~ CHERISH ME by J. Kenner ~ SHINE WITH ME by Kristen Proby

COLLECTION EIGHT
DRAGON REVEALED by Donna Grant ~ CAPTURED IN INK by Carrie Ann Ryan ~ SECURING JANE by Susan Stoker ~ WILD WIND by Kristen Ashley ~ DARE TO TEASE by Carly Phillips ~ VAMPIRE by Rebecca Zanetti ~ MAFIA KING by Rachel Van Dyken ~ THE GRAVEDIGGER'S SON by Darynda Jones ~ FINALE by Skye Warren ~ MEMORIES OF YOU by J. Kenner ~ SLAYED BY DARKNESS by Alexandra Ivy ~ TREASURED by Lexi Blake ~ THE DAREDEVIL by Dylan Allen ~ BOND OF DESTINY by Larissa Ione ~ MORE THAN POSSESS YOU by Shayla Black ~ HAUNTED HOUSE by Heather Graham ~ MAN FOR ME by Laurelin Paige ~ THE RHYTHM METHOD by Kylie Scott ~ JONAH BENNETT by Tijan ~ CHANGE WITH ME by Kristen Proby ~ THE DARKEST DESTINY by Gena Showalter

COLLECTION NINE
DRAGON UNBOUND by Donna Grant ~ NOTHING BUT INK by Carrie Ann Ryan ~ THE MASTERMIND by Dylan Allen ~ JUST ONE WISH by Carly Phillips ~ BEHIND CLOSED DOORS by Skye Warren ~ GOSSAMER IN THE DARKNESS by Kristen Ashley ~ THE CLOSE-UP by Kennedy Ryan ~ DELIGHTED by Lexi Blake ~ THE

GRAVESIDE BAR AND GRILL by Darynda Jones ~ THE ANTI-FAN AND THE IDOL by Rachel Van Dyken ~ CHARMED BY YOU by J. Kenner ~ DESCEND TO DARKNESS by Heather Graham~ BOND OF PASSION by Larissa Ione ~ JUST WHAT I NEEDED by Kylie Scott

*Discover Blue Box Press*

TAME ME by J. Kenner ~ TEMPT ME by J. Kenner ~ DAMIEN by J. Kenner ~ TEASE ME by J. Kenner ~ REAPER by Larissa Ione ~ THE SURRENDER GATE by Christopher Rice ~ SERVICING THE TARGET by Cherise Sinclair ~ THE LAKE OF LEARNING by Steve Berry and M.J. Rose ~ THE MUSEUM OF MYSTERIES by Steve Berry and M.J. Rose ~ TEASE ME by J. Kenner ~ FROM BLOOD AND ASH by Jennifer L. Armentrout ~ QUEEN MOVE by Kennedy Ryan ~ THE HOUSE OF LONG AGO by Steve Berry and M.J. Rose ~ THE BUTTERFLY ROOM by Lucinda Riley ~ A KINGDOM OF FLESH AND FIRE by Jennifer L. Armentrout ~ THE LAST TIARA by M.J. Rose ~ THE CROWN OF GILDED BONES by Jennifer L. Armentrout ~ THE MISSING SISTER by Lucinda Riley ~ THE END OF FOREVER by Steve Berry and M.J. Rose ~ THE STEAL by C. W. Gortner and M.J. Rose ~ CHASING SERENITY by Kristen Ashley ~ A SHADOW IN THE EMBER by Jennifer L. Armentrout ~ THE BAIT by C.W. Gortner and M.J. Rose ~ THE FASHION ORPHANS by Randy Susan Meyers and M.J. Rose ~ TAKING THE LEAP by Kristen Ashley ~ SAPPHIRE SUNSET by Christopher Rice writing C. Travis Rice ~ THE WAR OF TWO QUEENS by Jennifer L. Armentrout ~ THE MURDERS AT FLEAT HOUSE by Lucinda Riley ~ THE HEIST by C.W. Gortner and M.J. Rose ~ SAPPHIRE SPRING by Christopher Rice writing as C. Travis Rice ~ MAKING THE MATCH by Kristen Ashley ~ A LIGHT IN THE FLAME by Jennifer L.

## On Behalf of 1001 Dark Nights,
Liz Berry, M.J. Rose, and Jillian Stein would like to thank ~

Steve Berry
Doug Scofield
Benjamin Stein
Kim Guidroz
Tanaka Kangara
Asha Hossain
Chris Graham
Chelle Olson
Kasi Alexander
Jessica Saunders
Stacey Tardif
Dylan Stockton
Kate Boggs
Richard Blake
and Simon Lipskar

Made in the USA
Coppell, TX
18 June 2023

# The Challenge of Teaching Social Studies in the Elementary School

RETURN TO
**CARMAN CANTELON**
CONSULTANT

PROPERTY OF P-J DEPT.
ELGIN COUNTY BOARD
OF EDUCATION OFFICE

# The Challenge of Teaching in the

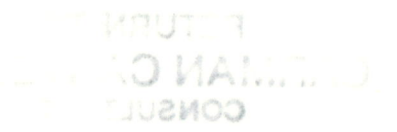

# Social Studies Elementary School *Third Edition*

Dorothy J. Skeel
*George Peabody College for Teachers*

*with assistance from*
Ronald E. Sterling

Goodyear Publishing Company, Inc. • Santa Monica, California

**Library of Congress Cataloging in Publication Data**

Skeel, Dorothy J
   The challenge of teaching social studies in the elementary school.

   Includes bibliographical references and index.
   1. Social science—Study and teaching (Elementary)
I. Sterling, Ronald E., joint author. II. Title.
LB1584.S52  1979      372.8'3'044     79-11315
ISBN 0-87620-150-8

Copyright © 1979 by Goodyear Publishing Company, Inc.
Santa Monica, California 90401

Y-1508-4

All rights reserved. No part of this book may be reproduced in any form or by any means without permission in writing from the publisher.

Current printing (last digit):
10  9  8  7  6  5  4  3  2  1

Printed in the United States of America

Cover and text design: Linda M. Robertson

To Jeff, Shelly, and Jill—

May they live in a world without conflict and prejudice.

## OTHER GOODYEAR BOOKS IN SCIENCE, MATH, & SOCIAL STUDIES

*DR. JIM'S ELEMENTARY MATH PRESCRIPTIONS*
James L. Overholt

*THE EARTHPEOPLE ACTIVITY BOOK People, Places, Pleasures and Other Delights*
Joe Abruscato and Jack Hassard

*ECONOMY SIZE From Barter to Business with Ideas, Activities, and Poems*
Carol Katzman and Joyce King

*LEARNING TO THINK AND CHOOSE Decision-Making Episodes for the Middle Grades*
J. Doyle Casteel

*LOVING AND BEYOND Science Teaching for the Humanistic Classroom*
Joe Abruscato and Jack Hassard

*MAINSTREAMING SCIENCE AND MATHEMATICS Special Ideas and Activities for the Whole Class*
Charles R. Coble, Paul B. Hounshell, Anne H. Adams

*MATHMATTERS*
Randall Souviney, Tamara Keyser, Alan Sarver

*MULTICULTURAL SPOKEN HERE Discovering America's People Through Language Arts and Library Skills*
Josephine Chase and Linda Parth

*THE OTHER SIDE OF THE REPORT CARD A How-to-Do-It Program for Affective Education*
Larry Chase

*SELF-SCIENCE The Subject Is Me*
Karen F. Stone and Harold Q. Dillehunt

*THE WHOLE COSMOS CATALOG OF SCIENCE ACTIVITIES For Kids of All Ages*
Joe Abruscato and Jack Hassard

For information about these, or Goodyear books in Language Arts, Reading, General Methods, and Centers, write to

JANET JACKSON
*GOODYEAR PUBLISHING COMPANY*
1640 Fifth Street
Santa Monica, CA 90401
(213) 393-6731

# Preface

Teaching social studies in the elementary school presents a challenge to any teacher, new or experienced. This challenge results from the unique content of the social studies and its contribution to the children's understanding of their world. The content of the social studies is derived from the social sciences, which investigate the actions of human beings. By teaching social studies, teachers attempt to help children understand themselves, develop an awareness of the multicultural composition of society and its global nature, and foster an atmosphere for acceptance of varying opinions and beliefs. In addition they must help them develop problem-solving and decision-making skills and foster an active participant role in society.

These challenges would be sufficient without the added concern of selecting appropriate content, teaching methods, and materials to successfully achieve the goals of social studies in the elementary school. The wide divergence in current social studies curricula, the many suggested methods of teaching, and an overabundance of available materials confounds the teacher's task. This text is designed to aid social studies teachers by presenting the current thinking in all these areas.

The text first introduces the reader to the variety of children, teachers, and classrooms that are found in our schools. Then it discusses the various positions held on social studies education and the decisions that a teacher must make. Then the text delineates the contributions of the social sciences and the curriculum development phases that affect teachers' program planning. Next, several methods are indicated—concept development, problem solving through inquiry, unit development, and multicultural education.

The second half of the text presents activities for practical application of the theories in teaching current affairs—including skill development in valuing, global education, interpersonal, communication, and map and globe skills. Also included is a discussion of the selection and utilization of materials and of the important aspect of evaluation of instruction at the classroom, local, state, and national levels.

One of the difficult but pleasurable tasks of an author is in some way to acknowledge the individuals who have assisted in the preparation of the manuscript. Dr. John D. McAulay, a faithful advisor and friend, is acknowledged as the person who stimulated my interest in social studies. Without that thoughtful stimulation, the original work and this revision would not have occurred.

My parents, Mr. and Mrs. Kenneth S. Skeel, surely must not be forgotten for they so frequently have provided the encouragement needed for me to continue my task of learning.

Those individuals who have made this revision possible are Ronald E. Sterling, University of Cincinnati, who contributed Chapter 9 on global education and reviewed the manuscript; James P. Levy, who had faith in my writing; Dr. Joseph Howard, Eastern Kentucky University, for his many helpful ideas; and the staff of Goodyear Publishing, including Chris Jennison and Nancy Carter.

DOROTHY J. SKEEL

# Contents

**PREFACE** vii

**PART ONE
INTRODUCTION** 1

**1 What Is Social Studies?** 2
Who Are the Children? *2*
Who Are the Teachers? *3*
What Are the Classrooms? *4*
What About Social Studies? *5*
Developing Objectives *8*
Objectives for Instruction *9*
    *Knowledge 10*
    *Understanding 10*
    *Attitudes and Values 11*
    *Skills 13*
Summary *14*

**2 The Social Sciences** 17
What Are the Social Sciences? *17*
    *History 19*
    *Geography 21*
    *Political Science 23*
    *Economics 26*
    *Sociology 29*
    *Anthropology 30*
    *Psychology and Philosophy 33*
Summary *33*

**3 Curriculum Development and Program Planning** 38
Local Conditions *42*
    *Community Environment, Socioeconomic Level,*
    *Experiential Background, and Ethnic and*
    *Racial Composition 42*
    *Intelligence and Aspiration Levels of Students 43*
    *Educational Goals of the School 44*
    *Materials 44*
    *A Sample Program 44*

State Requirements and Guidelines  50
   *Values and the Schools*  53
National Agencies and Projects  55
Decision Making and Program Planning  63

# PART TWO
# METHODOLOGY 69

## 4 Teaching Concepts 70
Social Studies Programs  73
Multidisciplinary Program  74
Interdisciplinary Program  76
Advantages and Disadvantages of Structured Programs  79
Introducing and Extending Concepts  79
   *Introduction of Concepts*  82
   *Extending Concepts*  84
Summary  85

## 5 Problem Solving Through Inquiry 88
Developing Thinking Skills  88
Questioning  89
Classroom Conditions  94
Role of the Teacher  94
Objectives  97
Problem Selection  98
   *Initiation*  99
   *Incident*  99
Problem-Solving and Inquiry Activities  100
   *Presentation of Facts*  100
   *Wastebasket Technique*  102
   *Discrepant Data*  103
   *Role Playing*  103
   *Tape Presentations*  104
   *Continuing Activities*  109
   *Responsibility of the Child in an*
   *Inquiry-Centered Classroom*  110
Advantages and Disadvantages of Problem
Solving Through Inquiry  110

## 6 Unit Development 114
Objectives  115
   *Role of the Teacher*  116
   *Role of the Children*  117
   *Conditions of the Classroom*  117
Unit Selection  117

Directing Children's Interests  119
Development of a Unit  121
   *Initiation*  121
   *Arranged Environment*  121
   *Exploratory Questioning*  121
   *Film or Filmstrip Presentation*  122
   *Reading Stories, Poetry, or Folktales*  122
Teacher/Pupil Planning for the Unit  122
Individual and Group Activities  124
Integrating Activities  125
   *Language Arts*  125
   *Art, Music, and Physical Education*  126
Culminating Activities  126
   *Committee Reports*  126
   *Tours*  126
   *Dramatizations*  127
   *Films and Filmstrips*  127
Bibliography  127
Evaluation  127
A Sample Resource Unit  127
Resources  133
Advantages and Disadvantages of Unit Teaching  134

## 7 Multicultural Education—Providing for All Children  136
Culturally Disadvantaged  136
Objectives  138
   *Conditions of the Classroom*  141
   *Role of the Teacher*  141
Selection of Content  142
Special Instructional Considerations  145
   *Organizational Patterns*  145
   *Teaching Methods*  146
   *Activities*  150
Role of the Child in the Classroom  152
Ethnic and Racial Minority Groups  152
Physically and Mentally Handicapped Groups  155
Sex Stereotyping  156
Summary  157

# PART THREE
# SELECTED CONTENT FOR EMPHASIS  161

## 8 Teaching Current Affairs—Social, Economic, Political, and Environmental  162
When to Start  163

Suggested Activities *164*
    *Bulletin Boards 164*
    *News Reporting 165*
    *Class Newspaper 165*
    *Role Playing, Discussion, and Debates 166*
    *Reading Newspapers 166*
Controversial Issues: Social, Economic, Political, and Environmental *169*
    *Social Issues 170*
    *Economic Issues 171*
    *Political Issues 172*
    *Environmental Issues 173*

### 9 A Global Perspective      177
Rationale for Spaceship Earth *177*
Objectives for a Global Perspective *178*
Curriculum Materials for Global Education *180*
Social Studies Textbook Series *180*
Supplementary Materials *182*
Atmosphere of the Classroom *184*
Activities to Implement Global Objectives *184*
Problems that May Be Encountered *187*
Other Activities *188*
Activities that Focus on Global Problems *189*
Summary *190*

## PART FOUR
## SKILL DEVELOPMENT      195

### 10 The Skills of Valuing      198
Rationale *198*
    *Cognitive-Developmental Approach 199*
    *Values-Clarification Approach 200*
    *Values Analysis Approach 203*
Summary *207*

### 11 Interpersonal Skills      209
Working in Committees *209*
    *What Is to Be Gained 209*
    *Organization 210*
    *Teacher-Pupil Planning 210*
    *"Magic Circle" or Group Meetings 212*
Summary *215*

### 12 Communication Skills      217
Reading *217*
Questioning Techniques *218*

Vocabulary Development  *219*
    *Flashcards  220*
    *Illustrated Concepts or Vocabulary Dictionary  220*
    *Language Experience Chart  220*
    *Varied Reading Materials  220*
Group Reading  *220*
Using Reference Materials  *221*
    *Locating Information  223*
    *Outlining and Notetaking  223*
    *Oral and Written Reports  224*
    *Panel Discussions  224*
    *Debates  225*
    *Role Playing  225*
    *TV or Radio Programs  226*
    *Dramatic Presentations  226*
    *Written Reports  226*
    *Graphic Reports  227*
Summary  *227*

**13  Map and Globe Skills**  229

Skills by Grade Levels  *230*
    *Kindergarten  230*
    *First Grade  230*
    *Second Grade  231*
    *Third Grade  231*
    *Fourth Grade  231*
    *Fifth Grade  232*
    *Sixth Grade  232*
Other Suggested Activities  *232*
    *Primary Grades  232*
    *Intermediate Grades  233*
Problems to Determine the Extent of Children's Skills  *233*
Using Interest Centers to Increase Skills  *236*
Urban Map Skills  *237*
Maps and Globes  *237*

# PART FIVE
# UTILIZATION OF MATERIALS  243

**14  Utilization of Materials in the Social Studies**  244

Children's Trade Books  *244*
Simulations and Games  *246*
Programmed Material  *248*
Cartoons  *249*

Graphs and Charts  *251*
Pictures  *254*
Textbooks  *255*
   *Utilization  255*
Multimedia Kits  *257*
Films and Filmstrips  *257*
Free and Inexpensive Materials  *258*

# PART SIX
# EVALUATION 263

## 15  Evaluation of Social Studies Instruction 264
In the Classroom  *264*
Methods of Evaluation  *266*
   *Observation  266*
   *Rating Scales  268*
   *Anecdotal Records  268*
   *Conferences  269*
   *Group Discussion  270*
   *Problem-Solving and Valuing Skills  271*
   *Analyzing Questions  273*
   *Teacher-Made Objective Tests  277*
   *Child Self-Evaluation  279*
Local Evaluation  *279*
National Evaluation  *281*
Summary  *283*

## Appendix 1—Criteria for Evaluating Textbook Materials 285

## Appendix 2—Evaluation of Teaching Aids 290

## Index 295

# The Challenge of Teaching Social Studies in the Elementary School

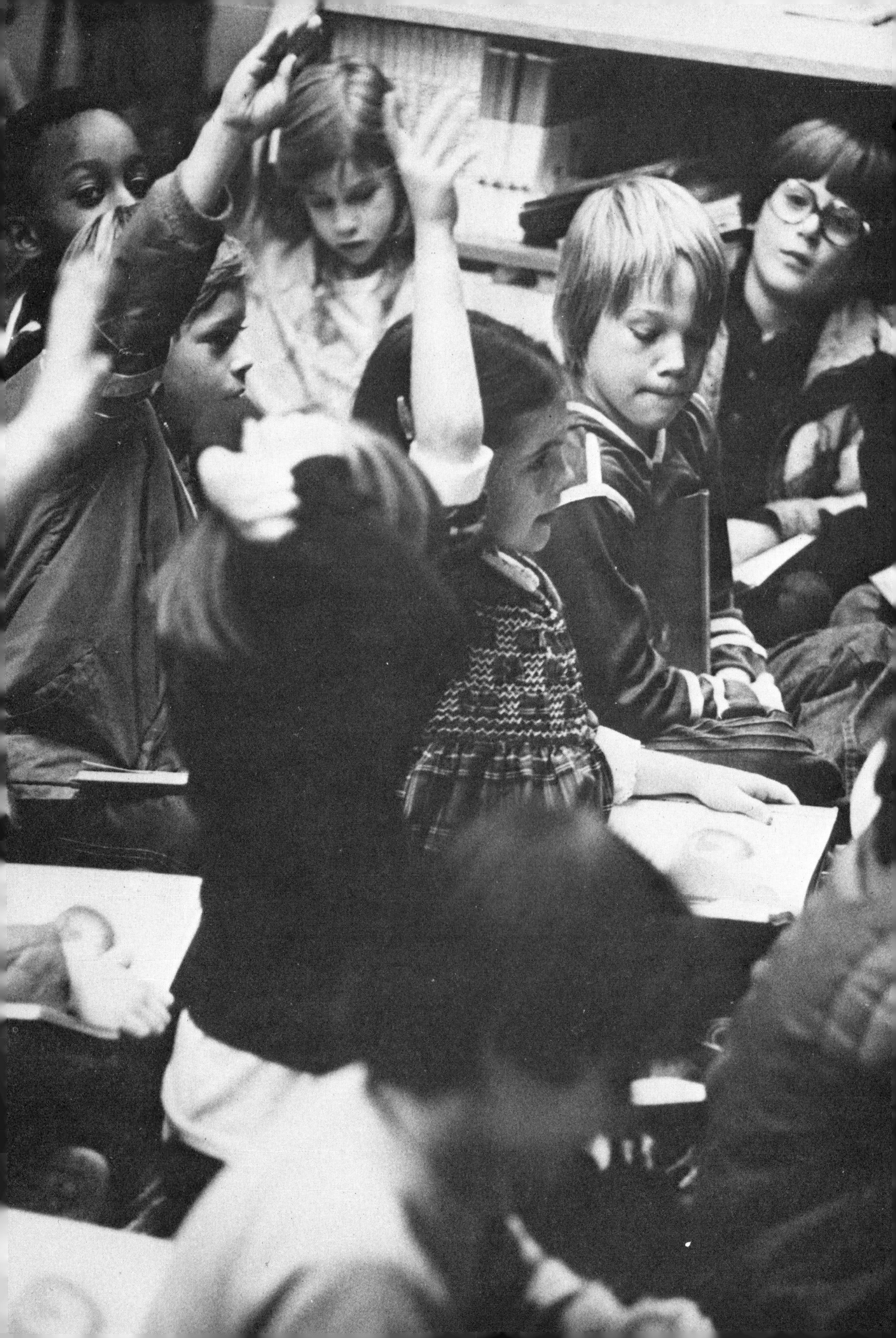

# Part One
# Introduction

What is social studies? What purpose does this subject serve in the elementary school curriculum? Teachers often ask these questions when they are planning a program of learning experiences for children. Many teachers are bewildered by the complicated problem of combining the proper mixture of reading, writing, arithmetic, science, art, music, health, and physical education, as well as numerous other suggested activities. They wonder how social studies can be included in an already crowded schedule, and even more relevant, if the subject is really that important.

Part One attempts to answer these questions by discussing the children and teachers that bring their hopes, fears, values, and aspirations to the classroom. In addition, the various positions on social studies education are outlined. The development of objectives for the social studies is discussed in behavioral or performance terms. The concepts and contribution of each of the social sciences are discussed in detail. This section also outlines the historical development of the social studies curriculum and the decision-making process of the teacher in program planning affected by local conditions, state requirements, and national guidelines.

# 1
# What Is Social Studies?

**WHO ARE THE CHILDREN?**

Children in the classrooms around our nation come in all sizes, shapes, and colors. They come with dreams, hopes, aspirations, hurts, frustrations, and resentment. They come eager to learn and are inquisitive about the world around them—liking people and happy about themselves. But they also come uncertain about learning, fearful of the unknown, and distrustful of people—not sure they have anything to offer.

There's Anthony, a bright and aggressive child, who spends most of his time in the classroom acting up, disrupting any group activity. Anthony begs to be noticed. His actions constantly say "Here I am," "See me," "Listen to me." Anthony comes to school clean and well dressed leading one to believe that his is a caring family. However, there are seven children at home and both parents work. There is never any time to answer Anthony's questions, listen to him, read to him, praise him for successes, or provide experiences outside the home or neighborhood. Anthony knows very little about his city other than it's full of hurrying, uncaring people. He observes how they push and shove one another on the streets, rushing to catch a bus or to be first in line at the food counter. His knowledge of the world beyond comes from watching television where he sees mostly violence. What ideas about the world and himself does Anthony bring to the classroom?

Gwen, on the other hand, is a happy, responsive child. She likes people, school, and herself. Her mother has spent much time with Gwen and her brother reading to them, and exploring with them on trips around our nation and Mexico. Gwen, even though she's only a third grader, realizes that people, although they may act differently and dress differently, have many of the same feelings and problems. She has played with Rosa, a Mexican girl, and knows you don't have to speak the same language to communicate with one another. What view of people and the world does Gwen bring to the classroom?

Robert is a child with a learning problem. He cannot read. This creates difficulties with many of his subjects. What is even worse is the way the children have treated him. Most of the time they refer to him as "dummy." The kids don't understand how badly he wants to learn. How will Robert react to social studies?

Ceci has lived a lifetime in the two short years she has been in school. She is fearful of her own shadow and rarely says anything unless asked a direct question. Ceci is a child who was bused to integrate a school. She remembers the taunts, "We don't want you niggers," "Go back where you belong." She has seen buses shaken and windows broken, people acting frenzied and hateful. The taunts and riots have stopped, but Ceci isn't sure that her teachers and classmates want her there anyway. Sometimes, the comments and looks she receives make her want to go home where she knows people love her and she can trust them. What is Ceci's view of the world?

Roya is a child whose parents came to the United States from a Middle Eastern country. Roya doesn't speak English nor does her mother and the other children in the family. She is aware of how different this new culture is from her own. She realizes that in addition to differences in dress and food, there are many customs of her country that are not practiced here. She misses the familiar sights and smells, plus she doesn't understand much of what is going on around her. The children in school behave differently toward the teachers and their friends. They tease Roya and laugh at her when she doesn't answer them. How will Roya's view of herself and the world develop?

Carl is a noisy, outspoken child. He comes from a family with a hard-working father who tries to provide for the family the best he can. Carl's father quit high school and has had to work at unskilled jobs all his life. He has some strong prejudices about society and people that he has passed along to his family. Carl's father believes that the many "foreign people" who have moved into this country have deprived him of a good job and the chances he deserves. He takes advantage of every opportunity to point out when "they" have done something unlawful, and that "they" should never have been allowed to come here. He doesn't want his taxes providing welfare for anyone, particularly "foreigners." Carl loudly announces his dislike for these people when his class is studying about cultures in other countries. What view of people and the world does Carl bring to the classroom?

## WHO ARE THE TEACHERS?

Teachers as well as children come in all sizes, shapes, and colors. They come with dreams, hopes, and aspirations. They come with values, beliefs, and attitudes about the world and themselves.

Rita is an attractive young woman who comes from a middle-class value-oriented family. She's had a good education and travel experiences that have exposed her to a wide variety of places. She has some strong opinions about teaching and people. She's rather cynical about her teacher preparation program believing that teaching is mostly giving the information that kids need. She's quite sure that methods of inquiry and discovery take too much time, but more importantly kids need to know the right answers. Rita is sure she knows the right answers. Rita doesn't have much patience with children who are different from her idea of a typical child. She doesn't think much of children from families on welfare because she believes everyone can get a job if they really want one. She doesn't understand children who come from backgrounds different from her own since she has had very little exposure to them. What effect will Rita have on the Roberts, Anthonys, Gwens, Cecis, Royas, and Carls?

Julie is a bubbly and enthusiastic individual. You can tell by the look in her eyes when she greets you that she likes people. She comes from a wealthy family. Her father is a doctor and he has given the family many experiences, including a year in the jungle while he operated a clinic. Julie has volunteered summers to work at the recreation center where she has encountered children from all types of neighborhoods. Julie enjoys teaching, but often feels that she hasn't reached a certain child. She realizes how difficult successful teaching really is. The children know she respects them and accepts them whatever their backgrounds or problems. They are comfortable in her classroom. How will Julie affect the learning environment for these children?

Hugo is a member of a minority group who believes that education is crucial to the improvement of the economic and social situation for all people. He chose teaching because he thought he would be an effective model for minority children. His classroom is a place where children can state their values and opinions without fear of being "put down." He wants children to recognize that people may have differences, but they can still try to work out solutions together. He cautions children to learn about all sides of an issue before drawing conclusions or making a decision. He knows that some children don't trust him because he is a minority person, but he tries hard to treat all children with respect. How will children respond to people and the world in Hugo's classroom?

## WHAT ARE THE CLASSROOMS?

Classrooms come in all sizes, shapes, and colors, too. There are classrooms in new, colorful, open-space buildings. There are classrooms in old, traditional, egg-carton-style buildings. There are classrooms equipped with a wide variety of materials that make teaching and learning an interesting experience. There are classrooms that are barren and unproductive. There are classrooms where children receive understanding, motivation, guidance, patience, and a learning environment that meets their needs. There are classrooms where children meet with indifference, hostility, and uncaring teachers.

One classroom in a traditionally styled building catches the eye. The building has been repainted with bright colors and the classroom is a soft yellow. Entering the room, one has a good feeling about it. There aren't any terribly neat and cold teacher-made bulletin boards. It's obvious that the room is for the children. One bulletin board depicts the cultures the children have been studying this year, showing pictures from magazines and newspapers as well as postcards and artifacts from the different countries. The children have pen pals in each country and letters are also in evidence. A globe and several maps are in constant use, and one map depicts the time and mode of transportation if traveling to the different countries. Another section of the board is entitled "How Are We Alike and Different?" which includes pictures of the children and their pen pals with a chart contrasting facets of their cultures such as school, clothing, houses, games, government, feelings, values, and problems. One anticipates that the teacher is probably a Julie or a Hugo.

Upon entering a pod in a modern open-space school, one is struck by the coldness of the atmosphere. The surroundings include brightly colored carpet and walls, but all the materials seem to be tucked away in the cabinets. There is limited bulletin board space and this is covered with a do's and don't's chart of rules, a neat teacher-made display of math sets, and a sterile set of pictures entitled "Our Community." No maps or globes are in evidence. One wonders if this is where a Rita is teaching.

## WHAT ABOUT SOCIAL STUDIES?

What does this mixture of children, teachers, and classrooms have to do with social studies? What is social studies? Just as children, teachers, and classrooms come in all sizes, shapes, and colors, ideas about what social studies is and should be are almost as numerous. An often quoted definition of social studies is "the study of man and his interaction with others and the environment." However, such a broad definition does not explore the points of possible disagreement.

Most definitions of social studies are functional, describing what it should do for the individual. A long-standing definition is one that believes that the major objective of social studies is to transmit culture, which requires acquisition of the knowledge of our nation's past history, with descriptions of its institutions and the responsibilities of its citizens. Thus, equipped with this knowledge, the child would become a good citizen. What effect would social studies presented in this tradition have on Anthony, Robert, Gwen, Roya, Ceci, and Carl?

Another position[1] suggests that social studies should be the acquisition of the structure and methodology of the social science disciplines (history, geography, economics, sociology, anthropology, and political science) since they are the parent disciplines of the social studies. By learning the organizing concepts of the disciplines such as scarcity, market, specialization, public policy, interdependence of economics, and how the economist acquires his or her knowledge, the child will, when necessary, apply these concepts to situations. Why should the child be expected to be a miniature social scientist? How will the knowledge of the social science concepts and the scientific inquiry skills of the disciplines be effective in the learning environment of these children and teachers?

Another defined function of social studies is that of reflective inquiry. Students inquire into beliefs, values, and social policies as well as assess the consequences and implications of possible alternatives. Students become problem solvers,[2] identifying a problem, hypothesizing a possible solution, gathering data, testing the hypothesis, and drawing conclusions. The emphasis is placed on the process of problem solving rather than the products of the research. Students can then apply this process to their own problems leading them to become rational decision makers. Would this process be most beneficial for an Anthony or a Ceci? How would it affect Carl?

A more recently defined function of social studies places emphasis on valuing and action. Students participate in the valuing process to become more aware of their beliefs and the actions precipitated by those beliefs. The students become active participants within the school and community. Are the Roberts, Anthonys, Gwens, Cecis, Royas, and Carls ready for the active participant role?

Social studies should be more broadly conceived than any one of the previously described positions and thus encompass something from each of them. As one reflects back on the descriptions of the children, teachers, and classrooms, one realizes the impact of the self-concepts, experiences, values, frustrations, resentments, and skills that the individual children and teachers bring to the social studies arena. What then should be the definition of social studies that will attend to the needs of the children, be intellectually sound, and develop necessary skills for effective participation in society?

The function of social studies should be to assist children in the development of a good self-concept; help them recognize and appreciate the global society and its multicultural composition; further the socialization process—social, economic, and political; provide knowledge of the past and present as a basis for decision making; develop problem-solving and valuing skills; and foster an active participant role in society.

As the children learn more about themselves and other people, they realize that others have similar feelings and problems, and they feel better about themselves. Children are then able to relate more effectively to others. A child dissatisfied with himself is unlikely to care much about the feelings and concerns of others.

Within almost any classroom will be children with a variety of cultural backgrounds, severe racial or ethnic prejudices, and a multiplicity of value beliefs. In addition, there will be different degrees of motivation, apathy, or disinterest, and different levels of intellectual capabilities and different feelings of self-worth. Hopefully, these children will be taught by teachers who respect them regardless of their backgrounds, capabilities, and value systems, and who try to provide a classroom atmosphere that is open and accepting—an atmosphere that recognizes our multicultural world and realizes that each culture's response to a common problem, however different, can still contribute something unique to the fabric of society.

Socialization (the ways people learn about their culture, i.e., roles, norms, values, customs) that occurs within such an atmosphere should give children a more objective view of the social, economic, and political processes of which they will be a part.

Content is selected which will illuminate an understanding of the past. Children cannot make decisions about the present or the future without some basic understanding of how we arrived at the present. This does not mean a chronological assemblage of facts that are soon to be forgotten, but rather a selection of the information necessary to understand current problems such as the decline of the cities, racial strife, or the oil crisis in the Middle East. Basic understanding also entails acquiring a respect for the cultural heritage of our country and other countries of the world.

The development of problem-solving skills provides a basis for the acquisition of decision-making skills. Children hypothesize a solution to a problem, but then need sufficient information to test the validity and feasibility of the hypothesis. Valuing skills are also necessary in the process since the action to be taken or the solution hypothesized should be guided by value priorities. Children must realize why they value as they do, that others may value differently, and the effect their values have on their actions. Decisions can then be made.

As children are given the opportunity to act on the solutions they evolve, they then see the efficacy of their roles in society. For example, when children arrive at the solution that a crossing guard is needed at a street intersection where several accidents have occurred, they take their solution to the proper authorities and observe the results after the authorities agree to add the guard; then they realize participation can be effective. Fostering this action is a necessity so that it will become a lifelong habit.

Goals established for the social studies from the above definition would be:

- To improve the individual's self-concept.
- To recognize the varying abilities of individuals and the worth of each individual.
- To acquire knowledge of and appreciation for the cultures within society.
- To increase awareness of and appreciation for the global society and its multicultural composition.
- To acquire knowledge of global problems.
- To acquire knowledge of past events and their influence on the present and the future.
- To acquire problem-solving and valuing skills that provide the basis for decision making.
- To acquire social skills that increase communication among individuals.
- To acquire knowledge of the economic and political systems for effective participation.
- To foster an attitude that encourages each individual to become an active member of society.

## DEVELOPING OBJECTIVES

Specific objectives developed for a social studies curriculum would be based upon the above-defined function and goals but with consideration for:

- The experiential background of the students; the attitudes, values, skills, and experiences that the students bring with them.
- The intellectual abilities of the students; the capabilities exhibited by the students.
- The availability of materials; the resources that are available within the school and community.
- The goals of the total school curriculum; the social studies objectives that should assist in attainment of the overall goals of the school.
- The societal factors that affect each and all of us; the changes in society to which the curriculum should respond.

WHAT IS SOCIAL STUDIES?

## OBJECTIVES FOR INSTRUCTION

Too frequently, objectives for instruction are stated in vague, meaningless terms. Objectives so stated are difficult to implement in the classroom and they do not communicate to others what is to be accomplished by the learning experiences. Numerous educators contend, however, that objectives stated in behavioral terms do lend themselves to observation and measurement. Robert Mager defines an objective as

> ... an intent communicated by a statement describing a proposed change in a learner—a statement of what the learner is to be like when he has successfully completed a learning experience. It is a description of a pattern of behavior (performance) we want the learner to be able to demonstrate.[3]

Mager indicates that when a teacher is writing objectives, either in behavioral or performance terms, it is advisable to include the following information:

First, identify the terminal behavior by name; we can specify the kind of behavior which will be accepted as evidence that the learner has achieved the objective.

Second, try to further define the desired behavior by describing the important conditions under which the behavior will be expected to occur.

Third, specify the criteria of acceptable performance by describing how well the learner must perform to be considered acceptable.[4] Each objective need not include all of the above information. Initially, objectives are written in broad terms to indicate the type of subject matter to be covered. Second, specific objectives are written in behavioral or performance terms to indicate the behavior expected of the individual after he or she has been exposed to the subject matter. An example of a broad objective is:

> *The student will acquire knowledge of the history of Mexico to enable him to understand the customs and traditions of that country.*

This objective made more specific and stated in behavioral terms might be:

> *The student will compare and contrast three of the Christmas customs and traditions of Mexico with those of the United States; identify two of the traditions sacred to Mexican families; list at least one of the Mexican holidays that is different from those celebrated in the United States.*

On the other side of the argument are those educators who believe that behavioral objectives standardize instruction and aim at only measurable results, thus eliminating learning that is self-directed, unstructured, and unpredictable. These educators would recommend objectives that are "specified" rather than "behavioral"—specified by a teacher according to a philosophy and taking into consideration the talents and choices of the children.[5]

The important aspect of stating objectives is whether the teacher has communicated what is to be accomplished by the instruction. Not all of the results of social studies instruction (e.g., values, attitudes) can be measured, nor is it necessary to attempt this, but teachers will want to have some means of determining the success of their efforts.

Objectives of the social studies are grouped into four areas: knowledge, understanding, values and attitudes, and skills. Knowledge and understanding are a part of the cognitive (knowing) domain; values and attitudes are a part of the cognitive, as well as the affective (e.g., prizing, feeling) domains; and skills are abilities or proficiencies.

## Knowledge

In the social studies, as in any subject, children should not be required to learn facts or knowledge merely for their acquisition. The knowledge they are to acquire should be selected on the basis of its capacity to further their understanding. For example, it would be better to learn that Washington became president of the new nation because the people trusted the leadership he exhibited during the Revolution rather than merely to memorize the fact that he was our first president. Rather than learn the names of the states and their capitals to reel them off in rote fashion, it would be better for students to learn that state capitals are generally located near the center of the states to better serve the people of that state.

Objectives developed in the area of knowledge are selected to further an understanding. An example of such an objective would be:

*The student will acquire knowledge of the minority groups of the United States to better understand how much they contribute to our society.*

## Understanding

One of the most important aspects of the social studies is the area of understanding. Obviously, facts are of little value unless they increase one's understanding of a subject or problem. Understanding requires the individual to synthesize several pieces of information and relate them to one another to comprehend the connection between the previous knowledge and the newly acquired information. Understanding of a problem is essential before an individual can attempt to solve it. With understanding, various pieces of information can be fitted together for a possible solution.

Measurement of an individual's achievement in the area of understanding becomes difficult unless the individual applies this synthesized knowledge to a new situation. Therefore, objectives under the heading of understanding must include this application.

Examples of objectives for the area of understanding are:

*The student will understand that individual abilities differ, and will show this understanding by ready acceptance of people with differing abilities.*

*The student will understand that the mobility of people is dependent upon a variety of individual goals such as adventure and greater opportunity, and will identify the different goals of groups he or she has encountered.*

## Attitudes and Values

Attitude is a continuing area of concern in the social studies, because it is believed that attitudes determine behavior. An attitude is defined as a relatively enduring organization of beliefs about an object or situation that causes an individual to respond in some manner. A belief

> within an attitude organization is conceived to have three components: a *cognitive* component, because it represents a person's knowledge, held with varying degrees of certitude, about what is true or false, good or bad, desirable or undesirable; an *affective* component, because under suitable conditions the belief is capable of arousing affect of varying intensity . . . when its validity is questioned; and a *behavioral* component, because the belief . . . must lead to some action when it is suitably activated.[6]

Therefore, the cognitive component may affect an attitude as knowledge is acquired about a particular situation. For example, viewing films of the modern cities in Africa would change the belief that Africans only live in grass huts. The affective component may be activated by confrontation with behavior that is inconsistent with the individual's belief "on how one should behave in that situation." For example, the teacher displays an interest in and appreciation for the primitive art of Africa and the child has always believed this type of art was "junky." The child will be required to reassess his attitude toward the artwork. The atmosphere of the classroom affects the attitudes developed. If a teacher is attempting to develop an attitude regarding the importance of recognizing the worth of the individual, but does not allow each person to express an opinion nor accept the contributions of each member of the group, it is doubtful that this attitude will be successfully conveyed to the students.

Measurement of attitude is best accomplished by observing the behavior of individuals in a given situation. Undoubtedly, there will be occasions when children will display the actions they feel are expected of them, thereby making measurement difficult. And there also will be times when teachers misunderstand or misjudge the behavior of children and are unable to assess their real feelings or emotions.

Examples of objectives for the area of attitudes are:

*The student appreciates that cooperative behavior is necessary to accomplish certain tasks and willingly offers to work with others.*

*The student values the contributions to our heritage of the many subcultures and expresses an appreciation for them.*

". . . A value, unlike an attitude, is a standard or yardstick to guide actions, attitudes, comparisons, evaluations, and justification of self and others."[7] "A person's value system may thus be said to represent a learned organization of rules for making choices and for resolving conflicts—between two or more modes of behavior or between two or more endstates of existence."[8] Values are much more difficult to change since they are generally learned early in the socialization process, at home and within the peer group.

Previously, values often were taught by the process of indoctrination, where the teachers indicated what was right or wrong based on their own value systems. However, studies have suggested that there are stages of development and that the school can best influence the child's values by helping him to grow into the advanced stages of personal development. Children can be helped to clarify their own value positions through the experience of analyzing conflicting value situations and exploring their own feelings and values in different situations. An example of an objective in the valuing area would be:

*The student will analyze his value position when confronted with a problem situation by listing alternative solutions, their consequences, and value issues.*

## Skills

A skill is defined as the ability to become capable or proficient at performing a task or tasks. In stating objectives for this area, the individual's potential should be determined. Because skills are developmental, an acceptable achievement level varies according to the individual's maturation level. For example, a primary-grade child cannot be expected to perform certain skills with the same proficiency as would an intermediate-grade child.

Skills are developed sequentially—some must be acquired before others. For example, children must learn to read before they can acquire skill in locating information; or, they must understand spatial relationships before they can develop skill in map reading. Skills are divided into three subgroups: social, intellectual, and motor.

Social skills are concerned with the interaction of individuals within a group. Obviously, children who are unable to get along with members of their own class or who constantly display uncooperative behavior will find it difficult to understand and appreciate the necessity for establishing cooperation among other groups or nations. A teacher must first strive to develop the social skills within the classroom. Examples of such objectives would be:

*The student will develop leadership ability by assuming the role of committee chairperson.*

*The student will acquire skill in cooperative planning by working in committees to the completion of a task.*

Intellectual skills include skill in doing research, critical thinking, problem solving, making oral and written reports, outlining, and taking notes. The development of these skills need not be limited to the social studies; they offer an excellent opportunity for integration, especially with the language arts. For example, critical thinking can be introduced in reading and then applied in the social studies. Examples of such objectives would be:

*The student will select the important point of a paragraph.*

*The student will demonstrate the use and understanding of the seven-color key of a map.*

Motor skills include proficiency in manipulative activities such as construction, painting, and drawing. Sample objectives would be:

*The student will demonstrate skill in the use of a variety of media, including paint, chalk, and charcoal.*

*The student will construct a relief map using plasticene.*

Continued practice is essential to ensure increased proficiency of skills. Some skills which will be practiced relate only to the social studies, while other skills could be used in any of the subject areas.

A crucial part of any social studies program is the development of a set of relevant objectives. Such objectives are related to purposes, understandable to all, and many can be measured by the student's behavior. For instruction to be valuable, the teacher should have a clear idea of how the instruction will affect student behavior.

## SUMMARY

As teachers consider social studies and its role in the curriculum, they must first think about the children in their classrooms. What value beliefs do they bring with them? What are their feelings about themselves and others? What are their prejudices? What are their experiences? What are their abilities and expectations?

Next, teachers must consider themselves. How do they feel about themselves and others? What are their value beliefs? Can they accept children who may hold different values? Will they attempt to impose their value beliefs? What are their experiences? Have they interacted with multicultural groups within the society or do they have a narrow view of culture? Can they accept children who come from cultural backgrounds different from their own? What expectations do they hold for children?

In addition, teachers need to consider their position on the function of social studies. Do they view it as training for becoming social scientists? Do they view it as a vehicle for transmission of culture? Do they view it as reflective inquiry or action and valuing? Or are they in agreement with the position that it is a composite of all these functions, with special consideration for improving the self-concepts of children, developing an awareness of the multicultural composition of society and its global nature, and fostering an atmosphere for acceptance of varying opinions and beliefs?

## NOTES

1. More detailed descriptions of these positions can be found in James L. Barth and S. Samuel Shermis, "Defining the Social Studies: An Exploration of Three Traditions," *Social Education* 34 (November 1970:743–751; Dale L.

Brubaker, Lawrence H. Simon, and Jo Watts Williams, "A Conceptual Framework for Social Studies Curriculum and Instruction," *Social Education* 41 (March 1977):201–205; and Robert D. Barr, James L. Barth, and S. Samuel Shermis, *Defining the Social Studies,* Bulletin 51 (Washington, D.C.: National Council for the Social Studies, 1977).
2. Brubaker, Simon, and Williams, "A Conceptual Framework," p. 203.
3. Robert F. Mager, *Preparing Instructional Objectives* (Palo Alto, Calif.: Fearon, 1962), p. 3.
4. Ibid., p. 12.
5. Robert M. Gagné and George F. Kneller, "Behavioral Objectives? Yes or No?" *Educational Leadership* 29 (February 1972):394–400.
6. Milton Rokeach, *Beliefs, Attitudes and Values* (San Francisco: Jossey-Bass, 1968), pp. 113–114.
7. Ibid., p. 160.
8. Ibid., p. 161.

## SELECTED REFERENCES

Brubaker, Dale. "A Conceptual Framework for Social Studies Curriculum and Instruction." *Social Education* 41 (March 1977):201.

Banks, James A. *Teaching Strategies for Social Studies.* 2nd ed. Reading, Mass.: Addison-Wesley, 1977.

Chase, W. Linwood, and John, Martha Tyler. *A Guide for the Elementary Social Studies Teacher.* Boston: Allyn & Bacon, 1972.

Ellis, Arthur K. *Teaching and Learning Social Studies.* Boston: Allyn & Bacon, 1977.

Gillespie, Margaret C., and Thompson, A. Gray. *Social Studies for Living in a Multi-ethnic Society,* p. 304. Columbus, Ohio: Charles E. Merrill, 1973.

Gronlund, Norman E. *Stating Objectives for Classroom Instruction.* 2nd ed. New York: Macmillan, 1978.

Jarolimek, John. *Social Studies in Elementary Education.* 5th ed. New York: Macmillan, 1977.

Joyce, Bruce R. *New Strategies for Social Education.* Chicago: SRA, 1972.

Kenworthy, Leonard. *Social Studies for the Seventies.* Waltham, Mass.: Blaisdell, 1967.

Lee, John R. *Teaching Social Studies in the Elementary School.* New York: Free Press, 1974.

Martorella, Peter. *Elementary Social Studies as a Learning System.* New York: Harper & Row, 1976.

Michaelis, John. *Social Studies for Children in a Democracy.* 6th ed. Englewood Cliffs, N.J.: Prentice-Hall, 1976.

Preston, Ralph C., and Herman, Wayne L., Jr. *Teaching Social Studies in the Elementary School.* 4th ed. New York: Holt, Rinehart & Winston, 1974.

Ragan, William B., and McAulay, John D. *Social Studies for Today's Children.* 2nd ed. New York: Appleton-Century-Crofts, 1974.

Ryan, Frank. *Exemplars for the New Social Studies Instruction in the Elementary School.* Englewood Cliffs, N.J.: Prentice-Hall, 1971.

Seif, Elliott. *Teaching Significant Social Studies in the Elementary School.* Chicago: Rand McNally, 1977.

Taba, Hilda, and Elkins, Deborah. *Teaching Strategies of Culturally Disadvantaged.* Chicago: Rand McNally, 1966.

Webster, Staten W., ed. *The Disadvantaged Learner: Knowing, Understanding, Educating.* San Francisco: Chandler, 1966.

Welton, David, and Mallen, John T. *Children and Their World: Teaching Elementary Social Studies.* Chicago: Rand McNally, 1976.

# 2
# The Social Sciences

**WHAT ARE THE SOCIAL SCIENCES?**

As an individual, you are different from any other person in the world. Your fingerprints are not like any other person's and your voice is uniquely your own. But there are things about you and things you do that are the same or similar to other peoples the world over. Most everyone you know has feelings, ideas, and problems similar to your own. From the earliest time that people lived on the earth, they have provided clues about themselves and their activities. Most of these human activities have resulted from people living together in groups. People had to communicate with others, so a language developed. People had to find ways to clothe and shelter themselves and to provide food. The physical environment required that people learn to protect themselves from heat, wind, or rain and to adapt themselves or the land when possible. As people satisfied their needs, they found ways to enjoy life through music, art, or games.

Living together in groups, people were confronted with problems. How could many people live together without fighting? Who would do the work? Who would be given the power to rule the people? Could one person take another person's life without being punished? Who would decide the punishment? These and many other problems resulted. The larger the number of people living together, the more problems seemed to occur.

In our modern world, we find this is also true. As people concentrate living in larger cities, the more problems they face. Many of these problems are difficult to understand and solve. The social sciences study the actions of humans engaged in the process of living in an attempt to explain why people behave the way they do. Each social science is identified as a discipline which is a body of knowledge about a subject, the individuals who investigate it, the methods of inquiry used by them, and the desired outcomes of the inquiry. Each of the social sciences (history, geography, political science, economics, sociology, anthropology, psychology, and philosophy) views humans from a different vantage point and uses different methods of inquiry to acquire its knowledge. This knowledge about human actions forms the basis for the content of the social studies.

This content is structured around organizing concepts in each of the disciplines. What is a concept? Possibly one of the difficulties in explaining concept is inherent in this definition: "A concept is something conceived in the mind—a thought, an idea, or a notion."[1] Another definition adds, "a concept is a mental image of something. The 'something' may be anything—a concrete object, a type of behavior, an abstract idea. The image has two basic dimensions: the individual components of the concept as well as the relationships of these components to each other and to the whole."[2]

While the above definitions discuss what a concept is, the following one suggests what the individual does: ". . . concepts are categorizations of things, events, and ideas—a convention, a carrier of meaning."[3] In the first two, the individual conjures up a way of thinking about "that something," while the third indicates that the individual must be involved in thinking processes—enumerating attributes of the concept, determining if a previous category is possessed for the concept or whether a new one will be necessary. This process is known as conceptualization. It is an ongoing process that operates as the individual encounters new experiences with the concept. Thus the "mental image of any given concept will vary according to the background or experience of whoever is conceptualizing."[4]

Concepts are stated in a number of forms: concrete or abstract; broad or narrow; single words, or phrases. Some concepts are concrete, for example, "man," while others are abstract, for example, "government." Some are so broad that they are difficult to conceptualize and must be broken down in order to be understood, for example, "culture," while others are so narrow they are of limited use, for example, "homes." Single words such as "work" are concepts as well as are phrases like "division of labor."

Why are concepts so important? Concepts permit individuals to organize the information or data they encounter. They place the information in categories or groups and by so doing recognize the relationships within the data. They ask questions about the data and gain meaningful insights. In the formation of the individual's conceptual framework, openings remain available for new information to be placed as it is encountered.

How are concepts acquired? The individual must formulate a mental image of a concept. Therefore, experiences must be provided where there are opportunities to encounter the concept in different situations.

How do concepts and structure or conceptual framework relate to the social sciences? Much discussion centers around the structure or conceptual framework of the social science disciplines. The discussion involves an identification of the concepts of the disciplines and the role of these concepts in teaching. It also involves determination of what learning experiences allow students to acquire knowledge of a discipline's conceptual framework.

What concepts and methods of inquiry do each of the social sciences contribute to the social studies?

## History

History has been identified as the awkward social science.[5] The narrative aspect of history is questioned as a scientific method of inquiry.

> The narrative, story-telling aspect of history is too easily treated as simply entertaining, or else didactic. But good history tells its stories about people and events in a spirit of inquiry so as to help each listener or reader do his own critical thinking about what really happened and why, and what is meant. Precise details, dates, and quotations from sources are only parts of a painstaking procedure for testing the truth by going through the story of precisely what happened.[6]

As historians attempt to find the pieces of that story, they search out information from two sources. A primary source such as a document, original letter, diary, log, or law is vital to them. Secondary sources such as accounts of events written in newspapers, interpretations of the events by other authors, will give historians additional insights. However, historians may not use all the information they have collected. As they organize it, test it, and reconstruct the facts, historians extrapolate, using the biases within their frames of references. Therefore, to fully understand historians' records of the past, one must know their particular frame of reference. For example, does the historian view most events from an economical or a political point of view? If it is economical, then the historian would tend to look for pieces of information that would support that point of view. In the process, other important facts might be overlooked.

The contribution of history is its accumulation of knowledge of the past, which provides meaningful insight into what is happening in the present and what to expect in the future. It can be the explanation of the cause-and-effect relationship of events. Events do not occur in a vacuum—something must precipitate them and something will be effected by them.

One of the difficult tasks of the teacher is the selection of historical knowledge. Neither is it possible nor desirable for students to learn the accumulated facts of history in some topical or chronological order. Rather, it is suggested that those facts or events be selected which are relevant to key questions of today, creating a postholing effect.[7] However, it is crucial that connections be built between the postholes so that an understanding of how the facts or events are related occurs. Students should investigate several accounts of an event so that they can use their own inquiry tools to determine how the pieces of information fit together.

In pursuing a key question facing the world today, "how can pollution be controlled?" a historical perspective may help us understand the basis for the problem.

Disposing of peoples' waste products, the historian learns, is not a new problem. As early as the Stone Age there is evidence of open sewers dug from house to house in the villages. The early problem was not one of concern for polluting the air, water, or earth, but whether it was a nuisance to other people. "Use your own property in such a manner as not to injure that of another" is a law repeated from Roman times. Before countries were heavily populated, this was not much of a problem. Homes and factories could be built such a distance away from other people that waste products would not be bothersome. However, with the coming of the Industrial Revolution, increased population, and people living more frequently in villages and cities, the historian finds that pollution became more of a nuisance.

In England, a Towns Improvement Clauses Act of 1847 required local authorities to discharge their crude sewage into rivers. However, with the additional industrial wastes being dumped into the rivers, it soon became obvious that some other method of sewage disposal was necessary. There were serious outbreaks of influenza and typhoid as well as an overpowering smell.

> The streets of this city are now in a condition of filth without parallel in the memory of this generation. We do not refer to the mud created by the week's rain. This is trivial and temporary. But the accumulation of garbage, ashes and all pollutions, the choked gutters, the reeking and deadly odors, in most of the back and side streets, is intolerable.

This article appeared in the *New York Times* on May 10, 1863. With the increased population, it is obvious that we no longer can rely on the idea that any pollution will not affect other people. Population doubles, production triples, and waste products increase at the same rate. There isn't any location where pollution will go unnoticed, so that we are neighbors one and all. Therefore, a historian might contend that the solutions should be global ones.

One of the difficulties in controlling pollution is knowing what is harmful and the quantity that can be absorbed into the environment without disastrous results. One historian suggests that those substances not found in nature, unless they are inactive, will cause changes in the environment and should be avoided. Those substances found in nature should be maintained at levels that will not be expected to cause biological change. The same historian claims that all human activities that release waste matter by reason of man's extraordinary proliferation and productivity are likely to upset the balance of nature. Historically, our laws have set a precedent not to release wastes that will be harmful to our neighbors. Therefore, the solution suggested is not a national, but an international one, of no-release of dangerous pollution.

The historian then uses the knowledge of the past to suggest a possible solution for future pollution control. Also obvious is the selection of events or postholing to explain the problem.

## Geography

Geography is concerned about the earth as the home for humankind. Geographers attempt to find out as much as they can about the earth. They are interested in "place," place in relation to a specific place like Chicago, Illinois, as well as in regard to classes such as mountain, desert, or farming areas. The second group is often referred to as a region which is an area identified by the specific criteria of its class.

The concepts most frequently used in geography are *location, position, situation, site, distribution,* and *arrangement.* To locate or find a place on the earth's surface requires relating it to other known places. Its actual position is determined by the lines of latitude and longitude. Site refers to the location of a given place with its local interval features or resources; situation refers to that location as related to other places. Distribution means where people live over the earth, and arrangement refers to how things are placed where people live.

How do geographers go about their inquiry? One of the most frequent methods used by geographers is mapping. After selecting an area or topic to study, geographers may make a detailed map of it. Some might study the desert areas of the world, comparing their characteristics and determining their similarities and differences. Other geographers would map a specific place to determine its characteristics and the relationship of those characteristics. What type of information do geographers learn about a place? After determining its exact position by means of degrees of latitude and longitude, geographers refer to its central location or the relationship of it to other places in the world. "Central location signifies being accessible to the flows of people, goods, and ideas."[8]

Next, geographers may study the physical features of the area, climatic factors, density of population, natural resources, land use, agricultural products, industries, exports, and imports. In addition to the above information, the geographer may collect facts about the culture such as birth/death rates, religious influences, and family traditions. Once the information is collected, the geographer attempts to determine how factors are related. For example, questions asked might be: How can a limited land space support such a high density of population? Is the climate a factor? Does it permit more than one crop to be grown each year? What about the soil? Do the chemical industries in the area produce fertilizers to increase the productivity of the soil? Does the area have easy access to other areas in the country which will supply it with food? Do the people have the necessary skills to develop the area's natural resources? How has the family tradition influenced the development of small factory units or are they a result of the lack of raw materials? It is obvious from these questions that the geographer is attempting to learn how the various factors of an area, physical and cultural, interact.

Therefore, the contribution of geography is the interaction of the relationship between people and places. Once again students are not expected to learn all the facts about these places, but rather how to obtain the information that is needed when studying a key question. Relating it back to the earlier problem of pollution, how does the geographer approach it?

The geographer does not look at the problem in terms of specific pollution, but rather in terms of the overall effects of pollution on the earth. "How is man changing the environment by the enormous waste products he deposits in the air, water, and earth?" One of the long-range problems that concerns the geographer is the effect of pollution on climatic changes. Can continued pollution of the earth cause irreversible changes in the climate? Not all geographers agree.

The manner in which a geographer measures climatic change is by the temperature of the atmosphere taken at the earth's surface over the whole earth. The temperatures are averaged over a year's time. Between 1880 and 1940, the average temperature increased by 0.4° C. During the last 25 years, it has decreased by 0.2° C.[9] How does this affect humanity? When the temperatures were increasing, the ice boundaries moved northward and the south-central regions of Eurasia and North America became drier. With the decrease in temperatures there has been a southward movement of ice boundaries and increased rain in these previously dry regions. The North Atlantic has an increased ice cover, which prevented Icelandic fishermen from completing their usual fishing season, but increased the rains in India, which improved the wheat harvest. What the geographer still cannot answer is whether these climatic changes were a result of humanity's technological advancement and pollution of the environment, or of natural phenomena. There are several ways human pollution could be changing the earth's atmosphere: burning of coal (fossil fuels), which increases the carbon dioxide in the atmosphere; urban pollution from industry, automobiles, and home heating units, which decreases the ability of sun to travel through the atmosphere (transparency); and increasing the amount of dust in the atmosphere from improper agricultural practices. The most concern is aimed at the increasing particle pollution of the atmosphere. The small particles of dust and smoke decreases the amount of solar radiation coming from the sun. Also, these particles aid the formation of fog and low cloud cover, which in turn reflects some of the sun's energy back into space. If this action increases at its present rate, the continual cooling of the earth's atmosphere could produce another ice age. Remember, this is something that geographers think might happen, but it is something of which they are not certain. However, since it is a possibility, geographers suggest there are certain precautions that can be taken. First, it is suggested that world-wide recognition, in each of the countries and the United Nations, be given to the long-term significance of human-made alterations in the climate. There should be world-wide programs to monitor the atmosphere to check for carbon dioxide, particle, and water content. The satellite programs should be developed to monitor the cloud cover and heat balance of the atmosphere on a global basis.

Geographers recognize the immediate concern of people over pollution, but believe there should be greater concern over the long-range effects that may be permanent.

## Political Science

The attempt of people to bring order to their lives is the concern of political scientists. They study methods of organizing society in terms of authority at all levels—from family, religious, and social groups to the national level. Political scientists seek to discover why people extend legitimacy of authority—whether by custom, morality, or legality. They are concerned with the functions and levels of the political system that extend to all people in society. Political parties, lobbies, and individual powers that provide decision-making policies are of interest to political scientists.

Concepts within political science that are necessary to its understanding include *political system, political socialization, authority, legitimacy, power, political behavior,* and *public policy.* The political system is that system of social control at the top of the hierarchy. Political socialization is the process by which individuals acquire their attitudes and knowledge about the political world. Legitimacy is the acceptance of the people that the political system has final authority over affairs of society. Power is the ability of individuals or groups to influence the behavior of others. Political behavior is the way in which individuals exercise their rights. Public policy is defined as "those authoritative decisions which carry out and enforce the wishes of the influential in the political system."[10] These "include laws, judicial decisions, treaties, executive rules and orders, local ordinances, administrative decisions—or any rule of conduct behind which stands the enforcing power of the political system."[11]

What forms of inquiry does the political scientist use? In recent years, many have become intent upon building a science of political phenomena to express political behavior "in generalizations of theories with explanatory and predictive value."[12] One application of the behaviorists' theory is evident in the study of voting behavior. The behaviorists attempt to discover who votes and why, and to generalize from these findings. They do not simply analyze the votes recorded, but rather interview voters several times during the political campaign and after it to determine their political attitudes and how they make political decisions.

Another form of inquiry is the case study, in which political scientists examine a specific unit of the political system or a particular event. An example might be the passing of a law. The case study would be comprehensive, examining all aspects of the particular law beginning with its historical background. Questions the political scientist might ask are: What happened to cause legislators to propose the law? Were they influenced by lobbyists? Were the voters responsible? How much opposition was there to the law? Who expressed the opposition? What is the impact of the law? When the study is complete it gives a realistic, descriptive picture of a certain aspect of the political system. From the study, new insights are gained about the political process. However, generalizations cannot be drawn from it since it represents the study of a single law.

Political scientists are also interested in comparative studies. They are interested not only in comparing political systems around the world, but comparing institutions such as parties or legislatures within a political system. As an example, political scientists would try to find out how countries vary in politically socializing the members of their society. In such a study, the attempt would be made to determine where children in the societies acquire their political knowledge and attitudes. Political scientists would interview individuals within those societies, make observations and study documents, laws, and the media to determine what most influences the child's political attitudes: parents, peer group, school, government, or media.

The contribution of political science, then, is to provide basic information concerning processes, behavior, and institutions of political behavior, political relations among nations, and public policies and ideas about government such as democracy, justice, and equality.[13]

How would political scientists approach the pollution problem? One of the first solutions that political scientists would pose is that of legislation. They would suggest that laws be passed to control the pollution problem. Laws would be written so that companies or individuals who are polluters would pay a fine if they broke the law. For example, the federal government passed The Air Quality Act of 1967, which set standards for the amount of air pollution that is permitted. Obviously all air pollution cannot be stopped immediately, nor will it ever be possible to stop it completely. The law gives the polluters a time limit when they must reach a certain level of pollution control without being fined. The Department of Health, Education and Welfare is the government agency that must see that the laws are enforced. The enforcement of these laws is accomplished with the aid of state and local governments. Some states may pass laws that are more strict than the ones passed by the federal government.

Since the people of the United States elect their representatives to make the laws—whether at local, state, or federal levels—the political scientists feel that the lawmakers will be forced to pass laws which will control pollution or the people won't re-elect them. However, there are some political scientists who say that because lawmakers represent a group of people from a certain area, they are forced to make decisions about pollution that might be best for their area, but not good for overall pollution control or best for the nation. Let's say a certain state has a large airline industry that wants to make planes that fly faster than the speed of sound. The airline industry is important to people of the state since it supplies them with jobs. Ecologists claim that too many planes breaking the sound barrier will not be good for the environment. When a law comes before Congress on whether the airline should be given financial support to continue building the planes, how will the representatives from that state vote? Will they vote to finance the planes because they believe they won't hurt the environment? Or will they vote to finance them since they know people back in their state need the jobs the airline industry can provide? In other words, are they more concerned about the environment or being re-elected by the people back home?

Another example would be when industries in one state are polluting waters that affect other states' water supply or recreation areas. Should the state lawmakers pass laws that will protect its industries or pass stricter laws which may be expensive for the state's industries, but will protect the other states' water supply and recreation areas? These decisions are difficult for the representatives to make, not only on the basis of whether they will be re-elected, but also because it is impossible for individual lawmakers to know what will be the total effect of an environmental law.

Some political scientists believe that all available information about a pollution or environmental decision should be fed into a computer, and then the computer can indicate what would be the probable results everywhere, not just in one area of the action. Not only would the lawmakers or representatives have access to the information, but the people who elect them would also be able to go to centers where the information from computers would be available. Political scientists feel it is important that the public be well informed about environmental factors if they are to make intelligent decisions in elections.

## Economics

An economist's major concern is the ability of people to adjust their unlimited wants to their limited resources. The economist is interested in peoples' use of these resources, both human and physical, in producing goods and services and distributing them among the people. The economist seeks to answer questions of what, how, when, and for whom to produce.

> Different societies produce different economic systems. A primary task of economics is to explain both the essential similarities and the nature of the differences in the economic life of different people, so that man may be better able to understand the conditions under which he lives and the alternatives that are open to him.[14]

The economic system of the United States is organized on the basis of the market system of making and spending money. Producers pay for resources and the services of people to make the products. People use the money they make in providing services to buy the products they want. This is a simplistic view of a complicated process of decision making and goal establishing by a society. If the goals of a society (for example, full employment) are not reached, economists attempt to explain this failure and to suggest solutions for fulfillment. Much economic information involves facts and figures, which are measurable and objective. However, the search for answers to economic questions also involves factors such as judgments of conflicting interests and goals, which are subjective. The economist contributes knowledge of economic activity in terms of the individual as well as how the system works and the problems encountered.

The most basic concepts in economics are *scarcity, specialization, interdependence, market,* and *public policy.* Scarcity means that a choice must be made in the allocation of material resources—there is not enough of a particular resource, whether money, time, or gas, to put it to all the uses that people want, and they therefore must make a choice. Specialization refers to making the choice of completing only one type of task. Sandy does only the cooking, while Ross does the cleaning, or the factory worker drills the holes in the steel plates while another installs the bolts. Market means there is need for goods or services that have been produced or provided. Interdependence demonstrates the fact that the individual cannot produce all the things needed and is dependent on others for goods and services. Public policy is the decision-making process to determine what will or will not be produced.

Economists collect, compile, and analyze data about economic systems. They may do historical studies to determine how the economic system developed and is changing. Another type of study would be the investigation of economic institutions such as consumers, businesses, governments, or markets. Questions asked by economists might be: What and how much are consumers buying? Who is and why are people unemployed? What type of industries are flourishing? What type of economic programs will the government support?

Also, economists study the efficiency of the economic system to determine if economic development is as rapid as it should be under the current conditions. Economists attempt to forecast what the future economic activity will be: Will the market go up or down? Will certain industries expand more than others? Economists use the facts of production, employment, tax cuts, and so on to hypothesize what future economic conditions will occur.

The economists contribute knowledge about how societies decide to use and allocate their resources, how economic systems develop and operate, and the problems encountered by individuals and the systems as they try to satisfy their wants.

How does the economist view the pollution problem? The economists claim that pollution can be reduced by producing fewer goods or a different variety of goods, by recycling more of what has been produced, or by changing the form of wastes or the manner of their disposal. The American people have worked hard to improve their standard of living through the production of goods. It is unreasonable to believe that production can be cut without causing a high rate of unemployment. We try to keep the unemployment rate down, but the more people work, the more goods they produce. However, it would be possible to cut down on the number of hours per week that people work and also encourage people to retire earlier. Cutting production is a doubtful solution to the pollution problem.

Changing the form of wastes or their disposal seems to be a more possible solution. The manner in which the economist approaches the pollution problem is in terms of the money to be spent for the control of wastes and the amount of value that would be received as a result of it. Will the costs exceed the benefits or benefits exceed the costs? How does the economist go about determining these amounts? Let's take air pollution as an example. What damages result from air pollution and how can the amounts be figured? Different economists have different ways of figuring the damages. For many years the cost of damages from air pollution was based on cleaning costs that had been figured in the Pittsburgh area. Pittsburgh was one of the first cities to recognize the need for pollution control. The steel mills were polluting the air and causing extensive damage to the paint on houses and plants. Using this figure of $20 per person per year, the cost for the United States comes to $11 billion.[15] What this does not include is the effect of air pollution on health. When costs for health are figured, hospital and doctor bills and the amount of wages lost by people who cannot work due to respiratory diseases are included. There is disagreement over health costs since there is some question whether air pollution is the only cause for the respiratory diseases. However, only 25 percent of respiratory diseases are blamed on air pollution. At this rate, $2 billion a year is estimated as the health cost.[16]

Another group of economists used property values to estimate the damages of air pollution. Property value means the amount it would cost a person to buy or rent the property. They found that as the level of air pollution went up, the value of property went down. Using these figures, they indicated the annual property-value losses in eighty-five cities would be $621 million.

On the other side of the problem, how much would it cost to control the amount of air pollution to reasonable levels? The National Air Pollution Control Administration has worked out the cost of control for these same eighty-five cities and estimates it would come to $609 million.[17] So we see, using these figures, that the cost of air pollution control would be less than the benefits that would result in just the property-value increases.

Now the question is, who should pay for the air pollution control — the industries that cause the pollution or the people who buy the products? The suggestion is made that measuring devices be placed on smokestacks, and industries would then pay a fee for the amount of pollution they discharged into the air, forcing them to control their pollution or pay heavy fines. This pollution control cost would then be passed on to the person who buys the products. Another example of this occurs when car manufacturers place pollution control equipment on cars, thereby increasing their cost to the buyer.

Another serious pollution problem is that of solid wastes—garbage. Each person in the United States throws away eight pounds of garbage a day. What can be done with it? Once again, the economist looks at the problem in terms of costs of disposing of it and the benefits derived from it. There are certain areas where solid wastes can be used for landfill, which could then provide recreational areas. The economist determines whether the cost of hauling the garbage to the location will be less than the profits from the recreation area. The next approach is the solution of the pollution problem from a financial standpoint—can we afford to permit pollution to continue? Can we pay to have it stopped? Who will pay? Economists see a sharing of the costs—the polluters, such as industries, paying for the controls as well as the consumers paying when they buy the products.

## Sociology

The interactions of individuals with one another and their associations are of concern to sociologists. They are interested in peoples' membership in groups such as the family, school, church, and government. They study groups—their internal organization, their maintenance processes, and the relations between members. They attempt to determine the influence of these groups upon their members—to recognize the behavioral changes exhibited by the members.

Sociologists contribute knowledge of social institutions (where people have organized in groups). They study their members, behavior, objectives, norms, roles, values, authority, realia, and location. They describe the social processes, from the simplest interaction to socialization, cooperation, competition, and conflict. They attempt to explain why members of a group behave as they do.

Sociologists are restricted in their inquiry to the information they can observe among and within groups and to that which people are willing to tell them. Many private aspects of human behavior are unavailable to them unless people reveal them through questionnaires, recordings, or interviews.

The major concepts in sociology include *group, institution, role, norm, value, socialization,* and *society.* A group is a number of people who are together to attain a goal or because they adhere to a set of organized meanings and values. An institution is a formalized set of interrelated roles established to reach certain goals like church, school, and government. A role is the part an individual plays in an institution or group such as the minister in a church or the leader of a gang. Socialization is learning that role. Norm is the type of behavior expected of an individual in a role. Value is what is important to an individual or group. Society is a set of interdependent groups or institutions that are self-sufficient.

Sociologists utilize a scientific method of inquiry. After establishing the need for the answer to a problem, they determine if there is any historical data or results from other studies that will help them hypothesize the possible answer. Once they have developed their hypotheses, they go about collecting data to prove or disprove them. For example, suppose there are problems in the neighborhood schools over what appears to be integration. However, the sociologist may believe that problems occur because there is a mixture of socioeconomic groups rather than the mixture of racial groups. This theory may have been developed as a result of researching from other studies or some historical precedents that have been set. Then the sociologist will use tools such as questionnaires and interviews to determine how the people feel about integration. Sociologists will want to learn how the children, teachers, and administrators perceive the effects of integration. They may begin by sending out questionnaires, but will generally follow up with interviews of a sample of the people so that it will be easier to interpret their responses. Sociologists will also interview people in the communities including parents, local government officials, and community leaders, to develop a more complete picture of the feelings within the neighborhoods. After the results have been compiled, sociologists may seek to do the study again in another similar community so that they may generalize from the findings. In other words, sociologists try to predict how people will react if they are placed in this situation with this group of people.

How will the sociologist perceive the pollution problem? Primarily, sociologists would be concerned about how the institutions of our culture have caused or effected the pollution of the environment. For example, are there certain religious teachings that have influenced peoples' behavior toward the environment?

Does economic motivation cause certain groups to display less concern for the environment? Some sociologists suggest that the desire for a better life increases the demand for goods and services. The result of this affluence is an exploitation of the resources to produce the goods plus additional waste from the consumption process.[18] The sociologist suggests that the social institutions have not been able to make adjustments to stress. Further discussion of the sociologist's ideas will follow the section on anthropology since many of the same concerns are shared by the two groups of social scientists.

**Anthropology**

The anthropologists view people as they adapt to their environment. These adaptations become their culture—customs, laws, beliefs, physical characteristics, and language. This accounts for the many different cultures that have developed dependent upon those adaptations. Anthropology is a relatively young social science which was primarily concerned with non-Western cultures, particularly with small communities, which enabled anthropologists to study all aspects of a culture. However, more recently anthropologists have begun to study complex modern societies including community studies in Japan, Europe, Mexico, and inside the United States.[19]

Some of the basic concepts in anthropology include *culture, custom, ethics, race, traditions, law,* and *beliefs*. Culture is the overarching concept in anthropology with the others subsumed under it. Culture is the learned behavior of a group of people. Another way of describing culture would be that which is added to the environment. Custom is the usual or accepted behavior or practice among a group of people. Ethics means the decisions within a group about what is right and wrong. Race identifies large groups of people having clearly distinguishable features that differentiate them from other groups of people. Laws are the formal sets of rules that a group agrees upon and establishes as a code of behavior. Belief is the acceptance of the truth of something without positive proof. Tradition is the handing down of beliefs and customs from generation to generation.

Some anthropologists search for the artifacts of early cultures, attempting to date their existence and trying to formulate an understanding of their structure and general characteristics. Their method of inquiry would be an archaeological dig for the remains of the early culture. The anthropologist analyzes and classifies the information collected.

Another form of inquiry would be the field study, in which anthropologists go to live with the group of people being studied. They would observe the people, conduct interviews, and participate in the activities of the culture. This type of study is an ethnography, where anthropologists acquire knowledge about the sources of words in the language, customs of marriage and religion, and behavior patterns of members of the culture. They attempt to learn about all the aspects of the culture and how each piece fits together to form a holistic view. In this way, anthropologists are different from the other social scientists, who may study only one aspect of the culture such as the laws or physical environment.

Suppose an anthropologist is interested in doing an ethnography of a community? What are some of the questions that would be asked? What are the customs of the community? Who participates in the weddings and funerals? Who helps out when someone is sick? What is the role of the family? Are parents strict with their children? Do the young people remain in the community? Are there community activities such as picnics, parades, and races? Are there any superstitions or tales of strange events in the community? Anthropologists would not necessarily ask people these questions, but as a result of living there over a period of time would observe the behaviors.

How do you persuade people to change their ways of living which have led to the present plight of the environment? Anthropologists and sociologists would view the pollution problem as indicated by the above question. Why would they view it as a need to change living patterns? Since anthropologists and sociologists study cultural patterns and the way groups behave in society, they would try to discover what elements in the cultures have created the current pollution problems. Anthropologists and sociologists are convinced that the pollution problem is a cultural problem and not a natural one. For example, as these social scientists look at the settlement of America, they find that the country was so rich with natural resources that the people quickly grew to believe that these resources could never be depleted. Actually, some of the resources we now prize were looked upon as nuisances. When the farmer wanted land, he cleared it of valuable trees and sod. Water was often a resource to be feared and controlled. Wildlife was a source of food, but often became a nuisance by destroying crops. As the people moved westward, these resources proved to be a challenge to their survival and once again they were looked upon as inexhaustible.

Other events occurred at this time which affected the political, social, and economic development of this country, and eventually the pollution problem. The French Revolution began the widespread form of democratic government. This provided for the redistribution of the means of production and resources among the people. Right from the beginning in America, the ownership of the land and the natural resources belonged to the people, and the decisions on the use and abuse of the natural resources are still being made today by millions of people.

Another event was the Industrial Revolution, which increased considerably the amount each worker could produce. With the development of factories, there began a concentration of population from the farmlands into the industrial cities. There was an increase in the wealth of a large portion of the population. This increase in wealth brought about a greater demand for goods and services. And as can be expected, increased production also increased the amount of waste products. Unfortunately, the concentration of people in the cities made the disposal of these wastes much more difficult.

Therefore, the anthropologist and sociologist feel that these three aspects of our culture have brought about the environmental crisis: the first is the feeling that our natural resources are here to be used and we cannot harm the environment to the extent that it can't be remedied; the second is the fact that decisions about pollution and natural resources are to be made by the people in terms of what they own, and also by voting for the regulations that will stop pollution. There is a wide range of concern about the environment. If the regulation appears to cost too much, such as a tax raise for the improvement of a local sanitation plant, many voters will not support the action. Some of the laws that have been passed by the national government to protect natural resources have not been strictly enforced.

The third factor is the importance that is placed upon the value of technology. Many people believe that with our advanced technology we can accomplish anything, even save our environment. It is believed if we are capable of sending a man to the moon, then we should be able to use that same technology to solve our pollution problems. Also, that same technology has given us a higher standard of living and the desire for a better life, a common goal of all societies.

What then would anthropologists and sociologists see as solutions to these problems created by our cultural patterns? Crucial to the success of any solution will be the understanding by the majority of Americans (or any democratic industrial nation) that natural resources, air and water included, are exhaustible and pollution must be controlled. The reliance on technology to find the answer to the problem must be revised. Certain technology damages the environment more than what it produces is worth. Since decisions about pollution are to be made by the people, then they must be informed of the effects of their affluent way of life and of the necessary steps that must be taken to correct it.

Thus, it is obvious that each one of the social sciences views the pollution problem from a somewhat different perspective. It is also quite obvious the contribution that each social science makes to the total understanding of the problem and the possible solution.

**Psychology and Philosophy**

Only recently have psychology and philosophy been included in the social studies, and their contributions become more important as we attempt to help children understand themselves and the values they possess.

Psychology is a study attempting to understand the individual and the actions of those around him or her. The discipline is involved with the search for the cause-effect relationships of human behavior, and thus the ability to make predictions about future behavior. Generally, the inquiry is directed toward individuals or small groups.

Philosophy is the search for and the accumulation of truths about reality, value, logic, and knowledge. It has been called the mother of the other sciences—as the individual areas of knowledge increased, they separated from the parent. Philosophy is broad and inclusive and has been described as "an attempt to discover the whole truth about everything."[20]

**SUMMARY**

Throughout the preceding discussion of the contributions of the social sciences, the tremendous overlapping of the subject areas is obvious. As a result of this overlapping, combinations of the sciences appear, such as social psychology, cultural geography, political sociology, cultural history, and economic geography.

The tables that follow should further clarify the contributions of the social sciences and their relationship to social studies.

Table 2.1 illustrates the major concepts and methods of inquiry of each of the social sciences. In addition, it identifies how each of the social sciences makes an important contribution to the social studies. Then in Table 2.2, the concepts, information (pertinent definitions), and generalizations from the social sciences are illustrated as was done with the pollution problem, but as each aspect relates to the topic of "The Community."

**TABLE 2.1** Major Concepts, Methods of Inquiry, and Importance of Each of the Social Sciences

## ANTHROPOLOGY

*Major concepts*
similarities and differences of physical and cultural characteristics of man
relationship of aspects of a culture to whole of a culture

*Method of inquiry*
archaeological excavations
field studies

*Importance*
describes the variety of human behavior and aids in the understanding of different cultures

## SOCIOLOGY

*Major concepts*
group life-institutions; small, voluntary stratified groups
relationships among groups
individual's role in the group

*Method of inquiry*
observation
theorizing
testing theories through questionnaires and interviews

*Importance*
deals with social forces in our lives and the forces in the lives of others applicable to us

## ECONOMICS

*Major concepts*
human wants are greater than available resources
scarcity, specialization, interdependence, market, public policy

*Method of inquiry*
definition of problems
analysis of causes
prediction of effects

*Importance*
deals in economic reality—an important part of everyday living

## HISTORY

*Major concepts*
understanding of the events of the past and how they are related to the present and future

*Method of inquiry*
collection of available information
testing of information

*Importance*
aids in understanding of the past, helps slow mistakes, and possible ways to avoid them in the future

## GEOGRAPHY

*Major concepts*
likeness and difference of earth's surface
relationship of physical environment to humans
origins and composition of a group of people as a result of its geography

*Method of inquiry*
regional method—one region is subdivided into climate, vegetation, land forms
mapping and direct observation

*Importance*
aids in understanding the relationship between man and his surroundings and in understanding physical features of the earth

## POLITICAL SCIENCE

*Major concepts*
public processes of political systems
ideas and doctrines about government

*Method of inquiry*
case study
historical development
comparative study

*Importance*
encourages active participation in the political process and clarifies cognitive images of governments

**SOCIAL STUDIES**

**TABLE 2.2** The Concepts, Information (Facts) and Generalizations from Each Social Science as Related to the Topic "The Community"

### ANTHROPOLOGY

*Concepts*
ethnicity
cultural contributions

*Information*
ethnic—relating to groups of people with the same ancestry
cultural contributions—shared and diverse values, activities, dress, customs, artifacts

*Generalization*
cultural contributions are not the monopoly of any one ethnic group

### SOCIOLOGY

*Concepts*
groups—family, friendship, peer, community

*Information*
A family is a group of people who live together—father, mother, children, aunt, uncle, grandparents
Each member of a family has certain responsibilities. Each family decides these for itself.
Friendship or peer-people who enjoy doing things together
Community—people who live in the same neighborhood who may or may not be organized in their activities

*Generalization*
man organizes many kinds of groups to meet his social needs

### ECONOMICS

*Concepts*
interdependence
public policy
market

*Information*
interdependence—community cannot produce everything it needs; it exchanges surpluses with other communities
public policy—goods and services are received as result of local government
market—supply and demand for local goods

*Generalization*
the development of a community is directly affected by its economic activities

### HISTORY

*Concepts*
origin of community
development
important events

*Information*
origin—when, who, and why community began
development—relating origin of the community to the present
important events—what and when they occurred and who was involved

*Generalization*
a full understanding of one's community requires understanding its past

### GEOGRAPHY

*Concepts*
population
land forms
climate

*Information*
population—number of people living within community
landforms—mountains, plains, rivers in the area
climate—temperature, rainfall, growing season, and winds

*Generalization*
man is influenced not only by people but by the climate and physical environment of the community

### POLITICAL SCIENCE

*Concepts*
political institutions
community rules
political roles in community

*Information*
political institutions—decision-making governing bodies that exist to make rules
rules—laws that groups of people abide by to maintain order
political role—part an individual assumes through interaction with other people

*Generalization*
there are many political groups within a community for varied reasons

**COMMUNITY**

## NOTES

1. Virginia D. Moore, "Guidelines for the New Social Studies," *Instructor* 79 (February 1970):112–113.
2. Barry K. Beyer, *Inquiry in the Social Studies Classroom* (Columbus, Ohio: Charles E. Merrill, 1971), p. 111.
3. Wisconsin State Department of Public Instruction, *Knowledge Processes and Values in the New Social Studies,* Bulletin No. 185, p. 6.
4. Beyer, *Inquiry in the Social Studies Classroom,* p. 126.
5. Paul Ward, "The Awkward Social Science: History," Chapter 3 in *Social Science in the Schools: A Search for a Rationale,* Irving Morrissett and William Stevens, eds. (New York: Holt, Rinehart & Winston, 1971).
6. Ibid., p. 28.
7. Ibid., p. 31.
8. Jan O. M. Brock, *Geography: Its Scope and Spirit* (Columbus, Ohio: Charles E. Merrill, 1965), p. 31.
9. Gordon J. F. MacDonald, "Caring for Our Planet," *Current* (January 1970):21.
10. Frank J. Sourauf, *Political Science: An Informal Overview* (Columbus, Ohio: Charles E. Merrill, 1965), p. 45.
11. Ibid.
12. David Easton, "Introduction: The Current Meaning of Behavioralism in Political Science," in *The Limits of Behaviorism in Political Science,* James C. Charlesworth, ed. (Philadelphia: American Academy of Political Science, 1962), p. 7.
13. Sourauf, *Political Science,* p. 7.
14. Richard S. Martin and Rueben G. Miller, *Economics and Its Significance* (Columbus, Ohio: Charles E. Merrill, 1965), p. 9.
15. Sanford Rose, "The Economics of Environment," *Fortune* (February 1970):183.
16. Ibid.
17. Ibid., p. 184.
18. Lewis W. Moncrief, "The Cultural Basis for Our Environmental Crisis," *Science* (October 1970):510.
19. Pertti J. Pelto, *The Study of Anthropology* (Columbus, Ohio: Charles E. Merrill, 1965), p. 31.
20. John U. Michaelis and A. Montgomery Johnston, eds., *The Social Sciences: Foundations of the Social Studies* (Boston: Allyn & Bacon, 1965), p. 243.

## SELECTED REFERENCES

Bacon, Phillip, ed. *Focus on Geography: New Concepts and Teaching Strategies.* 40th Yearbook. Washington, D.C.: National Council for the Social Studies, 1970.

Cartwright, William H., and Watson, Richard L., Jr., eds. *The Reinterpretation of American History and Culture.* Washington, D.C.: National Council for the Social Studies, 1973.

Michaelis, John U., and Johnston, A. Montgomery, eds. *The Social Sciences: Foundations of the Social Studies.* Boston: Allyn & Bacon, 1965.

Muessig, Raymond H., and Rogers, Vincent R., eds. *Social Science Seminary Series.* Columbus, Ohio: Charles E. Merrill, 1965.

# 3
# Curriculum Development and Program Planning

What constitutes an effective social studies curriculum for an elementary school classroom? Should the teacher religiously follow a textbook that has been selected by the school system? Is there a local curriculum guide that suggests topics, learning experiences, and references that may be utilized by the teacher? Has the school system initiated the use of national social studies project materials? Are there state requirements that must be met, such as civic education or state history? Or, is the curriculum a mixture of all these elements? Should it be?

Most teachers will find children in their classrooms with characteristics similar to those described earlier. Children come to them with *different experiential backgrounds* (Gwen has traveled quite extensively, but Anthony has never been outside the neighborhood; Roya has lived in two different cultures while Carl has a narrow view of one; Ceci has been exposed to much cruelty while Gwen experienced mostly love), *different value systems* (Carl's family believes in hard work while Robert's accepts welfare; Roya and Ceci both believe their families are most important while Anthony looks to the neighborhood gang for support), *different skills and abilities* (Robert has a difficult time learning his school subjects but Carl speeds through his without difficulty; Anthony is an expert with a basketball while Roya has trouble jumping rope), and *different interests* (Gwen wants to learn more about Mexico while Ceci would like to learn more about Africa), but many of them have the *same needs and aspirations:* to have a feeling of worth, to meet with success and to deal with failure, and to learn to live and work with others.

How do teachers accommodate for these differences? How can teachers plan a social studies program that will be meaningful for all the children? Agencies at the local, state, and national levels each develop social studies curriculums, but the ultimate decision about the proper curriculum for the individual classrooms rests with the teachers. Who will help them? How will they make those decisions?

A historical perspective on the process of social studies curriculum development should provide teachers with some basis for the decisions. During the colonial period, the main purpose of education in America was to teach religion and morality. The ability to read the Bible was a most important skill. However, after the Revolution, there was a need to promote patriotism and a knowledge of the new nation. History and geography became important subjects. In 1784, Jedidah Morse published *Elements of Geography,* which gave the combined history and geography of each state and country it included. *An Introduction to the History of America,* a textbook by John McCulloch published in 1787, introduced American history as a separate subject. Thereafter, separate history and geography texts were published. Most of the learning was memorization of facts and dates.

Free public elementary schools were legislated in 1835. These elementary schools were an important attempt to reunite the country after the Civil War. Civics, along with history and geography, became an important but separate subject area. The term *social studies* did not come into being until 1916 when the National Education Association Committee on the Social Studies began its use. With the beginning of social studies, the idea of practicing good citizenship began also. Students were not expected to learn facts, but to consider them in making decisions. Instruction was to be organized "on the basis of concrete problems of vital importance to society and of immediate interest to pupils."[1]

With some modifications in recent years, the widening horizons theory of social studies curriculum structure for the elementary schools was first initiated in the state of Virginia in 1930. Paul Hanna, one of its designers, continued refinement of its structure over the years. This theory advocates that the child should first study the environment around him in terms of familiar, basic human activities. For example, in kindergarten or in first grade, the child studies the activities of the family and home. In second grade, the environment is expanded to the school and the local community. Successively, throughout the remainder of the elementary grades, the child is introduced to the community, state, nation, western hemisphere, and world. The theory contends that, initially, a child understands best the environment that is most familiar to him. The curriculum content centers around the human activities involved in production, communication, government, transportation, protection, creation, religion, recreation, education, and the expression of aesthetic impulses.

Many conditions in our society have been responsible for suggested alterations in the widening horizons theory. Frequently, educators view

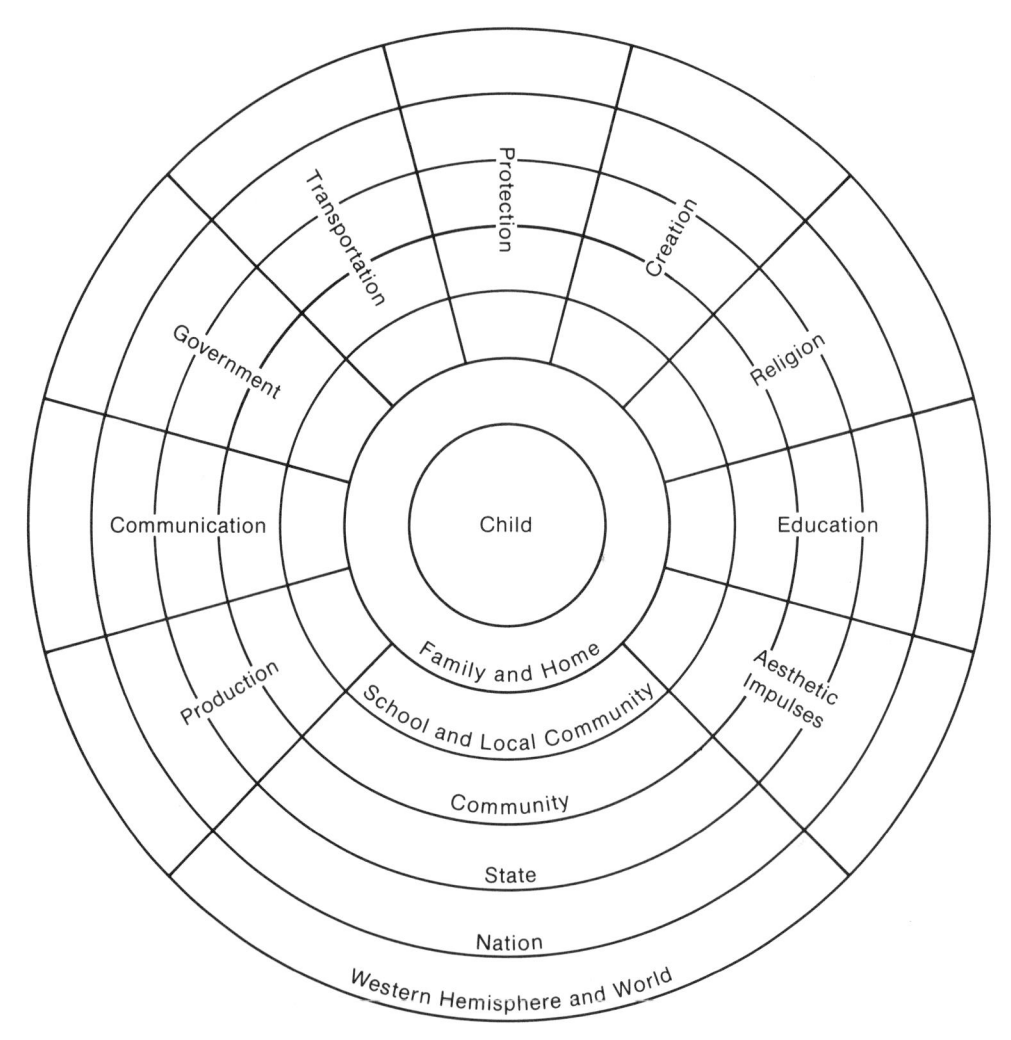

**Figure 3.1** Widening Horizons Curriculum Design Organized Around the Content of Human Activities

the advent of Sputnik as the impetus for radical changes in the educational programs. In the area of social studies, however, it would be unfortunate to fail to point out conditions that initiated change prior to Sputnik. For example, the position of the United States as a world power following World War II placed greater strain on the social studies to prepare citizens to accept that tremendous responsibility. The United States could no longer isolate itself without concern for what was happening in the rest of the world. The problems in international relations between the communist and noncommunist countries during the cold-war period necessitated a more thorough study of foreign ideologies. In addition, it was advocated that students needed a broader understanding of their American heritage in order to provide a basis for comparison. Equally important in the development of new educational programs was the emergence of underdeveloped nations seeking a place in the diplomatic world. Nations such as China, Egypt, and the African countries that in the past were rarely included in the social studies curriculum must now be a part of it.

Educators such as Jerrold R. Zacharias and Jerome Bruner influenced the social studies curriculum with their research and development programs, which stressed the structure of the disciplines and a major change in the theory of instruction. Social studies, however, was one of the last areas to be affected by these programs.

Project Social Studies, which was initiated by the U.S. Office of Education in 1962 to encourage social scientists and educators to develop new programs, added pressure to social studies education. These new programs emphasized the inclusion and extension in elementary social studies of content from all of the social sciences. They also emphasized that the skills of the social scientists should be acquired by the students.

Federal monies that placed emphasis on educating the culturally disadvantaged resulted in the development of programs and materials for these students. A natural outcome of this emphasis on individual differences was the establishment of programs for students of exceptional ability.

More recently, pressures around the world and within our society have influenced the teaching of social studies. The realization that problems of population, food and energy resources, and pollution are global, necessitate that students acquire knowledge about them and also learn what actions they can take to effect solutions. In other words, they are citizens of the world, not just citizens of a town, state, or nation.

The Civil Rights Movement, Women's Movement, and the recognition of the rights of the handicapped and the aging, necessitate that students receive a multicultural education. Multicultural recognizes the rights and contributions of the individual whatever the age, sex, race, religion, ethnic group, or handicap. Students need to learn about cultural diversity and different value systems as well as how to resolve conflict when it arises.

The rapid urbanization of our nation has changed the living patterns of people. The close contact of people in an urbanized and suburbanized society requires the development of better human relation skills and an understanding of the problems created by the crowded cities and suburbs. Skills are needed that permit individuals to cope with problems such as economic skills—how to buy wisely and where to go if products are faulty; political efficacy—knowing the power structure and the rights of the individual related to the laws that govern; and career possibilities—what jobs are available and how to train for them.

Technological advancements also have had their effect. Limited working hours provide more leisure time, which should be channeled toward worthwhile endeavors. Mechanization has virtually eliminated pride in craftsmanship and has created a need for some replacement for that reward. Unemployment has increased, which has necessitated retraining to acquire skills needed in the job market.

Family relationships have changed. The composition of families may be nuclear with mother, father, and children, or single parent, commune, and extended. Male and female roles within the family have altered. Communication within the family has been assaulted by the media. Divorce is becoming more prevalent. Both parents are often working. These conditions suggest that family members may not have as much influence on one another. Do children still acquire their values from their families or do they need to pursue value issues in school?

The above conditions have caused various groups to suggest changes in the social studies curriculum. Global education, career education, law-related education, economic education, political socialization, environmental issues, and moral development are some of the topics vying for a place in the curriculum.

How will teachers decide what is important? First, teachers must investigate what local conditions exist.

## LOCAL CONDITIONS

The type of social studies program established by the teachers will, in addition to considering individual children in the classroom, result from studies of the conditions inherent in the school community.

### Community Environment, Socioeconomic Level, Experiential Background, and Ethnic and Racial Composition

Environmental factors influence the type of social studies program that is introduced into a school system—a meaningful series of learning experiences for children in a rural area would not necessarily prove as fruitful for children in an urban community or in an affluent suburban district. The reason for this variation obviously lies in the everyday experiences of each group of children. Many of the situations confronting the children in the city, suburbs, and rural areas would differ greatly.

The socioeconomic level of the children in each area also affects their experiential background. The child from an affluent suburban home may have traveled extensively, been exposed to an enriching vocabulary, and been surrounded by books, magazines, and newspapers. The urban child from a poverty area may have traveled no more than four blocks from home, never have seen books until entering school, and received little direct communication from adults. Because they bring such different experiential backgrounds to the school situation, the children from these two environments certainly should not be confronted with the same social studies experiences. Children with rich, experiential backgrounds benefit from a program that builds upon their experiences and expands their horizons. They are able to handle more abstract material. In comparison, children with a paucity of experiences need a program to provide the experiences lacking in their backgrounds. A major portion of such a program would include field trips, a wealth of visual materials (such as pictures, films, filmstrips, books, and magazines), enriching cultural activities, and concrete experiences for vocabulary development. Obviously, programs for both areas would contain certain basic elements, although they would vary in their approach and content.

Large school districts with varying environmental areas within their boundaries may find it necessary to adopt several social studies programs to meet the needs of their children from divergent backgrounds.

The ethnic and racial composition of the community is important. Implementing the multicultural objectives studies of the racial and ethnic groups within the community will enrich the program, but more importantly will instill a feeling of pride in the children for their heritage.

## Intelligence and Aspiration Levels of Students

Home, community, and school environments play important roles in the intelligence and aspiration levels children achieve. Studies conclude that socioeconomic factors influence the intelligence level of children—those from lower socioeconomic groups score significantly lower on intelligence tests than those from middle socioeconomic groups.[2] School achievement apparently is related as well to socioeconomic status.[3] The aspiration level also is affected by the amount of motivation, interest, and support children receive from their environments, which include the home, the peer group, and the school. Obviously, social studies program planning should be influenced by these factors.

Children with apparent lower intelligence and aspiration levels need enriching experiences to stimulate their interest in learning and increase their motivation to achieve. Teacher expectations for them are important. Goals should not be outlined that would be unreasonable and frustrating to the children, but neither should the teacher possess the attitude that "they can't do anything."

The above-average in intelligence should be challenged by more in-depth studies of topics and extensive use of their own initiative in order to complete work; the quality of their work should be expected to be higher; they should be provided with material that will interest and excite them on their intellectual level. An important attitude for the superior student to acquire is one of respect for his or her own ability plus respect and appreciation for the contributions of those of lesser ability.

## Educational Goals of the School

The social studies program planned by the local school district should certainly contribute to the overall goals of the elementary school. If the school's intent is to help each child develop to the extent of his or her potential so that each may become an effective member of society, the social studies program should accept the responsibility for helping the student develop skill in and an understanding of human relationships.

## Materials

The extent of the materials necessary to make a program effective should be considered before the program is developed. Some programs require extensive libraries, resource materials, audiovisual aids, and artifacts that may not be available in some districts. However, often overlooked community resources such as the museum, public library, and community members can add considerably to the limited resources of a district.

## A Sample Program

A sample of a social studies curriculum that was developed by the teachers in a school after they considered the local conditions is shown in Table 3.1. The school had some specific concerns about its children and wanted to design a program that would attend to those concerns. Many of the children in the school came from lower socioeconomic homes and lacked social skills that permitted them to get along well with their classmates. As a result, there were frequent discipline problems. Materials that were used in the present program did not relate to the experiences of the children, and there was a lack of interest. The value orientations of the children often were different from those of their teachers.

**TABLE 3.1** (Roseville) School Social Studies Program

| OBJECTIVES (Attitude/Knowledge/Skill) | LEARNING EXPERIENCES | RESOURCES |
|---|---|---|
| I Knowledge of the democratic process and an understanding of its effect on their lives. | Children make their own rules in class, when possible. Organize a student council for the class or school, if there are decisions such a group can make. As a group such as family or school, etc., is studied, examine how and why rules are made. For example: families have rules; families depend on government that has rules; families teach their children to be good citizens and obey all the rules. | INTERMEDIATE<br>David Guy Powers *How to Run a Meeting, Book 1.* David Lavine *What Does a Congressman Do?* Alvin Schwartz *The People's Choice* (The story of candidates, campaigns, and elections). Ivan Klapper *What Your Congressman Does.*<br><br>RECORDS<br>Music of the American Indians of the Southwest, *The World of Man*, vol. 2. Religions Israel: Its Music and Its People. Head Start—With the Child, Development Group of Mississippi, John P. Sousa. G. Johnson Communism, *An American View.* I.A. McCarthy *Let's Go Vote.* E. Lundop *The First Book of Elections.* |
| II Attitude of the worth of each individual as a member of society; developing self-respect and respect for others. | Important considerations—Teacher's treatment of individuals in the classroom. Try to disassociate misbehavior from individual—"it's not you I dislike, but your behavior." Use assembly line to develop something of importance to children. Pull out any individual in the line and discuss what happens without them. | PRIMARY<br>Eva Knox Evans *People are Important.* Peter Buckley and Hortense Jones *Living as Neighbors, Five Friends at School.* Sandra Weiner *It's Wings That Make Birds Fly.*<br><br>INTERMEDIATE<br>Beryl and Samuel Epstein *Who Says You Can't?* Gudrum Alcock *Run Westy Run.* Robert Burch *Skinny.* Natalie Carlson *The Happy Orpheline, The Letter on the Tree.* Samuel Agabashian *All Except Sammy.* Madeline L'Engle *Meet the Austins.* Eleanor Estes *The Moffats, The Middle Moffat,* Rufus M. Elizabeth Sorenson *Miracle on Maple Hill.* Meindert DeJong *Shadrach.* |

*(continued)*

TABLE 3.1  Continued

| OBJECTIVES (Attitude/Knowledge/Skill) | LEARNING EXPERIENCES | RESOURCES |
|---|---|---|
| *Similarities in all individuals*<br>A. Awareness of traits shared by all people. All "are, feel, do, & have." Recognition of these similarities will be helpful for our students who may feel detached or alienated from other people.<br><br>*Similarities in groups*<br>B. Awareness of membership in many kinds of groups and similarities between us and other groups of people. Aids in development of positive self-concept. | *Timmy* (gr. K-6)<br>Objective: To stress importance of feelings. To discuss the inability to see feelings. To emphasize people's basic similarities as well as differences.<br>*Sameness and Difference* (gr. 2-4)<br>Objective: To help children see the basic similarities among people as well as their differences.<br><br>*Sameness and Difference* (gr. 2-6) See A.<br>*Perception of People* (gr. 2-4)<br>Objective: To sharpen children's perception of people. *Is, Feels, Does, Has* (gr. 2-4)<br>Objective: To help children to begin distinguishing between things people do, what they are, how they feel, and what they have. To get children to talk about themselves.<br><br>*Groups* (gr. 3-6)<br>Objective: To make children aware of the different groups to which they belong; to help children realize how allegiances to groups can overlap. To point out basic similarities of people, and yet show the differences among groups.<br>*Americans* (gr. 3-6)<br>Objective: To develop an awareness of what it means to be an American and how one becomes an American. | These learning experiences may be found in *The Intergroup Relations Curriculum*, John S. Gibson, Tufts University.<br><br>*The Magic Circle* activity may be used with all four topics (A, B, C, D). This concept is included in the Human Development Program. |

| OBJECTIVES (Attitude/Knowledge/Skill) | LEARNING EXPERIENCES | RESOURCES |
|---|---|---|
| *Differences in individuals*<br>C. An awareness of the uniqueness of each person can and should foster positive self-concept. | *Sameness and Difference* (gr. 2-6) See A.<br>*Perception of People* (gr. 2-4) See B.<br>*Is, Feels, Does, Has* (gr. 2-4) See B.<br>*Individuals* (gr. 1-6)<br>Objective: To start children thinking about people, what they are, do, feel, have.<br>*Describing Individuals* (gr. 1-6)<br>Objective: To develop awareness and to increase descriptive abilities.<br>*The Uniqueness of Individuals* (gr. 2-6)<br>Objective: To develop an awareness of: (1) the difficulty of judging a person by looks alone, (2) the fact that there are some things about a person that you can only know by asking.<br>*Hypothetical Individuals* (gr. 1-6)<br>Objective: To increase children's understanding of the complexity of people; to discover some of their stereotypes and prejudices and to help them become aware of their own mistaken generalities and definitions.<br>*Who Am I?* (gr. 1-4)<br>Objective: To increase awareness of the visible and invisible aspects of a human being. | These learning experiences may be found in *The Intergroup Relations Curriculum*, John S. Gibson, Tufts University. |
| *Difference in groups*<br>D. Awareness of differences between and among groups as well as differences of individuals within any one group helps to eliminate tendency to prejudge and misjudge people because they belong to a certain group. | *Role Playing* (gr. K-6)<br>Objective: To help children to gain an understanding of different roles of members of same group.<br>*Sameness, Difference* (gr. 2-6) See A<br>*Perception of People* (gr. 2-6) See B<br>*Is, Feels, Does, Has* (gr. 2-4) See B | |

*(continued)*

**TABLE 3.1** Continued

| OBJECTIVES (Attitude/Knowledge/Skill) | LEARNING EXPERIENCES | RESOURCES |
|---|---|---|
| | *Groups* (gr. 3-6) See B<br>*Americans* (gr. 3-6) See B<br>*Describing Individuals* (gr. 2-6) See C<br>*Skin Color* (gr. 2-6)<br>Objective: To put the socially laden fact of skin-color differences into a context that makes the matter primarily a question of: what is skin? what is color? To provide an opportunity for children to discuss skin-color differences without using the word *race*, while treating the fact of skin-color differences as a matter of shades. | The *Magic Circle* activity may be used with all four topics (A, B, C, D). This concept is included in the Human Development Program. |
| III Attitude toward the value of learning and its potential for future worth of the individual. | Apply knowledge to concrete situations such as buying groceries, using ads from the paper, buying a home, studying geography and cultures of countries where boys may go for military service, setting comparative clothing costs, learning where foods come from, selecting nutritious foods, understanding the concept of work and how we depend on one another, examining welfare-value whether temporary or permanent. Students also will give examples of knowledge needed for the future—what happens after you have all the money you need—how to appreciate other than material things. | PRIMARY<br>Muriel Stanek *How People Earn and Use Money.*<br>Frederic Rossomando et al *Earning Money, Spending $.* K. Guy *Money Isn't Everything.* J. Mother *Ideas About Choosing.* Shay *What Happens When You Put $ in the Bank.* |
| IV Ability to work with a group to the completion of a task. | Use committe work.<br>Establish guidelines<br>  1. responsibility of chairman<br>  2. responsibility of members.<br>Be sure a goal has been established for group—evaluate work of committees each day.<br>Play simulation game "Production Line." | |

| OBJECTIVES (Attitude/Knowledge/Skill) | LEARNING EXPERIENCES | RESOURCES |
|---|---|---|
| V Ability to control their behavior through understanding their feelings and those of others. | Use of children's literature books<br>Use of pictures displaying emotions<br>Games such as "Is, Feels, Does, Has and Go Away Prejudice"<br>School exchange—cultural, art pictures, writing letters, and play day. | Fannie R. Shaftel and George Shaftel, John Gibson (previously listed). Ruth Sawyer *Maggie Rose, Her Birthday Christmas.* George Smith *Wanderers of the Field.* Kate Seredy *A Tree for Peter.* Hel Griffiths *The Greyhound.* Lois Lenski *Strawberry Girl, Texas Tomboy, Corn Farm Boy.* James Garfield *Follow My Leader.* Eleanor Estes *The Hundred Dresses.* Jerrold Beim *Trouble After School, The Smallest Boy in the Class.* Emily Neville *Seventeenth Street Gang.* Mary Urmston *The New Boy.* Mary Stolz *The Noonday Friends, A Dog on Barkham Street, The Bully of Barkham Street.* |
| VI Ability to participate in the planning of learning experiences with the teacher. | Each activity planned with children and teacher.<br>Children set goals for what they want to accomplish.<br>Self-evaluate—how well goals were achieved. | |
| VII Ability to recognize problems and to find solutions to those problems. | Group focus on identification of problem—establish goals<br>Holding forces—why couldn't it happen?<br>Helping forces—what would make it different?<br>Brainstorm alternative solutions<br>1. smaller group chooses alternative and role-plays solution for larger<br>2. use situations from unfinished stories<br>3. "You Are There"—problems presented by roving reporter. | |

As the teachers worked to delineate the objectives for the program, it was obvious that the major focus had to be on developing good self-concepts, clarifying value positions, investigating one's feelings, acquiring the ability to work with individuals and groups, and acquiring the ability to recognize problems and to solve them.

Table 3.1 contains a selected number of the *key* objectives of the program, the learning experiences to develop them, and the necessary resource materials.

## STATE REQUIREMENTS AND GUIDELINES

In addition to the local conditions, teachers must be aware of state requirements and guidelines that will affect their social studies curriculum.

Responsibility for social studies curriculum development at the state level generally rests with the curriculum specialists of the state departments, often with assistance from public school personnel and university and college professors of social science and education. State departments establish broad guidelines for local districts, interpret state laws, and provide leadership for initiating change within the existing programs.

Previously, state departments issued curriculum bulletins that were followed religiously. Deviations from the established program were not encouraged, and few opportunities for creative teaching were possible. In addition, adjustments necessary to provide meaningful programs adapted to local needs were lacking. Now, however, a trend toward more flexibility in the use of these bulletins is apparent; generally, they are used as guides to instructional programs. The establishment of broad guidelines from the state departments gives the needed direction and continuity to the local programs, but permits the variations necessary for adaptation to local situations.

State requirements established by the legislature are interpreted to the local districts by the state departments, such as the requirement to study the history and geography of the state or the inclusion of consumer economics. Frequently, they are also responsible for establishing programs to implement state requirements. In states where textbooks are adopted on a statewide basis, it is the responsibility of the textbook committee of the state department to make these selections. Thus, the type of text materials to be utilized by the districts is often a state responsibility.

An example of a state curriculum guide is the one produced by Wisconsin. *A Conceptual Framework for the Social Studies in Wisconsin*

*Schools* was the result of collaboration between the Wisconsin Social Studies Committee and research scholars from colleges and universities. The bulletin's introduction gives an explanation of its basic philosophy:

> Factual knowledge is one aspect of the curriculum that most teachers recognize, teach, and test. Until recently most teachers, consciously or otherwise, have accepted the idea of the existence of a body of "conventional wisdom." This information answered the question "What should be known?" or "What should be taught?" Such a viewpoint is incomplete. While much of the knowledge that has stood the test of time will continue to merit consideration, much new, vital information has been generated. Not all facts can or should be learned; furthermore, these fragments of information often have little relevance in themselves. To resolve this problem, teachers should help students to collect and organize into concepts the multiplicity of facts that confront them.[4]

The bulletin contains introductory statements concerning the disciplines, history, geography, anthropology/sociology, economics, and political science. It also offers generalizations incorporating major concepts of each discipline and topic variants for each discipline for grades kindergarten through 12. Suggested use of the bulletin by teachers is identified thus:

> The pages within this bulletin attempt to demonstrate how the course content at each grade level can be used to develop these concepts and generalizations in a spiralling manner from kindergarten through the 12th grade. By following any strand, the reader will note that the developmental variants emerge in greater depth and sophistication at each succeeding grade level.
> This bulletin suggests the interrelated nature of history, geography, and the social sciences. An "orchestration" of these areas is implied in the developmental variants which appear at each grade level. This approach would encourage the teacher and students to draw against the concepts and structure of the several social studies areas in the consideration of any topic or problem.
> It is not intended that the statements of the basic concepts nor the variants will be taught as items to be committed to memory but rather as illuminating ideas or analytic generalizations which will emerge from what has been studied. Care should be taken that the concepts do emerge and then are applied to new situations. Mere verbalization of rules or masses of

information is not effective social studies education. Students should be helped to acquire meaning by use of the common elements presented. As students use the conceptual strands they should be given new challenges and presented with opportunities to see new applications at even higher levels until they gain the habit of arriving at valid analyses and generalizations of their own.[5]

The guide then lists the topics to be introduced at each grade level, selected major concepts from each discipline, and the developmental variants for each topic. Topics for each grade level include:

Kindergarten: Home and School

Grade One: Home, School, Neighborhood

Grade Two: Community Life

Grade Three: Community Life in Other Lands

Grade Four: Wisconsin

Grade Five: United States Geography and History

Grade Six: Selected Cultures (Food Gathering, Agrarian Handicraft, and Industrial Complexes)

Grade Seven: Man in His Political World

Grade Eight: Western Civilization

Grade Nine: Area Studies (Non-Western)

Grade Ten: United States History to 1896

Grade Eleven: United States History, 1896 to Present

Grade Twelve: Advanced Courses in History, Problems, and the Social Sciences

Thus, it can be seen from this example that the publication is intended to serve as a guide for the teachers.

Due to the constant demand for the publication and the increased concern for the inquiry, problem-solving/teaching-learning procedure and the valuing process, another pamphlet, *Knowledge Processes & Values in the New Social Studies,* was published. The first section of this guide deals with knowledge and its attainment through concept development and generalization attainment. In the second section, the eleven major social studies processes are identified and related to the problem-solving procedure. (See Figure 3.2.) We can look at the social studies processes and problem solving as being interdependent. The last section discusses the valuing process and how it relates to the school.

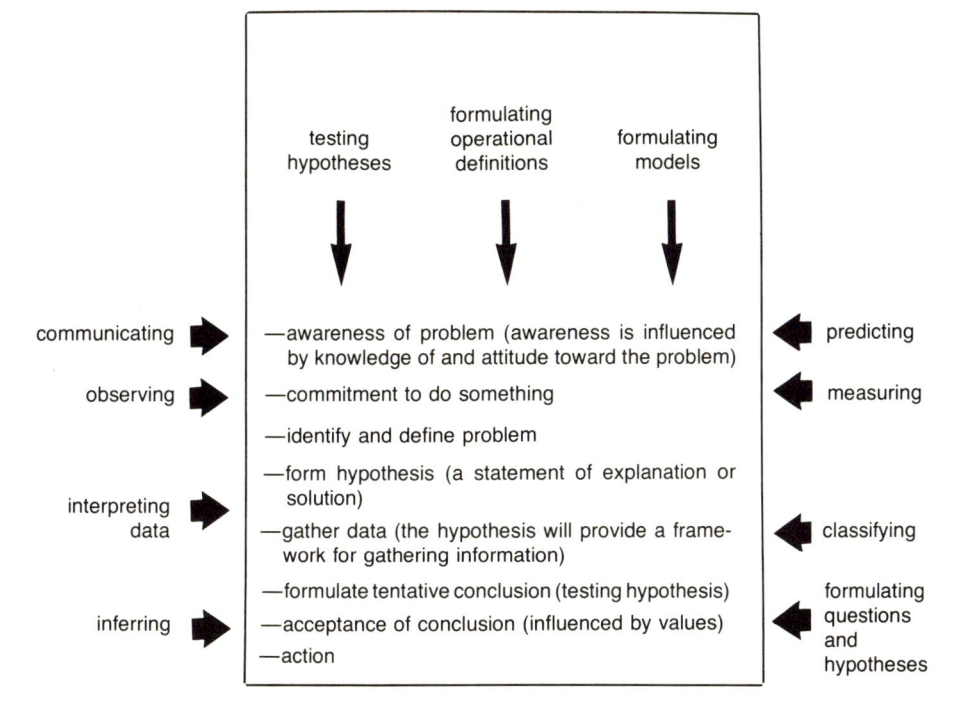

```
                    formulating
    testing         operational      formulating
    hypotheses      definitions      models
         ↓               ↓                ↓
```

communicating → —awareness of problem (awareness is influenced   ← predicting
                  by knowledge of and attitude toward the problem)

observing →     —commitment to do something                       ← measuring

                —identify and define problem

                —form hypothesis (a statement of explanation or
interpreting      solution)
data →          —gather data (the hypothesis will provide a frame- ← classifying
                  work for gathering information)

                —formulate tentative conclusion (testing hypothesis)  formulating
inferring →     —acceptance of conclusion (influenced by values)   ← questions
                —action                                               and
                                                                      hypotheses

**Figure 3.2** Problem Solving *(SOURCE: Knowledge Processes & Values in the New Social Studies (Madison: Wisconsin Department of Public Instruction, 1968–70), p. 35. Reprinted by permission.)*

## Values and the Schools

In a society in which there is general consensus on values, the public schools' role is quite clear. It is expected to reinforce and build into its curriculum and procedures the prevailing values. But in a situation of change and controversy about basic social norms, the position schools should take is not as easily determined. Each of the competing segments of the society—special interest groups, economic and business interests, political organizations, religious and ethnic groups, professional organizations, and so forth—all such groups believe that what they desire for themselves is also good for everyone, and they want to influence the training of the young in the desired directions. The school board, administration, teachers, and textbook publishers find they are being pushed and pulled by these interest groups, each of whom wants the schools to foster its values and beliefs.

Traditionally there was little question that the schools should promote such values as the following:

1. Respect property.
2. Be respectful of adults.
3. Say please and thank you at appropriate times.
4. Do not use profane language or bad grammar.
5. Be neat and clean.
6. Do not lie or cheat.

Now, however, in some situations these are quite controversial. Many lawsuits and community controversies have focused on the meaning of "neat and clean," for example. Several recent surveys indicate that cheating in school, rather than being unacceptable, has become the norm, and most students feel no guilt about cheating. Standards of profanity are constantly changing, and words that one rarely heard used in public a few years ago are now heard a great deal. While many may not like these developments, it is very necessary for teachers to recognize that they are taking place.

It is important to understand, too, that the school as a social institution, as a place where adults and youngsters live together for a large portion of the day, promotes many values simply in the way it is organized and run. Students may learn that:

1. Boys should be interested in sports. Girls should be interested in reading, clothes, and jump rope.
2. Fear and sadness are acceptable emotions for girls but not for boys.
3. As an individual, I don't amount to much. Or, as an individual, I have considerable skill and talent and people like me.
4. Teachers and adults generally have the answers and know what is good for me. Or, everyone affected by a social situation should share in controlling and assessing it.

While it is beyond the scope of this project to deal with the subtle but very powerful set of relationships that exist among students, teachers, and administrators in the school as a social structure, it is hoped that this brief mention will encourage teachers and administrators to look at it carefully. A somewhat polemical but very provocative commentary on the problem is Edgar Friedenberg's *Coming of Age in America*.[6]

Teaching strategies for valuing to use at the various stages of development complete the guide.

## NATIONAL AGENCIES AND PROJECTS

Another source for consideration by teachers in developing their social studies program is the national curriculum projects. These projects represent the areas of concern by scholars and educators relating their beliefs about what should be included in the curriculum.

At the national level there are a number of agencies that are involved in curriculum development, many of which influence social studies education. For a number of years, the National Council for the Social Studies has devoted itself to the improvement of social studies education. *Social Education,* the official journal of the organization, provides information representing the current thinking in social studies. Its yearbook and other publications pinpoint problem areas in social studies and supply needed guidance and material to aid in their solution.

The National Council for Geographic Education, through the *Journal of Geography,* and the American Historical Association expend considerable effort toward improving the teaching of their respective disciplines in the elementary school. Both provide leadership and materials to stimulate interest in and concern for social studies education.

The Joint Council in Economic Education is an example of a national group committed to the improvement of economic education. In 1964, the group initiated a project called the "Developmental Economic Education Program" (DEEP). The three major objectives of the project are "(1) to build economic understandings into school curricula, (2) to improve teacher education in economics and (3) to develop and test new teaching materials at all grade levels."[7] DEEP supplies a variety of materials for students in grades 1 through 12, a teacher training program via television, and clearing house services for economic materials.

By means of its financial assistance to Project Social Studies, a part of the Cooperative Research Program initiated in 1962, the U.S. Office of Education supplied a major impetus for curriculum change in the social studies. These projects, initiated at major colleges and universities across the nation and involving social scientists and educators, approached change from a variety of viewpoints. For example, Roy Price of Syracuse University sought to identify major social science concepts and to utilize them in developing instructional materials. John Michaelis of the University of California prepared teaching guides and materials on the Asian countries for grades 1 through 12. New approaches and materials for a sequential curriculum on American society for grades 5–12 became the concern of John Lee, Northwestern University. At the University of California, Los Angeles, Charlotte Crabtree was involved with teaching geography in grades 1- 3.

Project Social Studies at the University of Minnesota, under the direction of Edith West, developed concepts from each of the disciplines.

The interdisciplinary units for grades K–12 used culture as the core concept of the program. *The Family of Man* multimedia kits for grades 1–4 focused on a family or community such as the Hopi, Japan, Ghana, Israel, and New England. These materials have been adapted and produced commercially by Selective Education Equipment.

The *Social Science Laboratory Units* were developed at the University of Michigan with authors Ronald Lippitt, Robert Fox, and Lucille Schaible. These units, for grades 4–6, are concerned with the causes and effects of human behavior. First, children study what and how social scientists work. They learn to observe, make inferences, value judgments, and identify cause-and-effect relationships. Then, they work with hypothetical cases of social behavior, which they analyze with the tools acquired earlier.

*Intergroup Relations Curriculum* for grades K–6 was produced under the direction of John S. Gibson at the Lincoln Filene Center for Citizenship and Public Affairs, Tufts University, in Medford, Massachusetts. The objectives for the program are:

1. To advance the positive self-image of the child.
2. To reduce prejudicial thinking and discrimination toward all groups.
3. To help the child realize the many cultural and ethnic differences among people.
4. To give the student a realistic picture of America's past and present, including the contribution of its many groups.
5. To encourage the child to participate actively in the learning process.
6. To suggest ways individuals can foster a truly democratic society.[8]

With the political science concept of the "governing process" as the core, the materials focus on human behavior and why individuals, groups, and cultures differ.

*Development of a Sequential Curriculum in Anthropology for Grades 1–7* was instituted at the University of Georgia by Wilfred Bailey and Marion Rice. The Anthropology Project was a cooperative venture involving members of the Department of Sociology and Anthropology and the College of Education. The rationale of the project was based upon these premises:

1. Any field of knowledge, such as anthropology, consists of a system of symbols, or word labels, which is used to express ideas and describe relationships. An understanding or mastery of any field of knowledge begins with an understanding of the

symbol system, the meaning of which expands and develops as the knowledge of the discipline is extended.

2. Symbol systems are usually organized for transmission of a core of congruent ideas, usually referred to as subject matter, discipline, or field. For almost thirty years, the social studies movement has contended that a subject approach to the transmission of social studies is inappropriate for the elementary grades. It is thought that any type of organization of material, irrespective of its method, is designed to transmit knowledge, and there is nothing incompatible, except preference and tradition, with a subject presentation of a social science in the elementary grades.

3. Anthropological material is frequently used in the public school, but, in the absence of emphasis on anthropological concepts and terminology, the contribution that anthropology has to make to an understanding of man and of different cultures is frequently obscured. The material deliberately introduces anthropological terminology which may at first be somewhat difficult for the student. As his familiarity with these terms increases, however, it is expected that they will help him to organize and interpret in a more meaningful manner the world in which he lives.[9]

Organization of the program follows a cyclical pattern, with concepts developed in the primary cycle repeated and enlarged in the intermediate cycle. *The Concept of Culture* is the topic presented for grades 1 and 4. In grade 1, three ethnographies—the American, Kazak, and Aruntas—are presented through oral discussion by the teacher and with a picture text for the children. The comparison cultures of Kazak and Aruntas were chosen because they would be little known by teacher and pupil, and stereotypes of them would not have been established. Grade 4 develops the same topic; however, it emphasizes a more analytical approach with the organizing of cultural constructs.

*The Development of Man and His Culture* is the topic presented for grades 2 and 5. Units on *New World Prehistory* for grade 2 and *Old World Prehistory* for grade 5 are provided.

A project such as the Anthropology Project stresses the importance of social science content beyond the usual history and geography for children in the elementary school. It also stresses the value in helping the children to act as social scientists, learning their method of inquiry, and attempting to study the problems of society.

Other organizations at the national level have been responsible for the development of materials. One group is the Boston Children's

Museum, which developed MATCH units under the direction of Frederick H. Kresse. These unit kits, organized around topics of *The City, House of Ancient Greece,* and *The Japanese Family,* contain realia, films, filmstrips, pictures, games, maps, records, reference books, and a valuable resource—the teacher's guide. The philosophy guiding the development of these materials is that when children are involved with nonprint material, learning is real.

One of the curriculum projects designed for global education is entitled *Global Perspectives: A Humanistic Influence on the Curriculum,* edited by David C. King and Cathryn J. Long from the Center for Global Perspectives in New York. This is a sequential K–12 curriculum guide with suggested instructional strategies to add a broader world view in knowledge, attitude, and skill objectives organized around the concepts of interdependence, conflict, communication, and change.

*Career Development Curriculum* is the product of a University of Minnesota faculty and student team headed by Lorraine Hansen, Mary Klaureus, and W. Wesley Tennyson. The curriculum model is K–post-high school, developed around the broad concept of career development as self-development. The learning activities in the curriculum are designed to promote career maturity "so that as students grow and develop, they will have a systematic set of career exploration experiences that will help them to clarify goals: to obtain the skills, knowledge, and attitudes to achieve them; and to learn who they are, what they value, and how they define themselves in relation to others and to society."[10]

*The Rights and Responsibilities of Citizenship in a Free Society: A Law-Oriented Curriculum Guide for Grades K–12* is developed by the Missouri Bar Advisory Committee on Citizenship Education and the Missouri Department of Elementary and Secondary Education for the purpose of presenting educational activities for students on various aspects of the law such as "Why the Law?" and "The Bill of Rights and Individual Civil Liberties."[11]

*Man: A Course of Study* (MACOS) was produced by Education Development Center in Cambridge, Massachusetts, with Jerome Bruner and Peter Dow as directors. It is designed as a fifth-grade course with its focus on three questions: What is human about human beings? How did they get that way? How can they be made more so?

> *Man: A Course of Study* defines the subject matter, content, and grade-level classifications normally used in describing curriculum materials and underscores the notion that "all things that are, are in all things." The core discipline of the course is anthropology; but, because man is the subject, the scope of the curriculum ranges freely between the biology of man's origins and the humanities of his own creation.

Some organizing concepts of the course are life cycle, adaptation, and natural selection, which are introduced through the study of the salmon. In the herring gull studies, the same concepts are repeated, with the focus on adaptation, territoriality, parenthood, and aggression. The study of baboons includes all of the earlier concepts, but shows the unique social organization which allows the baboon to survive in his hostile environment. The highest-order concepts are introduced through a study of the Netsilik Eskimo. The examination of this microculture highlights the humanizing forces that have shaped man. The student must relate to this alien culture, and in the process of understanding the Eskimo, will understand the forces which have shaped his own culture and behavior patterns.[12]

*Taba Program in Social Science* was initiated in Contra Costa County, California under the leadership of Hilda Taba, San Francisco State College. A detailed look at this program will aid in comparison of programs developed at each level. The rationale of the program is outlined as follows:

> Today's curriculum must cope with many problems. One is the explosion of knowledge. A vast array of ideas has been added and is being added to the curriculum each year. Since the curriculum is already overcrowded, the pressure to cover an increasing range of content creates a severe problem. To encompass expanding knowledge without aggravating the problem of coverage, it is necessary to make a new selection of content. Otherwise, additions of content without deletions will dilute what is being offered.
> 
> Obsolescence of descriptive knowledge creates still another difficulty. Much of what is covered in schools, such as political boundaries or production statistics, changes constantly. This means, for example, that much of the descriptive knowledge learned by a fifth grader will be out of date before he reaches the twelfth grade.
> 
> There is also a need in curriculum for concepts from a wider range of the social sciences. If students are to acquire the needed knowledge and skills for effective living in the complex society of today, which includes an understanding of the many cultures in the world, it is necessary to introduce concepts not only from history and geography but also from anthropology, economics, sociology, political science, philosophy, and psychology.
> 
> The cumulative effect of these problems requires a new look at what kind of knowledge is most durable and valuable. We must

reconsider the role of specific descriptive knowledge in curriculum implementation. If descriptive knowledge changes rapidly, we are wasting time with any attempt to cover specifics for permanent retention. A new function must be found for descriptive knowledge.

To complicate this matter further, recent studies of learning and experimentation with curriculum have greatly extended the scope of responsibilities of the schools. For example, the current emphasis on creativity, on autonomy of thinking, and on the method of inquiry represents a renewed concern with thinking and cognitive skills. The development of cognitive powers now is recognized as an important aspect of excellence. This extension of objectives beyond the mastery of knowledge requires us to reexamine learning experiences. We no longer can assume that mastering well-organized knowledge automatically develops either autonomous or creative minds.

Another problem is that the range of ability and sophistication in any classroom has expanded both up and down. In many ways, the students of today are more knowledgeable and capable than we assume. At the same time, because of higher retention of students in schools, there are students in the ninth grade whose intellectual equipment is functioning on the level of an average second grader. This problem of heterogeneity may be severe enough to require measures other than ability grouping or changing the pacing while covering the usual ground. When the heterogeneity in ability is combined with the problems of emotional disturbance, frequently created by increasing urbanization, offering a fixed traditional curriculum becomes futile.

In other words, the curriculum must simultaneously build a more sophisticated understanding of the world, use a greater range of knowledge, be applicable to pupils having a greater range of abilities, and deal with expanding content. All of this has made it necessary to develop a new curriculum pattern.[13]

Objectives include the acquisition of selected knowledge, development of thinking skills, formation of selected attitudes, and development of academic and social skills. As an example, topics for grade 3 include:

*The Bedouin of the Negev*
    A Bedouin Family
    Winter at Wadi Juraba
    Spring in the Desert
    Summer Months

*The Yoruba of Ife*
    Twins in Yorubaland
    In the Country
    The Special Times

*The Thai of Bangkok*
    Bua Comes to the City
    Getting Ahead

*The Norwegians of Hemnesberget*
    The Time of Dark
    The Time of Light[14]

The topics are organized around the key concepts that follow. It is not expected that any of the key concepts will be developed fully in any one unit or even at any one grade level; they must be dealt with on all grade levels. The concepts must be visualized as threads which appear over and over again in a spiral which is always moving to a higher level. As the students' experience broadens and their intellectual capacities develop, they are provided with repeated opportunities in a variety of contexts to develop an increasingly sophisticated understanding of the key concepts. The sentences following each concept word provide illustrations of the way the word is used in The Taba Program in Social Science.

**Causality**
    Events often can be made meaningful through a study of their antecedents. Hence, to some extent, future events can be predicted.
    Events rarely have a single cause, but rather result from a number of antecedents impinging on one another in a given segment of time and space.

**Conflict**
    Interaction among individuals or groups frequently results in hostile encounters or struggles. Conflict is characteristic of the growth and development of individuals and of civilization as a whole.
    There are culturally approved and disapproved means for resolving all varieties of conflicts. Irrational conflict is reduced by recognition of the inevitability of differences and of the difficulty of determining their relative value. In most situations, some form of compromise is necessary because of the serious consequences of sustained conflict.

**Cultural Change**
    Cultures never remain static, although the context of change (economic, political, social, and technological), the speed of change, and the importance of change vary greatly.

Cultural change is accelerated by such factors as increased knowledge, mobility, and communication, operating both within and between cultures.

### Differences

The physical, social, and biological worlds (including human beings and their institutions) show extreme variation. Survival of any species depends on these differences.

Conflicts and inequities often result from assigning value to particular categories of differences, such as skin color or high intelligence.

### Institutions

Societies develop complexes of norms and roles which guide their people toward the satisfaction of needs. These complexes of norms and roles define proper and expected behavior.

Social institutions include organizations such as the family, and perform an important function in socializing the individual and establishing his status. Political institutions include rules and laws and serve to maintain order, to compel obedience to existing authority systems, and to provide the means for change in such systems. Economic institutions are organized around the production, distribution, and consumption of goods and services, and provide for the material needs of society members.

### Interdependence

All persons and groups of persons depend on other persons and groups in important ways. These effects on others are often indirect and not apparent.

The solution of important human problems requires human beings to engage in joint effort. The more complex the society, the more cooperation is required.

Cooperation often requires compromise and postponement of immediate satisfactions.

### Modification

As man interacts with his physical and social environment, both he and the environment are changed.

Man has often exploited his physical environment to his own detriment.

### Power

Individuals and groups vary as to the amount of influence they can exert in making and carrying out decisions which affect people's lives significantly.

As a strong motivating factor in individual and group action, the desire for power often leads to conflict.

### Societal Control

All societies influence and attempt to mold the conduct of behaviors of their members. The techniques used include precept, example, and systems of reward and punishment; the specifics of these techniques vary greatly from one society to another. Written laws are an attempt to clarify the rules by which society operates and to promote impartial treatment of its members.

Marked differences in child-rearing practices often exist among societies.

Everyone belongs to many groups with overlapping membership, different purposes, and often conflicting demands on members in terms of duties, responsibilities, and rights; each, by exerting social controls, shapes the personality structures and behaviors of its members.

### Tradition

Societies and the groups and individuals within them tend to retain many traditional values, attitudes, and ways of living and dealing with current problems, whether or not that behavior is appropriate.

Certain institutions in societies, such as family, religion, and education, tend to change less rapidly than do other elements of societies.

### Values

Those objects, behaviors, ideas, or institutions which a society or an individual considers important constitute values.

Whether or not a person holds a value can be inferred by others only on the basis of an extensive sample of his behavior.

Societies and individuals often differ significantly in the values they hold.

Values develop through both nonrational and rational processes.

The survival of a society is dependent upon agreement on some core of values by a majority of its members. The greater the variety of values within a society, the greater the likelihood of disagreement and conflict; in some societies such conflict is accepted as necessary to the realization of core values.[15]

## DECISION MAKING AND PROGRAM PLANNING

Teachers are faced then with curriculum frameworks from agencies at the local, state, and national levels that represent interpretations of what should compose social studies education. Local guides can provide specific objectives and a more detailed presentation of the program based on the needs and interests of the children and the community conditions. State guides are broad and general, indicating a framework which includes the state requirements. National programs exemplify the current thinking of educators and social scientists. They are designed to provide exacting information and guidance for teachers with the goal of affecting the development of their social studies programs.

Teachers must decide, then, how each of the guidelines will affect their individual classroom instructional programs, always considering the needs of the children. Figure 3.3 illustrates this decision-making process and the factors affecting it.

The result of this decision-making process should be the framework for a social studies program that is based on the special needs and abilities of the children in the classroom, but broadening the scope to recognize the importance of the community, local, state, and national guidelines.

Once the framework has been decided, then the instructional objectives as described in Chapter One should be developed for each of the following areas: knowledge, understanding, values, attitudes, and skills. These objectives will provide a basis for planning the learning experiences for the children. As indicated in Figure 3.3, teachers must select the instructional strategies and materials that will be employed in the learning experiences. Evaluation should be an ongoing process to determine the outcomes of those experiences.

The following chapters will discuss the different types of instructional strategies, materials, and evaluations that can be utilized within those learning experiences.

# CURRICULUM DEVELOPMENT AND PROGRAM PLANNING

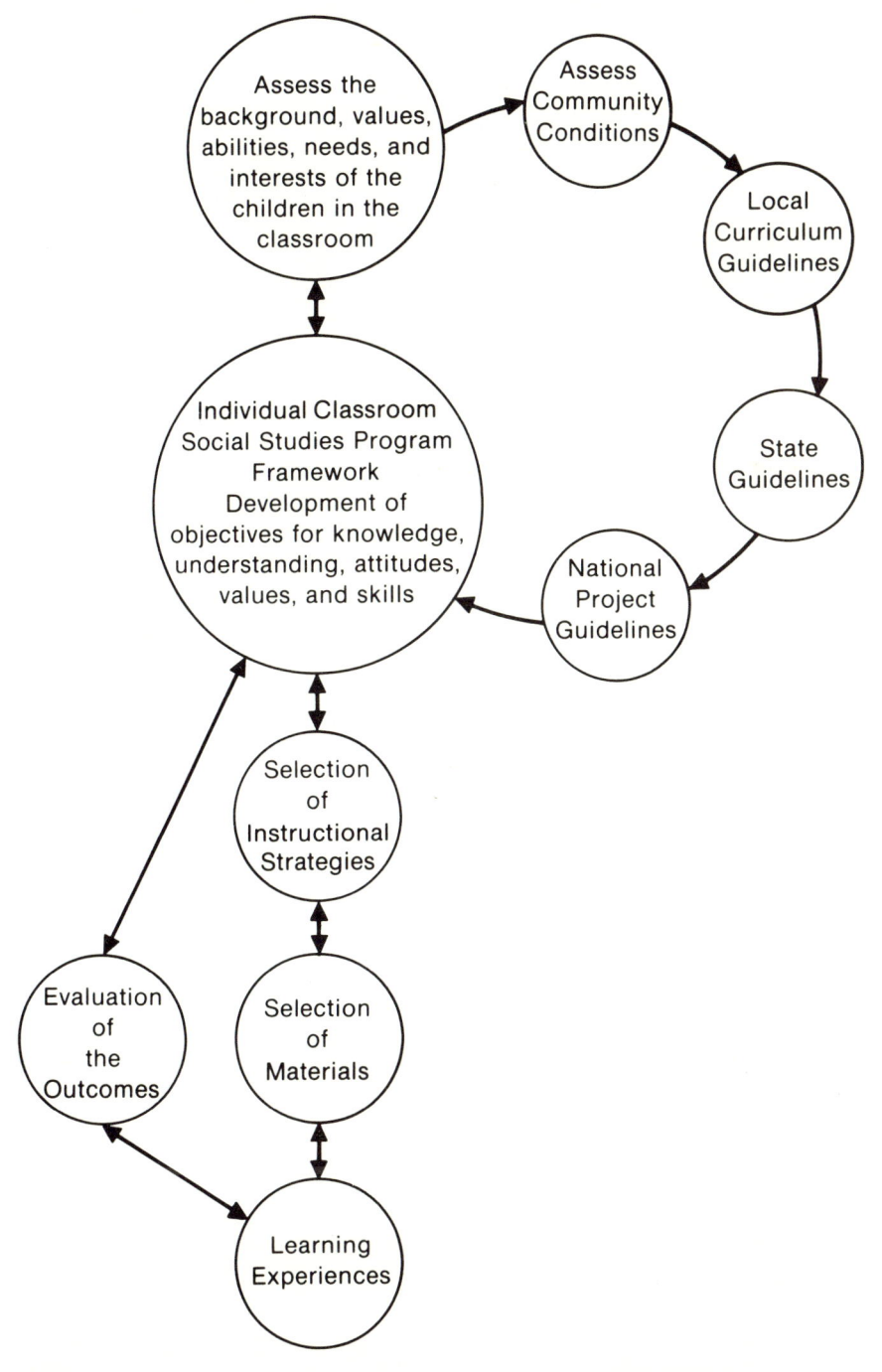

**Figure 3.3** Decision-Making Process for Individual Classroom Social Studies Program

## NOTES

1. National Education Association, *The Social Studies in Secondary Education,* Bulletin No. 28 (Washington, D.C.: Bureau of Education, 1916), p. 35.
2. Martin Deutsch and M. Brown, "Social Influence in Negro-White Intelligence Differences," *Journal of Social Issues* 20 (December 1964):24-35.
3. E. H. Hill and M. C. Giammatteo, "Socio-Economic Status and Its Relationship to School Achievement in the Elementary School," *Elementary English* 40 (March 1963):265-270.
4. *A Conceptual Framework for the Social Studies in Wisconsin Schools,* rev. ed. (Madison, Wis.: Wisconsin State Department of Education, 1967), p. 2.
5. Ibid., p. 3.
6. *Knowledge Processes & Values in the New Social Studies* (Madison, Wis.: State Department of Public Instruction, 1968-70), pp. 45-46.
7. John S. Gibson, *New Frontiers in the Social Studies* (New York: Citation Press, 1967), p. 96.
8. "Project Materials Analysis," *Social Education* 36 (November 1972):769.
9. *The Development of Man and His Culture,* No. 30 (Athens: University of Georgia, Anthropology Curriculum Project, 1966), pp. 1-2.
10. Lorraine Sundal Hansen and W. Wesley Tennyson, "Career Development as Self-Development: Humanizing the Focus for Career Education," *Social Education* 39 (May 1975):309.
11. Susan E. Davison, "Curriculum Materials and Resources for Law-Related Education," *Social Education* 41 (March 1977):184-193. The article lists extensive resource materials for law-related education.
12. "Man: A Course of Study," *Social Education* 36 (November 1972):743.
13. *Teachers' Handbook for Elementary Social Studies,* Introductory Edition by Hilda Taba, pp. 1-3. Copyright © 1967 by Addison-Wesley Publishing Company, Inc. All rights reserved. Reprinted by permission.
14. *The Taba Program in Social Science: Teacher's Guide* for *People in Communities* by Kim Ellis and Mary C. Durkin, pp. T3-T6. Copyright © 1972 by Addison-Wesley Publishing Company, Inc. All rights reserved. Reprinted by permission.
15. Ibid., pp. T3-T6.

## SELECTED REFERENCES

Banks, James A. "Ethnic Studies as a Process of Curriculum Reform." *Social Education* 40 (February 1976):76-80.

Beyer, Barry K. *"Teaching Basics in Social Studies." Social Education* 41 (February 1977):96.

Fox, R. S., and Lippitt, R. O. "Social Science in Early Education." *School and Society* 99 (December 1971):465-466.

"Global Education: Adding a New Dimension to Social Studies." *Social Education* 41 (January 1977):12–52

"Global Hunger and Poverty." *Social Education* 38 (1974):628–688.

Gross, Norman. "Law-focused Education." *Social Education* 41 (March 1977):168–184.

Hoffman, Alan J., and Ryan, Thomas F. *Social Studies and the Child's Expanding Self.* New York: Intext, 1973.

Jarolimek, John, ed. "The Status of Social Studies Education: Six Case Studies." *Social Education* 41 (November/December 1977):574–598.

*Knowledge Processes and Values in the New Social Studies.* Madison, Wis.: State Department of Education, 1968–70.

McCune, Shirley, and Mathews, Martha. "Building Positive Futures: Toward a Nonsexist Education for All Children." *Childhood Education* (February 1976):179.

Muessig, Raymond H. *Social Studies Curriculum Improvement: A Guide for Local Committees.* Bulletin No. 36. Washington, D.C.: National Council for the Social Studies, 1965.

*Social Studies Framework for the Public Schools of California.* Sacramento: California State Department of Education, 1962.

Taba, Hilda. *Teachers' Handbook for Elementary Social Studies.* Reading, Mass.: Addison-Wesley, 1967.

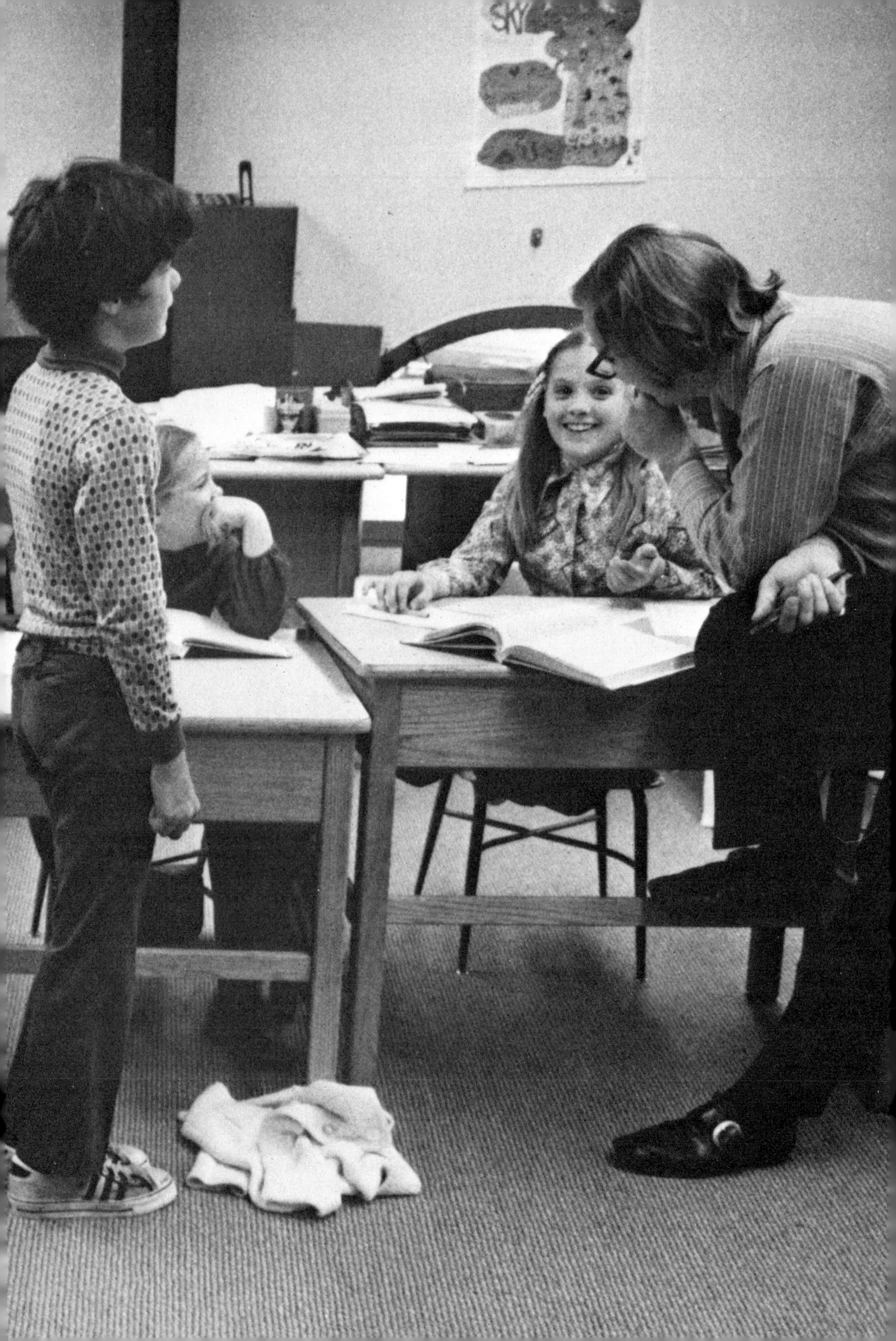
SKY

# Part Two
# Methodology

Although textbooks and state and local curriculum guides are provided for teachers, they ultimately must design a social studies program to meet the needs of the children in their classrooms. What methods will they use? Method here is defined as the procedures followed in achieving the goals of the social studies program. For example, should children learn to solve problems through the method of inquiry? Are learning experiences better organized with a unit approach? How should children learn social science concepts? Should children learn to think and behave as social scientists? How does the teacher provide a multicultural education for the children? Should a variety of approaches be used throughout the year?

This section will discuss several approaches: (1) concept development, (2) problem solving through inquiry, (3) unit development, and (4) multicultural education. Each discussion will include a definition of the method and an explanation of the objectives, philosophy, selection of content, and organization of the program, with an appropriate example.

# 4
# Teaching Concepts

Most of the current social studies programs are organized around the social science concepts. As indicated in Chapter Two, one of the difficulties is first identifying the structure or conceptual framework of the social science disciplines, and then second determining what learning experiences allow children to acquire knowledge of those structures.

Bruner relates, "To learn structure, in short, is to learn how things are related."[1] He claims, "In order for a person to be able to recognize the applicability or inapplicability of an idea to a new situation and to broaden his learning thereby, he must have clearly in mind the general nature of the phenomenon with which he is dealing."[2] In other words, the individual must know the structure of the subject. However, to know how things are related without developing "an attitude toward learning and inquiry, toward guessing and hunches, toward the possibility of solving problems on one's own"[3] is learning that is neither usable nor meaningful. Joyce explains structure as organizing concepts which formulate the way we think things are related.[4] These organizing concepts "provide the child with a systematic method of attack on areas where he seeks new knowledge."[5] The difficult task of the social scientist is to "translate the scholarly concepts and methods into forms that can be readily taught to children."[6] When these scholarly concepts have been selected and translated, experiences that permit children to discover their structure or organizing concepts can be selected.

Schwab states that the structure of a discipline is based on two components—concepts and syntax.

> The conceptual structure of a discipline determines what we shall seek the truth about and in what terms the truth shall be couched. The syntactical structure of a discipline is concerned with the operations that distinguish the true, the verified, and the warranted in that discipline from the unverified and the unwarranted. Both of these—the conceptual and syntactical—are different in different disciplines.[7]

Should concepts be presented in a sequence to provide an understanding of the discipline? Should all concepts be introduced at the beginning level and further developed at each succeeding grade level, or should a set of concepts be presented at each level? Figures 4.1 and 4.2 will help clarify this.

TEACHING CONCEPTS 71

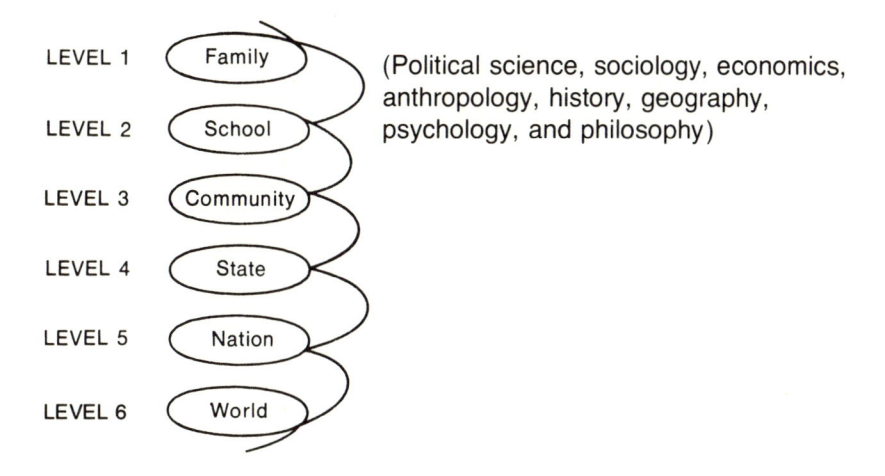

LEVEL 1  Family        (Political science, sociology, economics,
LEVEL 2  School         anthropology, history, geography,
                        psychology, and philosophy)
LEVEL 3  Community
LEVEL 4  State
LEVEL 5  Nation
LEVEL 6  World

**Figure 4.1**   Concept of Organizing Systems to Reach Certain Goals

**LEVEL 1**

Concept of interdependence of human beings
(family, school, community, other people)

Concept of human interaction with the environment
(clothing, food, shelter)

**LEVEL 2**

Concept of humans satisfying their needs with available resources
(money, work, division of labor)

Concept of producing goods and services

**Figure 4.2**   Selected Set of Concepts to Be Presented at Each Level

Figure 4.1 illustrates the method of introducing a concept at the beginning level and allowing it to increase in depth at each succeeding level. Figure 4.2 illustrates a set of concepts being presented at each level. In both examples, concepts are presented within a structure that is dependent (1) on the depth of the concept and (2) on one's previous set of concepts.

Social studies compounds the difficulty of introducing its structural framework, because it draws its content from a number of disciplines. Should the approach be interdisciplinary or multidisciplinary? Advocates of the interdisciplinary approach view "the social sciences as specializations of a common subject matter. According to this view, one thinks of social science as a substantial subject that proliferates like the branches of a tree."[8] (See Figure 4.3.) Each of the disciplines is related to the others through the common core of human behavior.

"Advocates of the multidisciplinary position see the social sciences as independent sciences concerned with aspects of human behavior that are related by the fact that the behavior is performed by the same organism. Here the social sciences are not part of a single tree, but are a number of independently rooted trees that happen to grow in the same earth, the study of human behavior."[9] (See Figure 4.4).

Those favoring the interdisciplinary approach stress the need to understand the interrelationships of the concepts of each of the social sciences. Presno and Presno explain that social science disciplines have some "common elements whatever their unique qualities and differences."[10] Each discipline "addresses itself to the description, explanation,

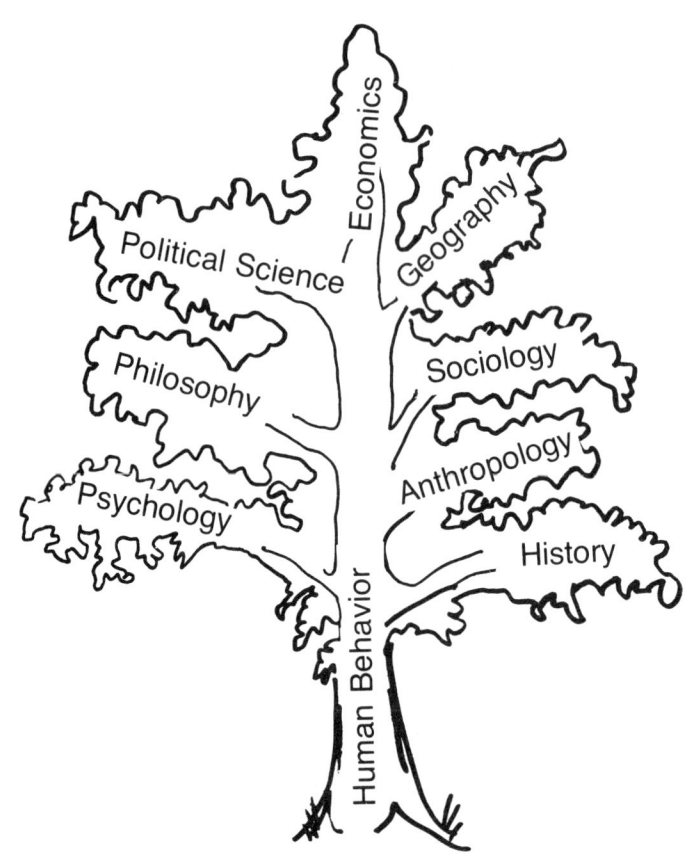

**Figure 4.3**    Representation of the Interdisciplinary Approach

TEACHING CONCEPTS 73

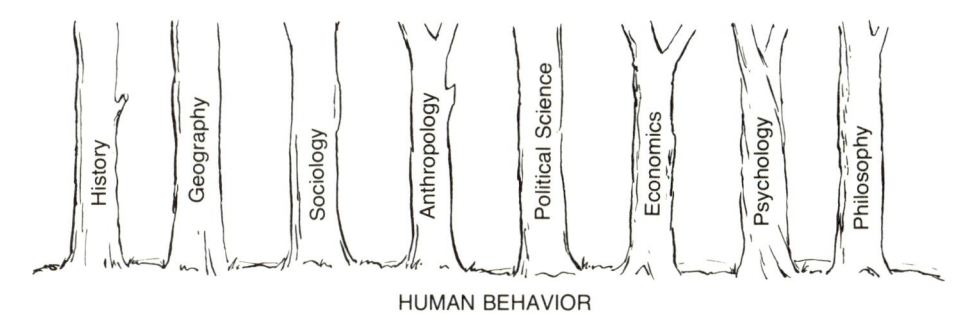

**Figure 4.4** Representation of the Multidisciplinary Approach

and classification of some aspect of the goal-direction behavior of human beings as they act, either individually or in groups, and as they are influenced by natural and cultural forces."[11]

Opponents of this theory argue that each discipline should retain its unique method of inquiry and conceptual structure. Scriven questions the interdisciplinary approach. He states that "the minute that you merge them, you get a smudge from which very little emerges."[12] Joyce, however, assumes "that the social sciences have much content in common and that a curriculum can be organized which emphasizes the unique concepts of each of them but does not establish separate courses for them."[13]

The multidisciplinary approach might be further identified as a separate-subject approach; however, acquiring knowledge of the discipline without the method of inquiry is not its intent. Programs using both models have been developed. Examples of each will be discussed.

## SOCIAL STUDIES PROGRAMS

Teachers often have difficulty arranging an effective sequence of activities for programs based on concepts. A study was recently conducted using beginning teachers to determine their ability in organizing a sequence of learning activities for a concept-based social studies program. Findings revealed "that the chief difficulty encountered had to do with selecting and providing relevant learning experiences for pupils. Relating specific learning activities to the attainment of specific concepts and generalizations proved to be particularly bothersome."[14] Social studies textbook series will provide teachers with a framework, selected concepts, and the sequence of activities to develop them.

These series are based on a structural framework with tight content boundary lines to avoid confusing the children with other concepts presented at the same time. A logical sequential program is planned, with each activity leading to the development of the intended concept. Each activity in the series builds upon the foundation provided by the previous activity. These programs suggest the procedures to be used to achieve the best results. As previously indicated, the structural framework is used to develop an understanding of the disciplines—their content, method of inquiry, and goals.

## MULTIDISCIPLINARY PROGRAM

The following program, selected as an example of a multidisciplinary approach, is *Investigating Man's World*. The philosophy of the series is as follows.

> *Investigating Man's World* is a multidisciplinary program that is meaningful now and will be meaningful for many years. No one social studies discipline—anthropology, economics, geography, history, political science, or sociology—offers all of the tools or experiences children need to learn about and understand man's past, present, and future societies. But children can learn about the world by making use of many social studies disciplines.
>
> The multidisciplinary structure of the material for each grade level leads children to simulate the working methods of anthropologists, economists, geographers, historians, political scientists, and sociologists. Children use the various social studies disciplines to inquire into the physical and man-made features, ideas, values, and problems of the world . . .
>
> *Investigating Man's World* accepts the principle that the key to knowledge and understanding lies in the structure and concepts of the social studies disciplines. *Investigating Man's World* is a conceptually structured program. It is organized according to the key concepts and generalizations—the primary ideas—of anthropology, economics, geography, history, political science, and sociology. *Investigating Man's World* asks children to think in terms of these key concepts and to begin to learn to work as specialists in these several disciplines.
>
> Within the framework and sequence of the program for *Investigating Man's World,* the social studies concepts are given extended and expanded treatment to coincide with the intellectual and social growth of children. For example, the basic nature of economic wants, scarcity, and choice are taught simply in a family context in the first primary-level materials. But as the framework of the series expands, the higher grade levels are

reached, these concepts of economics are discussed in more complex patterns in regional, national, and international settings.[15]

The basic framework of the series used the expanding communities theme. The following are the titles for each of the levels:

Family Studies
Local Studies
Metropolitan Studies
Regional Studies
United States Studies
Inter-American Studies
Atlantic Studies
Pacific Studies

*Regional Studies,* the fourth book of Scott, Foresman's program for *Investigating Man's World,* involves pupils in an examination of different kinds of regions beyond local communities. The first region investigated in *Regional Studies* is the state community: Because of its larger resources, the state community is able to provide through public and private institutions many services to the local communities that they themselves cannot provide effectively. Following the examination of the state, the investigation focuses on different regions of state communities.

*Regional Studies* is primarily a methods book designed to develop in pupils the skills of social scientists. Throughout the text many different states and regions of states are used as prototypes or as case studies to show the pupils how to investigate man's world. Once the methods of investigation have been presented, pupils are given the opportunity to apply them in an investigation of their own state, regions of states, and foreign regions.[16]

The books introduce the topics as they relate to each of the disciplines. The chart in Table 4.1 shows how the fourth book, *Regional Studies,* is organized enumerating the disciplines and the concepts introduced from each discipline.

Table 4.2, on page 77, is a sample page from the teacher's guide that is concerned with the concept of spatial location from the discipline of physical geography.

**TABLE 4.1**   Units (Italics) and Concepts

| *Physical Geography* | *Anthropology* | *Sociology* |
|---|---|---|
| Spatial Location | Ways of Life | Population |
| Territory | Early Man | Groups of People |
| Natural Setting | Races of Man | Change |
| Natural Resources | Culture | |
| | Cultural Change | |
| *Economics* | *Political Science* | *Human Geography* |
| Money | Constitutional Government | Population Density |
| Market System | Authority | Commercial Agriculture |
| Public Expenditure | Citizenship | Manufacturing and Transportation |
| Public Income | Laws | |
| Budget | Politics | |
| *History* | *Study of a Foreign State:* Bihar, India | *Part-One Activities* Study of Your State |
| Events | Concepts from Physical Geography, Anthropology, Sociology, Economics, Political Science, Human Geography, and History. | Concepts from Physical Geography, Anthropology, Sociology, Economics, Political Science, Human Geography, and History. |
| Natural Factors | | |
| Political Factors | | |
| Economic Factors | | |
| Social Factors | | |

SOURCE: *Regional Studies:* (INVESTIGATING MAN'S WORLD) by Paul Hanna, Clyde Kohn and Clarence VerSteeg. Copyright © 1970 by Scott, Foresman and Company, p. 12. Reprinted by permission.

## INTERDISCIPLINARY PROGRAM

*Windows on Our World,* a textbook series published by Houghton Mifflin, is an example of an interdisciplinary program. The philosophy of the program states:

> The social science disciplines are sources of facts, concepts, and generalizations that are worthwhile for children to learn .... Yet elementary social studies has a broader and more significant function: helping children develop an understanding of who we are .... *Windows on Our World* is built on the belief that there

**TABLE 4.2**  Sample Page from Teacher's Guide

### Each state has a relative location

States with coastal locations Ala., Alas., Conn., Del., Fla., Ga., Hawaii, La., Maine, Md., Mass., Miss., N.H., N.J., N.Y., N.C., Ore., R.I., S.C., Tex., Va., and Wash.

### A state has a location relative to natural features

Georgia has a coastal location. Kansas is far from any ocean. States with coastal locations on Atlantic (includes Gulf of Mexico) and Pacific Oceans are listed above. All others have interior locations.

### A state has a location relative to other states

Utah is west from Kansas
Missouri is east from Kansas
Utah is farther from Kansas
Missouri is closer to Kansas

Is your state near an ocean? What states are close to your state? What direction is your state from another state? When you answer such questions, you are describing the location of your state in relation to natural features and in relation to other states. You are describing your state's relative location.

Some states are close to and some are far from natural features such as oceans. States that have an ocean along one or more sides have coastal locations. States that are not near an ocean have interior locations. Look at the map on page 19 to discover how the location of Kansas compares with the location of Georgia in relation to oceans. Does Georgia have a coastal or an interior location? What kind of location does Kansas have in relation to oceans?

Name other states that have interior locations. What states have coastal locations in relation to oceans?

Each state has a relative location that can be described by its direction from other states. Use the map on page 19. In what direction is Utah from Kansas? In what direction is Missouri from Kansas?

Each state has a relative location that can be described by its distance from other states. Compare the distance from Kansas to Utah with the distance from Kansas to Missouri. Which is farther from Kansas? Which is closer?

The 48 states shown on the map on page 19 have a special relationship to one another. They are conterminous states. Each state shares a boundary with at least one other state. On the global map on page 18, you can see that Alaska and Hawaii are not conterminous states. They do not share a boundary with another state.

Answers to review questions.
1. Equator 2. Prime Meridian 3. Global grid 4. States with coastal locations border Atlantic or Pacific Ocean. States with interior locations do not border on an ocean. 5. No. Alaska and Hawaii are not conterminous. Conterminous states share a boundary with at least one other state.

Review of the Concept:
Spatial Location
1. Name the 0 east-west line.
2. What is the 0 north-south direction line?
3. What do you use to help you find exact location?
4. What is the difference between a coastal location and an interior location?
5. Are all states conterminous? What is a conterminous state?

SOURCE: *Regional Studies:* (INVESTIGATING MAN'S WORLD) by Paul Hanna, Clyde Kohn, Clarence VerSteeg. Copyright © 1970 by Scott, Foresman and Company, p. 20. Reprinted by permission.

are four particular dimensions of human identity of special relevance to social studies instruction. From this belief come the four overarching purposes that the Program is designed to further: to develop children's understanding of themselves as individuals, as members of groups, as human beings, and as inhabitants of Earth.[17]

Titles for each level in the program are as follows:

Me
Things We Do
The World Around Us
Who We Are
Planet Earth
The United States
The Way People Live

A chart lists the concepts that are developed at each level. Those listed for the Seventh Level, *The Way People Live,* are the following:[18]

| | | |
|---|---|---|
| behavior | goods and services | opinion |
| beliefs | groups | population |
| city | human beings | population explosion |
| consumers and products | human differences | race |
| cultural change | human likenesses | religion |
| cultural diversity | institution | rites of passage |
| culture | language | society |
| democracy | levels of industrialization | species |
| Earth | life cycle | suburb |
| education | market | technology |
| environment | metropolis | technology gap |
| fact | monarchy | urban explosion urbanization |
| family | needs | values |

Some of these same concepts also appear in the earlier levels. There is no designation that a concept is identified with any particular social science discipline.

There are four units in *The Way People Live.* They are: What Makes You a Human Being? How and Why Are Human Beings Alike and Different? How Does Culture Vary and Change? and Our Urbanized Earth. The last unit includes the lesson titles following.

# TEACHING CONCEPTS

From Cities to Supercities
Urban Living: Its Impact on Family and Friends
How Governments Cope With Urban Problems
Your Values and Planning for the Future

The beginning pages of the teacher's guide for Lesson 2 in this unit are presented on pages 80 and 81 (Figure 4.5) and will demonstrate how lessons are developed.[19]

## ADVANTAGES AND DISADVANTAGES OF STRUCTURED PROGRAMS

A program structured in a logical sequential pattern offers the advantage of providing a continuity of experiences. Too often, especially in the primary grades, the social studies program may be a haphazard collection of unrelated experiences. Children thus exposed to a wide variety of experiences may not develop an understanding of the social sciences concepts or how they are related to one another.

In a sequential program, the children's maturity level is considered to determine the placement of concepts at levels where most children will be able to comprehend them. This consideration prevents the presentation of concepts too difficult for the majority of children at any given level.

Disadvantages of the structured program are its failure to include incidents and problems that arise within the children's environment, the break in continuity caused by interrupting the sequential pattern to pursue an unrelated topic, and the program's possible failure to meet individual differences within the classroom. Obviously, some children may not have the necessary background of experiences to understand the concepts presented. Therefore, teachers will need additional understanding of and skill in the introduction and development of concepts.

## INTRODUCING AND EXTENDING CONCEPTS

If concepts are to formulate the curriculum framework for social studies instruction, then it is vital that students conceptualize—develop their own concepts or go beyond merely giving a name to a concept. As Beyer suggests:

Concepts help organize data into patterns which may provide meaningful insights into that data. That is, they provide a set of

LESSON 2             4–5 days

## Urban Living: Its Impact on Families and Friends

**FOCUS**

This lesson develops children's understanding of themselves as members of groups. It focuses on ways in which family and friendship patterns are affected by urban living.

The learning experiences in this lesson help to develop the skills of comparing, imagining, inferring, hypothesizing, and acquiring and reporting information from case studies and tables. The lesson also fosters respect for others and tolerance of uncertainty.

**PERFORMANCE OBJECTIVES**

The student should be able to:

- Extract and report from case studies evidence of change in ways of life.
- Infer feelings about change experienced by individuals described in case studies.
- Locate given countries on a world map.
- Compare changes in family patterns encountered by persons in various parts of the world who move to cities.
- Demonstrate increasing empathy by imagining and describing the possible feelings of a member of an urban family experiencing social change.
- Analyze the results of a questionnaire concerning the effects of urban living on friendship patterns.
- Hypothesize about the reasons for differences in friendship patterns in cities, suburbs, and more isolated towns.
- Use given statistics to construct a bar graph.

**MATERIALS**

student text: pages 406–417 and map on pages 452–453

*graph paper, writing materials (optional: tape recorder, reference books)*

*Teacher's Lesson Plan*

## Urban Living: Its Impact on Families and Friends

The young girl threaded her way among the hundreds of people crowding the city street. People were cooking, sleeping, and washing clothes. Others were selling fruits and vegetables. Several sat by old sewing machines. They waited for customers to ask them to stitch up clothes or blankets.

At last the girl stopped beside a fat letter writer. A sidewalk table served as his "office." The girl fished a sheet of paper and a few coins from her pocket. "Please tell my beloved brother that I am well," she said.

The letter writer didn't bother to look up at the girl. He yawned loudly and stretched his arms. Then he dipped his brush into an inkwell and began making marks on the paper.

Scenes like the one just described are happening in cities all over the world today. They reveal important changes that are taking place in family and friendship patterns. In this lesson you'll find out more about the changes that result from urban living. To start, you'll gain some firsthand knowledge from case studies.

As you read these case studies, fill out a chart like the one shown below. The case studies will not always give you exact information about the changes in family living or feelings. But you can infer the changes from what each individual says.

CHANGES IN FAMILY PATTERNS IN URBAN AREAS

| Case | Ways in Which the Family's Life Has Changed | Feelings About Those Changes |
|---|---|---|
| Meral | | |
| Chan | | |
| Sally | | |
| Stevo | | |
| Kenneth | | |

*Student Material*

**Figure 4.5**    Sample Pages from Teacher's Guide for Unit on "Our Urbanized Earth" *(SOURCE: WINDOWS ON OUR WORLD, edited by Lee F. Anderson, p. T-12. Copyright © 1976 by Houghton Mifflin Company. Reprinted by permission.)*

# Meral
Comes to Istanbul (Turkey)

I've been here two months now. My home was in a village more than 200 miles from here. We walked most of the way. My husband, four children, and mother came with me.

This one-room "lean-to" isn't much of a house. We built it ourselves with scraps of tin and wood that we found. We have no running water. We wash outside with water from a faucet in the yard. My mother does the cooking on a wood stove in the corner of our one room. I'm hoping we can get an apartment someday.

It's lonely for us here. But soon my cousins will be joining us. There's no way for young people to earn a living any more in the village where we lived. Maybe my cousins will be lucky the way we were. My husband found a job in a cloth factory three weeks after we arrived in Istanbul.

*Student Material*

**STRATEGIES**

*Opening the Lesson*  Read to the class the vignette which opens this lesson on text page 406. Ask the students if they can guess anything about what the life of the young girl might be like. Where could the scene have taken place? (You may want to share with the students the information that it actually took place in Hong Kong.) Ask the students: *Why do you think the young girl is living in a city? Where might her brother live? Do you think this scene could take place in different parts of the world? If so, how and why might details of it be different?*

After a very short opening discussion designed to motivate student interest, say that in this lesson the class will be looking into the lives of some real-life individuals. Say to the students: *Every person whose life story you are about to read lives somewhere in the world today. Every person you are about to meet will let you share the hopes, fears, and joys that living in an urban area brings.* (The Background Information on page T457 will be useful in your lesson preparation.)

*Developing the Lesson*  You might like to read aloud, or ask a good reader to read aloud, "Meral Comes to Istanbul." Then the class as a whole could suggest appropriate items to be included in the chart the students are to prepare (text page 406). Review how students can infer the feelings of the person featured in the case study even if those feelings are not stated explicitly. For example, Meral is unhappy at having to live in a ramshackle lean-to in the city but nevertheless hopes to find a better place to live in. Perhaps her old home in the village had been more comfortable.

*Teacher's Lesson Plan*

interrelated categories into which evidence gleaned from data or from experience may be placed.

Concepts also generate questions which can be asked of data in order to locate evidence for these categories. Knowing a specific concept enables us to use its elements as questions with which to probe data.[20]

Thus, it is important for teachers to be knowledgeable of different instructional strategies that may be used to introduce and extend concepts.

## Introduction of Concepts

Taba's model for concept formation relies on teachers asking sequentially ordered questions.

Concepts are formed as students respond to questions which require them: (1) to enumerate items; (2) to find a basis for grouping items similar in some respect; (3) to identify the common characteristics of items in a group; (4) to label the groups; and (5) to subsume items that they have enumerated under those labels.[21]

The following chart illustrates the questions that might be asked, the overt activity, and the covert mental activity.[22]

### CONCEPT FORMATION

| Overt Activity | Covert Mental Operations | Eliciting Questions |
| --- | --- | --- |
| 1. Enumeration | Differentiation | What did you see? hear? note? |
| 2. Grouping | Identifying common properties, abstracting | What belongs together? On what criterion? |
| 3. Labeling, categorizing | Determining the hierarchical order of items Super- and sub-ordination | How would you call these groups? What belongs under what? |

An application of Taba's model would be to present a map to the students which is color-coded to represent land, water, mountains, and which indicates other physical features. The concept to be introduced is natural features. The initial questions asked by the teacher, the possible responses, and student overt activity are listed in the following chart.

## CONCEPT FORMATION

| Teacher Question | Possible Response | Student Overt Activity |
|---|---|---|
| What do you see on the map? | harbor, blue, green, coastline, rivers, brown | Enumeration and listing |
| What belongs together in a group? | blue rivers<br>brown harbor<br>green coastline | Grouping |
| What would you call these groups? | colors natural features | Labeling Categorizing |

Further development of the concept would continue through Taba's next two cognitive tasks: interpretation of data and application of data. These will be discussed in more detail in the next chapter on inquiry. Taba's model would exemplify an inductive approach whereby the student arrives at a determination of the label for the concept.

Gagné's model is an example of a deductive approach to the introduction of a concept. The steps in the model are listed as follows:[23]

## CONDITIONS FOR A CONCEPT-LEARNING TASK

1. Show the subject an instance of the concept and specify its name.
2. Show the subject another and different exemplar (or several) and again specify the concept name.
3. Show the subject a negative instance of the concept and specify that it is not the concept name.
4. Show the subject still another positive exemplar and, pointing appropriately to the positive and negative examples, respectively, specify the concept name and specify that it is not the concept name.
5. As a test, give the subject a context and request that he illustrate or select the instance of the concept.

To apply Gagné's model to the teaching of the concept of "group," first present the students with the picture of a group (basketball team). Then state, "This is a group." Show several pictures of a group (girl scouts, play group, band) each time stating, "This is a group." Then present a negative example (individual person) stating, "This is not a group." Then present another positive and negative example stating, "This is a group, but this is not a group." To determine if the students have learned the concept, give them a series of pictures which are examples and nonexamples and request that they place them in the appropriate stacks.

## Extending Concepts

**Brainstorming**   After the students have had some introduction to a concept or to determine what their ideas are about a concept, the following instructional strategy can be used.

> Give the students an envelope and a sheet of paper. The concept to be extended is culture. Ask them to list five things they think about when they hear the word culture. Then have the students place their lists inside the envelopes and pass them around until no one can determine whose envelope they are holding. Before they open it, have them write on the outside of the envelope the one thing they are sure is on the list inside. When they open the envelopes, determine if they were correct.
>
> Then ask students to call out the lists so that they may be written on the board. After the list is complete, ask students if there are any things that are similar and could be put together. After grouping has occurred, label the groups and then ask if anyone disagrees with any of the things listed to describe culture. Discuss those items that are in question. Then ask if someone will generalize about the meaning of culture. What is culture? What is not culture?

**Series of Pictures**   In an attempt to extend the concept of home, collect a series of pictures that represent different types of homes (single family dwelling, row houses, apartment highrise, trailer, boat, nomad's tent). These examples can also represent styles from different cultures.

> Show children the first picture and ask the question, "What do you see?" If children do not enumerate the attributes of the home such as windows, doors, etc., then ask specific questions, like "What is this?" After the visible attributes have been listed, ask questions such as "What does this provide for people?" "What do we call it?" Then present each one with the questions, "How is this alike?" "How is this different?" After all of the pictures have been utilized, ask the children if they can generalize about homes. An example of a response might be: "Homes may look different and be made from different materials, but they all provide shelter for people." If it has not come up in previous discussion, ask the question, "What is the difference between a 'house' and a 'home?'" This question should stimulate further extension of the concept.

**Storybooks**   Younger children are delighted by the antics of their favorite friends in storybooks; however, those same antics provide excellent opportunities for concept development. Read Virginia Lee Burton's *The Little House* (New York: Houghton Mifflin, 1942), which is a story about a house that is in the country, but growth causes a city to build around it. Extend the concept of change with questions such as: What was happening to the house? Why didn't the house like all the hustle and bustle of the city? Why did people ignore the house? Has anything similar to what happened to the house happened to you? Are there other changes in your life? What can you do about them?

The concept of group is easily understood by children when reading Leo Lionni's *Swimmy,* a story about a small fish that organizes many little fish into a big group. "Why did Swimmy need all the other fish? What might have happened to Swimmy if he tried swimming alone? What are the advantages of a group? Disadvantages? Do you belong to any groups?" The above questions will further clarify the understanding of the concept of group.

## SUMMARY

As indicated in an earlier chapter, concepts may be concrete or abstract; broad or narrow; single words or phrases. The ease with which children can acquire concepts will be dependent upon their level of abstractness, broadness, or length and difficulty. As indicated by Taba,

> Because concepts are hierarchical, or of different levels of abstraction, complexity, and generality, concepts of a high order can be learned only gradually over a period of time and by repeated return engagements in new contexts.[24]

Therefore, teachers will find concepts embedded in the conceptual frameworks supplied by the social studies textbooks, but will need to determine what additional experiences are needed by children for those concepts to be learned.

## NOTES

1. Jerome S. Bruner, *The Process of Education* (Cambridge, Mass.: Harvard University Press, 1960), p. 7.
2. Ibid., p. 18.
3. Ibid., p. 20.

4. Bruce R. Joyce, *Strategies for Elementary Social Science Education* (Chicago: Science Research Associates, 1965), p. 26. Reprinted by permission of the publisher.
5. Ibid., p. 29.
6. Ibid., p. 37.
7. Joseph J. Schwab, "The Concept of the Structure of a Discipline," *Educational Record* 43 (July 1962):197–205.
8. G. W. Ford and Lawrence Pugno, eds., *The Structure of Knowledge and the Curriculum* (Chicago: Rand McNally, 1964), p. 89.
9. Ibid.
10. Vincent Presno and Carol Presno, *Man in Action Series: People and Their Actions,* Teachers' Ed. (Englewood Cliffs, N.J.: Prentice-Hall, 1967), p. ix.
11. Ibid.
12. Ford and Pugno, *Structure of Knowledge,* p. 95.
13. Joyce, *Strategies for Elementary Social Science,* p. 13.
14. Agnes M. Inn, "Beginning Teacher's Problems in Developing Social Studies Concepts," *Social Education* 30 (November 1966):540.
15. *Regional Studies: Investigating Man's World* by Paul Hanna, Clyde Kohn and Clarence VerSteeg. Copyright © 1970 by Scott, Foresman and Company, pp. T4–5. Reprinted by permission.
16. Ibid., p. T7.
17. *Windows on Our World,* edited by Lee F. Anderson. Copyright © 1976 by Houghton Mifflin Company, p. T12.
18. Ibid., p. T29.
19. Ibid., pp. T446–447.
20. Barry K. Beyer, *Inquiry in the Social Studies Classroom: A Strategy for Teaching* (Columbus, Ohio: Charles E. Merrill, 1971), p. 15.
21. Hilda Taba, *Teachers' Handbook for Elementary Social Studies* (Palo Alto, Calif.: Addison-Wesley, 1967), p. 92.
22. Ibid.
23. Robert M. Gagné, "The Learning of Concepts," *The School Review* 73 (Autumn 1965):191.
24. Cited in Hilda Taba, "Implementing Thinking as an Objective in Social Studies," in *Effective Thinking in the Social Studies,* Jean Fair and Fannie Shaftel, eds. (Washington, D.C.: National Council for the Social Studies, 1967), p. 36.

## SELECTED REFERENCES

Beyer, Barry K. *Inquiry in the Social Studies Classroom: A Strategy for Teaching.* Columbus, Ohio: Charles E. Merrill, 1971.

Bruner, Jerome S. *The Process of Education.* New York: Random House, 1960.

*Conceptual Framework: Social Studies.* Madison: Wisconsin State Department of Education, 1967.

Ford, G. W., and Pugno, Lawrence, eds. *The Structure of Knowledge and the Curriculum.* Chicago: Rand McNally, 1964.

Fraenkel, Jack R. *Helping Students Think and Value: Strategies for Teaching the Social Studies.* Englewood Cliffs, N.J.: Prentice-Hall, 1973.

Joyce, Bruce R. *Strategies for Elementary Social Science Education.* Chicago: Science Research Associates, 1965.

Martorella, Peter H. *Concept Learning in the Social Studies Models for Structuring Curriculum.* Scranton, Penn.: International Textbook, 1971.

Moore, Virginia D. "Guidelines for the New Social Studies." *Instructor* 79 (February 1970):112–113

Morrissett, Irving, ed. *Concepts and Structure in the New Social Science Curricula.* West Lafayette, Ind.: Social Science Education Consortium, 1966.

Price, Ray A.; Hickman, Warren; and Smith, Gerald. *Major Concepts for Social Studies.* Syracuse: Social Studies Curriculum Center, Syracuse University, 1966.

Schwab, Joseph J. "The Concept of the Structure of a Discipline." *Educational Record* 43 (July 1962):197–205.

Thomas, John L. "Concept Formation in Elementary School Social Studies." *Social Studies* 63 (March 1972):110–116.

Womack, James G. *Discovering the Structure of Social Studies.* New York: Benziger Press, 1966.

# 5
# Problem Solving Through Inquiry

## DEVELOPING THINKING SKILLS

The method of teaching problem solving through inquiry often has been misunderstood and misused because of discrepancies in the definitions given for the terms "problem solving," "inquiry," "reflective thinking," "inductive reasoning," and "discovery." Frequently, these terms are used interchangeably without explanation of their different meanings.

Problem solving is the process whereby an individual identifies a problem situation, formulates tentative explanations or hypotheses, verifies these tentative hypotheses by gathering and evaluating data, and restates the hypotheses or arrives at generalizations. The individual may then apply these generalizations to new situations.

Many authors use reflective thinking and inductive reasoning to identify the problem-solving method. Early in the thirties, Dewey referred to the identification of the problem as the prereflective period, to the search for an answer as the reflective period, and to the dispelling of doubt as the postreflective period.[1]

Inductive reasoning or inductive teaching is described as the process of leading an individual toward solving a problem by providing him with sufficient stimulation and a direction based on hypotheses. Inquiry is the method of searching for the solution to a problem.

> Inquiry is not conducted as an indiscriminant search for facts; it is instead, an organized, directed search.[2]

> Hypotheses direct its activities.... Hypotheses determine what facts will be selected as relevant to the problem. They influence what interpretations are formulated and accepted in the end.[3]

Discovery may occur as the individual is conducting his or her search—the person reassembles or reorganizes information based on previous and newly acquired learning and gains insight into the problem.

Bruner states that discovery

> ... is in its essence a matter of rearranging or transforming evidence in such a way that one is enabled to go beyond the evidence so reassembled to new insights. It may well be that an additional fact or shred of evidence makes this larger transformation possible. But it is often not even dependent on new information.[4]

Therefore, inquiry and discovery can be defined as steps in the problem-solving process.

The problem-solving approach in teaching rests solidly on the ability of children to think effectively. Taba relates, "The task of instruction is to provide systematic training in thinking and to help students acquire cognitive skills which are necessary for thinking autonomously and productively."[5] There is a sequential order, as Piaget shows, in the development of forms of thought from childhood to adulthood; each step is a prerequisite to the next. A student should manipulate concrete objects in order to develop an intuitive grasp of the abstract concepts before engaging in abstract reasoning. Teaching strategies require the following for a proper developmental sequence.[6]

> The teaching strategies which helped students advance to higher levels of thinking involved what questions were asked; what the teacher gave or sought and at which point in the proceedings; or bypassed elaboration and extension of ideas; and whether or not there were summaries of ideas and information before inferences of higher order were sought.[7]

As Taba so aptly points out, teaching children thinking skills depends more on what we get out of the children than on what we put into them.[8] The basic philosophy of the problem-solving approach is one of developing thinking skills in children that enable them to formulate generalizations about a given situation. These generalizations should be ones that can be applied in new situations, specifically in the problems in the everyday lives of the children, as well as the problems of our global world.

## QUESTIONING

If teachers are to help children develop thinking skills, they must know how to ask the right questions at approximately the right time—when the child appears ready for the question. Research has indicated that teachers tend to ask questions that are at the lowest level of the hierarchy of questioning, concrete questions that require the individual to recall information. Several models of questioning have been advanced to increase the teacher's ability to ask questions at higher levels of thought. One example is Taba's model based on three cognitive levels: concept formation, interpretation of data, and application of principles. At the first level, *concept formation,* as was described in Chapter Four, the child is asked to list, group, and categorize through such questions as: What did you see, hear, note? What belongs together? On what criterion? What would you call these groups? What belongs under what?

Next, the child is requested to *interpret the data* collected, draw inferences, and generalize through questions such as: What did you notice? See? Find? Why did so and so happen? What does this mean? What picture does it create in your mind? What would you conclude?

The last level, *application of principles,* requires that the child hypothesize about what he or she thinks will happen in the new situation and to support this prediction. These questions might include: What would happen if? Why do you think this would happen? What would it take for so and so to be generally true or probably true?

Figure 5.1 represents a chart of Taba's model illustrating the eliciting questions, covert mental operations, and the overt activities.[9]

In the previous chapter, the first-level questions were used to develop the concept of natural features. Look at the map drawing below of the transparency that should be used to introduce the learning experience. Figure 5.2 illustrates how Taba's three levels of questioning would be applied. Remember that these questions are only the key ones and others would be asked dependent upon the responses from the children.

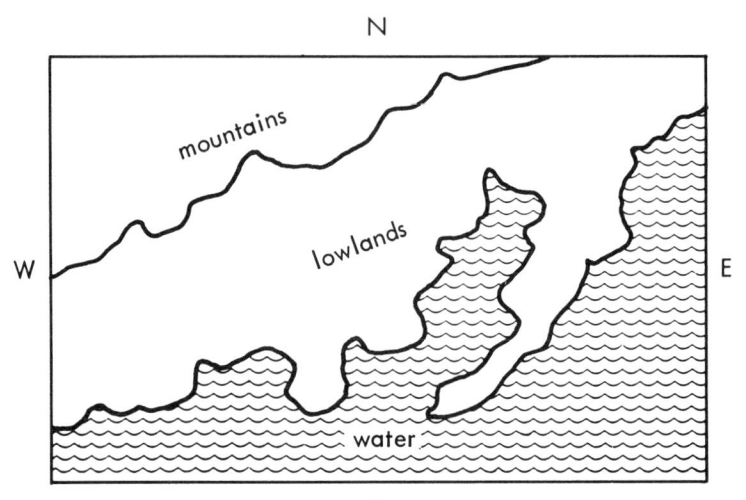

# PROBLEM SOLVING THROUGH INQUIRY

| | CONCEPT FORMATION | |
|---|---|---|
| 1. Enumeration and listing | Differentiation | What did you see? hear? note? |
| 2. Grouping | Identifying common properties, abstracting | What belongs together? On what criterion? |
| 3. Labeling, categorizing | Determining the hierarchical order of items Super- and subordination | How would you call these groups? What belongs under what? |

| | INTERPRETATION OF DATA | |
|---|---|---|
| 1. Identifying points | Differentiating | What did you notice? See? Find? |
| 2. Explaining items of identified information | Relating points to each other; determining cause and effect relationships | Why did so-and-so happen? |
| 3. Making inferences | Going beyond what is given: Finding implications, extrapolating | What does this mean? What picture does it create in your mind? What would you conclude? |

| | APPLICATION OF DATA | |
|---|---|---|
| 1. Predicting consequences; explaining unfamiliar phenomena | Analyzing the nature of the problem or situation; retrieving relevant knowledge | What would happen if . . . ? |
| 2. Hypothesizing; explaining and/or supporting the predictions and hypotheses | Determining the causal links leading to prediction or hypothesis | Why do you think this would happen? |
| 3. Verifying the predictions | Using logical principles or factual knowledge to determine necessary and sufficient conditions | What would it take for so-and-so to be generally true or probably true? |

**Figure 5.1**  Taba Model of Cognitive Tasks

| CONCEPT FORMATION |||
| --- | --- | --- |
| Teacher Question | Possible Response | Student Activity |
| What do you see on the map? | blue, green, rivers brown, harbor, coastline | Enumeration and listing |
| What belongs together in a group? | blue    rivers<br>brown  harbor<br>green  coastline | Grouping |
| What would you call these groups? | color key—<br>natural features | Labeling, categorizing |
| INTERPRETATION OF DATA |||
| What are some factors to be considered in selecting the location for building a city? | Climate, physical features, space, water supply, harbor protection from elements, natural resources | Identifying |
| Why would you want to build your city near a good harbor? | Cheaper transportation; case of access | Explaining items identified |
| How do climate and physical features of an area influence the development of a city? | They determine type of building, heating, or cooling. | Making inferences |
| APPLICATION OF DATA |||
| Where would you build a city? | Beside that big harbor along the coast | Predicting, hypothesizing |
| Why would you build it there? | It would be protected, access to interior, etc. | Supporting prediction |
| What would you need for the city to grow? | Harbor would be deep enough for large vessels, natural resources nearby | Verifying the prediction |

**Figure 5.2** Taba Questioning Model Applied to Location of a City

Another application of the model would be through the use of the following picture. Several concepts can be developed by redirecting the focus of the questions.

PROBLEM SOLVING THROUGH INQUIRY

CONCEPT ONE — Humanistic — self-concept

Generalization: *Many people feel the same way when they face problems.*

*Questions*

What do you see in the picture?

How do you think the boy is feeling?

Why do you think he feels that way?

What makes you think he feels that way?

Have you ever felt that way? When?

Why do you think he set up the lemonade stand? What are some possible reasons?

Have you ever wanted to have a business of your own? Why?

CONCEPT TWO — Economic — supply and demand

Generalizations: *There must be a demand for your product in order for it to sell. Costs cannot exceed money taken in if you are to make a profit.*

*Questions*

What is the boy in the picture doing?

Is there something wrong?

What expenses does he have?

Why do you suppose he wants to make a profit?

Why do you suppose business is bad?

What could the boy do to improve his business?

CONCEPT THREE—Citizenship Education—responsibility

Generalization: *Responsibility must be accepted as a part of individual freedom.*

Questions

Do you think the people in the neighborhood would mind having the lemonade stand?

What are some problems that might occur?

How could the boy avoid these problems?

Why must we think of others when we plan to do things?

## CLASSROOM CONDITIONS

If children are to receive maximum benefit from the questioning strategies and continue the problem solving, the atmosphere of the classroom must foster a feeling of trust and security within the children. Students need to know that they will receive help and understanding from the teacher and that they can ask questions and offer acceptable answers without fear of being wrong. The classroom environment should provide excitement and stimulation for learning. Materials should be available to supply the needs of searching minds. The teacher should create an atmosphere of mental freedom that enables each individual to think without concern for boundaries.

How can this be accomplished? The responses given by a teacher, verbally and nonverbally, will relay much to the children. Encouraging responses such as "that sounds interesting," "what a thought-provoking solution," "good thinking," and "what a good idea," should be utilized. However, facial expressions and tone of voice should convey the same messages. To state flatly "you're wrong" or "what a ridiculous answer" to children in front of their peers will cause them to be much more cautious with their next responses, if they respond again.

## ROLE OF THE TEACHER

In an inquiry-oriented classroom, the concept of the teacher's role undergoes a change in emphasis. Previously, the teacher assumed the major roles of information giver and disciplinarian with only minor roles of

# PROBLEM SOLVING THROUGH INQUIRY

motivator, referrer, counselor, and advisor. (See Figure 5.3.) However, in an inquiry-centered classroom, the teacher assumes the primary role of motivator, while remaining an information giver, disciplinarian, counselor, referrer, and advisor. (See Figure 5.4.)

As motivator, teachers stimulate and challenge the students to think. They initiate problem situations for the children to identify. Their questioning provides the focus and direction for the children's search. They assume the role of information giver only when the students request it or when it becomes necessary to redirect activities that may have wandered from the original goal. As referrer, they guide children to materials and sources of information. As advisor and counselor, they supply children with encouragement when it is needed and diagnose difficulties and give assistance. Discipline is necessary to avoid chaos; however, it is vital that children be guided toward self-discipline, which is important in the problem-solving approach.

To summarize the teacher's role, it is one that:

1. Helps children seek an answer rather than being a fountain of knowledge.
2. Provides motivation and direction for the inquiry.

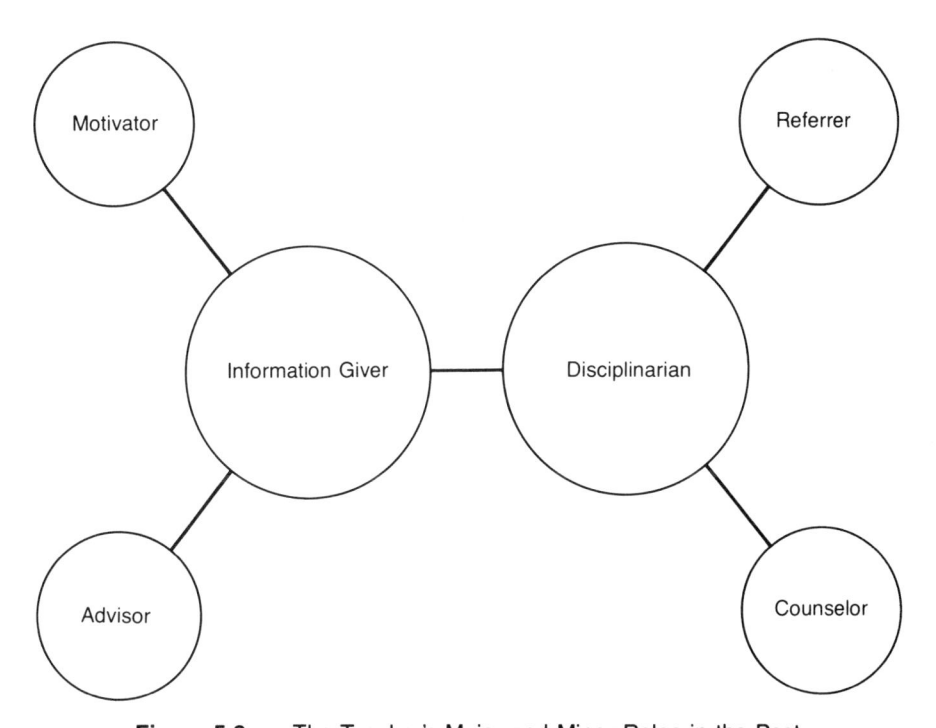

**Figure 5.3**   The Teacher's Major and Minor Roles in the Past

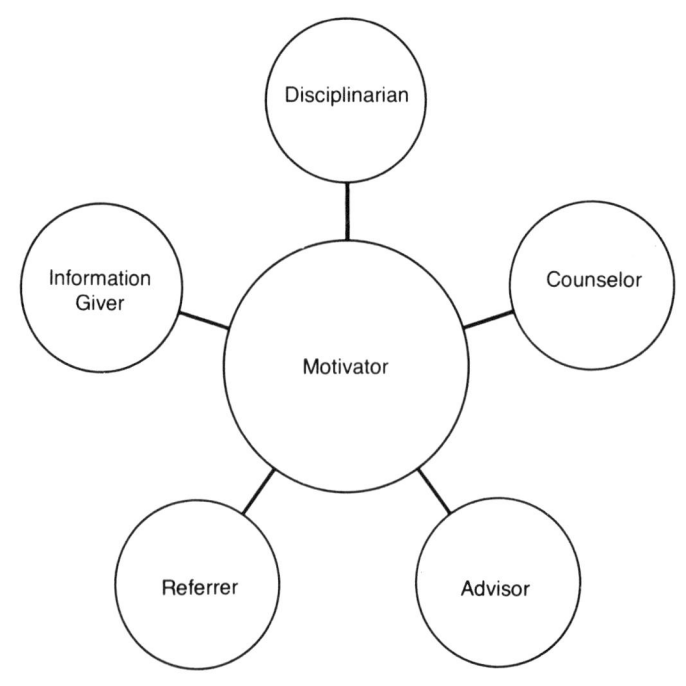

**Figure 5.4** The Teacher's Major and Minor Roles in an Inquiry-Centered Classroom

3. Establishes an effective classroom climate where children can question and can seek answers without fear of being penalized for wrong answers.
4. Provides materials expressing different points of view.
5. Helps children to learn to accept the opinions of others.
6. Helps children develop an organized method of thinking about and dealing with information so that they will become independent thinkers.
7. Becomes an effective questioner—leading children from the concrete to the abstract level of thought.

Teachers should be aware that the use of the inquiry process in the classroom does require more planning time on their part. They must know how they will initiate the activity, what questions they will ask, and how to refocus the thinking of children. To accomplish these tasks it is necessary to have sufficient background knowledge of the problem from a variety of sources.

## OBJECTIVES

The objectives of the method of problem solving through inquiry are based on the processes or steps in which children are involved (identifying a problem, stating and testing hypotheses, and generalizing).

These broad objectives are outlined as follows:

*Develop the student's ability to:*
   *Identify and define a problem situation in relation to the social sciences and to apply this knowledge to everyday life.*
   *Formulate hypotheses for tentative problem solutions utilizing the information presented and previously acquired knowledge.*
   *Compare and evaluate various theories, data, and generalizations in testing tentative hypotheses.*
   *Select relevant facts necessary for testing hypotheses.*
   *State generalizations from results and apply them to new situations.*

*Acquire skill in:*
   *The use of a variety of materials to secure information relative to the problem.*
   *Discovering the relationships between previously and newly acquired information to acquire new insight into the solution of a problem.*
   *Rational thought processes by constructing hypotheses and testing, revising, and refining these hypotheses.*
   *Expressing opinions on issues after an analysis of available information.*

*Acquire knowledge of:*
   *Problem-solving techniques.*
   *Methods of inquiry used by social scientists.*
   *Recall information necessary for problem solution.*

*Develop an attitude of:*
   *Open-mindedness toward all sides of an issue before arriving at a decision.*
   *Accepting opinions of others and understanding why opinions vary.*
   *Concern and interest in the problems of society by active participation in problem-solving activities.*[10]

These objectives are general and based on the major values of the problem-solving methods as purported by its many advocates. More specific behavioral objectives should be developed within the content boundaries and needs of the individual classroom.

## PROBLEM SELECTION

Quickly acknowledged is the fact that the success of the problem-solving method lies in the selection of problems for inquiry. Dunfee and Sagl suggest the following criteria for problem identification:

1. Does the problem challenge the children intellectually, stimulate critical thinking, allow them to seek cause-and-effect relationships, and offer opportunity for formulating and testing generalizations?
2. Does the problem relate directly to the lives of the children, based on their past experiences, and have an impact upon them presently?
3. Is the problem concerned with a basic human activity and does it thus illumine man's efforts to meet his needs?
4. Are there sufficient community and classroom instructional resources available for developing the problem?
5. Does the problem offer opportunities for expansion of interests?[11]

Does following the guidelines of a structured plan restrict the problem-solving method? Should teachers be permitted to provide alternatives to the suggested outline of study? Freedom of choice in what Clements, Fielder, and Tabachnick call "Big Questions" for inquiry study is "justified by the demands of a particular teaching-learning situation and its potential for increasing the efficiency with which children learn."[12]

The "Big Questions" or problems should be interesting and should initiate inquiry. It should be possible to translate them into small questions that can be answered by simple observation and lead to increased understanding. By selecting concepts and ideas that help answer the small questions, answers to the "Big Questions" can be formulated.[13]

Fox, Lippit, and Lohman, of the University of Michigan, assume "that the way for children to inquire in a social science area is to begin with incidents that are microcosms of the larger scene—incidents that are representative of their own life experiences."[14] An adaptation of their model of inquiry is presented:[15]

1. *Identify problem.*
   Set goals.
   Make design for study.
   Why do people behave in this way?
2. *Observation data collection.*
   Children look for clues to determine why things turn out the way they do.
3. *Advance theories for causes of behavior.*
4. *What behavior might lead to better consequences?*
   Make hypothesis.
   Test hypothesis.
5. *Draw conclusions.*
6. *Research theories of others.*
7. *Generalize.*
   How can I apply this to my own life?

An example of the method of problem solving through inquiry will be developed with adaptations from the above model.

## Initiation

The initiation (designated in the model as Step 1) sets the stage for the problem-solving situation. It should stimulate inquiry and develop a continuing interest in the problem. Unless sufficient background is provided, problem identification will be difficult; however, too much information may stymie the quest. The initiation establishes the focus or direction of the search and serves as a springboard for action. The most effective initiations are those that actively involve the children, either mentally or physically. Possibilities for this stimulation are contained in these illustrations of initiations.

## Incident

This next example from a sixth-grade classroom is designed to initiate inquiry.

*Step 1.* The teacher, without giving any reason for the action, uses chairs and desks to build a separating wall between two sections of children in the classroom. The teacher deliberately separates good friends and any brothers or sisters. The children soon ask questions: Why are you doing this? What have we done to deserve this? My best friend is on the other side—when will we get to sit together again? How long are you going to leave this here? As a result of this experience, the children began to analyze the motives for and results of such actions. The remaining steps of the model are easily identified.

*Step 2.* Observe the behavior of the children as the incident takes place. Help the children look for clues to understand their own behavior.

*Step 3.* Advance theories about causes—what negative or positive feelings were produced?

*Step 4.* What behavior might lead to better consequences? Was there some way to avoid the building of the wall? Make and test a hypothesis by classroom action.

*Step 5.* Draw conclusions and summarize learnings.

*Step 6.* Discuss places in the world where cities or countries have been divided in such a manner—Berlin, Korea, Vietnam.

By introducing questions and materials, the teachers can provide direction or focus toward one of these areas if they desire. The inquiry can now take on as much emphasis as necessary through research, reading, and discussion.

*Step 7.* Generalizations can be drawn from the study. Final applications are made to the children's own life—a possible question might be, "What behavior leads to hostile feelings toward me?"

## PROBLEM-SOLVING AND INQUIRY ACTIVITIES

### Presentation of Facts

Another activity designed to initiate inquiry is this graduated presentation of a series of facts about a country to a fifth-grade class.[16]

FIRST TRANSPARENCY

| Information About a Country | Information About a State |
|---|---|
| *Country* | *Texas* |
| Area: 760,000 sq. mi. | Area: 267,339 sq. mi. |
| Population: 48,313,438 | Population: 11,196,730 |
| Birthrate: 42.5/1000 | Birthrate of U.S.: 18.2/1000 |
| Suicides: 1.6/100,000 | Suicides in U.S.: 11.1/100,000 |
| Life expectancy: 1940–39 | |
| 1968–67 | |

### Questions

As you compare the area and population of this country with those of Texas, what conclusions can you draw?

What does the comparison of birthrates indicate?

What does the comparison of suicide rates suggest about the country?

From your limited knowledge of this country, identify any problems you think it might have.

Some problems the children might suggest would be overpopulation and lack of food.

## SECOND TRANSPARENCY

*Major Crops*

| | | |
|---|---|---|
| coffee | tobacco | bananas |
| corn | garbanzos | sisal (50% of world's |
| rice | cocoa | production) |

### Questions

What indication of the physical features of the country do these products give you?

What type of climate do these crops suggest?

What discrepancies in the climate might these crops suggest?

Do the crops indicate the country's location?

## THIRD TRANSPARENCY

*Minerals*

| | | |
|---|---|---|
| silver (world's leading producer) | copper | tin |
| gold (7.5 million; U.S. 63.1 million) | zinc | coal |
| lead | antimony | iron ore |

### Questions

Do the minerals indicate anything different about the physical features?

What can you hypothesize about the technology and industries of the country?

## FOURTH TRANSPARENCY

*Industrial Products*

| | | |
|---|---|---|
| cotton | iron and steel | rubber |
| cloth | chemicals | paper |
| beer | electrical goods | handicrafts |
| sugar | | |

### Questions

What can you conclude about the country from its industrial products?

Would you change any of your previous hypotheses as a result of this added information?

## FIFTH TRANSPARENCY

*Imports:* $2,442,000
*Exports:* $1,374,000

| | |
|---|---|
| cotton | cattle |
| coffee | fruit |
| ($1,000,000 annually) | |
| cane sugar | fresh and frozen meat |
| tomatoes | |

**Questions**

What does the imbalance between exports and imports suggest about the economy of this country?

Do the products indicate any of the industries in the country?

Hypothesize concerning the problems you see this country facing.

## SIXTH TRANSPARENCY

*Tourism*

| | |
|---|---|
| $320 million long-stay/yr. | Texas |
| $540 million short-term | $500 million/yr. |

**Questions**

Does the information about added income from tourism change any of your hypotheses?

Try to identify the country.

The country is Mexico. The class can now begin to seek information to test their hypotheses about the country. The information on the transparencies was selected to focus primarily on economics, but other facts can be selected to change the focus.

**Wastebasket Technique**

The teacher collects assorted articles from the wastebasket in one of the rooms of the house or one from another classroom in the school. For example, items from the kitchen might include a cereal box with the vitamins listed, a soft-drink can (be sure to include the pull ring), frozen orange juice can, other vegetable or fruit cans, a pair of scissors, a box or can that has a person's picture on it, a knife and fork, an ice-cube tray, a penny, a plastic milk carton, can opener, and glass bottles. Other materials may be added as the teacher plans to focus the search for information. Pose the problem thus: If you were an archaeologist in the year 2500 and during a dig had unearthed these articles from a lost culture, what could you hypothesize about that culture? Could you draw any generalizations about the culture without further information?

This type of activity should increase the child's skills of observing, classifying, and interpreting data and formulating hypotheses. Another approach to this same type of activity would be to substitute artifacts from other cultures such as a piece of fine china, chopsticks, or a silk painting from Japan.

## Discrepant Data

The utilization of the discrepant data technique[17] is intended to create cognitive dissonance within the individual, which should help break down stereotypes.

For example, to introduce the study of another culture, choose slides or pictures that would reinforce the stereotypes about that culture—such as wooden shoes, windmills, tulips, and chocolate from Holland. Present the slides or pictures to the children and ask them to formulate a generalization about the culture. An example of the generalization they might arrive at would be: Most people in Holland wear wooden shoes and grow tulips.

Then introduce the discrepant data in the form of slides or pictures featuring large cities and factories to show the modern aspects of Holland. Ask the children to restructure their generalization to accommodate the new information. The restructured generalization might be formulated thus: Some people in Holland still wear wooden shoes and grow tulips, but many live in modern cities and work in factories.

## Role Playing

Role playing is an activity that can be used for initiation in any grade. Following is an example of its use at the primary level. The teacher presents and discusses a particular situation with several selected children who, in turn, role play for the class. Their dialogue follows:

>KEVIN:   Did you hear what happened to Billy on the playground yesterday?
>
>SARAH:   No, I was absent.
>
>KEVIN:   He was sliding backwards down the slide and cracked his head.

**JESS:** He's in the hospital with a concussion.

**SARAH:** I'm sorry, but he knows we shouldn't slide backwards.

**KEVIN:** He always did like to show off.

**JEFF:** Other kids do it all the time and don't get hurt, so why shouldn't he?

**Question**

Why do you suppose Billy behaved this way?

The class discusses the situation and recognizes the problems and consequences of breaking safety rules. They try to understand why things turn out as they do. Why did Billy get hurt when others do the same thing without being hurt? What type of behavior would lead to better consequences? The class makes and tests hypotheses and draws conclusions. Teachers may then direct the search for information in any direction they prefer—for example, bike safety, home safety, or highway safety.

A variation of this initiation can be accomplished by role playing using an unfinished story for which the children seek solutions. An example might be:

> Terry had borrowed a great snake book from Kim to finish his report for science. While he was working at the kitchen table (where his mother had told him not to do his homework), eating cookies and drinking a glass of milk, his baby brother knocked over the milk, drenching Kim's book. What should he do? His mother wouldn't allow him to go on the trip to the zoo Saturday if she knew he had disobeyed, but he couldn't return Kim's book the way it looked now.

Children can take turns playing the roles of mother, Terry, and Kim as they work out the solutions to the problem. Other similar role-playing situations can be found in *Role-Playing for Social Values* by Fannie R. Shaftel and George Shaftel (Englewood Cliffs, N.J.: Prentice-Hall, 1967).

## Tape Presentations

Another interesting technique to utilize is a taped presentation which provides the opportunity to include several voices and sound effects. Taping segments of historical diaries or fiction stories that introduce problem situations can be quite effective. An example of one follows.

Rob Nelson added a flashlight to the collection of clothes and other articles he had placed in his gym bag. He thought he'd better go to the kitchen and get some cookies and a sandwich or two since he didn't know when he might find food again. Rob was running away from home. He was tired of all the rules, rules, rules. Go to bed by 9:00 o'clock, you can't watch TV on school nights, and on and on.

Rob left the house and started for the main highway, where he hoped to get a ride. Rob walked for a long time, but no one seemed interested in giving him a ride. When he spied a police car coming down the road, he quickly dashed off into the woods. All of a sudden from the direction of his city came a blinding flash and loud booms. Rob dove for a covered ditch and that was all he remembered.

Hours later Rob came to; he ached all over. Gradually he crawled toward the opening, which was almost closed with debris. He looked out and was stunned at what he saw. The landscape was scarred and nothing could be seen. No sound, human or mechanical, could be heard. No birds sang.

For a while he just stood there. Then he. . . .

The generalization to be reached by the children from a discussion of this episode is:

*Written laws are an attempt to clarify the rules by which society operates and to promote the impartial treatment of its members.*

Dialogue between teacher and children might go like this:[18]

T: What would be one of the first things you might do?
S: I'd run.
S: I'd look around and maybe just go back and see what happened.
S: I'd just run as fast as I could the opposite way.
T: Well, suppose you did look around; what might you look for?
S: Some way to survive.
S: For people.
T: Why would you look for people?
S: To see if any were alive.
S: You heard the big sound (on tape) and then you couldn't hear anything after that.

T: Is there any reason that you would look for people? Do you think that perhaps others escaped?

S: Yes.

S: Yes, you need to start working together and build to survive. Everything is barren.

S: It's natural to look for somebody else.

T: Why do you say that?

S: I don't think one person could live in a destroyed city by himself.

S: Yeah, he's right there—you need someone to help you. You can't do everything yourself. You need help.

T: Good!

S: If the city was destroyed, I'd try to get out of there and go someplace else.

T: Suppose you do find a few more survivors; perhaps some had hidden in a cave, and soon you found five or six people. What would be one of the first things that you people might do?

S: Look for food and shelter.

S: Yes, you would be hungry after a day and you can't go without it.

S: You need shelter.

T: Remember, everything was destroyed. What would you use for food and shelter?

S: You would look for plants and stuff in the ditch.

S: I think you would look for food or anything left over you might be able to find.

T: What might be the safest thing for you to eat?

S: Something that was in your ditch because everything else could have been poisoned by the explosion.

T: What kind of food would you look for?

S: Mostly plant life—that would be about the only thing left.

T: Could you eat the top of the plant?

S: You could eat the root.

T: Why would the roots be the only thing left really?

S: Because the top of the plants would be destroyed and the roots would be left underground.

T: You're right; you remembered in the story that everything was scarred. Do you know anything about plants that might tell you about a water supply? What do you know about plants?

S: They need water, sunlight. . . .

S: The roots, they collect something like that so I guess you might get something out of the roots to eat.

T: Good! Now we've discovered people. We've discovered our next basic need is our food, water, shelter. . . .

S: Well, water, that might be our first. It depends. It may be way back in a cave and there would be blind fish, lobster, crab. . . .

T: OK, after we get our food, water, and our little group of people, what are we going to have to do now? For example, when you go on a camping trip, what do you do to make things easier?

S: You work together.

S: Yeah, you work together in groups.

T: How do you work together?

S: Have somebody go get firewood, and some get water.

S: Some get water, and you know—everything that wasn't destroyed?

T: Yes, that's good. I'm glad you came up with the idea of organizing; this is what you have to do. Now suppose you have this group of people, how are we going to make sure everyone plays fair? For example, if we have a big, strong man over here and also someone who was hurt in the blast and is not too strong, who do you think should get the most food?

S: He would.

T: Who would?

S: The injured guy.

T: Why?

S: Because he'd need the nourishment.

S: I don't agree with that because there may be so little food that they will have to fight over it and the stronger one is going to take it.

T: Do you think the strong should take it?

S: No, I think that it should be divided, but that's not the way it is. If I was in that position, I'd probably take the most if I could, or as much as I could.

T: But what do you think we could do to make this a little more fair? We may have some strong people and some weak people. . . .

S: I think we should give the weak person more food and he might get better and then we would have another person helping. I don't know.

T: What can we do to make sure this doesn't happen, that one person gets all of it?

S: Split it up evenly or something like that.

S: Depends on how many people you had in on this. It might be easier, you know, if we had five or six people, or it might be harder to find that much food. But if there were three or four people it might be easier, I think.

S: Make rules.

S: Make the rules and everybody gets the same amount of everything.

S: Like in Monopoly you would get the same amount of money, even though you aren't equal at the end of the game.

T: That was the important thing; you said you need a set of rules, good!

S: And Rob was trying to get away from rules. (referring to tape)

S: Ah-hh.

T: Yes, he was, wasn't he?

S: Uh-huh.

T: What do you think might happen if we didn't have any rules at all?

S: You couldn't do a thing. If you wanted to play a game, you couldn't play it.

T: Why not?

S: Because one guy could say, well, there's no rules and I can have as much money as I want.

T: And who do you think is going to?

S: The stronger person.

S: It's right there. If you don't have rules, the stronger person always gets it. You know it's that way!

T: Suppose someone breaks the rules?

S: Give him a penalty.

T: What kind of penalty?

S: Depends on what you're doing.

T: Suppose we catch one of the people in our group stealing food.

S: Make his next ration less than he usually gets.

S: See how much he took. If he took an awful lot and if he had any extra, put it back and he can't eat for the rest of the day or something.

T: What else could you do? What do you think some people might want to do to him?

S: Physically hurt him.

S: That's a good idea—ha, ha!

T: How could we decide on a proper punishment to give a person? If we find someone taking more than his share—in other words, breaking a rule—how can we punish him?

S: Make him have a little less than his share.

T: OK, thinking over the little story you have just heard and the discussion we've had, what would you consider an important idea you developed? Everyone think carefully! What is one important idea you came up with from today's story and our talk?

S: Well, rules are very important because if somebody breaks them, the stronger person always gets his way, then it's just no fair to the weaker person.

T: Anyone else have an important idea?

S: Well, if a person is going to participate in something, everyone has to work together....

S: And play fair and not break the rules.

S: Because there are too many people in the world to live without rules.

S: Laws you mean.

## Continuing Activities

After the problem has been initiated with the class, testing the hypotheses may take many forms, depending on the needs of the class. For example, the class could be divided into committees (to be discussed in Chapter Nine), with each committee selecting a hypothesis to test and then reporting back to the class on their findings. At that time, the class can decide, on the basis of the information given, whether to accept or reject the hypothesis or determine whether additional information is needed. Another approach would be for each child to test his or her own hypothesis.

Gathering data may take many forms—such as viewing films or filmstrips, listening to tapes or records, interviewing people in the school or community, and utilizing resource books or textbooks. After the hypotheses have been tested utilizing the data collected, the children should draw generalizations based on their new knowledge. When possible, these generalizations should be applied to the child's own life.

### Responsibility of the Child in an Inquiry-Centered Classroom

The children become active inquirers into their own education. They make decisions about their learning experiences and interact more with teacher and peers. They are active thinkers—seeking information, probing, and processing data, and asking questions rather than always being questioned. The children pose the problem to be solved, suggest the hypotheses to be tested, search for the necessary information, determine the discrepancies in the information, accept or reject the hypotheses, and draw generalizations. They participate in the self-discovery of certain basic concepts and principles as they move from observation, classification, interpretation, and application to generalization. The children acquire insight into their own behavior that will enable them to apply the generalizations to their own lives. They also learn to express themselves so that all may understand their views while learning to be open-minded and willing to accept the thoughts and opinions of others.

## ADVANTAGES AND DISADVANTAGES OF PROBLEM SOLVING THROUGH INQUIRY

Advocates of the method of problem solving through inquiry stress the value of developing rational thought and of the act of discovery encountered during the search for solutions to a problem. Bruner hypothesizes that discovery in learning "helps the child to learn the varieties of problem solving, of transforming knowledge for better use, helps him to learn how to go about the very task of learning."[19] Retrieval of the information learned through discovery is more easily accomplished.[20] Research indicates that as the child progresses through elementary grades his inquiry ability increases.[21]

Motivation for learning becomes internal for learners in the problem-solving situation because they are actively seeking knowledge to solve a given problem. The excitement of discovery encourages them to continue their search; they learn by doing. The problems presented to the learners are concrete and are related directly to their own experiences. The children can suggest a variety of solutions, but the situations remain open-ended, which can lead to further study.

Those who question the emphasis on the act of discovery of the inquiry method suggest that it places too little attention on the crucial role played by facts and skills in a student's mastery of a body of knowledge. Ausubel relates that "abundant experimental research has confirmed the proposition that prior learnings are not transferable to new learnings unless they are first overlearned."[22]

Friedlander questions the value of a child's curiosity in operating as a motivator and incentive for academic learning. He claims that children's curiosity may be unsystematic, noncumulative, immediate, and easily satisfied. He suggests that a child's curiosity may be satisfied with incorrect or partial information and that it may be strongest with issues not necessarily the proper concern of the school.[23]

Concern is voiced by many for the inquiry method's practice of accepting "any answer." This group stresses the fact that the children might not have the opportunity to test all of their answers and it questions how the children will know if their answers are right or wrong. Continued research is necessary to answer the claims of both the advocates and the opponents of this method.

# NOTES

1. John Dewey, *How We Think* (Boston: D. C. Heath, 1933), p. 106.
2. Joseph J. Schwab, *The Teaching of Science as Inquiry* (Cambridge, Mass.: Harvard University Press, 1962), p. 14, cited in Charlotte Crabtree, "Supporting Reflective Thinking in the Classroom," in *Effective Thinking in the Social Studies*, Jean Fair and Fannie Shaftel, eds. (Washington, D.C.: National Council for the Social Studies, 1967), p. 89.
3. Fair and Shaftel, *Effective Thinking*, p. 89.
4. Jerome Bruner, *On Knowing* (Cambridge, Mass.: Belknap Press of Harvard University Press, 1962), pp. 82–83.
5. Hilda Taba, *Teacher's Handbook for Elementary Social Studies* (Reading, Mass.: Addison-Wesley, 1967), p. 87.
6. Ibid., p. 88.
7. Ibid.
8. Ibid., p. 89.
9. Ibid., pp. 92, 101, 109.
10. The writer acknowledges the use of Benjamin Bloom and David Krathwohl, *Taxonomy of Educational Objectives: Handbook I. The Cognitive Domain* (New York: David McKay, 1956).
11. Maxine Dunfee and Helen Sagl, *Social Studies Through Problem Solving* (New York: Holt, Rinehart and Winston, 1966), pp. 23–24.
12. H. Millard Clements, William R. Fielder, and B. Robert Tobachnick, *Social Study: Inquiry in Elementary Classrooms* (Indianapolis: Bobbs-Merrill, 1966), p. 117.

13. Ibid., p. 68.
14. Robert Fox, Ronald Lippitt, and John Lohman, *Teaching of Social Science Material in the Elementary School,* USOE Cooperative Research Project E-011 (Ann Arbor: University of Michigan, 1964), cited in Fair and Shaftel, *Effective Thinking,* p. 156.
15. Fair and Shaftel, *Effective Thinking,* p. 157.
16. Luman H. Long, ed., *The World Almanac* (New York: Newspaper Enterprise Association, Inc., 1974), p. 585.
17. Adapted from materials produced by the High School Geography Project, Association of American Geographers.
18. Dialogue from classroom presentation by Ronald E. Sterling and a group of fifth- and sixth graders.
19. Bruner, *On Knowing,* p. 87.
20. Ibid., p. 95.
21. J. S. Allender, "Some Terminants of Inquiry Activity in Elementary School Children," *Journal of Educational Psychology* 61 (1970):220–225.
22. D. P. Ausubel, "A Teaching Strategy for Culturally Deprived Pupils: Cognitive and Motivational Considerations," *School Review* 71 (1963):456.
23. Bernard Z. Friedlander, "A Psychologist's Second Thoughts on Concepts, Curiosity, and Discovery in Learning," *Harvard Educational Review* 35 (1965):25.

## SELECTED REFERENCES

Beyer, Barry K. *Inquiry in the Social Studies Classroom.* Columbus, Ohio: Charles E. Merrill, 1971.

Brubaker, Dale L. "Indoctrination, Inquiry, and the Social Studies." *The Social Studies* 41 (March 1970):120–124.

Bruner, Jerome. *Toward a Theory of Instruction.* Cambridge: Harvard University Press, 1966.

Ellis, Arthur K., ed. "The Child's Environment: A Living Laboratory for Social Science Research." *Social Education* 39 (November/December 1975):483–496.

Fair, Jean, and Shaftel, Fannie R. *Effective Thinking in the Social Studies.* Washington, D.C.: National Council for the Social Studies, 1967.

Goldmark, Bernice. *Social Studies, a Method of Inquiry.* Belmont, Calif.: Wadsworth, 1968.

Massialas, Byron G., and Cox, Benjamin C. *Inquiry in Social Studies.* New York: McGraw-Hill, 1966.

Massialas, Byron; Sprague, Nancy F; and Hurst, Joseph B. *Social Issues Through Inquiry—Coping in an Age of Crises.* Englewood Cliffs, N.J.: Prentice-Hall, 1975.

Ryan, Frank. *Exemplars for the New Social Studies: Instructing in the Elementary School.* Englewood Cliffs, N.J.: Prentice-Hall, 1971.

Ryan, Frank, and Ellis, Arthur K. *Instructional Implications of Inquiry.* Englewood Cliffs, N.J.: Prentice-Hall, 1974.

Schwab, Joseph J. *The Teaching of Science as Inquiry.* Cambridge: Harvard University Press, 1963.

Skeel, Dorothy J., and Decaroli, Joseph G. "The Role of the Teacher in an Inquiry-Centered Classroom." *Social Education* 33 (May 1969):547–550.

Suchman, J. Richard. *Developing Inquiry.* Chicago: Science Research Associates, 1966.

# 6
# Unit Development

Current interpretations of unit teaching are equal in variety and number to those of problem solving. The *Dictionary of Education* defines the unit as "an organization of learning activities, experiences, and types of learning around a central theme, problem, or purpose developed cooperatively by a group of pupils under teacher leadership."[1]

Michaelis identifies a unit as "a plan to achieve specific objectives through the use of content and learning activities related to a designated topic."[2] Another definition suggests that "the unit represents a way of organizing materials and activities for instructional purposes."[3] Each definition recognizes the importance of organizing learning activities. This organization is the key to unit planning—one learning experience must be related to another in order to avoid fragmentation. A unit contains learning experiences that are related to other curriculum areas—for example, language arts, math, science, physical education, art, and music. Problem solving may be incorporated in the unit, but a unit can be developed without its use.

Basically, there are two types of units—the resource unit and the teaching unit. Resource units, as the label indicates, contain extensive suggestions of learning experiences, content, and materials for developing a selected topic with children. In contrast, a teaching unit is created to meet the needs and interests of a specific group of children. The teacher may draw upon the contents of a resource unit for the development of a teaching unit. A teaching unit may become a resource unit when used by another teacher with a different group of children.

The organization of a unit consists of:

1. Purpose—the reason for teaching the unit.

2. Objectives—the goals that will be reached in the process of teaching the unit.

3. Content—primarily the background information for the teacher or an organization of the knowledge necessary to achieve an understanding of the topic.

4. Activities—including initiation, individual and group experiences, integration with other subject areas, and culmination.

5. Bibliography—references for the teacher and children and materials such as records, films, filmstrips, and games.
6. Evaluation—a measure to determine the success achieved in accomplishing established objectives.

Variations occur in this suggested organization, but most units contain the same components.

## OBJECTIVES

Objectives established for the unit method of teaching overlap with those of problem solving, because both methods are concerned with similar goals although they attempt to achieve their goals by different means. Broad objectives for unit teaching include:

*Acquire skill in:*
*Working cooperatively with members of a group through committee participation and planning.*
*The use of a variety of materials including books, primary sources, magazines, and pamphlets.*
*Communicating with members of a group through reports, plays, panel discussions, and interviews.*

*Develop an understanding of:*
*The importance of establishing effective human relationships to achieve established goals.*
*The interrelationship of content areas.*
*The importance of social studies in relation to everyday life.*
*The democratic process and the responsibility of each individual to make the process effective.*

*Acquire knowledge of:*
*Facts and information sufficient to develop an understanding of the topic under study.*
*Methods to secure accurate information about the topic.*

Obviously, these objectives are quite general and are based on the elements of unit teaching that are emphasized. More specific behavioral objectives should be formulated with a definite topic in mind.

Unit teaching is based on the theory that the children are motivated to learn material that they help to select and to plan in cooperation with the teacher. The theory also suggests that children can understand a topic more readily if they study it in the context of various subject areas, for they are then able to realize the interconnectedness of the content areas. For example, following this method, children who are attempting to understand Russian culture learn about the country's music and art and participate in games played by Russian children in addition to learning about Russia's government, education, history, geography, and economics.

The unit is a blueprint for broad or depth coverage of a topic. Topics can be covered in breadth, including as many aspects as possible, or in depth, emphasizing only selected aspects. A unit generally requires a longer period of time than does a problem-solving situation. However, a problem-solving situation may be included as a part of the unit. The unit method places more emphasis on content acquired than does the method of problem solving, but content is not its primary goal. The processes children use (communicating, cooperating, researching, and analyzing) as they acquire their information are still the primary goals. The fact that a unit-teaching situation provides opportunities to meet individual differences is one of its vital facets.

**Role of the Teacher**

The teacher's major role in unit teaching is one of motivator; however, more of the initial motivation should come from the child's involvement in the planning. Since the teachers have developed the unit plan, they supply more guidance for the organization of the study. There is cooperative teacher/pupil planning of the learning experiences to permit children to participate in the decision-making processes. The teacher plans activities particularly designed to meet individual needs. If Janice is shy and needs the experience of working with others, the teacher places her in a group where she won't be dominated, but where she can accept responsibility and develop her leadership skills. Or, the child like Terry who has exceptional art skills can be utilized in the development of an authentic African war mask.

The referrer role is expanded since more information is provided directly by the teacher in the initiation and by supplying materials for research and suggesting activities for reporting. Advisor and counselor roles may be expanded particularly if the groups have difficulty working together. It may be necessary for the teacher to counsel groups on ways in which they can work out their problems. For example, Jimmy isn't doing his share of the research and the committee wants to drop him from the group. The teacher talks with Jimmy about his responsibility and also

# UNIT DEVELOPMENT

with the rest of the committee to find out how the issue can be resolved. Much of the discipline is handled through group participation and decision making.

## Role of the Children

Children's responsibilities during the development of a unit are extensive. They should actively participate in the planning stage of the unit, fulfill their committee obligations, enter into discussions, and report research findings to others. The children are involved in some discovery in pursuit of information, but it is not as greatly emphasized in unit teaching. In addition, they should exhibit interest in the other children's reports, ask questions, and evaluate the performance of themselves and others.

Guidelines for procedures are formulated by the children, and it is each individual's responsibility to abide by the established rules. Group cooperation is essential to accomplish the selected goals.

## Conditions of the Classroom

The atmosphere of the classroom is created by the group's decisions concerning the regulation of their activities. Through cooperative planning, the children and teacher develop suggested behavior standards for working in committees, doing research, and presenting information to the class. The teacher's primary responsibility is to guide the children's thinking toward reasonable decisions. Extensive materials are necessary for research, and physical conditions should lend themselves to small group activities.

# UNIT SELECTION

Numerous criteria are suggested for selecting units of study around children's interests. Some of these criteria are:

1. The unit's general utility.
2. Its social significance.
3. Its ability to increase and extend the children's background knowledge.
4. Consideration of the needs and demands of society.[4]

If the processes in which children are involved (communicating, cooperating, researching, and analyzing) constitute the primary goal of unit development, should the content of the unit be based on the interests of children? Will children become more involved in a unit based on their interests? What are the interests of children at the various grade levels? Research indicates that children are interested in different topics at each of the grade levels:

*First grade*—Trips or journeys to extraordinary and different places such as dry, wet, hot, or cold lands. Also, cowboys and Indians of early American history.

*Second grade*—Areas of the earth different from their own immediate environment such as Africa, Japan, the North Pole. Historical background of national symbols such as Fourth of July, Statue of Liberty, the President.

*Third grade*—Big oceans and big continents, historical background of people such as Indians, soldiers of the Revolution, the person who discovered New York.

*Fourth grade*—Genuine interests in particular areas of the earth—Japan, England, the Congo and general social features of these, such as the Queen of England, the religion of Japan.

*Fifth grade*—Those geographic areas which dominate the current news—Middle East, Russia, China and the historical reason for some of the large social problems that appear on the national and international scene.

*Sixth grade*—Similar interests as the fifth grade, but more penetrating. Also, interest in the poverty of the masses in Latin America, social differences in East and West, beginnings of Communism, and development of the Cold War.[5]

Do the children's interests change as the times change? Are their interests universal, or do they differ from school to school and from classroom to classroom? How can teachers determine the interests of the children in their classroom?

The teacher can develop an interest inventory to aid in determining the focus of the students' interests. The children answer the teacher's questions by checking the appropriate column—for example, "like," "dislike," or "not sure." Sample questions might be:

1. Do you like to learn about the following:
   a. People from countries such as Japan?

Vietnam?
Africa?
b. The way a country runs its government?
c. Why many people in the world cannot find work and do not have enough to eat?
d. Famous people such as
Jesse Jackson?
Anwar Sadat?
Queen Elizabeth?
e. How people transport goods from place to place by
Trains?
Airplanes?
Ships?

Teachers formulate questions based on current topics in the news, suggested topics from curriculum guides, textbooks, and knowledge of the children's interests gleaned from class and informal discussions. Other types of interest inventories might involve short-answer questions, children's autobiographies, or individual pupil/teacher conferences.

## DIRECTING CHILDREN'S INTERESTS

Children's interests can be directed toward topics that teachers deem important for study. The techniques that teachers employ to introduce the topic as well as the interest displayed by them are important factors. What topics should be developed? The basic activities involved in the expanding human communities (in the family, school, neighborhood, local county and metropolitan area, state, region of states, U.S. national, U.S. and inter-American, U.S. and Atlantic, U.S. and Pacific, and in the world), as identified by Hanna, are frequently used as a basis for determining content. Also, the outline of content in textbooks can be the basis for unit topics.

Equally important to consider for inclusion in a social studies unit are topics that aid in developing the selected concepts and generalizations from each of the social sciences: history, geography, sociology, economics, political science, anthropology, philosophy, and psychology.[6] An awareness of our current social, economic, environmental, and political problems should certainly direct the teacher's selection of topics. Figure 6.1 gives sample topics that may be developed for each grade level.

*Kindergarten*
Who Am I?
Where We Live
Where Other People Live
Our Animals
Animals from Other Lands
Working Together

*First Grade*
Our Community
Pollution in Our Town
How Do We Communicate?
Homes in Other Lands
   Japan
   Mexico
   Africa

*Second Grade*
Our Shopping Center
Interdependence of People
How Do We Transport
   Our Goods?
Our Wants and Needs
Our National Parks

*Grade Three*
How Communities Grow
Big Cities
   New York
   Boston
   Los Angeles
   Houston
Other Communities
   Bombay, India
   Melbourne, Australia
   Manila, The Philippines

*Grade Four*
Pollution of the World
How Do We Govern
   Ourselves?
How Do Other People
   Govern Themselves?
Our State and Its Problems

*Grade Five*
Our Nation Today
How Did It Grow?
What Problems Did It Face?
Our Nation and Its Neighbors
Our European Neighbors
People of Latin America

*Grade Six*
World Neighbors
What Are the Problems?
People of China
What's Happening in the
   Middle East?
People of East Africa

**Figure 6.1**   Sample Unit Topics for Grades K–6

## DEVELOPMENT OF A UNIT

### Initiation

The teacher is responsible for providing the setting for the study. Sufficient information is necessary to stimulate continuing interest in a topic. However, too much information will not leave enough questions to be answered and may stifle interest. The ability and experiential level of the children will serve as possible guidelines for determining the amount of information to include in the initiation. A problem-solving situation, as suggested in Chapter Three, can be used for the introduction in order to combine the methods of problem solving and unit organization. Other initiation activities might include an arranged environment, exploratory questioning, films, stories, poetry, and folktales.

### Arranged Environment

Use of a number of prepared exhibits and bulletin boards creates a classroom atmosphere that lends itself to the topic for study. Bulletin boards supply two types of stimulation: (1) information about the topic—presented by charts, pictures, and newspaper clippings, or (2) the presentation of a series of searching questions to be answered during the study.

Displays would include books and magazines that present discussions of the topic at varying levels of reading difficulty. The books should contain stories as well as facts. Other displays might show selected artifacts relative to the topic. Criticism of the arranged environment points out that it lacks pupil/teacher planning and creates an artificial beginning for the pursuit of the study. Gradual development of the bulletin boards and exhibits by the children throughout the study is suggested.

### Exploratory Questioning

Teachers need to know the extent of their students' understanding or misunderstanding about a topic before beginning the study. Introducing a topic through a stimulating question period provides teachers with information to help them plan the direction and depth of the study. It also creates excitement about the topic. Such questioning can be incorporated with any initiation or used exclusively for the initiation. For example, when the topic is concerned with the study of Africa, the teacher might have the children react to questions such as: What do you think of when someone mentions Africa? How would your life change if you moved to Africa? What are some of the contributions that Africans have made to our heritage?

Generally, more information about individual understanding can be obtained when children are requested to write their answers; however, oral questioning stimulates more interest in the topic. Assessment of the answers in terms of general misconceptions as well as the amount of present knowledge about the topic should direct the focus of the study.

### Film or Filmstrip Presentation

A film or filmstrip used to introduce the study can present information and/or questions. Those that provide provocative information may foster immediate interest that may not be sustained.

### Reading Stories, Poetry, or Folktales

Stories relative to the topic that present situations similar to those in the children's lives provide stimulation. Poetry and folktales also catch the interest of children. *Children's Books to Enrich the Social Studies*[7] is a good source for information concerning this type of material.

## TEACHER/PUPIL PLANNING FOR THE UNIT

After the initiation, the course of action for the study should be planned cooperatively by the pupils and the teacher. The initiation in this example presents on a transparency a map of Africa indicating the natural resources of the continent (Figure 6.2).[8] The dialogue that follows might introduce the transparency and continue the pupil/teacher planning.

> TEACHER: What can you learn about Africa from the map?
>
> SANDRA: It has many natural resources.
>
> TOM: Not so many when you think how large Africa is.
>
> TEACHER: Can you tell anything about the physical features from the resources?
>
> JEAN: Many of those minerals are found in mountainous regions.
>
> BUZ: Not all. Oil is found in flat areas, also phosphate.
>
> JIM: Yes, and I've seen copper mines on plateaus.

UNIT DEVELOPMENT 123

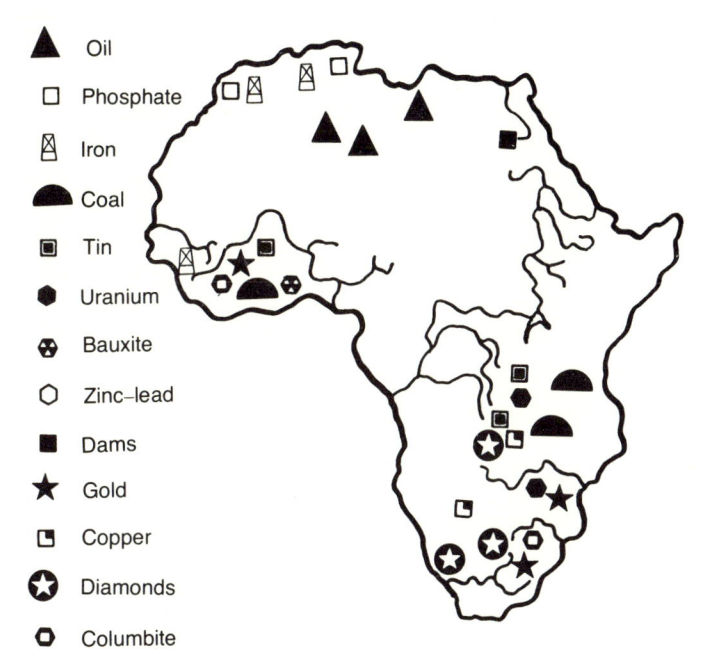

- ▲ Oil
- ☐ Phosphate
- Iron
- Coal
- Tin
- Uranium
- Bauxite
- Zinc-lead
- ■ Dams
- ★ Gold
- Copper
- ✪ Diamonds
- Columbite

**Figure 6.2** Natural Resources of Africa

**TEACHER:** So far we think there are mountains, plateaus, and plains. What do the rivers tell you about the land?

**MYRTLE:** Usually, the sources of rivers come from mountains.

**TODD:** Look at that large area where there aren't any rivers. That must be all desert.

**TEACHER:** Can you hypothesize about where people might live?

**SHERMAN:** It seems more would be concentrated near the resources and rivers—the eastern and southern sections.

**REED:** They have so many different resources, there must be lots of industries.

**MARIA:** No, I don't think Africa has that much technology. Those are different countries with the resources and maybe they don't trade with one another.

**SCOTT:** Don't some European countries control the resources in Africa?

**TEACHER:** You've raised a number of questions about Africa. Suppose we list them.

**SCOTT:** What are the physical features of Africa?

**REED:** What industries do you find in Africa?

ANGELO: Shouldn't we find out the different countries in Africa?

TEACHER: Why do you think so?

ANGELO: To understand how the continent is divided.

TEACHER: How would you state the question?

ANGELO: What are the countries in Africa and their governments?

MARIO: What is the history of the countries and how did they develop?

RON: What are the industries in the countries? Most of the time you think of jungles and huts.

RUTH: What is the climate like and how do the people dress?

TINA: What type of music and art is there in Africa?

SCOTT: What kinds of traditions are important to the people? You know, what do they value?

TEACHER: Africa is such a large area, do you think we should try to learn about the entire continent?

SCOTT: Let's find out general information about all of Africa, then we can decide if there's an area where we might want to concentrate.

TEACHER: Is that satisfactory to everyone? We've listed a number of questions to research. Look at them carefully and decide which one you'd like to choose.

SCOTT: Can we work in committees, so several people can look for information on each topic?

TEACHER: Good idea—we should find more information when we work together on a problem.

Children become more actively involved in their learning experiences when they have an opportunity to share in the planning. Teachers can easily guide the discussion toward the goals they plan to accomplish.

## INDIVIDUAL AND GROUP ACTIVITIES

Unit organization has the advantage of providing the opportunities to meet individual needs. Children who have special interests or skills can be guided toward tasks that fulfill these needs. Research can be conducted in areas of a study that are of particular interest to individual children. Those of exceptional ability can engage in research in greater depth and thus can acquire skills beyond the normal level. Children who have talent in music, art, writing, or drama have an opportunity to use these skills.

In the above dialogue, it's obvious that Scott is outgoing and probably possesses leadership ability. He easily can assume the responsibility for organizing a committee where he can help other children. Maria, on the other hand, would prefer to pursue the topic of history on her own. Tom and Reed are both talented in music and art. Continuing in this manner, other group or individual activities may be organized around the interests and abilities of the other children.

Group activities contribute to the individual's development. For example, the child who has difficulty in getting along with other children and who is assigned to a group activity of real interest to him or her hopefully will acquire skills of cooperative behavior. Equally important is the opportunity for the child with leadership ability to channel this energy into worthwhile activities. Shy children who would hesitate to enter into activities and discussions in front of the whole group will often do so within small groups. Activities that encourage discussion of important aspects in the study aid the development of oral language skills.

## INTEGRATING ACTIVITIES

The development of an understanding of the relationship of one subject area to another is made possible through integrating activities, which helps children realize that knowledge in one subject is related to other subject areas. These activities also provide meaningful practice of skills acquired in other areas.

### Language Arts

Skills introduced in the language arts acquire more meaning when they are applied in the content areas. Children realize a purpose for acquiring skills when they can put them to use. Unit teaching provides numerous opportunities for the use of language skills.

Methods for encouraging the development of oral language skills might include reports of individual or committee research, panel discussions or debates on facets of the study, role-playing incidents to clarify understandings, and class discussions about the topics. Interviewing individuals to secure information also develops oral language skills. Listening skills, too, are sharpened during these experiences.

Outlining, note taking, and preparing written reports are skills needed for research activities. Critical reading skills are necessary to determine if the source of the information is fact or opinion. Locational skills involving the use of the table of contents, index, cross references, and appendix are necessary when seeking information during the study.

### Art, Music, and Physical Education

Construction activities such as building a model Indian village or a salt and flour relief map add considerable understanding to a study and correlate learning experiences. Painting or drawing murals provides opportunity for interpreting events. Making artifacts from various cultures (for example, making cornbread when studying Indians) makes a study more realistic.

Frequently, topics provide opportunity for integration with music (for example, constructing maracas or drums when studying Mexico or listening to the music of the country). Learning the dances native to a country helps develop an understanding of its people. Children enjoy learning the games that are played in the countries under study.

## CULMINATING ACTIVITIES

Culminating activities draw together the learning experiences of the unit. These activities should emphasize the main points, identify the interrelated ideas, and provide a compositive view of the topic. As a result of these activities, children should be able to formulate generalizations that can be applied to new situations. Examples of culminating experiences follow.

### Committee Reports

The completed research of the committees can be presented in a variety of ways—TV or radio productions; talks illustrated with prepared charts, bulletin boards, and realia; or a movie roll that includes information from every committee.

### Tours

The study of a country provides the opportunity for planning a guided tour to emphasize the important historic, recreational, and geographic points of interest. Illustrative materials such as maps, murals, and pictures supply background.

## Dramatizations

The production of dramatic presentations requires interpretation of the information secured and insures better understanding of the topic. Children portraying the landing of the Pilgrims or the Boston Tea Party will understand better and retain longer the information acquired.

## Films and Filmstrips

Audiovisual aids such as films and filmstrips can be used effectively for culminating activities when they review information previously investigated.

# BIBLIOGRAPHY

An extensive bibliography listing the materials available for the teacher and the children should be included in the unit. Resource books, films, tapes, records, pictures, community resources, and suggested field trips should be included for reference.

# EVALUATION

The methods of evaluation to be utilized during and at the completion of the unit must be planned. These evaluations are attempts to determine whether the objectives of the unit were successfully achieved. Evaluations must be made in terms of the success with which individual and group performance meets the objectives. Continuous evaluation throughout the unit guides its direction. Teachers should be evaluating their teaching procedures and their effectiveness in guiding the activities of the children. An assessment of the kinds and uses of materials is also important. Evaluation methods will be discussed in greater detail in Chapter Fifteen.

# A SAMPLE RESOURCE UNIT

Africa will be the topic used to illustrate the development of the aspects of a resource unit: purpose, generalizations, objectives, activities, daily lesson plans, and bibliography. The content or background information for the teacher is too extensive for inclusion here; however, a skeletal outline is provided.

## Africa—A Land of Contrasts

*Purpose:* Africa is a continent that is experiencing rapid changes. Countries that for many years were ruled by European nations have gained their freedom and are struggling with the problems that face all new governments attempting to be recognized by the modern world. For too long, the ideas and impressions that children have had about Africa are those from a TV world of animals and jungles. This unit presents a view of Africa with its cities, industries, and problems similar to other countries of the world. An overview of the continent will be developed and will be followed by an in-depth study of one country—Kenya.

*Generalizations:*

Geography influences the culture developed within a country and thus modifies the environment.

Culture is the pattern of interaction within a given group of people; it is determined by the people's shared values, beliefs, and opinions on what constitutes acceptable behavior and customs.

The historical background of a country affects its development.

Government is an attempt to provide a society with order and stability.

Africa is a country rich in tradition, but struggling with social changes.

*Objectives:*
1. To acquire knowledge of the physical features of Africa and to determine their effect on the cultural development.
2. To acquire knowledge of the different cultural patterns of Africa.
3. To acquire knowledge of the historical development of countries within Africa, particularly Kenya.
4. To develop an attitude of respect for the traditions and cultural contributions of Africa.
5. To recognize the problems faced by developing nations and their effect on other nations of the world.
6. To develop locational skills in using maps and globes.
7. To develop skill in using a seven-color key on a map or globe.
8. To develop skill in locating information through a variety of sources.
9. To develop skill in the ability to work cooperatively through participating in committees.

10. To develop oral language skills by reporting information to the class.
11. To develop skill in valuing through role playing.
12. To develop psychomotor skills in art, music, and physical education activities.

*Initiation:* The unit can be introduced with survey type questions as indicated on page 122, or with the use of the natural resources map on page 123. Another possibility would be the use of discrepant data, where you first present a set of pictures or slides that reinforce the usual stereotypes of Africa (jungles, animals, grass huts, tribal costumes) and ask the children to draw a generalization about Africa from these pictures. Then you would introduce the discrepant data with pictures or slides of the modern cities, industries, western dress and entertainment and ask children to restructure their generalization about Africa. What has changed their ideas? Do they have sufficient information about the country? If not, what questions do they need to research? Organization of these research activities can follow a similar pattern as the one indicated for the resource map.

## DAILY LESSON PLANS

**First Day:**
*Objectives # 1, 6, 7*
*Outline of Content*

I. Geography
A. Area
B. Population
C. Location
D. Land Forms
  1. Desert
  2. Plateau
  3. Mountains
  4. Great Rift Valley
  5. Rivers
E. Vegetation
  1. Rain Forests
  2. Savanna
  3. Veldt
  4. Oasis
F. Natural Resources

*Materials:* Relief maps and globes of Africa with the land forms and rivers, maps with types of vegetation, natural resources, and population.

*Procedure:* Utilize the maps and globes in a discussion of location of Africa in relation to the United States and other areas of the world. Locate the major land forms and the rivers.

Form committees to research the different types of vegetation, distribution of population, and natural resources.

## Second and Third Day:
*Objectives # 8, 9, 12*

*Materials:* A variety of maps and globes, books with data about population, natural resources, paper for murals or maps, transparencies, paints, and pastels.

*Procedure:* Give committees an opportunity to work. Be sure each group understands its task. Help groups decide how they will present the information through preparation of a mural, map, or guided tour of the continent.

*Evaluation:* Observe committees to determine the following:

1. Are the chairpersons effective?
2. Are groups sharing materials?
3. Is each person doing his/her share of work?
4. Are there any interpersonal problems?
5. Are the children having any difficulty locating information? What are the problems, if any?

## Fourth Day:
*Objectives # 1, 6, 7, 9, 10*

*Materials:* Maps, murals, and reports prepared by committees. Overhead projector.

*Procedure:* Committees present information they have acquired through their research. There are maps and murals which provide a backdrop for an imaginary tour through the country. Transparencies are projected to present the information on the distribution of population and natural resources.

Questions asked after the presentations to help children formulate generalizations:

1. How might the different vegetations and distribution of natural resources affect the culture?
2. What does the distribution of population tell you about the different sections of the continent?

*Evaluation:* Observe the children during their presentations:

1. Did each speak so all could hear?
2. Were the children listening to one another?
3. Was the information presented so that it was easily understood?

## Fifth through Ninth Day:
*Objectives # 2, 4, 8, 9, 12*

*Materials:* Books on African cultures written on varying reading levels. Films, filmstrips, musical instruments, game books, and artifacts from Africa. Materials for constructing murals and artifacts.

*Outline of Content*
- I. People of Africa
  - A. Hamite
  - B. Nilote
  - C. Bantu
  - D. West African Negroes
- II. Cities of Africa
  - A. Nairobi
  - B. Addis Ababa
  - C. Dar-es-Salaam
  - D. Salisbury
  - E. Capetown
  - F. Lagos
  - G. Brazzaville
  - H. Algiers
  - I. Tunis
  - J. Cairo
- III. Village Life
- IV. Music
- V. Art
- VI. Religion
- VII. Recreation

*Procedure:* Show film with an overview of the many types of African cultures.

Discuss: How might your life change if you moved to an African country?

Form committees or have individual research done on some aspect of the African culture. One group does an overview of the history of the African countries to learn of the different groups that come to the continent. Have them prepare a time line of the major events.

## Tenth Day:
*Objectives # 3, 4, 9, 10*

*Procedure:* Have an African festival with the artifacts, murals, music, foods, and games prepared by the committees. Invite any African people who may be in the community.

*Evaluation:* Observe children to determine how they react to the different activities.

1. Are they willing to participate—dance, play games, try the foods?
2. What type of reactions do children display when introduced to a different food, game, etc.?
3. Children write a story about what their day would be like if they lived in one of the African countries.

**Eleventh Day:**
*Objectives # 3, 4, 5*

*Outline of Content*
    Kenya
    I. Historical Background
       A. European Influence
       B. Independence
       C. Struggle for Nationhood
       D. Government
    II. Problems of the People
    III. Traditional versus Modern

*Materials:* African folklore book, films, books on historical and cultural aspects of Kenya.

*Procedure:* Introduce the study of Kenya with a folktale. Read the tale and discuss how it is similar to folktales from other countries. Discuss the lesson it is attempting to teach. Talk about tradition. What does it mean to you? What does it mean to other people? What happens when traditions are broken?

**Twelfth through Fourteenth Day:**
*Objectives # 3, 4, 5*

*Materials:* Same as previous day.

*Procedure:* Read and discuss the historical development of Kenya concentrating on the war for independence (1952–57). Read story "The Devil at Yalahun Bridge," which depicts the reaction of educated Africans to the British before independence. Discuss the effect on the people—family life was disrupted, many fathers were killed, traditions were changing, employment was difficult to find.

    View films on different life styles in Kenya.

**Fifteenth Day—Culmination Activity:**
*Objectives # 4, 5, 11*

*Materials:* Story about father having difficulty finding work to pay for his family needs. Role-play cards with descriptions of family members.

*Procedure:* Read story about family in Kenya that lives in small village Nyeri outside Nairobi. The father, Patrick, was a freedom fighter, but cannot find work and the family does not have enough food to get along. Patrick is a carpenter and might find work in Nairobi, but that would mean leaving his family. It is possible that Patrick might only find a job as a shoeshine person. One of the boys, Kimani, is old enough to go to the city to find work, but he has no skills. If he goes to the city, it is doubtful he would find work except as a car park attendant and if he is lucky, maybe as a waiter. Another boy, named after the Olympian Kipchoge, is a runner and hopes to be famous too, in the Olympics, some day. He does not have time to work. The mother, Ruth, does not want the father or son to leave home. She would rather have her daughter, Grace, marry someone with money. Grace wants to marry a poor goatherder. What should the family do?

Have children discuss and list the possible alternatives that are open to the family. Also, list the consequences that would occur with each alternative. Discuss the values that would be most important to the family.

Make masks from construction paper for each one of the family members.

Have children wear masks and role play the family discussion in an attempt to solve their problem.

Discuss the following questions at the end of the role playing session: How did you feel when you took Patrick's, Kimani's, etc., role? How did it help you understand the problems that the family was facing? Were their problems similar to any that you face in your family?

*Evaluation:* The children's ability to place themselves in the roles of the family in Kenya and their discussion would demonstrate their depth of understanding about the country, its people, and problems.

Another form of evaluation could be a debate on the problems of developing nations.

## RESOURCES

Jarolimek and Davis. *The Ways of Man.* New York: Macmillan, 1971.

Shorter; Starr; Kenworthy. *Eleven Nations.* Chicago: Ginn, 1972.

O'Hern. *Man and His World.* Morristown, N.J.: Silver Burdett, 1972.

*Hi Neighbor.* U.S. Committee for UNICEF. 331 East 38th St. New York, N.Y. 10016.

Changing Africa: A Village Study Unit. Cultural Initiative Series: Africa. InterCulture Associates, Box 277, Thompson, Conn. 06277

*Children of African People.* Almeric Publications, 231 E. 32nd St., New York, N.Y. 10002.

Efua Sutherland, *Playtime in Africa.* Atheneum Press.

Leonard Doob. *A Crocodile Has Me by the Leg.* Walker and Co., 720 5th Ave., New York, N.Y.

*Fun and Festival in Africa.* Friendship Press, 120th St. and Riverside Dr., New York, N.Y. 10027.

*African Song Book.* Recreation Services, Delaware, Ohio.

*African Musical Instruments.* D.C.A. Education Products, 4863 Stenton Ave., Philadelphia, Pa.

*Kenya.* Scott, Foresman: Glenview, Ill.: Spectra Program, People of the World.

Film: "Two Life Styles in East Africa." Bailey Films.

Film: "Malawi: Two Young Men." Churchill Films.

*East African Packet,* postcards, charts. African-American Institute, 866 UN Plaza, New York, N.Y. 10017.

Abioseh Nicol, "The Devil at Yalahun Bridge," in *Two African Tales.* New York: Cambridge University Press, 1965.

Kathleen Arnott, *African Myths and Legends.* New York: Henry Z. Walck, 1963.

## ADVANTAGES AND DISADVANTAGES OF UNIT TEACHING

Most proponents of unit teaching claim that its major advantage is broad or in-depth coverage of a topic, which provides opportunities for integration with other curriculum areas. A unit also aids in the efficient organization of learning experiences. The boundaries of content for a topic are established to determine the skills, knowledge, attitudes, and understanding a child will acquire in a specified period of time.[9] The variety of possible activities in a unit provides opportunities for meeting individual needs. Also, this variation promotes the development of a wider range of skills.

The disadvantages of unit teaching are centered primarily on its less effective means of developing thinking skills. Problem solving through inquiry, which can be part of a unit, accomplishes this goal to a greater extent. The boundary lines drawn for the unit's content often do not permit children to pursue interests that may arise spontaneously.

Possibly the most effective way of overcoming the disadvantages of both unit teaching and problem solving is to combine both methods. Hanna relates "that when the problem approach is used as the basis for unit organization the overall problem is analyzed into subproblems and questions, the answers to which are necessary before the overall problem can be solved. Sometimes the larger problem grows out of a perplexity about a smaller, related problem."[10]

Obviously, some topics that should be presented by unit organization don't lend themselves to problem solving or present such weak problem situations that they are ineffective. There are also some problem situations that can't be effectively organized as units because of their short-term duration. Teachers must select the most effective method by considering a topic in relation to the interest, ability, and motivation of their children.

## NOTES

1. Carter V. Good, *Dictionary of Education* (New York: McGraw-Hill, 1945), p. 436.
2. John U. Michaelis, *Social Studies in a Democracy* (Englewood Cliffs, N.J.: Prentice-Hall, 1968), p. 199.

3. John Jarolimek, *Social Studies in Elementary Education* (New York: Macmillan, 1967), p. 56.
4. Ibid., pp. 44–45.
5. William Ragan and John D. McAulay, *Social Studies for Today's Children* (New York: Appleton-Century-Crofts, 1964), pp. 201–202.
6. *Social Studies Framework for the Public Schools of California* (Sacramento: California State Department of Education, 1962), pp. 90–109.
7. Helen Huus, *Children's Books to Enrich the Social Studies* (Washington, D.C.: National Council for the Social Studies, 1966).
8. Mary E. Greig, *How People Live in Africa* (Chicago: Benefic Press, 1963), p. 17.
9. Ragan and McAulay, *Social Studies for Today's Children*, p. 217.
10. Lavonne A. Hanna, Gladys Potter, and Neva Hageman, *Unit Teaching in Elementary School* (New York: Holt, Rinehart and Winston, 1963), pp. 233–234.

## SELECTED REFERENCES

Hanna, Lavonne A.; Potter, Gladys; and Hageman, Neva. *Unit Teaching in the Elementary School.* New York: Holt, Rinehart and Winston, 1963.

Hill, Wilhelmina. *Unit Planning and Teaching in Elementary Social Studies.* Washington, D.C.: U.S. Office of Education, 1963.

Hopkins, Lee, and Avenstein, Misha. *Partners in Learning: A Child Centered Approach to Teaching Social Studies.* New York: Citation Press, 1971.

Jarolimek, John. *Social Studies in Elementary Education.* 5th ed. New York: Macmillan, 1977.

Joyce, Bruce, R.; Wiel, Marsha; and Wald, Rhoda. *Three Teaching Strategies for the Social Studies.* Chicago: SRA Inc., 1972.

Michaelis, John U., ed. *Teaching Units in the Social Sciences: Early Grades, Middle Grades, Intermediate Grades.* Chicago: Rand McNally, 1966.

Nerbouig, Marcella H. *Unit Planning: A Model for Curriculum Development.* Belmont, Calif.: Wadsworth, 1970.

Ragan, William, and McAulay, John D. *Social Studies for Today's Children.* New York: Appleton-Century-Crofts, 1964.

Skeel, Dorothy J. *The Challenge of Teaching Social Studies in the Elementary School: Readings.* Santa Monica, Calif.: Goodyear, 1972.

# 7
# Multicultural Education— Providing for All Children

To provide a chapter in a methods text that can effectively discuss the needs of all types of children in the classroom is not an easy task. One does not wish to label children (lest the label might remain with them), but without identifying these groups with particular needs, it is impossible to design educational programs that can adequately develop their potential. The groups identified here are those who are "culturally disadvantaged," racial or ethnic minorities, physically or mentally handicapped (mainstreamed), and sex stereotyped. Even though these groups are singled out, multicultural education is for all children.

Multicultural education has been narrowly defined by some authors to mean ethnic studies or learning about other cultures, but it is defined here to be far more inclusive. It is not intended to detract from ethnic or cultural studies, but rather to expand the definition to mean education that builds upon the uniqueness of the individual and the resolution of conflict over the differences. Special provisions need to be made in the curriculum and the teaching strategies to provide a truly multicultural education for children. Let's look, then, at the special needs of these groups of children.

## CULTURALLY DISADVANTAGED

These children have worn many labels, from "culturally deprived," "culturally disadvantaged," and "underprivileged" to "low socioeconomic backgrounds." Research indicates that socioeconomic class does affect the level of mental abilities of children and that there are certain patterns of mental abilities found in ethnic groups. Children from lower-class families were found to score lower on mental ability tests than children from middle-class families.[1] "Ethnicity does affect the pattern of mental abilities *and,* once the pattern specific to the ethnic group emerges, social-class variations within the ethnic group do not alter this basic organization."[2] How then do we identify the disadvantaged? How is the term to be defined? To identify them as children who come from lower socioeconomic levels or minority groups is unfair. Granted, concentrations of the disadvantaged may be found in minority groups and in areas of low socioeconomic levels, but it is incorrect to label all children from these groups as such. It is also incorrect to assume that disadvantaged children are not to be found in affluent majority groups.

A definition of the term disadvantaged is difficult since different factors contribute to the condition. Larson and Olson identify disadvantaged children as those children affected by the following:

1. Language development—underdeveloped expressive and receptive skills as well as speech patterns which conflict with dominant language norms.
2. Self-concept—inadequate self-image which will lead to self-doubt and insecurity resulting in low school achievement and a lessened feeling of personal worth.
3. Social skills—possess a minimal amount of skill in conventional manners and social amenities; unskilled in relating socially to peers and authority figures; and unable to function effectively in school group.
4. Cultural differences—most come from lower income and minority groups and will possess beliefs and behaviors which may differ from dominant groups in school.[3]

The reader must be aware that these children have developed language abilities to function within their own groups, but their language frequently conflicts with the expectations of the school. Most teachers react negatively to these children, who come to school with experiences, values, languages, and behaviors different from those expected of them. Teachers find three basic problems in their adjustment to teaching these children: (1) presenting learning experiences, (2) discipline, and (3) moral acceptability. These students do not meet the specifications of the "perfect student," and the usual teaching techniques are inadequate.

Disadvantaged children have been present since schools were established, but their increasing numbers and our lack of effective programs have created tremendous educational and social problems. The impetus for alleviating this situation has been provided by federal monies directed toward improving educational programs for the disadvantaged. This effort, however, may be too little too late. Unless individual teachers accept the responsibility for adapting their educational programs to the needs of the disadvantaged, a portion of the potential talent of our nation will be lost.

Whether all of the members of a class or only one or two fit into the category of disadvantaged, the teacher of that class faces a number of challenges:

1. Possessing and exhibiting the proper attitude toward these children.
2. Compensating for their learning problems.
3. Selecting appropriate materials or preparing them if acceptable ones are not available.
4. Adjusting teaching techniques to coincide with learning styles.

These challenges are present no matter what the subject area. Possibly, the challenges are even more demanding in the social studies because the concepts developed are so dependent on the extent of previous experiences.

## OBJECTIVES

Social studies objectives for the disadvantaged are formulated with consideration for their learning problems and environmental factors. Broad general objectives include:

*Acquire knowledge of:*
*The history of minority groups and their contributions to the cultural heritage of the nation.*
*The children's immediate environment in order to enable them to understand its relationship to the larger world.*
*The democratic process and the importance of the individual assuming his or her responsibility.*

*Acquire an understanding of:*
*The contribution that each individual makes to the group in which he or she is a member.*
*The reasons prejudice occurs and its effect on society and the relationships of people.*
*The problems of poverty and prejudice that occur in other cultures of the world.*

*The relationship of what is learned in school to the child's everyday activities.*

*To develop an attitude of:*

*The worth of each individual as a member of society.*

*The value of learning and its potential to provide a better future for each child.*

*Develop skill in:*

*Communicating with others through oral and written methods.*

*Getting along with others in the immediate group and in society.*

*Acquiring information through critical reading, listening, and observing.*

These objectives vary according to the specific needs and background of the group. The emphasis here is placed on the necessity for experiences in social studies to compensate for the disadvantages the children bring with them to school. Obviously, most of the problems disadvantaged children face as they enter school are the result of cultural experiences in their early formative years. Nursery and "Headstart" programs are aimed at attempting to add to these experiences. However, the children still enter school disadvantaged in the previously outlined areas. Their future appears quite different to them from that of average children. They see little offered by the traditional school that applies to their life. Therefore, teachers must adapt their programs to meet the needs and interests of these children; but what adaptations are necessary?

Before planning educational programs, the teacher would be wise to investigate common conditions in the experiences of disadvantaged groups that have contributed to their early learning. These factors, however, are not to be used as excuses for lack of success with disadvantaged children; rather, they should increase the teacher's understanding of the experiences and expectations they bring with them.

Most of these children come from large families, which precipitate crowded living conditions, limited parental attention, and excessive inappropriate stimuli such as shouting, crying, and loud radio or TV playing. The children's parents often lack formal education and social know-how, are unemployed or are in low-paying, unskilled jobs, and move frequently; these same conditions are often perpetuated in their children. Discipline in the home is often of a physical nature—authoritative, inconsistent, and immediate—to alleviate a present situation as soon as possible. Patriarchal authority reigns in the home with the exception of the black family, which may be dominated by the mother.

Children are given responsibilities early—for example, the care of younger children or particular household chores. This tendency results in less concern for the self and more group orientation. Early independence gives way to peer domination, which replaces the family as a socializing agent and source of values.[4] Frequent illness and lack of proper food, health, and dental care decrease the learning efficiency of the children.

Equally and possibly more important, as Riessman points out, are some of the positives of the culture of the disadvantaged. Riessman feels that these include an interest in vocational education; parents' and children's respect for education in spite of their dislike for school, where they sense a resentment toward them; the children's slow cognitive style of learning; hidden verbal talent; freedom from self-blame and parental overprotection; lack of sibling rivalry; and informality, humor, and enjoyment of music, games, and sports.[5] These positives may provide a basis on which teachers can build a more adequate educational program.

Initially, experiences offered these children should be vital and motivational. They should build upon the children's present backgrounds. First, the children should be reintroduced to their immediate environment and helped to understand it. Then, their horizons should be expanded to a wider environment. Have the children ever been on a bus, gone to the supermarket, visited a museum, baked cookies, had someone really listen while they talked, or experienced approval upon completion of a task?

Bereiter and Engelmann claim that enriching experiences are not enough. They claim that the disadvantaged do not have enough time to participate in the same experiences as privileged children. Therefore, selection and exclusion of experiences is necessary to provide those activities which will produce a faster-than-normal rate of progress.[6] Their discussion primarily is aimed at the preschool program; however, it certainly should be considered when planning programs at any level.

Cultural deprivation is synonymous with language deprivation. It is apparent that the disadvantaged child has mastered a language "that is adequate for maintaining social relationships and for meeting his social and material needs, but he does not learn how to use language for obtaining and transmitting information, for monitoring his own behavior, and for carrying on verbal reasoning."[7] The disadvantaged child cannot use language "to explain, to describe, to instruct, to inquire, to hypothesize, to analyze, to compare, to deduce, and to test."[8] If such language deprivation has not been corrected by the time the child enters the formal school, it certainly should affect the approach used for teaching social studies.

Research indicates that the following factors should be considered in planning educational programs for the disadvantaged:

1. Children's interest and concern for the here and now.
2. Extensive concrete examples are necessary for their cognitive style of perception and learning.

# MULTICULTURAL EDUCATION

3. The children experience difficulty in classifying, relating, and integrating knowledge.
4. Learning is most successful when the process is self-involving and of an active nature.
5. The teacher should show an expectation of success.
6. Repetition of information is necessary through a variety of approaches.
7. There should be continuous feedback to the student on his progress.[9]

## Conditions of the Classroom

More than any other single factor, the importance of providing an interesting and stimulating classroom cannot be overemphasized. Children need to feel that the classroom is a place where they will learn and be respected as individuals, not rejected because they have had different experiences. Examples of some items that should be included in the environment are small animals such as rabbits, snakes, or birds, or a plant. Such items present the children with an opportunity to learn to care and be responsible for living things, which are often not a part of their world. Equally important is the experience of sharing the responsibility for the upkeep of the classroom. Pictures of people and places within the community should be used to help children to identify school with the outside world. Books, books, and more books are needed at varying levels of difficulty and should contain stories of experiences relating to and expanding upon the child's experiences. Vast amounts of concrete materials and visual aids are necessary.

## Role of the Teacher

The presence of teachers who can be trusted is crucial to the success of disadvantaged children in school. Teachers must understand and be sincerely interested in the children. They must be cognizant of the most effective teaching techniques for these children. Also, they must be willing to accept the children as they are and help them to learn as much as possible.

Teachers with middle-class backgrounds will need to learn about the cultures of the disadvantaged and about how to work cooperatively with the parents to achieve the best results. The teachers are an important link between the home and the school. They should never discredit the values, beliefs, and customs of the disadvantaged, yet they should offer the children an awareness of another way of life. Parents are interested in the practical value of schooling for their children, and they should be made to feel welcome and involved in school activities.

A tremendous responsibility is placed on the teacher, since motivation for learning is often lacking in the disadvantaged. Generally, such motivation can be created by a responsive teacher using carefully selected materials, methods, and topics.

## SELECTION OF CONTENT

As previously pointed out, there are certain factors inherent in the social studies that are not as problematic in other subject areas. Webster relates the following: "The content in social studies is of a highly verbal nature—more reading is required than in almost any other subject; topics are frequently removed from realities of life chronologically and spatially; and many of the values, attitudes, and behaviors advocated are contrary to those of the disadvantaged."[10] Also, the materials available portray experiences that are often remote from the lives of the disadvantaged. An awareness of these factors will permit teachers to compensate for them. Considering the learning experiences of the disadvantaged as well as the problems inherent in the social studies, what should be included in the content of the social studies program?

The goal of such a program is for the disadvantaged to learn the same basic concepts of social studies as any elementary school child; however, adaptation will be necessary to relate the content to their everyday lives. The following model serves as a basis for planning programs for the disadvantaged, whether they be urban or rural.

| IMMEDIATE ENVIRONMENT | REMOVED ENVIRONMENT |
|---|---|

*Kindergarten—Grade 1*

| | |
|---|---|
| Home, family, and school—Discussion centers on the type of family relationships that occur in the environment of the child. An example might be the presence of additional adults in the home, such as aunts, uncles, grandmothers, or the absence of a father. No attempt should be made to place emphasis on the typical mother-father-child relationship of the middle-class home. To develop the self-concept, stress | Select a culture that has a similar family relationship—for example, have Mexican-Americans study Mexican customs. |

| IMMEDIATE ENVIRONMENT | REMOVED ENVIRONMENT |
|---|---|
| \multicolumn{2}{c}{*Kindergarten—Grade 1*} |

| | |
|---|---|
| should be placed on individuals and their roles. | |
| Values of individual. | |
| Comparison of values in classroom. | |
| Local community—Stress available libraries, museums, parks, recreation areas, and community services. | |
| Important people—Discuss leaders in the community and nation but, most important, select leaders from the children's culture, such as Martin Luther King for black children. | |

*Grade 2*

| | |
|---|---|
| Democratic processes—Discuss the problems of minority groups, using those apparent within the classroom, for example, the failure to choose a favorite game or the presence of more girls than boys. | Group minority problems in national relationship. |
| National heritage—Stress contributions from their particular culture such as music, art, and so on. | Symbols such as flag, holidays, freedom. |
| Economic concepts—Work in the family, neighborhood, school. | Other areas of the nation with similar problems. |
| Study problems of lack of money, resources, unemployment. | |
| Environmental problems—Neighborhood playground, garbage, streams, air. | Worldwide pollution problems. |

*Grade 3*

| | |
|---|---|
| Historical—Choose a local memorial, monument, or early settlement of the area. | Early pioneers, Indians, people who came from lands specific to the group's ancestry. |
| Relationship of urban and rural areas—Children in rural areas | Cities or rural areas beyond local environment. |

| IMMEDIATE ENVIRONMENT | REMOVED ENVIRONMENT |
|---|---|
| *Grade 3* | |
| learn about their contributions to cities in terms of food, labor, and purchases; children in the city learn of their contributions to the country. | |
| Communication—Within the classroom, use methods beyond spoken language, for example, facial expressions, actions. | Systems including different languages relating to their cultural background. |
| Transportation—Stress modes used in their community and the problems presented. | Link to previous study of cities and their available modes of transportation. |
| *Grade 4* | |
| Geographic concepts of locale—Study climate, rainfall, and terrain. | Similar geographic conditions in other areas of the world. Contrasting geographic conditions existing in close proximity to the local environment and in other parts of the world. |
| Social, economic, and political problems of the community. How values affect decisions that are made. | National and world problems of a similar nature. |
| *Grade 5* | |
| Governmental processes—Begin with class organization, school, and community. | State and national government and relation to early development and birth of the nation. Contrasting governments. |
| Local racial or nationality problems. | Discuss the Civil War, Spanish-Cuban-American War, etc., to help the children understand the possible origins of the problems. |
| *Grade 6* | |
| Family background of children in classroom. | Nations of children's ancestors. |
| Neighboring community's ancestral background. | United Nations. |

IMMEDIATE ENVIRONMENT    REMOVED ENVIRONMENT

*Grade 6*

Community projects—Neighborhood improvement, visiting home for elderly, vocational opportunities.

This model does not provide an exhaustive list of the content to be included in the social studies, nor are the grade lines intended to be restrictive. The model attempts to show a pattern of relationships between the concerns of the immediate environment and the removed environment. This model stresses the necessity of beginning with the here and now and expanding to that which is distant and past.

## SPECIAL INSTRUCTIONAL CONSIDERATIONS

Adaptation of the content is important, but it is not sufficient to allow the disadvantaged learner to receive maximum benefit from the instruction. Other necessary considerations involve organizational patterns, teaching methods, activities, and materials.

### Organizational Patterns

The organization of the class affects subject areas other than the social studies, and it is an important consideration. Team teaching has been used successfully with disadvantaged children.[11] A faculty team comprised of a team leader, four teachers (each with a class), a college intern, and a team mother provides more individualized instruction, increased motivation for learning, different teaching styles, and flexibility in scheduling. Disadvantaged children need the opportunity provided by the team to identify with many adults. Discipline is maintained more readily and neophyte teachers are more effectively introduced to working with disadvantaged children in a team-teaching situation.

Organization based on nongraded continuous progress is beneficial because it removes the failure complex and emphasizes individualization of instruction. Children are grouped by ages; they begin working at their respective levels and move ahead as rapidly as possible. Interest grouping across class or grade lines, specifically in social studies, provides increased motivation because children are encouraged to select their own group based on their interest in a topic. Within-class grouping, organized according to specific skills or friendship groups, adds to both the interest and the flexibility of the program. Children can learn to work more effectively with others and more freely from group to group.

## Teaching Methods

This chapter previously stated that disadvantaged children have difficulty with abstract reasoning and need more concrete experiences to facilitate learning. Teachers must adapt teaching methods to avoid pursuing abstractions without providing concrete examples. However, it is important for teachers to move from the concrete to the abstract.

The teacher should use open-ended questioning to motivate thinking and to remove the block of the "one right answer" syndrome. Repetitive use of this method is necessary because first experiences may be discouraging. An example of the type of open-ended inquiry that should be used with the children to help them understand their problems is portrayed by the following dialogue.[12] There has been an argument between two children in the group. The teacher pursues the causes of the argument with the children:

T: What was the fight about?

P: About Tanya and him shooting each other.

T: Why do you suppose he pulled the chair out from under Tanya?

P: Because Tanya was hitting him.

T: Why was she hitting him?

P: Because he was bothering her. She was bothering me.

T: Why was she bothering you?

P: Because I didn't let her use my Footsie [a toy attached to the foot for jumping].

T: So what seems to be the trouble between the two of them? What was the problem?

P: That Michael....

T: What really was the problem?

P: He could of told on her.

T: Now stop and think about it. What really was the trouble? What do you think the real problem was?

P: That I didn't let her use my Footsie.

T: In other words, she wanted something that you had. So what really was the problem then? What do you think it was? Yes, he wouldn't share with her. Can you think of what might have been a different way to behave?

P: Everything would have been all right—if he hadn't pulled the chair from under her.

T: You think that if they had shared, everything would have been all right. Tanya and Michael, will you show us how it would have been if you had shared? Show us what would have happened if you would have shared.

[The children role play the sharing process.]

T: All right, what makes the difference here?

P: He shared with her so no fight would start.

T: Why do you suppose people behave the way they do? Who do you suppose....

P: Because they don't want to get in trouble.

T: Stop and think a moment, Tanya, why is it that people don't want to share? Or why is it that they behave the way they do?

P: Because they don't like the other people. Sometimes they are spoiled.

T: What do you mean by spoiled?

P: They always want their way.

T: Anyone else?

P: They aren't bothering other people. But Tanya asked Michael for a Footsie and then they ask someone else and they say no. Like if they ask someone else and they say yes, they are a nice guy.

P: Like if Tanya had a Footsie and Michael asked for it and Tanya wouldn't let him, so if Michael had a Footsie....

P: If Lanie and Robert had a Footsie and Lanie asked Robert could he use his Footsie and Robert went home and Lanie came back with his Footsie, Robert asked him and Lanie said no.

[The teacher switches to another incident that had occurred in the hall.]

T: Now something happened out in the hall while these children were out there—you tell us what happened.

P: There was a boy out in the hall and his name was Brian and he was looking at us while we were playing our play and then Jeffrey went over there and pushed him.

T: All right, why did Jeffrey push him?

P: Because he was nosey. Because he was waiting for somebody and Jeffrey didn't know it.

T: Why did he push him, Tanya?

P: Because he was going to tell everybody else.

P: He could have been meddling, picking at him and stuff.

T: You boys aren't thinking carefully enough. Why do you suppose—here we are out in the hall and Brian is not really a part of our group you see out there. He was just standing there; now, what did Jeff really do when he went over and pushed him?

P: Meddling. . . .

T: No, I think you are using a word you don't really know. What do you mean by meddling?

P: Picking on him.

T: He wasn't picking on him.

P: They don't know. They weren't even out there.

T: That doesn't make any difference. Don't you think they can tell just by thinking about it? Why do you suppose—now picture us out there in the hall. Here we are, the four of us, talking and standing over there in the corner and the boys here think, "he is listening to our conversation and what we are doing," and so Jeff goes over and pushes him. Why do you suppose he went over and pushed him? What was he saying to Brian by pushing him?

P: To get out of here.

T: Why do you suppose he wanted him to get out of here?

P: So he couldn't listen.

P: Now can I tell the rest? He was waiting for somebody. . . .

T: Wait a moment, before you tell us that. . . .

P: Jeffrey didn't know he was waiting there for somebody and then Jeffrey pushed him.

T: We still haven't really answered why he pushed him.

P: I know, I know. Because Jeffrey didn't know Brian was waiting for the lady and the girl.

T: This is very true. But don't you think there is some real reason behind it?

P: Brian might tell somebody or something.

T: Do you think that he was worried about Brian telling someone? What do you think was his real reason for pushing him?

P: He didn't want nobody to know about it.

T: All right. Here we were, a small group, and he didn't want him to get into the group, did he? Can you think of other times when people do this?

P: When they don't want nobody to listen in their conversation.

T: Is it only listening in their conversation? What are some other times when you don't want someone to get into some activity or something that you are doing?

P: Because they are disturbing you?

T: Do you think it was because they are disturbing you? What is another reason?

P: They are supposed to be in a classroom and they might be tardy. They might be tardy and we don't want them to get in trouble.

P: They would get a bad report on their report card.

T: All right, can you tell me what would have been a different way that he could have acted toward Brian? What could he have done?

P: He could have said, "Why are you waiting out in the hall when you should be in the room?"

T: All right, he could have said to him, "Why are you waiting out in the hall?" All right, what else could he have done?

P: I could have said, "What are you doing out there, Brian?" He could have said, "I am waiting for somebody." I could have said, "Ain't you going into the room?" and then he would say no, he was waiting for somebody there.

T: Think of another thing.

P: That is a good way to start a fight.

T: So what might have happened?

P: They might have had a fight in the hall and get a paddle from Mr. Gregory.

P: Jeffrey could have said, "You are going to be tardy."

T: All right, that is another thing he could have done.

P: I know another one. He was getting kind of cold as he was soaking wet.

T: That is true. Brian was wet. Now what would you say would have been the best way for him to behave?

P: Just go over there and ask him why he was waiting in the hall. And Brian could have told him and Jeffrey would have walked back and sat down and started listening to what you are saying.

T: That is right. So why do you suppose people behave the way they do?

P: Because they don't want other people to listen to their conversation and they don't want to start a fight.

P: And they don't want other people—they want other people to mind their own business.

The main difficulty for the children in this discussion was the ability to concentrate for any length of time and to stick to the line of questioning. However, they have sophisticated insight into their own and others' behavior. The repeated use of this same approach will lead to improved concentration on the part of the children, and they will be better able to follow the questioning. In this activity, the children were participating in inquiry; they identified a problem (group behavior problem), suggested hypotheses (other ways to behave to avoid the problem), tested out their ideas and arrived at some generalizations (they think most want people to mind their own business). By beginning the inquiry process with a problem that is a part of their daily experiences, the teacher is able to motivate more active participation on the part of the children in the class. Everyone has had the experience of an argument and can contribute to the discussion. This activity then leads to the presentation of a problem that is abstract or out of the immediate environment, such as a community problem: Why can't people agree on a location for the new school? or Why is there pollution in our city or local community?

It should be remembered that in addition to enabling children to acquire inquiry skills, this activity is contributing to the alleviation of aforementioned factors that define the disadvantaged. The children are improving verbal skills and their own self-images through successful participation, and are learning the social skills of give and take in a discussion.

It is important to relate the activities of school to the children's outside world. Therefore, current affairs and controversial issues must be a part of the instruction. Children soon realize that what they are learning aids them in solving their daily problems and provides an understanding of the problems of others. They soon realize that history is happening right now and that there is a relationship between the past and current events.

A variety of approaches to the same topic should be used. Only unlearned content should be repeated. Ausubel suggests that material should be thoroughly learned before new material is presented.[13] Disadvantaged children need more guidance from the teacher; however, eventually this guidance should lead to independent action. Both problem-solving and unit-teaching methods should be used.

## Activities

Role playing is regarded as a most effective technique to use with the disadvantaged.[14] It permits children to physically work out a situation, or to be active participants in an incident.

An increasing number of experiences should be provided for the use of oral language. Verbalization in discussions, role playing, reporting, and dramatizations are all vital methods to be used. Talking first in small groups will increase the child's confidence in meeting a larger group situation. By reading information and stories to the children, the teacher facilitates learning for the disadvantaged reader and increases listening skills. However, care should be exercised in making certain children understand the vocabulary and the concepts of what is being read. Concrete materials should be used to illustrate the reading.

It is important to get the children out into the community to become acquainted with the conditions and problems that exist. For example, the students could do a local traffic survey, inspect housing conditions, make a photo scrapbook of the community, interview local public officials and community members about community problems, or tackle some local clean-up problem or help some elderly members of the community. These types of activities have been successfully initiated in many school districts.[15]

Simulations, or simulation games, as they are frequently called, present a possible way for more active involvement in learning. A simulation, through its materials—whether films, tapes, graphic prints, or printed material—is intended to recreate a situation as close as possible to real life. The players take the roles of the individuals in the simulation. A problem with several alternatives (with no one *correct* alternative) is presented for the players to solve through the simulation. The more sophisticated games produced commercially, such as Ghetto and Sunshine (originally for high school, but can be adapted for the elementary school), are aimed at improving race relations; the City Game[16] gives children the chance to engage in planning to improve conditions in the city during the next twenty years.

A less sophisticated form of simulation is the role-playing situations developed by Shaftel and Shaftel,[17] which are problem stories for children to portray.[18] Teachers can produce their own simulation games inexpensively and thus build them around the problem areas that are most relevant to their particular classrooms.

Games and simulations are purported to be motivating and competitive and should help in the development of decision-making skills. However, further research is needed to prove this assertion. Research questions needing answers include: Are there lasting effects upon children's values? Does competitiveness developed in the game carry over into other daily activities? Can children handle the power they acquire in the game situation?

Situations for children to express their feelings and emotions must be provided. Honest appraisal of feelings such as hate, love, trust, distrust, and honesty should be included. These experiences help children understand themselves and others. Experiences in which each child meets with repeated success are vital to the disadvantaged. Praise and encouragement should be built-in factors of every experience.

## ROLE OF THE CHILD IN THE CLASSROOM

Teachers need to explain the role expected of the children in the learning situation. This explanation frequently has not been reinforced by the home environment. The children first must be motivated to learn. By showing they expect the children to be successful, teachers assist them in building good self-concepts. As the children gain confidence, they become less dependent on the teachers. As they become involved in learning activities, their interest increases. Hopefully, they will then understand their role as learners.

In the beginning, the environment should be more structured in order that the children may learn the advantages of organized behavior. Freedom of decisions and choices can be permitted as the children learn self-discipline.

## ETHNIC AND RACIAL MINORITY GROUPS

A prime objective of multicultural education is to correct ethnic and racial myths and stereotypes by providing students with accurate information on the histories, lives, and cultures of ethnic groups. Too often school curricula have omitted blacks, Puerto Ricans, American Indians, Cubans, Mexican Americans, and Asian Americans entirely, or depicted them in negative ways. Multicultural curricula can correct these distortions by explaining the contributions these minorities have made to American history and culture, and by presenting honest, comprehensive portrayals of their life experiences. This means including information about their status in American society in contemporary and historical perspective and their characteristics as functional cultural entities, as well as their contributions.[19]

How can this goal of multicultural education be accomplished? It won't be accomplished by developing a unit about an ethnic or racial minority and adding it to the current social studies curriculum. It will be accomplished when ethnic studies become an integral part of the curriculum. For example, when children in first grade study the family, they would study the customs and beliefs of various ethnic family groups with the goal of understanding how these customs and beliefs affect relationships within families as well as relationships within the broader society. Another example would be in studying a historical event; it would be viewed from several different ethnic perspectives. Separate studies of ethnic or racial groups tends to set those groups apart, giving a we-they perspective. As Banks relates, "Comparative approaches to ethnic studies are needed to help students to understand fully the complex role of ethnicity in American life and culture."[20]

H. Prentice Baptiste, Jr. and Mira Baptiste suggest that teachers begin with a subject-integrating concept. They use slavery as an example, indicating that it has typically been introduced with the Civil War and linked with Afro-Americans. They suggest that, "Historically, numerous groups of people at one time or another have been slaves or enslavers. Ancient history or modern times offer starting points for this concept. The multicultural process is reflected in an exploration of the slavery concept which involves the use of many groups of people as both slaves and enslavers. A more valid conception of the term can be realized when students are given the opportunity to study slavery from a comparative perspective, which uses the underlying economic structure, religious beliefs, cultural values, and geographic environments."[21]

Key factors in the success of integrating cultural diversity into the curriculum are the role of the teachers and the type of classroom atmospheres that they establish. Children need the opportunity to explore the diversities that exist among them and to share their unique experiences. They need to learn how to resolve conflicts that arise from these diversities. Teachers must be sensitive to these needs and provide appropriate learning activities. Examples of some activities that teachers have tried follow.

> Children divide into groups of six or eight and sit in a circle. They should remove all rings or bracelets. One student is blindfolded while another in the group comes forward to allow that student to explore his or her hands. They should note the texture, size, nails, fingers, and similar features. Then remove the blindfold and have the student go around the circle exploring the hands of those in the group until he or she identifies those explored. Repeat until all have had a chance to participate.
>
> Call the class back together and discuss the following questions:
> Were there obvious differences among the hands?
> Were you surprised when you found out whose hands they were?
> How did you feel about touching or being touched?
> How did others react when you touched them?

Why do we react in different ways (racial, cultural, social, familial, and sexual customs)?

Can the diversity of responses to touching result in misunderstanding between people?[22]

The teacher initiates a discussion about culture as follows:
1. What is culture? . . . Tradition?
2. Are people born knowing how to act in ways acceptable to their culture? Why or why not?
3. What do people learn from others in their culture?

Have students divide into groups of four to six. Using materials describing various cultures, list the traits that reflect these cultures such as languages, foods, clothes, customs, arts, ideas, the way people act. Have the students make lists of the cultural traits and their meanings within their groups. Record them on posters or the blackboard. Discuss the similarities and differences listed and the significance of various traits.[23]

The inquiry process can be used to explore stereotypes. As previously mentioned, the discrepant data technique is used whereby pictures or slides are shown to reinforce the stereotype such as Mexicans riding burros, wearing straw hats and serapes, and eating tacos. Students develop a generalization about Mexicans. Then discrepant data is introduced showing the modern cities, industrial plants, and Mexicans involved in a variety of occupations. This then broadens the students' concept of the Mexican culture and the generalization would then be restructured.

Have students develop a collage of Indians (or any other group). Examine the collages for possible stereotypes. Show pictures of contemporary Indians teaching, practicing law, or at work in other professions. Ask students if they would recognize Indians on TV, in the movies, or anywhere in society without buckskins and feathers. What does this tell us?

To help students understand conflict and to resolve it when it arises, first start with a discussion of conflicts they face within themselves. Should I buy a new bike or save my birthday money? Do I hit my sister when she bothers me or try to discuss the matter with her?

After children have identified some conflicts, talk about how they resolve them. How do they make their decisions?

Then discuss conflicts that arise on the playground or in the classroom. How can these be resolved?

Investigate conflicts that occur in the community or society. Try to determine what causes these conflicts. Is it cultural beliefs and customs? If people understand their differences, can they be resolved?

## PHYSICALLY AND MENTALLY HANDICAPPED GROUPS

Just as with any other group, when physically and mentally handicapped children are mainstreamed into the classroom, teachers must adapt instructional procedures and content so all children can participate.

A prerequisite to concern about instructional procedures and content is a sensitizing to the needs of the handicapped. These children may come to the classroom with very low self-esteem in addition to their handicaps. They may not have learned the necessary interpersonal skills to get along with their peers. Most of these children have been faced with negative and hostile attitudes toward them from people they have encountered.

In exploring differences and disabilities in each child in the classroom, understanding and appreciation can be achieved. To understand the handicap and its effect on the person is important. Children can relate the unobserved heart murmur as well as the observable confinement to a wheelchair and the effects of these handicaps on each child. Exploring the strengths of each child is equally important.

When children who are not handicapped have the opportunity to work and share with handicapped children, encounters outside the school setting then become more meaningful, eliminating the stereotypes previously learned. Handicapped children can benefit when participating in the mainstream of society by increasing their self-esteem and by making a contribution.

Children should learn about the contributions of the many famous handicapped people such as Thomas Edison, Franklin Roosevelt, Helen Keller, and others. Also, handicapped adults in the community can come into the classroom to discuss the problems they face in society and how they have coped with them.

Children can make posters for "Hire the Handicapped" week. This gives them an opportunity to relate the contributions that the handicapped make to society.

Adaptations in instructional strategies and content will vary depending upon the type of handicap. Children who are mentally handicapped will need instructional materials to match their level of ability. Different instructional approaches will be necessary to meet the learning styles for auditory, visual, and physical learners. Many opportunities for the children to meet with success will be needed. Teachers should capitalize on their strengths such as artistic or mathematical ability. Topics chosen for study should be of interest to the children. Children with visual and auditory handicaps will require more effective use of materials. Concrete experiences are a necessity for the visually handicapped. An opportunity to explore the faces of classmates to know them better and feel more comfortable with them is an example. A map with raised features increases their understanding of the concept of mountain or valley. When pictures are used, a more detailed description of them will be necessary.

Taping information for the auditorily impaired is a necessity. Classmates can do the taping. Children in the classroom can learn a few phrases in manual communication to help the children feel more comfortable. Another possibility is a project whereby a group of children or the class designs a new form of communication, such as picture drawing or knot tying.

Children working in pairs can draw on the strengths of each and compensate for a handicap, whatever it might be. Also, older children coming into the classroom can provide individual or small group assistance. Sometimes, children prefer help from older children rather than their peers.

## SEX STEREOTYPING

There have been practices within the schools which develop or reinforce sex stereotyping. For example, textbooks and materials have frequently depicted women in the home or as nurses, clerks, or secretaries. Men have been stereotyped as strong and nonemotional, working in leadership roles. Often, women who have made contributions in history have not been included in the text materials.

Many times children are assigned tasks that are sex stereotyped—the boys do jobs that require strength while the girls water the plants. In addition, games or physical education classes may be segregated so that girls and boys are not permitted to participate in the same type of games. Toys or play centers may segregate children when girls are encouraged to go to the doll and homemaking areas while boys investigate the math and science centers. Forming separate lines for leaving and entering the classroom reinforces segregation.

Additional sex stereotyping may occur in the school faculty and administration. Women may stay in the classroom and not take on the administrative role, while men may be pressured to be administrators.

Some positive steps that can be taken include the following.

1. Selecting textbooks and materials that depict males and females in traditional and nontraditional roles.
2. Providing career education that presents the full range of options available to males and females.
3. Studying the contributions of men and women equally, both in historical and contemporary times.
4. Providing role-playing situations where both sexes can explore all types of feelings and emotions.
5. Having children analyze advertising and TV programs for sex stereotyping.

## SUMMARY

The aim of multicultural education is to provide an environment where children of either sex and of any racial, economic, ethnic, or handicapped group can grow intellectually, develop good self-concepts, and participate in meaningful human relationships. Teachers will need to assess materials, teaching strategies, physical environments, and curriculum to determine that particular mix which will be needed by the children in each classroom.

## NOTES

1. Susan S. Stodolsky and Gerald Lesser, "Learning Patterns in the Disadvantaged," *Challenging the Myths: The Schools, the Blacks, and the Poor, Harvard Educational Review* No. 5 (1971), p. 43.
2. Ibid.
3. Staten W. Webster, ed., *The Disadvantaged Learner: Knowing, Understanding, Educating* (San Francisco: Chandler, 1966), p. 491.
4. A. Harry Passow, ed., *Education in Depressed Areas* (New York: Teachers College Publications, 1963), p. 113.
5. Frank Riessman, "The Culturally Deprived Child: A New View," *School Life* 45 (April 1963):57.
6. Carl Bereiter and Siegfried Engelmann, *Teaching Disadvantaged Children in the Preschool* (Englewood Cliffs, N.J.: Prentice-Hall, 1966), pp. 6–19.
7. Ibid., p. 42.
8. Ibid., p. 31.
9. Webster, *Disadvantaged Learner*, p. 477.
10. Ibid., p. 586.

11. Helen K. MacKintosh, Lillian Gore, and Gertrude Lewis, *Educating Children in the Middle Grades* (Washington, D.C.: Department of Health, Education, and Welfare, Office of Education, 1965), p. 39.
12. From Dorothy J. Skeel, *Children of the Street: Teaching in the Inner-City* (Santa Monica, Calif.: Goodyear, 1971), pp. 47–52.
13. Webster, *Disadvantaged Learner*, p. 593.
14. Fannie R. Shaftel and George Shaftel, *Role Playing for Social Values: Decision Making in the Social Studies* (Englewood Cliffs, N.J.: Prentice-Hall, 1967), p. 149.
15. W. A. Gill, "Innovative Social Studies in the Urban Elementary School," *School and Community* 58 (May 1972):6; L. Rich, "Instead of Molotov Cocktails," *American Education* 33 (June 1970):11–15.
16. Glenys G. Unruh, "Urban Relevance and the Social Studies Curriculum," *Social Education* 33 (October 1969):710.
17. Shaftel and Shaftel, *Role Playing for Social Values*.
18. Josie Crystal, "Role Playing in a Troubled Class," *Elementary School Journal* 69 (January 1969):169–179.
19. Geneva Gay, "Curriculum Design for Multicultural Education," in *Multicultural Education: Commitments, Issues, and Applications*, Carl A. Grant, ed. (Washington, D.C.: Association for Supervision and Curriculum Development, 1977), p. 97.
20. James A. Banks, "Ethnic Studies as a Process of Curriculum Reform," *Social Education* 40 (February 1976):77.
21. H. Prentice Baptiste, Jr. and Mira Baptiste, "Developing Multicultural Learning Activities," in *Multicultural Education*, pp. 110–111.
22. Michael G. Pasternak, *Helping Kids Learn Multicultural Concepts* (Nashville, Tenn.: Nashville Consortium Teacher Corps, 1977), pp. 21–22.
23. Grant, *Multicultural Education*, p. 123.

## SELECTED REFERENCES

Banks, James A., ed. *Teaching Ethnic Studies: Concepts and Strategies*. 43rd Yearbook. Washington, D.C.: National Council for the Social Studies, 1973.

Dunfee, Maxine, and Crump, Claudia. *Teaching for Social Values in Social Studies*, ASCD, 1974.

Giese, James. *Multicultural Education: A Functional Bibliography for Teachers*. Omaha: Teacher Corps, Center for Urban Education, The University of Nebraska, 1977.

Grambs, Jean Dresden, ed. *Teaching About Women in the Social Studies: Concepts, Methods, and Materials*. Bulletin 48. Washington, D.C.: National Council for the Social Studies, 1976.

Grant, Gloria, ed. *In Praise of Diversity: Multicultural Classroom Applications*. Omaha: Teacher Corps, Center for Urban Education, The University of Nebraska, 1977.

*Harvard Educational Review.* "Challenging the Myths: The Schools, the Blacks, and the Poor," No. 5, 1971.

Passow, A. Harry; Goldberg, Miriam; and Tannenbaum, Abraham J., eds. *Education of the Disadvantaged.* New York: Holt, Rinehart and Winston, 1967.

Skeel, Dorothy J. *Children of the Street: Teaching in the Inner-City.* Santa Monica, Calif.: Goodyear, 1971.

Wisniewski, Richard, ed. *Teaching About Life in the City.* 42nd Yearbook. Washington, D.C.: National Council for the Social Studies, 1972.

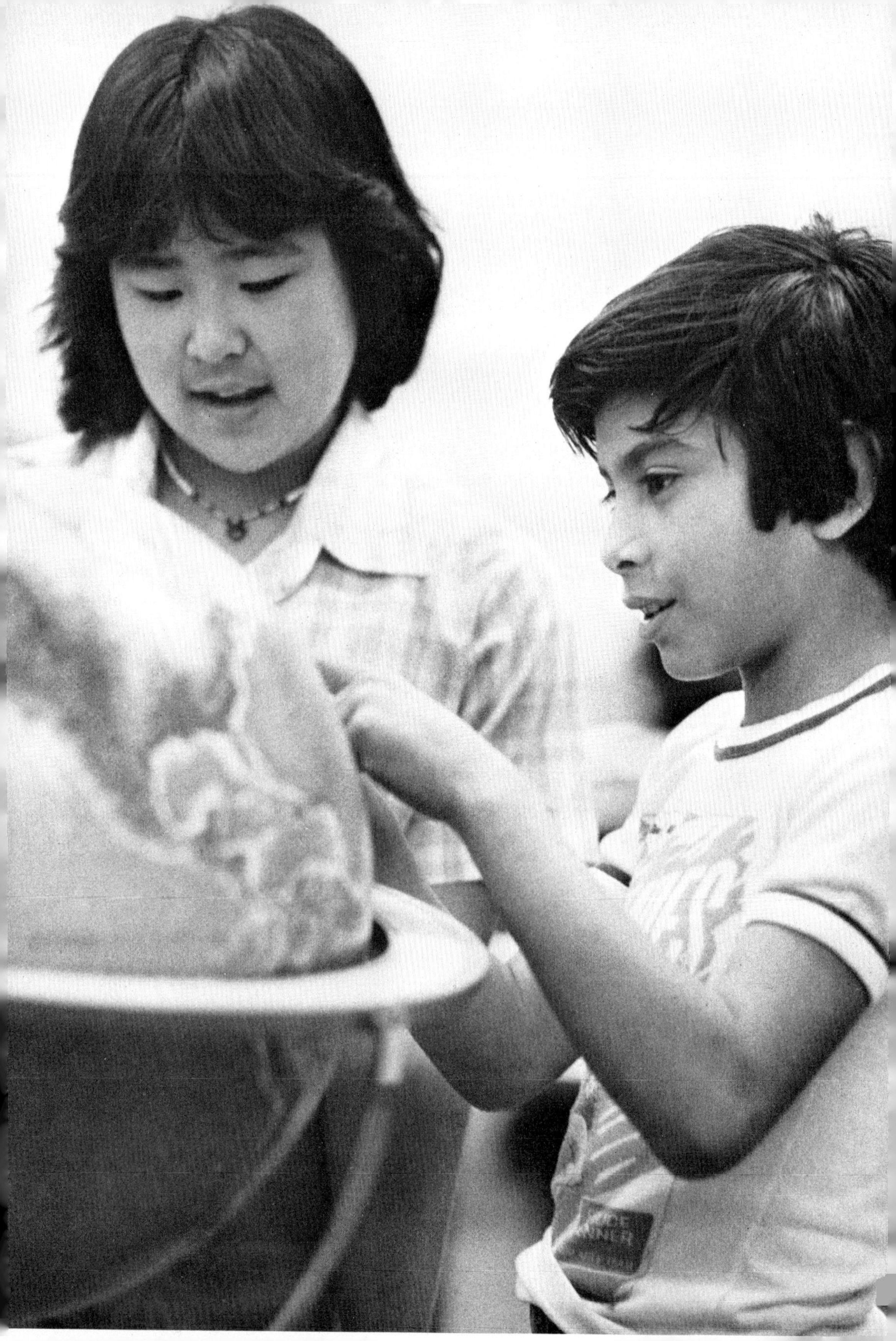

# Part Three
# Selected Content for Emphasis

The national and international problems facing our country today require that particular emphasis be placed upon current affairs and global issues in our elementary schools. If children are to be active participants—assuming the responsibility that citizenship affords them—they should begin early to be knowledgeable about the events that happen around them. Controversial issues should be presented with an open mind. All sides of an issue must be viewed, and children should be encouraged to take a position on the issues in question. Only through intelligent, critically thinking citizens will we find solutions to our domestic and world problems.

Our world has grown too small, as a result of our fast transportation systems, to allow us to be unfamiliar with the customs and cultures of people around the world. The close contacts today between all peoples require that children build an understanding of cultures different from their own and an appreciation of the similarities among all peoples. In their home or community environment, children are often exposed to unfavorable attitudes toward other cultures. Consequently, the school must assume the responsibility for fostering better relationships among people. Many problems must be faced from a global perspective.

This section discusses the rationale for teaching current affairs and global issues and presents activities that can be initiated for the development of these topics.

# 8
# Teaching Current Affairs—Social, Economic, Political, and Environmental

Numerous purposes can be listed for teaching elementary school children about the daily events that happen around them; however, none is so pressing as the need for helping children become knowledgeable citizens—interested and active participants in the affairs of their world. Perpetuation of our democratic way of living requires the attainment of this goal.

Another vital purpose involves the development of children's awareness concerning the social and political problems that exist in our country. The discrimination against racial and minority groups that causes serious difficulties within many cities and towns, the extreme poverty that deprives people of a decent living, the differences of opinion in our political parties concerning important issues, and the environmental concerns are only examples of the many problems that we face. The early attitudes that children develop about these problems and their ability to attempt to solve them are important outcomes of instruction in this area.

Our rapidly changing world affects each child's life. Failure to understand the reasons for and the effects of change is frustrating. Through the study of current affairs, the child becomes aware of and is more willing to accept the changes in the world. Because our nation is so often affected by events in other parts of the world, children must be aware of the complicated relationships that create these situations. Out of this understanding will come an awareness of the power wielded by their own and other nations.

Research and discussion of the events that happen in their daily lives permit children to relate school to the outside world. They realize that what they learn in school aids them in solving their own daily problems and provides them with an understanding of the problems of others. Children soon begin to see that history is also what is happening right now and that there is a relationship between past history and current events.

Through the study of current affairs, children will acquire the habit of reading newspapers, listening to news reports, and discussing these events with others. This habit should be retained throughout adult life. The children will find it difficult to understand completely many of the items they hear or read about, and it is important to discuss and clarify these items. The children can also increase their skills in critical reading, looking at all sides of an issue, evaluating the source of information, oral language (through reporting and discussion), vocabulary, recognizing propaganda techniques, recognizing important news events, and summarizing news reports.

Objectives for teaching current affairs are:

*To develop knowledgeable active citizens of the community, nation, and world.*

*To develop an awareness of the tremendous social, economic, political, and environmental problems of our nation.*

*To facilitate the understanding of the nature of change.*

*To appreciate the position of the United States as a power in the world community.*

*To enhance the relationship between school learning and events in the children's daily lives.*

*To increase proficiency in the language art skills of critical reading, thinking, evaluating, oral language, vocabulary, and summarizing.*

## WHEN TO START

As soon as children come to school, they should be introduced to the current events within their understanding. As an introduction, teachers can start with reports of events in the children's lives. The first concept to be learned is that events make news. The next step is to learn what news is important. Many teachers start the day with the development of a class newspaper containing items about the children's lives. After the children understand what a newspaper should contain, items are included from other rooms in the school, the community, the nation, and the world. An example of what such a newspaper might contain follows.

Today is October 24, 19___. The weather is warm and sunny.

Sharon Gray's house burned last night. It is located at 24 Locust Street.

Shadyside School will hold an Ice Cream Social. It will be Wednesday at 8:00 in the evening.

The Riverside Community Park will build a swimming pool. Boys and girls can learn to swim.

Learner Creek is polluted. Plans are being made to help clean it.

National elections will be held next month. Our parents will elect a President of the United States.

A variation of this activity might be for small groups of children to prepare their own newspaper or draw pictures of current events and discuss them with the class. Or, teachers can clip pictures from newspapers and magazines and discuss them with the children, who can then develop captions that demonstrate their understanding of the events in the pictures.

To provide children with a thorough understanding of important events occurring locally, nationally, or world-wide, the teacher should plan problem-solving situations or units of study. Examples of such events might be: a natural catastrophe such as flood, tornado, or hurricane; political campaigns; space events; wars and confrontations; and events that relate to past or current topics of study.

Continuation throughout the elementary school grades of these and other activities concerning current events will foster favorable attitudes toward and natural concern about the world affairs. The enthusiasm and interest displayed by the teacher are vital factors in the success of these activities.

## SUGGESTED ACTIVITIES

### Bulletin Boards

A bulletin board should be reserved for displaying news items or pictures relating to current affairs. An important point to remember is the necessity for the frequent change of its contents. Captions on the board such as "What's New?" "What in the World Is Going On?" or "News of Our World" stimulate interest.

Division of the board into areas for local, state, national, and international items helps children differentiate the news events. The use of a world map on the board enables children to locate the area of the news event and helps them develop map skills. A thread of yarn attached to the location of the event and leading to the written report helps the children associate the place with the event. Responsibility for the bulletin board can be assigned to committees of children or can be a dual obligation of the teacher and the children.

## News Reporting

A variety of organizational patterns can be used to assign children the responsibility of reporting the news. For example, one child might be assigned the responsibility for the news of one day or one week, or committees of children can be assigned the responsibility for a certain period of time. Tape recordings of these reports provides some variety.

The establishment of a mock radio or TV station within the classroom supplies greater reality for the news-reporting situation. Special broadcasts or programs can be planned when outstanding events take place. Some classrooms may wish to conduct a daily morning news broadcast with reporters assigned specific areas of the news. Intermediate-grade children may provide the news program for the entire school over the public address system. Included in these programs may be school news of interest to all.

Items for children to remember when reporting the news should include:

1. Do I understand what is happening in the news event?
2. Can I discuss it with the other children?
3. Do I know enough about it to answer most of the questions the children might ask?
4. Are there any words that I'll need help in pronouncing?
5. Is the event of interest to most of the children, or will it add knowledge to a topic we are studying?

## Class Newspaper

The organization of the class into a newspaper staff to publish and distribute a school newspaper provides realistic experience for news reporting. Reporters can be assigned to secure news of the different classes, the school office, and special events. Additional reporters can use outside sources to obtain significant local and national news. Many language skills, as well as social skills, are developed by interviewing people and writing news reports. A sample front page from a school newspaper is shown opposite.

The entire school can be organized to prepare the newspaper if an individual class doesn't want to take on the total responsibility. Generally, one of the intermediate grades handles the organization of the paper, and reporters are selected from the other classes.

A field trip to a local newspaper provides background information and increased interest in newspaper publication. If a field trip is not possible, a resource person from the newspaper could visit the classroom.

## Role Playing, Discussion, and Debates

Role playing can be used to advantage with news events. It requires that children have a thorough understanding of the event before they attempt to act out the situation for others. Dramatizing a summit meeting or the speech of a famous person helps children realize what the event was like.

Discussions can be organized in many ways. The total class might research a specific topic and attempt to present different points of view, or a news program might be watched on TV—either at school or at home—and discussed. When differences of opinion occur within the group, a debate provides a valuable experience. Both sides can present their views and the children in the class can decide which side presents the best argument. Before the debate takes place, ground rules must be established for time limits on speaking, the use of notes, and the manner of answering the opposition.

## Reading Newspapers

The presence of a daily newspaper in the classroom or library is excellent stimulation for developing the habit of reading newspapers. It is also advisable to secure several popular news magazines to complete the resources. Even primary-grade children can benefit from the pictures presented.

Mere reading of news material without learning to recognize biased presentations and propaganda techniques is useless. Providing children with news materials that relate differing points of view helps them to understand how the same news events can be reported quite differently, depending on the viewpoint of the reporter. Propaganda techniques such as the use of emotionalized words, vague, general statements, name calling, or the bandwagon, testimonial, or plain-folks treatments are examples that elementary school children can recognize.

# U.S.N. Strikes Again

| VOLUME NO. 2 | NASHVILLE TENNESSEE | MARCH 1979 |

**SPOTLIGHT ON MRS. MARTIN by Julie**

Mrs. Martin lived in Chattanooga when young. Her favorite dessert is chocolate pudding. She has friends but no brothers or sisters. She has loved green peas since she was 12. Her favorite school subject was reading.

## MOVIE REVIEW CORNER
By Lauren

THE SPY WHO LOVED ME

It was a movie that is very hard to describe, so it won't be so good. It was a good movie that some people should see. It was a movie that a lot of people love, like me. I loved the movie.

BEN

## SPORTS
By Reed

U.S.N. girls played Harding Academy girls. The score was 22 to 44. We won the game.

"Rah! Rah!"

## "Portraits" by Tina

MRS. MARTIN

SAY THIS VERY FAST!!!!!!

How much wood
   can a woodchuck chuck
      if a woodchuck
         could chuck wood.

By Claire

## Classroom Chatter
By Karen Doochin

Timmy has gone to Disney World for a week.

Leah lost her voice for a long time.

March birthdays:
   Scholle - 19th
   Scott   - 23rd
   Shelbie - 30th

We have a week off this month. This is where some of us might go:
   Shelbie - Panama City
   Karen   - White Bluff
   Scholle - Knoxville or Oregon
   Diane   - Washington DC
   Elwyn   - Miami

## What is this?

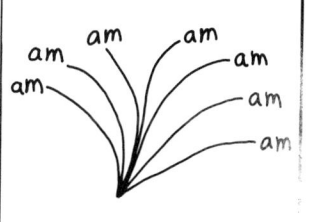

am  am  am
am       am
         am
         am

ANSWER: AN AMBUSH

---

(SOURCE: Supplied by Mrs. Susan Adler, student teacher, University School, Nashville, Tenn.)

Emotionalized words are those that stir very strong feelings within us whenever we hear them. "Loved ones," "mother," "home," "our rights," and "our duties" are examples of words used to blind us with emotion, and thus distract us from the main point of the discussion. An example of their use might be "Vote for Joe Doakes, he'll protect your home and loved ones." We are so concerned about our home and loved ones that we are willing to vote for Joe Doakes without first determining if he has the proper qualifications. Newspapers and magazines use emotionalized words to excite people about reading certain articles. We frequently see headlines such as "Mother Loses Home," "Rights Are Blocked," or "Children Beaten."

Children often use the bandwagon technique to secure permission for something they wish to do—it is the "everyone's-doing-it, why-can't-I," trick. It is the idea of following the crowd or jumping on the bandwagon to attain a goal.

The testimonial is frequently used in advertising. If a famous personality uses a product, then the product must be good for everyone. In politics, too, a candidate supported by a person who is well-known gains additional support from the public.

The plain-folks technique is used by politicians. They appear to dress, act, and think like the people from whom they are seeking votes. An example of this is the politician who visits the farm, milks the cows, pitches hay, or drives the tractor to convince the people that he is really one of them. Actually, he may never have done these things before.

Name calling is used by various individuals and groups to label someone favorably or unfavorably. Many people automatically stop listening to or reading about someone who has been labeled by a name that is unsavory to them. Names such as "communist," "liar," and "traitor" influence people against the individual so labeled. "Good guy," "patriot," and "democrat" are names that may influence a person favorably.

Vague, general statements about a topic confuse individuals. Failure to include any proof about a claim makes it difficult to determine its accuracy. "Many politicians are crooked" is an example of a vague, general statement.

Children should be able to identify and give examples of the different propaganda techniques, and they should relate this understanding to the material they encounter in newspapers and magazines and on television. Here are some sample statements:

1. *Plain folks.* Sam Arthur, a man of the people, one who came from humble beginnings, is the man for you.
2. *Name calling.* Joe Doakes is a communist and should not be permitted to run for office.

3. *Testimonial.* Mr. President endorses candidate John Smith for governor. You'll want to vote for him.
4. *Emotionalized words.* He is a protector of our rights.
5. *Bandwagon.* Millions of people use Granny's Glue and so should you.
6. *Vague, general statement.* Everyone agrees that new sidewalks are needed in Jonesville.

Examples of activities that provide children with the opportunity to recognize these propaganda techniques follow:

1. Bring a radio to class and listen to some popular newscaster as he or she makes statements such as those listed above.
2. Suggest that children listen to TV at home and bring to class examples of these statements.
3. As the children become more sophisticated, they can identify how people use voice inflections and facial expressions to convey the same messages.

## CONTROVERSIAL ISSUES: SOCIAL, ECONOMIC, POLITICAL, AND ENVIRONMENTAL

For a variety of reasons, many teachers step lightly when controversial issues arise in the news or in the classroom. Fear of losing jobs, prejudices, lack of knowledge of the issue, school policy, community feelings, or a lack of concern are all possible causes for a teacher's timidity in this area. Controversial issues—from racial problems to the population explosion—are found in almost every newspaper or newscast. How can they be avoided? Should they be avoided?

Certain controversial issues should be discussed in the elementary school, for children need the opportunity to study all sides of an issue and to make their own decisions. Teachers should use discretion when selecting issues for study. Several criteria should be applied:

1. Are the children mature enough to thoroughly understand the issue?
2. Do the children have sufficient background experiences to critically appraise the issue?
3. Will the study of the issue help attain the goals of the school and the community?

4. Is the issue of social, political, economic, or environmental significance?
5. Does the policy of the school permit the study of such an issue?
6. Will the children become better-informed, thoughtful citizens as a result of the study?

The manner in which a teacher approaches the study of controversial issues is of vital importance. Teachers who have a chip on their shoulders about an issue, or those who are prejudiced, opinionated, or possess an extreme point of view and teach only one side of an issue would be wise to ask someone to assist them with the study. Teachers who feel they cannot discuss an issue without showing their prejudice do the children a disservice in attempting the study. One of the main purposes in having children research issues is to develop in them the habit of approaching any issue with an open mind, securing the facts on all sides, and then making a decision when necessary. A prejudiced teacher who permits that prejudice to show defeats this purpose.

Most controversial issues can be so charged with emotion that it is difficult for the teacher to ask children to assess all sides of an issue unemotionally. A teacher may not always be successful in this task, but should encourage students to attempt to control their emotions and view issues objectively. Simple issues, such as resolving the fair treatment of others in the classroom, may be the starting point for understanding differences of opinion.

## Social Issues

The teacher must decide whether the social issue will require an extensive study or can be handled in several class discussions with individual and group research. This decision will depend upon the children's expressed interest in the issue and the issue's relation to the previously stated criteria for selection. The approach to a social issue requires objectivity on the part of the teacher and the supplying of materials that present all sides of the issue.

Suppose some type of confrontation among groups in the community took place in your town last night. Today, depending upon the person reporting the event, it is being given labels such as "racial," "vandalism," "a demonstration against injustice," or "an attempt to overthrow the law." The children arrive in school very excited about the event and eager to discuss it. What do you do? How do you approach it? Obviously, you can't ignore the issue because it is a part of the children's world. Rather than permit the children to tell what they have heard about the event, the teacher might suggest that they list a series of questions for which they will be required to secure answers.

1. How did the confrontation start?
2. Where did it start? or, Why did it start?
3. Is it known who was responsible for starting it?
4. How much damage was done? or, What were the outcomes?
5. Why did the confrontation begin?
6. Will it happen again?
7. What can be done to prevent it from happening again?

Answers to these questions should be found by listening to news reports (in school when possible) presented by many stations, reading papers, and talking to several people who were in the area, if this can be arranged. All children should record the answers they secure, give the source, and then compare them the next day in school. If it is determined that the event was caused by some deep-seated community problem, a thorough study of the issue should be undertaken by children in the intermediate grades, if school policy permits. Young children should pursue the topic to the depth of their understanding and ability to secure information. Children should interview citizens of the community, assess their feelings about the problem, find out what laws govern the problem, and determine whether the laws are being enforced. The teacher should provide the opportunity for children to discuss possible solutions to the problem. Children should learn that the true facts involved in this type of situation are often difficult to find. They should assess the validity of the information they secure. Other examples of social issues that could be researched and discussed are abortion, population control, capital punishment, drug abuse, and school busing.

**Economic Issues**

Most communities are faced with economic problems similar to those faced by the nation—welfare programs, high prices, unemployment, strikes, and so on. To study a local issue first may prove beneficial before attempting to understand a national problem because some of the children's families may be affected by the local problem. If this is true, care should be exercised to avoid embarrassment for these children.

Within any community, there is an area where people in lower socioeconomic levels are living. Depending on the community, conditions will vary, from run-down tenements along garbage-lined streets to neat, small dwellings. People here have few modern conveniences; many live on welfare or have low-paying jobs where they do not earn sufficient money to care for their families. Frequently, this means that children do not receive adequate medical and dental care, do not have clothes for school, and do not have recreation opportunities such as playgrounds, pools, or any type of camping or vacation experiences. Some communities provide these services for lower-income families while others do not. How should teachers approach this issue—or should they? It is extremely difficult for children to understand why these conditions should continue to exist, especially if they live within them, and equally as difficult to comprehend, if they live in affluent areas. Why do some people live in large, beautiful homes and are able to take care of all their own needs while others live in crowded, run-down areas and need welfare programs to care for their families?

Older children should tackle such an issue. Questions similar to the following should be pursued:

1. Are there sufficient jobs available in the community?
2. If not, why not?
3. Do the unemployed have the training or skills for the available jobs?
4. If not, why not?
5. Does the community provide the same services for the poor areas as for the affluent—garbage collection, playgrounds, pools, recreation programs, schools, vocational training?
6. Can volunteers provide medical and dental care?
7. Are there any solutions available? What are they?

Much of this information will have to be secured from public officials through interviews or letters as well as through public documents in the library and court house. Any follow-up action that can be taken should be done—such as writing letters to public officials discussing the findings or any solutions the children might have concluded. If it is a solution the children can accomplish, such as cleaning up a park or helping to paint houses, then these should be attempted.

**Political Issues**

During any preelection period there are political issues that should be pursued. For example: there are two candidates running for office and it appears from the newspapers and TV ads that one candidate is using smear tactics to try to win the election. The children should attempt to investigate the charges by either attending speeches made by the candidates and asking questions, or by inviting the candidates to the classroom. It may not be possible to determine whether the charges are true or false by these activities, but the children will better understand the candidates and their positions. If additional investigation is warranted, the children may interview residents in the community to learn their feelings about the candidates, or utilize any records—such as previous issues of the newspapers—which might contain information about the candidates' charges.

## Environmental Issues

In our nation, historically the people have not been concerned about preserving the environment or our natural resources. When the country was founded, it was believed that there were unlimited resources for humans to use in any way they wished. Trees and sod were destroyed to clear land for farming without any concern for their replacement or for what ecological imbalance this might create. Disposal of wastes was not a problem as long as one did not contaminate another person's water supply. As the population increased and the industrial revolution advanced, pollution became a critical problem; but unfortunately, the cultural habits of the people had been established. Those who have worked hard for an improved standard of living do not want to give up the goods and services they have earned, even though the increased production of these goods and services increases pollution. Also, historically we have believed that the people should make decisions about pollution control and protection of natural resources. Often, lawmakers do not pass strict control laws if these would cause financial burdens to certain interest groups; or, local voters won't support a bond issue for improved sanitation if it will increase their taxes. Another difficulty in fighting pollution is the importance that is placed upon technology. Many believe that technology can accomplish anything—including saving our environment, or producing synthetic resources when the natural resources are depleted. How can these cultural habits be changed? Obviously, it is crucial that young children develop an awareness of the gravity of the issue.

The issue is not only a national one, for humankind has advanced technologically to the extent that its activities affect the rest of the world. There are no local problems any more that can be left to local economic or political convenience. "We have now reached a point in human affairs at which the ecological requirements for sustaining the world community take precedence over ... the more transient value systems and vested interests of any local society."[1] But how does humankind solve these tremendous problems? What solutions does it seek? "The next fifty years may be the most crucial in all man's history.... The knowledge with which we might make the correct decisions is barely adequate—yet our gross ecological errors may reverberate for many generations."[2]

Environmental issues may appear to be more difficult to approach since they are global, but are they different from others in terms of the number of different views that are held, solutions advanced, and positions represented? Possibly they are different in that the individual does not really know how grave the situation has become. Will we be without air to breathe, water to drink, and food to eat? Are our energy sources in danger of depletion? Many danger signs point in this direction, and thus it is of utmost importance that children learn about the environmental issues if they are to survive.

How does the teacher present these issues? There are a number of approaches that might be used, but it is crucial that children be confronted with an actual situation, since reading about it or watching films will not bring about the same level of awareness.

One first-grade class filled their aquarium with water and threw litter into it. They observed what happened to the water and the debris in a very short time. You may want to place a fish in the water to demonstrate how difficult it is for it to get sufficient air when the water is polluted. With the cooperation of the custodian, you could permit each child in the class to throw one piece of paper on the floor each day and leave it there until the end of the week, so the children will realize how rapidly they can pollute their room with litter.

Another type of activity that is a confrontation situation is to shut off the drinking fountains for a day and not permit the children to have any water. This type of activity should be done only after a letter has been sent home informing the parents of the purpose of the activity. You may want to extend this activity to the elimination of lunch for a day to emphasize what it would be like to go without food. After the environmental issues have been brought to the awareness level of the children, it is important that they apply the problem-solving and decision-making skills to these issues.

The teacher may want to approach the issue from the viewpoint of one of the social science disciplines as was done in Chapter Two. Suppose the children start with the economist, since everyone claims that pollution control would cost too much, either in terms of money or jobs, if it were strictly enforced. There are numerous newspaper and magazine articles which express the views of the economist on pollution. Children can discover that the economist expresses the view that pollution can be reduced by producing fewer goods or a different variety of goods, by recycling more of what has been produced, or by changing the form of wastes or their manner of disposal. Here, the decision-making skills of the children can be increased. How do you decide which goods you would be willing to go without or have in limited amounts? Do you cut down production of goods and be faced with unemployment? Is this the best solution?

Changing the form of wastes or their disposal seems to be a more possible solution. The economist looks at the amount of money to be spent to control wastes and the amount of value that would be received as a result of it. For example, the disposal of solid wastes—garbage—is one that plagues every large city. Each person in the United States throws away eight pounds of garbage a day. What can be done with it? There are areas, such as outside of Chicago, where garbage is used in landfill projects to provide recreational areas. This landfill area has been constructed with alternating layers of clay and garbage to become a ski and toboggan slope. The economist determines whether the cost of hauling the garbage to the location will be less than the profits gained from the recreation area. The cost of this eventually will be paid by the people who use the recreation facilities. Also, property values around the area will increase once the landfill has been completed. The main problem is moving the garbage from areas of concentrated population, where there is limited use of landfill techniques, to areas where the garbage can be used. The economist will question—does it pay? In most cases, the answer would be yes.

However the teacher chooses to approach environmental issues, it is important that an awareness of the problems be accomplished with young children. Any vital social studies program must include the study of current affairs. If this study is omitted, the children are growing up outside the mainstream of society.

## NOTES

1. John McHale, "Global Ecology: Toward the Planetary Society," in *It's Not Too Late,* Fred Carvell and Max Tadlock, eds. (Beverly Hills, Calif.: Glencoe Press, 1971), p. 29.
2. Ibid., p. 39.

## SELECTED REFERENCES

Berryman, Charles. "One Hundred Ideas for Using the Newspaper in Courses in Social Studies and History." *Social Education* 37 (April 1973):318–320.

Chase, W. Linwood, and John, Martha Tuler. *A Guide for the Elementary Social Studies Teacher.* 2d ed. Boston: Allyn & Bacon, 1972.

"Controversial Issues: Can You Keep Them Down?" *Grade Teacher* (February 1969).

Crowder, William W. "Helping Elementary Children Understand Mass Persuasion Techniques." *Social Education* 31 (February 1967):119–121.

Gratz, Pauline. "The Environment and the Teacher." *Social Education* 35 (January 1971):58–62.

Howitt, Lillian C. *Enriching the Curriculum With Current Events.* New York: Teachers Practical Press, distributed by Atherton Press, 1964.

Jarolimek, John. *Social Studies in Elementary Education.* New York: Macmillan, 1977.

Long, Harold M., and King, Robert N. *Improving the Teaching of World Affairs: The Glen Falls Story.* Washington, D.C.: National Council for the Social Studies, 1964.

Meadows, Douella H., et al. *The Limits to Growth.* New York: Universe Books, 1972.

Michaelis, John U. *Social Studies for Children in a Democracy.* 5th ed. Englewood Cliffs, N.J.: Prentice-Hall, 1972.

Sheridan, Jack. "Thursday Is Current Events Day." *Social Education* 32 (May 1968):461.

Ward, Barbara, and Dubos, Rene. *Only One Earth.* New York: W. W. Norton, 1972.

# 9
# A Global Perspective

## RATIONALE FOR SPACESHIP EARTH

You are one of the nearly four billion passengers now on spaceship earth as it slowly makes its appointed rounds in space. Soon there will be more of us aboard this tiny craft. In a short time there will be four billion of us. Then five billion. Then six billion. And then—more?

We are going to have to learn to live together or perish together. Our choices are limited; our alternatives, few. It is international community or international chaos. It is international society—or international suicide. Or possibly one more alternative—the precarious position of competitive coexistence.[1]

Although the figures are well-known, they are worth repeating if for no other reason than to forestall the complacency that comes from too much familiarity with unpleasant facts. It required 1,600 years to double the world population of 250 million of the first century A.D. Today, the more than three billion on earth will double in thirty-five years' time, and the world's population will then be increasing at the rate of an additional one billion every eight years.[2]

Frightening claims, scare tactics, or cold facts, however one wishes to perceive them, they must be faced and they do have an impact on social studies instruction. As Jayne Millar Wood indicates:

> Teaching about the increasing interdependence of nations, global hunger and poverty, and the problems of development of more than three-fourths of the world's people is important if one wishes to prepare students for the world of tomorrow. Today's students must begin to develop an awareness of global community, for within another generation such an awareness may be essential for human survival.[3]

How do children perceive their world? Do they understand the meaning of spaceship earth, global society, and world community?

A study conducted in a midwestern state demonstrated that confusion still exists for sixth-grade students in their understanding of global dimensions. The curriculum guidelines for the state specified content that was intended to move children from an understanding of their own country toward the goal of understanding their position in a world setting.[4]

Evidence of confusion existed when students in the study were asked to identify their nationality. Forty percent indicated a correct response, thirty percent had confused responses, and many others had incorrect responses that related to race, religion, and ethnic group. When asked for the meaning of nationality the most popular response was "don't know," followed by incorrect responses referring to race and religion.

Further confusion was indicated when children were asked about their foreign experiences such as living in another country, or having friends in another country. Of those who indicated positive responses regarding their foreign experiences, less than half were able correctly to qualify their responses. Typical incorrect responses to "other countries" were East Chicago, Michigan, Ohio, Indianapolis, Pittsburgh, Evansville, and Vincennes. The confusion was mixed at times when some students indicated they had lived in other countries like Puerto Rico, Mexico, and East Chicago, or had visited other countries all the way from Indiana to California.[5]

Examining curriculum guides for elementary social studies might suggest that students have sufficient exposure to content aimed at preparing future citizens to meet the challenge of a lifetime of existence in a diverse multicultural nation and world. However, the above study, while certainly not completed on a national scale, does indicate a possibility that students experience difficulty with basic concepts in global understanding. As teachers attempt to teach global education to young children, they should not assume that merely covering the content will achieve the objectives outlined in this chapter. The atmosphere of the classroom, the materials selected, the mood of the community, and teachers' interest and preparation, all play major roles in determining the outcomes in global understanding for children.

## OBJECTIVES FOR A GLOBAL PERSPECTIVE

Global living will require a change in education for the young. That education must provide not only the understanding and skills to live effectively in a global society today, but also the ability to cope with the realities of the future and to appreciate those of the past.

How do teachers determine what children need to experience to become responsible citizens in an interdependent world? What skills are necessary to confront the perplexing problems of the human community? What should the objectives be?

A major objective is for children to develop the ability to perceive the world as an interdependent human community made up of cultures that have more similarities than differences. In addition, one must recognize that an individual's perception of the world is that person's own, shaped by his or her experiences, and is not necessarily a perception shaped by others.

A second objective is for children to realize that the interdependent human community faces problems of overpopulation of the planet, pollution of the air and water, food shortages, energy and resource depletion, health, education, conflict, poverty, deprivation of human rights, as well as coping with an urbanized and technologically advanced society.

A third objective for global living is to develop within children a willingness to recognize the inevitability and benefits of diversity among peoples and cultures and the constantly changing status of the world. This recognition of diversity and change requires a human being with knowledge about and appreciation for the world's cultures and an understanding of the causes and effects of change.

With this knowledge and appreciation the fourth objective, human relations skills, can develop. These skills enable the children to relate and interact with people from diverse groups within their culture and diverse cultures of the world.

A fifth objective for children is to develop the ability to apply skills of inquiry and analysis to information about the world, and to critically assess the information and review it from a global perspective.

A sixth and overarching objective of the children's education is to evolve a philosophy and value system that takes account of the realities of world living. Examination of values such as cooperation, justice, responsibility, standards of living, and peaceful resolution of conflict would be appropriate. The acquisition of decision-making skills which are then applied to that philosophy and value system is necessary.

The seventh and crucial objective is to help the children develop good self-concepts and the self-realization of their worth as individuals in the human community. When this has been accomplished, it is possible for them to relate more effectively to other members of that humanity.

Realistically, the above objectives are most difficult to achieve, but optimistically one must pursue them. In such an attempt one must continually assess the components of the school. What are the attitudes, skills, and abilities of the teachers? What are the attitudes, skills, and abilities of the children? What materials or resources are available in the school and community? What is the feeling of the community?

The approach should not be piecemeal, adding studies of world cultures as problems to the existing curriculum, but rather it should be a continuous development of a world perspective that permeates all aspects of the curriculum.

Children need to learn to function effectively in their own community, but learn also to view that community as just one of many within the world community.

Individuals who see global education as a threat to the continuation of a nationalistic identity will become concerned that children are developing an ambiguity about their own country in an attempt to understand other countries' cultures and their values. Therefore, it would be emphasized that a culture develops as a result of a number of different factors and that each way of life may be best for that group or culture, but may not necessarily be best for everyone. Thus one should avoid stating, "this is the way 'we' do it, but 'they' do it differently," but rather develop an attitude of "let's look at how each group does it."[6]

## CURRICULUM MATERIALS FOR GLOBAL EDUCATION

One of the perplexing problems in pursuing global education is the difficulty in finding curriculum materials that avoid a narrow view of the world and give children sufficient information for them to draw their own conclusions.

## SOCIAL STUDIES TEXTBOOK SERIES

The following textbook series provide a practical and realistic approach to the implementation of global education into the existing social studies curriculum. These series are structured and comprehensive programs.

The Taba Program in Social Science, published by Addison-Wesley (1972), consists of texts for grades one through seven. *People in Families* (grade one) provides an introduction to families of cultures around the world. *People in Neighborhoods* (grade two) does not follow the pattern found in grade one. It emphasizes only American neighborhoods, but does introduce families that have immigrated to these neighborhoods from other countries. *People in Communities* (grade three) once again introduces communities around the world to show how families relate to the more extensive social organization of which they are a part. *People in*

*States* (grade four) presents states in four foreign cultures and follows each with a series of activities to relate to the student's own state. *People in America* (grade five) examines the pluralistic nature of American society at different periods of history.[7]

Conceptually the series is well organized and develops the child's ability to arrive at generalizations based on the Taba model. Problem situations are introduced minimally, with an occasional interpersonal problem. Globalism is not introduced as a concept, but cultural pluralism and interdependence—important elements in a global perspective—are included.

Harcourt Brace Jovanovich's *Principles and Practices in the Teaching of the Social Sciences: Concepts and Values* (1975), has taken a conceptual-schemes approach to social studies. Five conceptual schemes are carried through six levels of texts: (1) people are the products of heredity and environment; (2) human behavior is shaped by the social environment; (3) geographic features of the earth affect human behavior; (4) economic behavior depends on utilization of resources; and (5) political organizations resolve conflict and make interaction among people easier. All five schemes readily lend themselves to global education.[8]

In the lower-level texts, these conceptual schemes cover topics such as human variability, rules, and interaction in families and peer groups. All are treated cross-culturally. The higher levels deal with topics such as mediation, peace keeping, and the relevance of conflict resolution and economic interdependence to our lives. The global emphasis is retained throughout the series and seems to be broadly conceptualized and developmental.

*Windows on Our World,* published by Houghton Mifflin (1976), structures elementary social studies content into understandings about individuals, groups, human beings, and planet Earth. The series' textbook titles reflect this structure: *Me, Things We Do, The World Around Us, Who Are We?, Planet Earth, The United States,* and *The Way People Live*. The series places emphasis on accepting and appreciating similarities and differences of people around the world.[9]

Science Research Associates' series, *Our Working World* (1971), has a system orientation. At level one, families are studied as systems, with goals and interrelated parts (family members). This approach is applied to neighborhoods, cities, regions, and the nation, as well as the world. The systems approach lends itself to problem solving by avoiding the study of problems in isolation. In this program, problems are studied in relation to other phenomena.[10]

Although *Our Working World* does not introduce the concept of globalism per se, it does treat a variety of cultures effectively. *Families, Cities,* and *Regions of the World* contain good examples.

## SUPPLEMENTARY MATERIALS

The district of Glen Falls, New York, has long been recognized as a leader in international education. Their latest proposal, *Project Survival,* outlines objectives for incorporating the study of international problems across all school subjects. Their objectives are similar to those outlined in this chapter.[11]

*Spaceship Earth* curricula have been developed in a number of school systems across the United States. The Joint School System, Cedar Rapids, Iowa, has a three-year program that focuses on the following: world-wide cultural diversity, the historical tracing of a previous environment, and the biological needs of man. The program tends to be multidisciplinary as opposed to interdisciplinary.[12]

John L. Goodlad and his associates (Macmillan, 1974) have proposed the development of mankind schools. Their proposal is a model for educating children for a mankind perspective. It entails school-wide alterations in attitudes, values, behavior, as well as in the curriculum. Their objectives are similar to those in this chapter. Their ultimate intent is to pervade all aspects of schooling with knowledge of and concern for unity of men. Therefore, unlike most of the materials listed in this chapter, the proposal goes beyond mere curriculum changes.[13]

*The Family of Man* (Selective Education Equipment, 1972) is discussed in Chapter Fourteen. These materials consist of a series of kits focusing on cultures in this country and in other parts of the world.[14]

*Teaching About Interdependence in a Peaceful World,* developed by Donald Morris for the United States Committee for UNICEF, is a series of units on the topics of Worldwide Health, Food, and Mail Service. They use simulation and role playing to help learners see how the world is becoming increasingly interdependent.[15]

Children's books are excellent sources for children of any age, and are especially helpful with young children. Generally, these books contain stories about children from other countries, and they describe their customs and cultures in terms that children can easily understand. It is important that the information in the book is accurate. Care in the selection of books should prevent the use of those that present only the differences between cultures and fail to show the similarities among all children, no matter where they live. Teachers can compare the folktales, fables, and myths of other lands with those of our own country.

There is an unlimited supply of children's books that can be used to introduce concepts, to increase understanding, and to improve attitudes about our global society.

The Asia Society, in *Asia: A Guide to Books for Children,* describes children's books on Asia in general and also on specific Asian countries.[16]

*Children's Books on Africa and Their Authors: An Annotated Bibliography,* is a helpful tool for use in locating English-language children's books that have Africa as their setting or subject.[17]

The U.S. Committee for UNICEF provides *Africa: An Annotated List of Printed Materials Suitable for Children,* which is a selective guide to more than 300 English-language items. UNICEF also produces similar annotated bibliography lists for Latin America and the Near East. All three of the above are updated by individual country and subject lists published in mimeographed form by the Information Center on Children's Cultures, U.S. Committee for UNICEF, 331 East 38th Street, New York, New York 10016.[18]

Simulations are other supplemental materials that are helpful in achieving the objectives for global education. *Bafa Bafa: A Cross Culture Simulation,* explores the meaning of culture and contact among cultures. It examines how prejudice and stereotyping occur.[19] *Guns or Butter* is a simulation that allows upper elementary students to explore the problems of world peace and prosperity.[20] *Humanus* allows a small or large group of students to work as survival cells making decisions on how to cope with world disaster.[21]

The objectives of a global education curriculum cannot be accomplished through the introduction of a set of materials. More important is the recognition by the teachers of the need for global education and the knowledge and skills necessary to implement such a program.

Teachers interested in implementing global education into the classroom need to acquire the following knowledge and skills:

1. Knowledge about the world's population, food supply, energy and resources, and developed and developing nations.
2. Knowledge about theories being advanced to solve problems from a world perspective (Buckminster Fuller, Harlan Cleveland, Henry Kissinger, and so on).
3. Skills necessary to introduce a problems approach to young children in a variety of ways (for example, inquiry and analysis, simulation, role playing, case studies).
4. Skills to introduce analysis of conflicting value systems.
5. Refinement of human relations skills that allow the teacher to work effectively with children from all racial and ethnic groups and help children develop these skills using such programs as *Magic Circle, Schools Without Failure, The Other Side of the Report Card,* and others.
6. Awareness of available materials, and resources for developing improved programs in this area of study.

7. Skills necessary to adapt available materials to meet global objectives.
8. Decision-making skills to decide what to teach and how to locate sources and materials.

## ATMOSPHERE OF THE CLASSROOM

The attitude of the teacher and the atmosphere that is established in the classroom are vital to the development of global education. A teacher who displays anything but complete acceptance of every child in the class regardless of race, religion, or national origin would most probably fail in an attempt to teach the children to accept those from other cultures.

A classroom where there is an attitude of mutual respect for and sensitivity toward the feelings of others provides the proper atmosphere for developing empathy with peoples of different cultures. Such an attitude does not just happen—activities must be planned to aid its growth. Children have a natural tendency to be concerned about themselves and their own problems, but they need to discover the pleasure that comes from assisting others. A classroom partner plan for helping one another with school work, committee assignments that continually change members after tasks are completed, and assisting in the school library, kitchen, or office are examples of activities within the school that help children develop the ability to empathize with others. Projects initiated in the community such as cleaning up a local lot for a playground, collecting toys or clothes for underprivileged children, singing or performing at a home for the elderly, and participating in fund-raising drives are identified as representative of the type of activity needed. It is doubtful that children will be able to develop empathy for people of another culture with whom they have no contact if they have little feeling for those with whom they associate daily.

## ACTIVITIES TO IMPLEMENT GLOBAL OBJECTIVES

1. Develop the ability to perceive the world as a human community made up of cultures that have more similarities than differences.
   a. Supplement texts with pictures that show people of other cultures expressing the same kinds of emotions as American children—for example, laughing, crying—and point out problems children in both cultures share. Stress how people are alike

even though they dress differently or live in different homes. (Many text series do not take a human community view and tend to stress the differences among peoples rather than similarities. More specifically, they exemplify cultures by extreme contrasts with American culture.)

   b. Divide the class into the major cultures of the world, to provide a microcosm. Research cultures so each group can understand and present the perspective of "their" culture. Stress how overpopulation, interdependence, urbanization, and technology affect the total world population. Children need to visualize that their nation makes up a small proportion of the world's population but uses a large portion of the world's resources. For example, the United States has six percent of the world's population but consumes thirty percent of the Earth's energy. The United States has approximately sixty percent of the Earth's wealth.[22] Dramatize the situation in a class of twenty-five by dividing the class up proportionately according to population and wealth. Set desks together to act as continents for Asia, Africa, North America, and Europe. Allow twenty-five pieces of candy to act as the entire wealth of the world. Place fifteen of the twenty-five students on the continent of Asia, five on the continent of Europe, three on the continent of Africa, and two on North America, to stand for world population distribution. Pass out the candy by giving fifteen pieces to the two people on North America, six pieces to the five people on Europe, three pieces to the fifteen people on Asia, and one piece to the three people on Africa. Ask students how they felt on their respective continents before the "wealth" was divided. After "wealth" is distributed ask students how they feel.

   c. Utilize the simulation *Spaceship Earth* as described in Torney and Morris (1972).[23]

2. Develop a willingness to recognize the inevitability of diversity among cultures and peoples, and the constantly changing status of the world.

   a. Demonstrate the concept of diversity in the classroom by discussing that because children have different parents, they each look different, but because they are all human beings they too have much in common.

   b. Treat geographic diversity and how it affects homes, clothing, food, and employment.

   c. Locate children's books that demonstrate how change occurs, such as *The Little House*[24] and discuss how change occurs within each family and community.

d. Develop case studies of individuals in different culture groups.
   e. Visit schools that are ethnically or culturally different from the children's and invite students for a return visit.
   f. Invite a foreign family into the classroom to demonstrate aspects of their culture.
   g. Trace the change of the local community through pictures and discussion with senior citizens.
3. Develop the ability to apply skills of inquiry and analysis to information about the world, and to critically assess the information and review it from a global perspective.
   a. Utilize newspapers, news magazines, television programs, and other news services to acquire information about the world.
   b. Introduce the idea that records about events may be recorded from different perspectives and should therefore be closely analyzed. Introduce descriptions of events written from different perspectives and analyze them. The article written about Japan may serve as an example.

*Jammed Tokyo's Crime Rate
Is Far Below New York's*

TOKYO—People in Tokyo rarely cross the street against a red light. They do not scrawl graffiti on subway walls. And they do not commit many murders either.

... That Japan's capital is the least crime-troubled of any big city in the world is itself not news. Tourist brochures regularly make this point: Even on dark, lonely streets in the dead of night, you need not be afraid of lurking shadows.

Consider a few of the "why's": The gun control and drug laws are severe, and they are enforced by an efficient police force. Public respect for law and authority is traditionally strong. Arrest is a deep disgrace both for oneself and for one's family. The level of education is high. Unemployment is low.

... "In Japan most people agree on what is right and what is wrong," said a young businessman who had just returned from the U.S. "In America different groups have different ideas about what is right and wrong."

... In brief, while cities in Europe and the U.S. have seen their crime rates double and more over the last ten years, crime in Tokyo has not increased. In the category of major crimes, the rate has actually dropped despite steady growth in population.

Are the Japanese less criminally inclined than other urbanized people, or are the Japanese police simply more effective in preventing crime?[25]

4. Develop human-relations skills to the extent that the individual can relate and interact with people from diverse groups within his or her culture and diverse cultures of the world.
   a. Participate in Magic Circle activities where children have the opportunity to express personal feelings and to listen to others express theirs.
   b. Establish a classroom atmosphere in which he or she demonstrates that each person is accepted. For example, if daily awards such as "Worker of the Day" are given, make sure that a record is kept of who receives the award so that in time all have the opportunity to participate in the honor.
   c. Role play interpersonal problem situations.
5. Evolve a philosophy and values system that faces the realities of world living. The acquisition of decision-making skills which are then applied to that philosophy and value system is necessary.
   a. Develop the idea that decisions of individuals often affect other nations of the world (for example, oil pricing, sugar pricing, coffee pricing, coal strike). Older children can participate in simulations such as Dangerous Parallel.
   b. Discuss how value systems develop. Have children establish an artificial value system for the classroom and abide by it.
   c. Role-play decision making of world problems (Panama Canal, nuclear power testing, Israeli-Arab Middle East conflict, South Africa apartheid policy).
   d. Pinpoint current events on a large world map with pictures and articles.
6. Develop good self-concepts and the self-realization of worth as individuals in the human community.
   a. Make each child aware of higher contributions to the classroom situation.
   b. Have young children draw outline maps of each other and fill in feelings and emotions.
   c. Make a list of all things that the children use that are from other countries to heighten their awareness of themselves as consumers and producers in a world community.

## PROBLEMS THAT MAY BE ENCOUNTERED

1. Teachers may not have been exposed to the concepts and knowledge necessary for implementation of global education.
2. Skepticism is exhibited about global education, indicating that its

inclusion in the curriculum is close to being unpatriotic. Almost any daily newspaper pinpoints a global problem, whether it's an oil spill that contaminates the oceans for all, food shortages caused by drought that unbalances the world market, or terrorism inflicted upon a group that did not necessarily trigger the hostility. What further documentation is needed?

## OTHER ACTIVITIES

To actively participate, whenever possible, with people of another culture is certainly more worthwhile than merely reading about them in a book or seeing a film. Activities that provide participation are:

    1. Pen pals—Children acquire names of those in other lands who wish to correspond with someone. These relationships may produce interesting sidelights, as illustrated in the following anecdote. While visiting Expo '70 in Osaka, Japan, a conversation was started with a young Japanese girl at one of the exhibits. Throughout the course of the conversation it was learned that Toyoko had been corresponding with a pen pal in Phoenix, Arizona, for the past seven years and that this pen pal had invited Toyoko to stay with her family for one year and attend the last year of college with her in the United States. It so happened that the college was located in a town in Pennsylvania only a few miles from where the author had recently finished his undergraduate work. Talk about a small world! Try this and see what experiences await your youngsters.

    2. Exchange programs—Classes exchange samples of artwork, scrapbooks, and other items with classes in another country. (Write: Art for World Friendship, Friendly Acres, Media, Pennsylvania.) Another illustration will attest to the effectiveness of this activity. While teaching in a sixth-grade classroom at Eleele School, on the island of Kauai in Hawaii, this author began such a program with a friend who was teaching in a fourth-grade rural school in Pennsylvania. The classes exchanged letters, pictures, and other odds and ends. Some excitement was created when the class in Hawaii elaborately decorated a coconut, signed all their names, dropped it in the mail, and surprised an unsuspecting Pennsylvania secretary who opened the mailbox to find the coconut staring her in the face! I'm sure the reaction it evoked from the class was just as stirring.

    3. Visitors—Visitors from another culture are invited to the school for discussions of their country, demonstration of their language, and display of any realia they may have. The contact with a resident of another culture makes the culture appear more realistic to the children.

4. Adopting children—There are several plans that permit financial assistance to children in countries where special help is needed. An example is the Christian Children's Fund, Box 511, Richmond, Virginia 23204. The agencies send a picture of the child with background information and permit the exchange of letters.

5. Ship adoption—Children become affiliated with one of the boats in the Merchant Marine for one year and exchange letters with sailors aboard ship, who write about the places they are visiting. They may even come to visit the class when they return to the area.[26] Information about the Adopt-A-Ship-Plan may be obtained through The Propellor Club of the United States, 17 Battery Place, New York, N.Y. 10004.

6. The study of other cultures was introduced in Chapter Six with the unit on Africa. This format may be applied to any culture.

## ACTIVITIES THAT FOCUS ON GLOBAL PROBLEMS

The cafeteria may provide the setting to demonstrate to children what it might be like to live in a part of the world where there is not enough for everyone to eat. The teachers and two-thirds of the class may go without lunch and watch the other one-third of the class eat their usual, plentiful meal. A follow-up discussion should indicate some significant results.

Further sensitivity to the problem of hunger and food distribution might be developed—particularly in the upper elementary grades—by planning and preparing meals that correspond to the diet of undernourished people, both in terms of the portion and the balance of basic food groups. An average, suburban child who sits down to a small portion of rice would gain more in empathy and sensitivity than he or she would lose in nutrition.

How do we help children understand their ethnocentric bias? One way is for children to see discrepancies between their own perception of a situation and that of others. Although there is little material available at the elementary level, teachers can get copies of history books printed in the United Kingdom, Canada, and other English-speaking areas of the world, and read to the class those portions that describe historical periods of interaction of these nations with the United States—for example, the Revolutionary War and the War of 1812. Such readings should be followed by accounts of how and why these historical accounts may differ significantly.

Another project would be to send for newspapers from English-speaking countries around the world and then compare the coverage given to the same topics in their local paper. Ethnocentrism can be observed not only in the way the "news" is dealt with, but also in the selection and relative space given to various news stories.

Another way to develop an awareness of ethnocentric bias is by an examination of the language used in describing our relations with other peoples and cultures—past and present. Why was it a "massacre" when the Indians killed white men, but a "battle" when Indians were slaughtered?

Also, a primary teacher could point out the left-to-right pattern we use in reading and writing and call attention to the variety of ways people in other cultures read and write—both with vertical patterns as well as right-to-left. An example of the development of an awareness of one child to his own ethnocentric view is illustrated by this hypothetical response to a lesson: "They write backwards, don't they? But I bet they think we write backwards."

A limited form of ethnocentrism can be exhibited by children with the blue eyes/brown eyes simulation activity. All the blue-eyed children in the classroom are told that they are "better" than the brown-eyed children and the way that they decide to do things that particular day is the "best" way. The teacher lets the blue-eyed group dictate the games to play, the way they are to proceed to the lunch room (blue-eyed children first, of course), and all other activities that the class participates in for that day. Afterwards, the experience should be discussed and roles exchanged on another day. It has been reported that those children who experience the position of being inferior first seem to exhibit a greater degree of empathy and do not display as much bias in their behavior as did the first group.[27]

## SUMMARY

How children view themselves and their world will determine the future of that world. To develop a global perspective, children, in addition to learning about who they are, must learn about the billions of people beyond the borders of their country and how everyone contributes to the human community.

## NOTES

1. Leonard Kenworthy, *The International Dimension of Education,* Association for Supervision and Curriculum Development, NEA (1970), p. 115.
2. Robert S. McNamara, "The Gap Between the Rich and Poor: A Widening Chasm," *Social Education* 38 (November/December 1974):631.

3. Jayne Millar Wood, "Adding a Global Outlook to Our Secondary Curriculum: Classroom Teaching Strategies," *Social Education* 38 (November/December 1974):664.
4. Ronald E. Sterling, *Determining the Attributes That Sixth Grade Children in Indiana Attach to the Concepts of Nationality and Religion.* Doctoral Dissertation, Indiana University, Bloomington, 1974.
5. Ibid.
6. Dorothy J. Skeel and Sally Oldham, "Curriculum Development in Global Education for the Elementary School" (Washington, D.C.: Longview Foundation for Education in World Affairs and International Understanding, Inc., 1976).
7. *The Taba Program in Social Science* (Menlo Park, Calif.: Addison-Wesley, 1972).
8. *Principles and Practices in the Teaching of the Social Sciences: Concepts and Values* (New York: Harcourt Brace Jovanovich, 1975).
9. *Windows on Our World* (Boston: Houghton Mifflin, 1976).
10. *Our Working World* (Chicago: Science Research Associates, 1971).
11. *Project Survival: International Education for the Seventies in Glen Falls* (Glen Falls, New York: Glen Falls City Schools, 1970).
12. D. N. Morris, "Developing Global Units for Elementary Schools," in D. C. King, ed., *International Education for Spaceship Earth* (New York: Foreign Policy Association, 1970).
13. John L. Goodlad, M. R. Klein, J. M. Novontney, et al., *Toward a Mankind School* (New York: Macmillan, 1974).
14. *The Family of Man,* Selective Education Equipment, 1972.
15. Donald Morris, *Teaching About Interdependence in a Peaceful World,* United States Committee for UNICEF.
16. Asia Society, *Asia: A Guide to Books for Children* (New York: Asia Society, 112 East 64th Street, New York, N.Y. 10021).
17. Nancy J. Schmidt, *Children's Books on Africa and Their Authors: An Annotated Bibliography* (New York: Africana, 1975).
18. U.S. Committee for UNICEF, *Africa: An Annotated List of Printed Materials Suitable for Children* (New York: UNICEF, 331 East 38th Street, New York, N.Y. 10016).
19. R. Gary Shirts, *Bafa Bafa: A Cross Culture Simulation* (La Jolla, Calif.: Simile II, 1977).
20. William Nesbitt, *Guns or Butter* (La Jolla, Calif.: Simile II, 1972).
21. Paul A. Twelker and Kent Layden, *Humanus* (La Jolla, Calif.: Simile II, 1973).
22. Isaac Asimov, *Earth, Our Crowded Spaceship* (New York: The John Day Co., 1974).
23. J. V. Torney and D. N. Morris, *Global Dimensions in U.S. Education: The Elementary School* (New York: Center for War/Peace Studies, 1977).
24. Virginia Lee Burton, *The Little House* (New York: Houghton Mifflin, 1942).
25. *New York Times,* 17 April 1974. © 1974 by The New York Times Company. Reprinted by permission.

26. Malcolm P. Douglas, "Ship Adoption May Be Your 'International Thing.'" *Social Education* 34 (January 1970):56.
27. These activities have been taken from Donald N. Morris and Edith W. King, "Bringing Spaceship Earth Into Elementary Classrooms," *Social Education* 32 (November 1968):676–677.

## SELECTED REFERENCES

*Global Perspectives: A Humanistic Influence on the Curriculum.* Center for Global Perspectives, New York, 1975.

Millar, J. C. *Focusing on Global Poverty and Development: A Resource Book for Educators.* Washington, D.C.: Overseas Development Council, 1974.

Nesbitt, W. A., ed. *Data on the Human Crisis: A Handbook for Inquiry.* New York: Center for International Programs. New York State Department of Education, 1972.

Palomares, Uvaldo, and Logan, Ben. *A Curriculum on Conflict Management: Practical Methods for Helping Children Explore Creative Alternatives in Dealing with Conflict.* Human Development Training Institute, San Diego, 1975.

Reischauer, E. O. *Toward the 21st Century: Education for a Changing World.* New York: Alfred A. Knopf, 1973.

Remy, R. C.; Nathan, J. A.; Becker, M. J.; and Torney, J. V. *International Learning and International Education in a Global Age.* Bulletin 47. Washington, D.C.: National Council for the Social Studies, 1975.

Ward, B., and Dubos, R. *Only One Earth: The Care and Maintenance of a Small Planet.* New York: W. W. Norton, 1972.

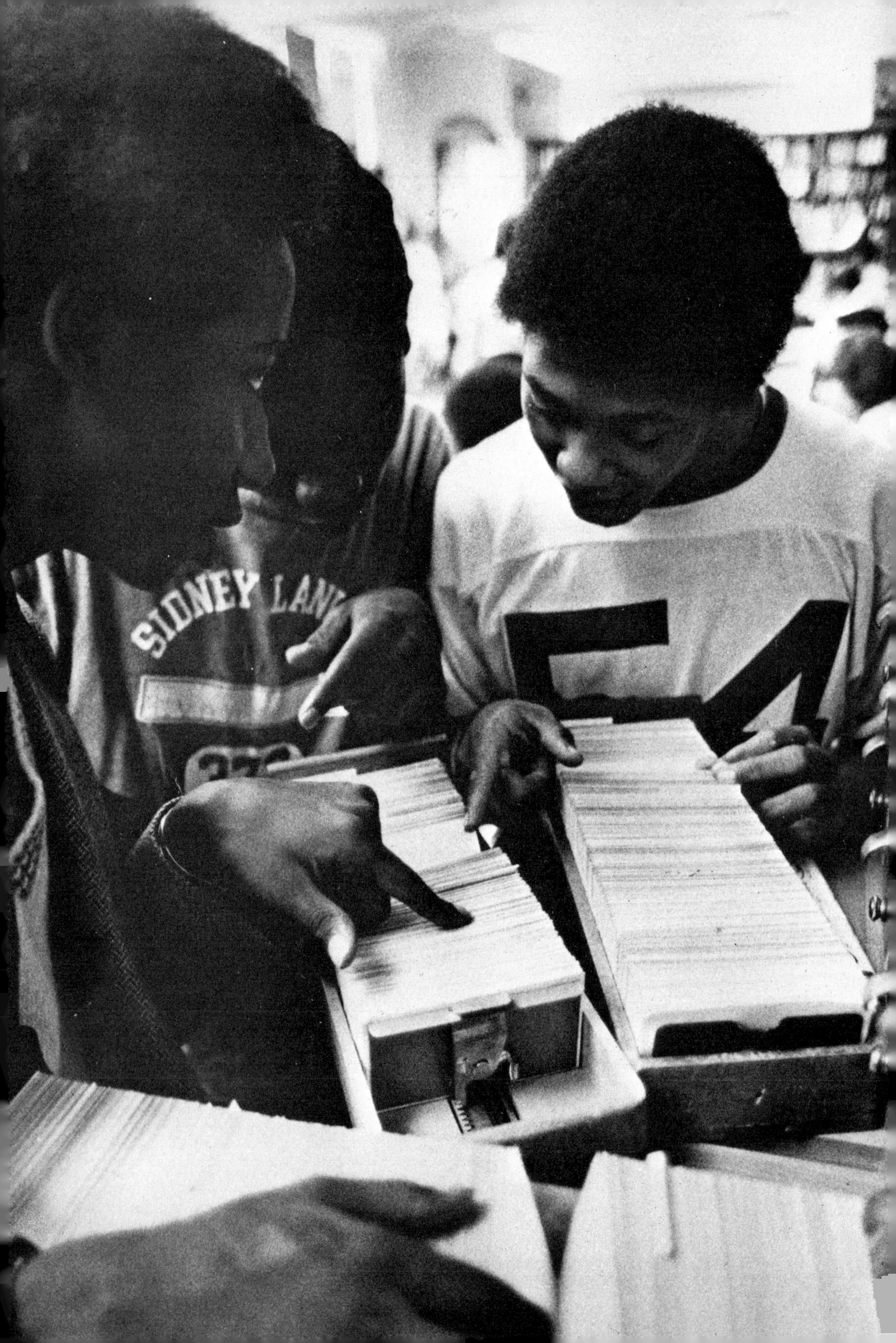
SIDNEY
54

# Part Four
# Skill Development

Opportunities for skill development in the social studies are numerous. In addition to the specific skills needed in the social studies, the subject provides a real purpose for use of the skills introduced in other curriculum areas such as language arts, science, mathematics, art, music, and physical education. The 33rd Yearbook of the National Council for the Social Studies analyzes skills of shared responsibility and those pertaining specifically to the social studies.

I. Skills that are a definite but shared responsibility of the social studies:
   1. locating information
   2. organizing information
   3. evaluating information
   4. acquiring information through reading
   5. acquiring information through listening and observing
   6. communicating orally and in writing
   7. interpreting pictures, charts, graphs, and tables
   8. working with others

II. Skills that are a major responsibility of the social studies:
   1. reading social studies materials
   2. applying problem-solving and critical-thinking skills to social issues
   3. interpreting maps and globes
   4. understanding time and chronology[1]

The Council suggests that development should be based on the following principles of learning and teaching.

1. The skill should be taught functionally, in the concept of a topic of study, rather than as a separate exercise.
2. The learner must understand the meaning and purpose of the skill, and have motivation for developing it.
3. The learner should be carefully supervised in his first attempts to apply the skill, so that he will form correct habits from the beginning.
4. The learner needs repeated opportunities to practice the skill, with immediate evaluation so that he knows where he has succeeded or failed in his performance.
5. The learner needs individual help, through diagnostic measures and follow-up exercises, since not all members of any group learn at exactly the same rate or retain equal amounts of what they have learned.
6. Skill instruction should be presented at increasing levels of difficulty, moving from the simple to the more complex; the resulting growth in skills should be cumulative as the learner moves through school, with each level of instruction building on and reinforcing what has been taught previously.
7. Students should be helped, at each stage, to generalize the skills by applying them in many and varied situations; in this way, maximum transfer of learning can be achieved.
8. The program of instruction should be sufficiently flexible to allow skills to be taught as they are needed by the learner; many skills should be developed concurrently.[2]

Part Four discusses (1) the skills of valuing, (2) interpersonal skills, (3) communication skills, and (4) map and globe skills.

Valuing is included in the skills section since it should be emphasized that the children are learning skills in evaluating and making judgments.

Interpersonal skills include working in committees as well as specialized activities such as "magic circle" and self-concept development.

Communication skills include reading, with emphasis on concern for individual differences, research, writing, and reporting. Since map and globe skills are of a particularly specialized nature and are frequently neglected by the teacher, they are given special emphasis.

## NOTES

1. Helen McCracken Carpenter, ed., *Skill Development in Social Studies,* 33rd Yearbook (Washington, D.C.: National Council for the Social Studies, 1963), pp. 310–311.
2. Ibid., pp. 311–312.

# 10
# The Skills of Valuing

**RATIONALE**

Value issues confront children daily as they attempt to make decisions about their lives. Should I take the money in Sylvia's desk? Will I be a friend to Herby who is black? All the other kids are going to boycott Mr. Jim's market because he won't hire Puerto Ricans: should I? My mother wants me to be a doctor and make lots of money; I want to drive a truck. What should I do? How do children make these decisions? What values do they possess? Where and how did they acquire their values? Does the family influence values more than does the peer group? Why don't people behave the way they say they should?

Possibly now, more than at any other time in our history, children observe tremendous conflicts in the values that people say they possess and what they actually exhibit by their behaviors. Equality of opportunity for all is a phrase often heard, but children witness discrimination against minority groups and women particularly for jobs and schooling. Children find to be untrue advertising claims on television suggesting the virtues of certain products. Parents warn children against breaking laws, but serve as poor examples by exceeding speed limits when they are late. Everyone talks about how important it is to protect the environment, but litter is everywhere and the local strip mining company attempts to leave without reforesting the area. Government is supposed to operate for all people, but some officials can be bribed to grant special favors. In light of these conflicts, what values should children possess? How does the school affect the children's value system? How should it?

Different subcultures and life styles in our society possess varied value beliefs. Children from these homes come to school with different value structures, as was witnessed by the description of the children in the first chapter. Often, the teacher does not possess the same values as those of the children. What set of values will be accepted? *Hopefully, no one particular set of values will be indoctrinated, but rather the teacher will aid the children in acquiring the skills that will help them evaluate and clarify the values they possess.*

Obviously, the teacher's behavior will demonstrate value beliefs as will the policy statements of the school. For example, if the teacher tells the children that each individual is unique and important, but disregards individual differences in planning learning experiences and expectations, children will question whether the teacher values the worth of the individual. If school policy requires that children form lines to move about the school, but teachers and the principal tell students that they are to develop self-control, children will quickly observe the discrepancy.

There are numerous approaches to values education or moral education. Moral education is defined by Purpel and Ryan as "direct and indirect intervention of the school which affects both moral behavior and the capacity to think about issues of right and wrong."[1] Three of these approaches will be discussed: cognitive-developmental, values clarification, and values analysis.

## Cognitive-Developmental Approach

The cognitive-developmental approach is most frequently identified with Lawrence Kohlberg. Research findings by Kohlberg suggest that children achieve the ability to make value judgments dependent upon the stage of development in moral concepts they have reached. He indicates that there are six stages through which a child must go step by step. These are as follows:

Level I—Premoral
- Stage 1. Obedience and punishment orientation.
- Stage 2. Instrumentally satisfying the self's needs and occasionally others'.

Level II—Conventional Role Conformity
- Stage 3. Good-boy orientation.
- Stage 4. Authority and social-order maintaining orientation.

Level III—Self-Accepted Moral Principles
- Stage 5. Recognition of an arbitrary element or starting point in rules or expectations for the sake of agreement.
- Stage 6. Orientation to conscience as a direct agent and to mutual respect and trust.[2]

This developmental view strengthens the position of the school to stimulate the individual child's moral judgment and character rather than teaching fixed values.[3] "... The sign of the child's moral maturity is ability to make moral judgments and formulate moral principles of his own, rather than his ability to conform to moral judgments of the adults around him."[4] Therefore, it is the responsibility of the school to provide opportunities for the child to assess real and challenging conflict situations. These should be situations that do not have the obvious adult answer at hand to discourage the child's own moral thought.[5]

If the developmental stages of Kohlberg are to be followed, it is suggested that the teacher first determine the stage that the children have reached before deciding on the types of instructional materials to use.[6] Research indicates that posing value judgments that are one level above the children's present stage of development proves most effective.[7] Kohlberg uses examples of moral dilemmas to determine the levels of development. These can be used as instructional materials in addition to those developed by the teacher. An example of one of them follows:

> In Europe a woman was near death from cancer. One drug might save her, a form of radium that a druggist in the same town had recently discovered. The druggist was charging $2,000, ten times what the drug cost him to make. The sick woman's husband, Heinz, went to everyone he knew to borrow the money, but he could only get together about half of what it cost. He told the druggist that his wife was dying and asked him to sell it cheaper or let him pay later. But the druggist said, "No." The husband got desperate and broke into the man's store to steal the drug for his wife. Should the husband have done that? Why?[8]

What effect does the classroom peer group have upon the child's value structure? Kohlberg found that children with extensive peer-group participation advance more quickly through the stages of moral judgment than those who are isolated from participation.[9] Once again, it is obvious that active participation with value issues in the classroom with peers will foster the development of the valuing process.

Criticism of Kohlberg's approach says that he ignores other forms of morality and that he fails to recognize the "affective side of morality, of moral emotions such as 'guilt,' 'concern for others,' 'remorse,' and so on."[10]

## Values-Clarification Approach

A second approach to the classroom process of valuing is advanced by Raths, Harmin, and Simon, who suggest that teaching strategies should help children clarify their values. The process of valuing as posed by them is based on the following criteria:

1. Choosing from alternatives.
2. Choosing after careful consideration of the consequences of each alternative.
3. Choosing freely.

4. Prizing, being glad of one's choice.
5. Prizing, being willing to publicly affirm one's choice.
6. Acting upon one's choice, incorporating choices into behavior.
7. Acting upon one's choice repeatedly, over time.[11]

This approach, labeled values clarification, "... is based on the premise that none of us has the 'right' set of values to pass on to other people's children."[12]

As an example, headlines from the newspaper are given to children and they are asked to rank them in order of importance to them.

Consumer Suit Bill Passes, Faces Veto

Explosion Unleashes Pesticide Gas Cloud

Nuclear Industry Must Face Problems

Liquor by Drink Wins in Close Vote

Afterwards, children are requested to write and then discuss the reasons behind their rankings. This gives children the opportunity to think about what things are important to them and why.

Newspaper articles also provide excellent situations for values clarification. The article on page 202 is used with the strategy as presented in Figure 10.1.

The news article may present only one side of the issue, and it will be necessary to search out factual information and possibly opinions from other sources. Children should not be forced to make their own value decisions until they are ready. It should be pointed out that with the addition of new information, new experiences, or hearing other opinions, their original decisions may change.

Another source for ranking values is the Values Survey developed by Rokeach. There are two lists, each containing eighteen items—instrumental (preferred modes of behavior) and terminal (end states of existence). The individual is requested to rank these values in order of importance to him- or herself in guiding his or her daily life. Fifth- and sixth-grade children should be able to rank these and discuss why they are so ranked. Of equal importance is the teacher's ranking. Such ranking may indicate wide discrepancy between the teacher's and the children's value beliefs.

Sidney Simon[13] suggests the following activity to help children find out what they really want. He suggests that the teacher provide Western Union telegram blanks or have children write on paper headed "Telegram." Ask each child to think of someone in their own lives to whom they would send a telegram that begins with the words *I urge you to*. These

## 'Deplorable conditions' cited
# Migrants satisfied, state senator says

**Special to The Courier-Journal**

BEDFORD, Ind. — Migrant farm workers who come to Indiana each fall to harvest tomatoes live like animals because they want it that way in the opinion of state Sen. Earl Wilson of Bedford.

Wilson, chairman of the Indiana Legislative Council's Migrant Workers Interim Study Committee, and two other members of his committee, Rep. Wilma J. Fay, R-Indianapolis, and Rep. Glen R. Harden, D-Columbus, visited four migrant workers' camps early this month in Henry and Delaware counties.

Wilson said he came away with the feeling that conditions cannot be greatly improved for migrant workers, because they do not want them to. Efforts in the past to improve conditions have largely met with failure, he said.

What is needed, the senator said, is legislation to provide some standardized regulations, with inspections of the camps, preferably by local health authorities, to ascertain that the minimum standards are maintained.

"We have to be careful," he said, "not to impose more severe restrictions on Indiana farmers and packers than exist in other states, because that would put Hoosier farmers at a disadvantage competitively with farmers in other states."

"We probably need some federal legislation with which all employers of migrant workers would have to comply," he said.

Wilson said his committee found generally unsanitary conditions in the camps, and some conditions that could be classed as deplorable. "But generally speaking, the deplorable conditions were much of the workers' own doings," he said. "You can't make a silk purse of a sow's ear," he declared.

"They complained of cesspools stinking," he said, "but in some quarters the toilets had been used a dozen or more times without being flushed. I flushed them to see if they were working properly, and they were.

"We found screens deliberately torn from the windows. Maybe that was so there could be fast exit out windows if the wrong person came in the door. Management people said they could repair the screens, but the workers would promptly tear them out again.

"Garbage pails were outside some living units everywhere we went, but in some cases the cans were empty and garbage was strewn all over the floor inside. In a matter of five minutes, 75 per cent improvement could be brought about in this situation," the state senator said.

Wilson said it is his recommendation that there be daily inspection of the migrant worker camps, with supervision, to see that the recommendations and regulations are carried out. This, he said, should be done by the employer and local or state health authorities—preferably by local health boards if possible.

Wilson said many of the workers with whom he talked said they were perfectly satisfied and that conditions in Indiana were better than in some other states.

Despite the bad conditions under which the migrants live, Wilson said there didn't seem to be any illness to speak of.

Wilson said that one of the better camps which his committee visited was at Sulphur Springs in Henry County. There a new mobile home village was created two years ago for the migrant workers. The project cost $250,000, he said, but the first year the migrant workers did $36,000 damage.

The migrant workers committee will meet again Nov. 4 at the Indianapolis State House and expects to come up with recommendations for stop-gap legislation for 1972. Wilson said the committee will work toward a more comprehensive bill for introduction in the 1973 legislature.

(SOURCE: *The Courier-Journal* (Louisville), October 27, 1971.)

# THE SKILLS OF VALUING

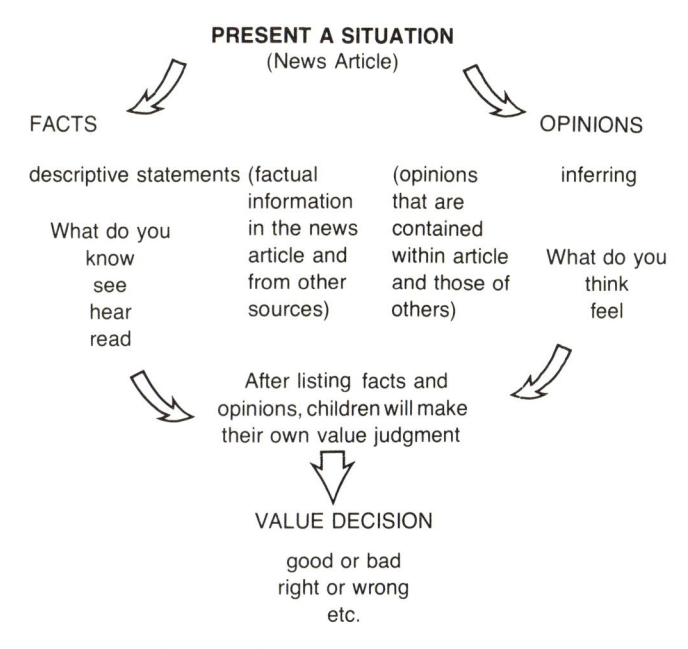

**PRESENT A SITUATION**
(News Article)

**FACTS** — descriptive statements (factual information in the news article and from other sources)

What do you
know
see
hear
read

**OPINIONS** — (opinions that are contained within article and those of others) inferring

What do you
think
feel

After listing facts and opinions, children will make their own value judgment

**VALUE DECISION**

good or bad
right or wrong
etc.

**Figure 10.1** Situation for Valuing

telegrams are used several times a year and are kept by the children so that they may refer back to them and write "I learned statements" from the messages carried by the telegrams.

The critics of values clarification indicate one of the major criticisms is the superficiality. As Stewart claims, "it deals primarily with the content of values and somewhat with the process of valuing, but ignores the most important aspect of the issue—namely, the structure of values and valuing, especially structural development. To oversimplify a very complex subject, the content of values/moral judgments is the 'what' that is expressed by the person, the answer to a question or a dilemma; whereas the structure is the underlying cognitive logic on which the content is based, or the 'why' that generated the answer."[14] In other words, individuals may be expressing what they believe, but may not be requested to think about and explain the why of their beliefs. Also, individuals may not know how to use their beliefs to guide their decision making and behavior.

## Values Analysis Approach

Another approach is that of values analysis, whereby individuals discuss or list the alternative forms of action that are possible to resolve the value conflict. Then, the consequences of each of those actions are discussed or

**PRESENT A PROBLEM OR DILEMMA**
(Unfinished Story)

What are the possible alternative solutions to the problem?

What are the consequences of each of the alternative solutions?

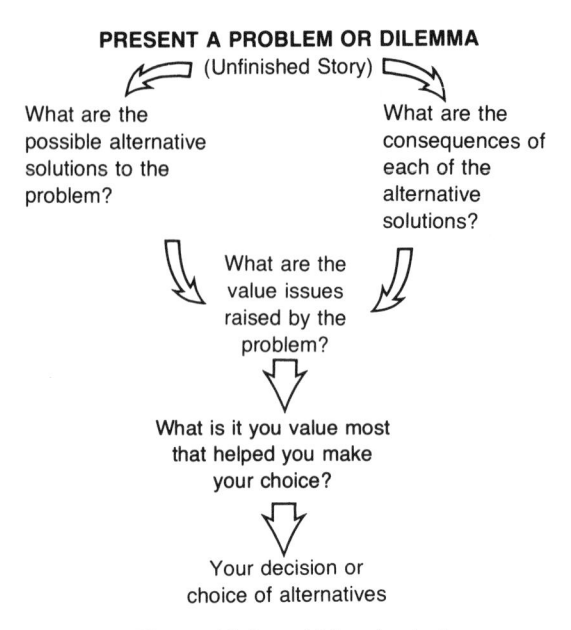

What are the value issues raised by the problem?

What is it you value most that helped you make your choice?

Your decision or choice of alternatives

**Figure 10.2** Value Analysis

pursued in an attempt to realize how the action will affect all those concerned. The value issues that are raised by the conflict are listed and discussed. Individuals must decide which of the value issues are most important to them and why they are important. A choice of the action to be taken should be based on what is most important to you or what you value most. Figure 10.2 outlines the process of value analysis.

The above strategy can be implemented in a variety of ways. The problem can be presented to the children for discussion of the alternatives and consequences, or children can be requested to list their own alternatives and consequences to be discussed later with the class. Children should not be forced to express their solutions and value choices if they show any hesitation. The teacher should indicate that it is a free choice. The following is a sample problem presented to younger children and the classroom dialogue that it initiated.

## What Should David Do?

David had the reputation for being the "character" of the class. He enjoyed his success of being the "unpopular star" of the class. It was the only time he received any attention. If something happened, David was the first to be accused. One morning Susan discovered that her week's lunch tickets were missing. David was the first person to be mentioned as the culprit. However, David did not take the lunch tickets and he knew Sammy had done it.

# THE SKILLS OF VALUING

Sammy had told him that morning that his mother did not have any money for his lunches that week. What should David do?

**TEACHER:** What are some ways in which David might solve the problem?

**SARAH:** He could pretend he doesn't know anything about it.

**JIM:** Tell the teacher what happened.

**TEACHER:** What about Sammy?

**JIM:** Let the teacher talk to Sammy.

**KARA:** Go to Sammy and ask him what he's going to do.

**NANCY:** Yes, and tell him that otherwise David will take the blame.

**JUAN:** That won't work. Sammy probably wouldn't care if David took the blame.

**NANCY:** No, I think Sammy would feel bad about that.

**BOB:** David should tell everyone that he isn't guilty, but that Sammy is.

**SARAH:** No, he should give Sammy a chance to confess.

**BILL:** If David tells everyone, it will hurt Sammy. Maybe it is the first time he has taken anything. Maybe he was hungry.

**BOB:** You can't take things just because you are hungry.

**SARAH:** Have you ever been hungry and not had any money?

**NANCY:** It isn't that Sammy was right in what he did, but how do we work things out so that neither David nor Sammy will be hurt any more than necessary?

**TEACHER:** Do you have any more ideas about what David might do? No? Then let's look at the consequences of each possible solution.

| *ALTERNATIVE* | *CONSEQUENCES* |
|---|---|
| Ignore the situation. | David will be blamed for taking the tickets. |
| | The kids won't trust David. |
| | Sammy would get away with it. |
| Tell the teacher. | David would not be blamed. |
| | Sammy would be punished. |
| | Sammy would be angry at David. |

| | |
|---|---|
| Talk to Sammy. | Sammy may not be willing to confess. |
| | Sammy may confess. |
| | David may lose Sammy as a friend. |
| Tell everyone that Sammy took the tickets. | Sammy will be hurt. |
| | David won't be blamed. |
| | The kids may not believe David. |

**TEACHER:** What are the value issues involved with the problem?

**TRACEY:** I don't understand what you mean.

**TEACHER:** What important things are a part of the problem? Is it a matter of money, trust, friendship?

**TRACEY:** Oh! I see! It's trust. The kids don't trust David.

**KIM:** Also, friendship. David's friendship with Sammy.

**JASON:** How about the value of each person?

**BILL:** Self-respect. When you are guilty and want to somehow make up for your mistake.

**SKIP:** Honesty.

**BOB:** If you tell everyone, then they will know you didn't do it.

**TEACHER:** Think about which of these values is most important to you. Ask yourself, "Why are they important?"

**SKIP:** Suppose honesty and friendship are equally important to you.

**TEACHER:** Then think about the effect on others as well as yourself.

The teacher then asked if any of the children were ready to role play their choice of solution. Role playing any of these value situations can be most effective. Children can be asked to suddenly reverse roles to get the feel of another view. Bob quickly volunteered and opted to tell everyone what had happened. Several of the children argued with him and role played their own solutions. This did not change Bob's mind and the teacher remained out of the discussion. The children completed this activity by recording in their logs their choice and the reasons for it.

The previous example is included to emphasize the point that the teacher should not attempt to tell Bob his position is "wrong," because it is his choice and he feels strongly about it. If the teacher moralizes with Bob, he may not be as open in future discussions and the teacher's position is not likely to change Bob's basic value beliefs. You may question whether the previous experience was worthwhile for him. The answer is "yes," because he is very much aware of what values are most important to him and why. It is possible that the other children's discussion with him may have quite an effect on similar future value decisions.

Frequently, specific problem-solving situations or units of study will contain value issues that should be confronted instead of avoided. When a fifth-grade class studied the pollution problems of a local factory, the value issues of profit versus nonpolluted air were pursued. In playing the simulation game *Sunshine,* the children identified the value issue of equality versus inequality. The unit of study that focuses on India identified the religious value placed on the sacredness of animals, particularly the cow, versus the lack of food. An example of this type was given in the unit on Africa on page 132. Young children, in their study of the community, encountered the value of community pride versus encouraging more industry to settle there.

One of the major concerns of this approach is that the value issues are most complicated and children have had limited experience with logical or moral reasoning. It is suggested that children will be too quick to make a decision without having all the knowledge or facts that are necessary to understand the issue.

## SUMMARY

Discussions that give children the opportunity to express how they feel about important things in their lives are becoming increasingly more useful. Teachers have been learning that the things that they value are not always valued by others and that moralizing with a group of children has less effect on them than providing a forum where they can pursue these value issues with their peers. Valuing situations where children can talk (rather than be talked to) about what they believe and why should help them grow in their ability to understand what they value and be prepared to act upon those values.

## NOTES

1. David Purpel and Kevin Ryan, "Moral Education: Where Sages Fear to Tread," *Phi Delta Kappan* (June 1975):659.
2. Lawrence Kohlberg, "Moral Education in the Schools: A Developmental View," *School Review* 74 (Spring 1966):7.
3. Ibid., p. 19.
4. Ibid., p. 20.
5. Ibid., p. 23.

6. James A. Mackey, "Moral Insight in the Classroom," *Elementary School Journal* 73 (February 1973):35.
7. Kohlberg, "Moral Education," p. 24.
8. Lawrence Kohlberg, "Stage and Sequence: The Cognitive-Developmental Approach to Socialization," in David A. Goslin, ed., *Handbook of Socialization Theory and Research* (Chicago: Rand McNally, 1969), pp. 347–480.
9. Kohlberg, "Moral Education," p. 17.
10. Richard S. Peters, "A Reply to Kohlberg," *Phi Delta Kappan* (June 1975):678.
11. Louis E. Raths, Merrill Harmin, and Sidney B. Simon, *Values and Teaching* (Columbus, Ohio: Charles E. Merrill, 1966), p. 30.
12. Sidney B. Simon, "Values Clarification vs. Indoctrination," *Social Education* 35 (December 1971):902.
13. Ibid., p. 904.
14. John S. Stewart, "Clarifying Values Clarification: A Critique," *Phi Delta Kappan* (June 1975):684.

## SELECTED REFERENCES

A Special Issue on Moral Education. *Phi Delta Kappan* (June 1975).

Bernstein, Jean, et al. "Examining Values in the Upper Grades." *Social Education* (December 1971):906–909.

Brown, Ina Corrine. "What Is Valued in Different Cultures." *Educational Leadership* 27 (November 1969):151–514.

Fraenkel, J. R. "Strategies for Developing Values." *Today's Education* 62 (November 1973):49.

Greer, Mary, and Rubinstein, Bonnie. *Will the Real Teacher Please Stand Up?* Santa Monica, Calif.: Goodyear, 1972.

Kohlberg, Lawrence. "Moral Education in the Schools: A Developmental View." *School Review* 74 (Spring 1966):1–30.

Mackey, James. "Moral Insight in the Classroom." *Elementary School Journal* 73 (February 1973):33–38.

Metcalf, Lawrence E., ed. *Values Education*. 41st Yearbook. Washington, D.C.: National Council for the Social Studies, 1971.

Raths, Louis; Harmin, Merrill; and Simon, Sidney. *Values and Teaching*. Columbus, Ohio: Charles E. Merrill, 1966.

Rosen, Bernard C. "Family Structure and Value Transmission." *Merrill-Palmer Quarterly* 10 (January 1964):59–76.

Simon, Sidney B. "Values Clarification vs. Indoctrination." *Social Education* 35 (December 1971):902.

Skeel, Dorothy J. "What Values Are Important." *Today's Education* (January/February 1977).

Williams, Marianne E. T. *A Study of Effectiveness of a Systematic Instructional Model on the Rational Decision Making Behavior of Sixth Grade Students*. Unpublished doctoral dissertation, Indiana University, 1972.

# 11
# Interpersonal Skills

One of the most important aspects of social studies should be its ability to foster the growth and development of interpersonal skills. The topics and learning activities of social studies lend themselves to children talking about the interactions of people as well as participating in those interactions. Children learn what is required to get along with people, resolve conflict, and work together to complete a task. As an example, committee work develops many of these skills.

## WORKING IN COMMITTEES

### What Is to Be Gained

Experience in working in committees for the attainment of specific goals develops skill in cooperative behavior. The ability to get along with others is a skill that should be acquired as early as possible. As children enter school, they are often self-centered and frequently unwilling to share materials with others. They learn the skills of cooperative behavior by sharing playthings, working on projects with other children, and participating in group activities such as singing, dancing, and listening to stories. At the kindergarten level, committees should be small, consisting of two or three children; their task should be of a simple nature. Building a house with blocks, getting the milk, or cleaning up materials in the play areas are suggested as beginning activities for committee work. Later in kindergarten and in first grade, more formal tasks can be assigned, such as preparing a story for creative dramatics, drawing a movie roll of a story, or finding answers to questions by looking at pictures. One first-grade class organized a pet show with committees of children responsible for invitations, judging, refreshments, prizes, and care of pets. Children soon learn that the success of such an activity is dependent upon each person cooperating and completing his or her share of the task.

Continual involvement in committee work throughout the elementary grades is necessary to maintain and refine skill in working together. As children mature, they are capable of working in larger groups (of perhaps five or six members) and of completing more difficult tasks. It is crucial that the teacher establish a definite purpose for committee work and that the children understand this purpose.

## Organization

The method of selecting members for committees can vary, depending upon the group of children and the purpose. Classes of children who have few discipline problems and get along well with one another generally can be permitted to select committee memberships of their choice, based on each individual's interest in a particular subject or task. However, classes of children who experience considerable difficulty in getting along, have discipline problems, or have too many leaders should be organized in committees by the teacher. At times, it is beneficial for the teacher to select particular students for a committee in order to meet individual differences. For example, the child who is exceptional in art may be placed on a committee in which he can use his talent. Or, the child not very adept in research skills should receive help when placed on a committee of children more capable. It is not necessarily good, however, to place outstanding children with the very slow, for too great a discrepancy in ability may result in frustration for all concerned.

The teacher who has never worked with committees before or a class that has not had experience in working in committees may wish to begin the activity one committee at a time. Using this method, the teacher organizes one committee to work on a task; at the completion of its responsibility, she organizes another committee. This method allows the teacher more time to work with each group to guide its activities. After all members of the class have participated in this experience, the whole class can be organized into committees.

## Teacher-Pupil Planning

Successful committee experiences depend considerably upon the routines established within the classroom. Children respond more favorably when they have the opportunity to aid in developing the guidelines for a project. The following is an example of the dialogue of a class planning for committee work. The children are fourth graders who have had previous but limited experience working in committees.

    TEACHER:   What is the first thing a committee should do after the members have been selected?

    GEORGE:   We should decide on someone to be a chairperson.

    TEACHER:   How do you make this decision?

    JANE:   We can hold an election and nominate people and then vote.

    BILL:   Yes, but that takes too long. You can have each person decide who he or she wants and write the name on a slip of paper.

## INTERPERSONAL SKILLS

**TEACHER:** What type of person makes the best chairperson?

**SALLY:** Someone who isn't too bossy and always telling you what to do.

**SAM:** Someone who will do his or her share, but also help you if you need it.

**TEACHER:** Suppose we list the responsibilities of a chairperson.

The children's completed list of responsibilities for the chairperson follows.

The chairperson should:

1. Understand the responsibility of the committee.
2. Help each person understand the task.
3. Be sure each person completes the task.
4. Accept the opinions and suggestions of committee members.
5. Report the committee's progress and problems concerning materials to the class.
6. Be sure members share materials.

**TEACHER:** What responsibilities do the members of the committee have?

**JIM:** We need to be sure that we do our share of the work and not wait to be told.

**MISSY:** Don't forget that sharing materials is a committee member's responsibility too.

The completed list was placed on a chart for all to observe when needed. These are the points listed:

Committee members should:

1. Share materials with others.
2. Listen to the committee members' and the chairperson's suggestions.
3. Complete their tasks on time.
4. Do their share of the work.
5. Be willing to help others.

**TEACHER:** Are there certain things we should all remember when working in committees?

**MARY:** Work quietly, so you won't disturb others.

**RICK:** Clean up your materials at the end of the period.

BILL: I think that the big thing is to get your work done on time so others won't have to wait for you.

SHELLY: Also, stick to your topic and don't spoil someone else's report.

The types of responses listed here are typical to those most classes will offer. The crucial aspect is not the content of the response but rather the process involved, whereby the children take an active part in the decision making which affects their behavior as they work in committees. With young children, teachers may find it necessary to be more directive in their questioning. For example, the teacher might ask questions such as: When we play a game and choose a leader, how do we do this? What is the leader's job?

The guidelines that have been established by the class should be referred to daily before beginning the work. In addition, when a problem arises the teacher should suggest that the children analyze the cause of the problem and check the guidelines for a solution. Children become more self-reliant and self-disciplined when they share in the process of making the rules.

Interpersonal skills, which are so necessary in any society, are developed through most learning experiences in school; however, committee membership provides many fine opportunities for their practice. Learning to get along with others, sharing materials, the giving and taking of opinions, and assuming responsibility are important skills to be acquired if the committees are to be successful. If these skills are acquired during committee work, the results should carry over into activities in other areas, such as on the playground, during other classwork, and after school in the neighborhood.

The organization of a committee necessitates getting along with others. Each member must be willing to accept the guidance of the chairperson. The membership of a committee may not consist of each person's best friends; the child must therefore learn to cooperate with any classmate. If committee tasks are to be completed, members must be willing to share materials and readily respect the opinions of others. Committee members have responsibilities that they must assume if success is to be achieved. Frequently, classes that have failed to develop any real group feeling or "esprit de corps" will be more successful after the experience of working together in committees.

## "Magic Circle" or Group Meetings

When groups or classes of children are placed together, there are bound to be disagreements and difficulties with children who are working with one another. Several programs have been developed to increase communication and improve the interpersonal relationships among groups. One of them, frequently called the "Magic Circle" by Harold Bessell and Uvaldo Palomares of the Human Development Training Institute, has been used quite extensively.

As explained in the *Theory Manual,* children form a circle with the teacher (ranging from a small group of six to nine in preschool kindergarten to the entire class in the other grades, where two circles will be necessary) to increase the communication possibilities. The authors explain: "As a geometric figure, the circle has always had magic in it, and when people sit in a circle, there is social magic. People feel physically a part of something; they feel closer and less unconnected with each other. They feel less inferior or superior to each other, because pecking orders or hierarchies need straight lines and lots of space for definition. When children sit in a circle with an adult, they feel flattered; they feel that they have been granted a share in his status, and they have. Politeness and courtesy are fostered in a circle."[1]

The manual continues with an extensive discussion of how to prepare for the circle session, leadership skills that are necessary, transferring leadership from teacher to child, and examples from the activity guides for the grades. Then the authors discuss the teacher and how the program may affect him or her. The manual goes on to discuss the three themes of the program: *awareness* (knowing what your thoughts, feelings, and actions really are), *mastery* (knowing what your abilities are and how to use them), and *social interaction* (knowing other people).[2] The authors caution that it may take a year or more for the teacher to really be comfortable with the program. Inservice training sessions are offered to aid teachers in acquiring skills necessary to initiate and implement the program.

Another less formalized program, contained within the pages of a book entitled *The Other Side of the Report Card: A How-To-Do-It Program for Affective Education* by Larry Chase, is concerned with the social and emotional development of children. Chase explains the book as follows:

> This book is a smorgasbord of ways to help children learn some of the survival skills they need today and tomorrow. It was written because of my conviction that a teacher in a classroom *can* significantly affect the social and emotional growth of students in positive, healthful ways. The activities, directions, and topics described in this book are relevant. They have all been used with kids and grownups, and most have worked most of the time.[3]

The beginning chapters discuss affective education and how to prepare for awareness sessions. Then there are a series of units to be used with children in the sessions. They do not need to be used in any particular order. Examples of topics are: friendship, fear, trust, self-control, tolerance, self-concept, lying, and problem solving. Each unit establishes the objectives for the topic and provides a series of activities to meet those objectives. Following is an example of the unit objectives for Decisions and the beginning activity.

## Objectives

Students will:

a. Become sensitive to the importance of wise decision making and the number of decisions they have to make.
b. Identify the components of a critical decision.
c. Identify available resources for help in making important decisions.
d. Become aware of how risk is involved in decision making.
e. Take a public stand on how they see themselves as decision makers.
f. Begin to think about their future as being controlled by decisions they make now.

## Activity 1

*Purpose:* To enable students to gain experiences at making forced choices and in publicly defending their choices.

*Process:* Explain that today one corner of the room will represent one choice and another corner will represent an opposite, or different choice. Begin the activity by saying, "In that corner is McDonald's, and in that corner is Mr. Steak. Go to the corner of your choice." When they have all gone to their chosen spot, approach one group and, pretending to be a reporter, ask someone, "Why are you here?" Elicit responses in this manner from three people in each group; then ask them to regroup in the center of the room. Repeat this process for at least six or seven different choice pairs. Follow each choice episode by asking some why they are where they are.

Select your choice pairs from this list (or make up some of your own):

1. Are you more of a leader or a follower?
2. Are you a grouper or an aloner?
3. Are you spring or autumn?
4. Are you more yes or more no?

INTERPERSONAL SKILLS

5. Are you more like, "Two heads are better than one," or "Too many cooks spoil the broth"?
6. Are you more like "A stitch in time saves nine," or "Better late than never"?
7. Are you more like a question or an answer?
8. Are you more like a teacher or a student?
9. If you needed advice would you go to your mother or your father?
10. Are you more parent or child?

After you have gone through the forced-choice process several times, ask the class to come up with other choices. The more involved they get now, the better.

Take at least ten minutes to discuss, as a whole group, the problem of choosing between two opposite choices. At this point, you are making students aware of their choices. Later they will examine strategies for choosing more wisely.[4]

The remaining chapters include developing your own lesson plans, what ifs, and evaluating awareness sessions. It concludes with a bibliography of reading materials and an annotated listing of affective films.

## SUMMARY

Whether as a teacher you choose to use committee work, the "magic circle," or some other affective education program, it is crucial that children improve their interpersonal skills. Learning becomes more pleasurable when children have respect for and listen to one another. In addition, our fast-changing impersonal world requires these skills if children are to cope with that world and participate effectively in it.

## NOTES

1. Harold Bessell, *Methods in Human Development Theory Manual,* 1973 Revision (San Diego, Calif.: Human Development Training Institute, 1973), p. 14.
2. Ibid., p. 1.
3. Larry Chase, *The Other Side of the Report Card* (Santa Monica, Calif.: Goodyear, 1975), p. xi.
4. Ibid., pp. 151–152.

## SELECTED REFERENCES

Borton, Terry. *Reach, Touch and Teach.* New York: McGraw-Hill, 1970.

Castillo, Gloria A. *Left-Handed Teaching Lessons in Affective Education.* New York: Praeger, 1974.

LaBenne, Wallace D., and Greene, Bert I. *Educational Implications of Self-Concept Theory.* Santa Monica, Calif.: Goodyear, 1969.

Miller, John P. *Humanizing the Classroom: Models of Teaching in Affective Education.* New York: Praeger, 1976.

# 12
# Communication Skills

Whereas interpersonal skills focus on the ability to communicate with people, this chapter takes an in-depth look at specific ways of communicating through reading, research, writing, and oral reporting. Social studies, as does every content area, gives children the opportunity to apply the reading and language arts skills.

## READING

One of the most frequent criticisms leveled at social studies materials is that children cannot read the material that is necessary for background information, whether it's a textbook or a library resource book. Most recent studies, analyzing textbooks for readability, disclose that in the intermediate grades it may range within the texts from an age level of two to twelve years.[1] Often, the difficulty is increased by the number and method of introducing new concepts. Concepts may be presented too frequently without giving sufficient exposure for development. Also, concepts may be presented without explicit enumeration of their criterial attributes. Therefore, the reader does not understand the concepts and cannot comprehend the material read. In Chapter Four, which discussed concepts, teaching suggestions were outlined for teachers to introduce and extend concept development. It is important that these concepts be introduced before the children begin to read the materials.

When teachers are teaching reading, they do not hesitate to group children according to their instructional levels and provide materials on those reading levels. Teachers need also to provide some similar opportunities for social studies reading. Some suggestions follow:[2]

1. Tape record important sections of the textbook so children can listen as they follow along in the texts. More able readers can help with the recording.

2. Have children work in pairs on reading assignments, matching a less able with a more able reader.
3. Have children prepare summaries or outlines of textbook sections. Use language experience techniques for younger children. These can be used year after year.
4. Use picture analysis questioning skills to focus on the important concepts.
5. Have the class prepare a "cartoon" narrative of part of the text, depicting the major concepts.
6. Cut illustrative material and pictures from old texts and magazines. Make unit scrapbooks and bulletin boards to illustrate main concepts of text.
7. Develop "textbook learning centers" where groups of children are each responsible for developing learning experiences for the other children for a small section of the text.

## QUESTIONING TECHNIQUES

The use of the Taba questioning strategies with reading social studies textbooks will increase the thinking skills of children as well as the comprehension of the material read. The following is an example of a page from the third-grade Sadlier text by John D. McAulay, *Communities Around the World*.[3]

### *The Land Has Helped the Americans*

North America is a very rich <u>continent</u>. There is much good <u>farmland</u>. There are many <u>metals</u>, <u>minerals</u>, and <u>rivers</u>. The Americans use the metals and minerals. They use the rivers and other waterways to send things from one place to another. You may have seen <u>ships</u> or <u>boats</u> on a river. You certainly have seen <u>trucks</u> and <u>railroad trains</u>. These are other ways of moving things. Ways of moving things from place to place are called means of <u>transportation</u>.

North America's land is needed by the farmers. Farmers need good land and enough rainfall to grow food. The whole center of North America has much of this good land. This area is level, or flat. It is called the "<u>Great Interior Plain</u>." On the plain, farmers grow much wheat, corn, and barley. But some of this land is too dry to grow food. There is not enough rainfall. On this land ranchers raise <u>cattle</u> and <u>sheep</u>. The cattle provide meat and leather. The sheep provide meat, wool, and leather.

COMMUNICATION SKILLS                                                                 219

After the children have read this section, the teacher can utilize the following key questions on each of the levels: concept formation, interpretation, and application. Also, listed are the possible student responses.

### CONCEPT FORMATION

| Teacher Questions | Possible Student Responses |
|---|---|
| Find the continent of North America on your map. What countries does it include? | United States, Canada, and Mexico |
| What resources did our book tell us we could find within the continent of North America? | farmland, minerals, metals, rivers |

### INTERPRETATION

How do we use these resources?

| | |
|---|---|
| farmland | grow food, raise cattle |
| metals, minerals | make trucks, ships |
| rivers | move things (transport) |

### APPLICATION

What could we do if these resources were not here?

| | |
|---|---|
| farmland | find other things to eat<br>buy from other countries |
| metals, minerals | we might use wood<br>buy from other countries |
| rivers | move things overland |

These same levels of questions can be formulated for study guides to provide a purpose for reading the material.

## VOCABULARY DEVELOPMENT

Since social studies materials frequently introduce a multitude of new vocabulary words, teachers will need to use similar techniques with social studies vocabulary as they do with reading or other content areas.

As an example, in the previous selection from the third-grade textbook the underlined vocabulary words are introduced to the children prior to the reading in the following manner. Teachers should find pictures that illustrate the vocabulary words. Write the words on the board, leaving sufficient space. Using tape or magnets, have children match the pictures with the words and explain them. Leave them on the board during the reading so that children can refer back to them if they have any difficulty.

**Flashcards**

Make flashcards of the concepts or vocabulary words for a chapter in the social studies textbook. Place pictures of them on the back of the cards. Have children work in pairs, learning the new words before beginning the reading. Games also can be played with them.

**Illustrated Concepts or Vocabulary Dictionary**

Have children cut out pictures from magazines or draw pictures to illustrate the concepts or vocabulary words in the social studies. Develop an illustrated dictionary of them. Children can refer to the dictionary as they are reading.

**Language Experience Chart**

After children have read a selection from their textbook, ask them to tell you about it in their own words. Prepare an experience chart with their responses. Have children illustrate the chart where appropriate. Use the chart as review the following day before beginning the next section.

**Varied Reading Materials**

Children's trade books and paperbacks can add variety to the reading task. They also can provide different levels of reading that are needed by students. Helen Huus's *Children's Books to Enrich the Social Studies* (Washington, D.C.: National Council for the Social Studies, 1966) and Doris Paine's *Teaching With Paperbacks: A Multi-Title Approach* are excellent resources for choosing books for the classroom.

## GROUP READING

One of the most common practices in utilizing the social studies textbook is for the children to "take turns" reading a paragraph or two. After the reading is completed, the teacher will conduct a discussion, generally asking information questions. If the purpose of the reading is to acquire information, then poor readers won't help others achieve this goal or retain it themselves. Children usually fidget, look out windows, or create some disturbances while poor readers are stumbling along. This type of experience does nothing to improve the skill or the self-esteem of the poor reader. What are some alternatives if the teacher wants to use the textbook as a group experience?

1. The teacher reads while the children *do* or *do not* follow along.
2. Teachers choose the best readers to read sections.
3. Children who are good readers from older grade levels read the selection.
4. The children read the selection silently; then, in response to teacher questions, read a sentence or two that contains the answer. In addition, teachers ask questions that go beyond facts to include interpretation and application.
5. Good readers from the class read sections of the textbook, stopping when appropriate.

## USING REFERENCE MATERIALS

As children search for information pertaining to particular topics, they will need assistance in using a variety of resource materials.

1. Library—In preparing to use the library, the children should learn the arrangement of the card catalog, the placement of books on the shelves, and the procedure for checking out books. The topic under study may be used as an example to be located in the card catalog, and so forth.
2. Encyclopedia—One of the favorite sources of information for young children is the encyclopedia, because its organization makes it easy for them to locate topics. Frequently, children copy information from this book without any understanding. The vocabulary may be too difficult, and the children do not look up words in the dictionary that they do not understand. Guidelines should be established for using the encyclopedia.
    The children should ask themselves these questions:

    a. Do I understand the information given about the topic?
    b. Are there any vocabulary words I do not know?
    c. How can I best report this information to the class?

d. Will an outline of the information be enough or should I take notes?

e. Are there cross-references where I might secure additional information about the topic?

f. If I prepare a written report, can I complete it in my own words?

3. Textbook—The textbook can be used for background reading by the entire class. The teacher should be sure that the children understand the organization of the text and that the reading level is suitable. When available, a variety of texts or multitexts provide the opportunity to compare viewpoints and information presented by different authors.

4. Primary sources—Work with primary source material (original source of information without some other person's interpretation) is valuable in helping children draw their own conclusions, interpret the facts presented, and evaluate the validity of the material. G. P. Putnam and Sons have produced "Jackdaws," which are kits of primary source material. Each kit is organized around a topic, such as "Columbus and the Discovery of America." They include reproductions of actual documents from this early historical period.

Another primary source of information is obtained by conducting interviews and surveys. Children should prepare their questions for the interview in advance. An example of an interview the children might conduct would be questioning an official about the building of a recreational park for the city:

a. Where will the park be located?

b. What type of equipment will it include?

c. How much will it cost the taxpayers?

d. When will it be completed?

e. Why is it being built?

After securing information from a primary source, the child should compare it, if possible, with its coverage in the newspaper. The children should try to answer these questions:

- Does the paper report the same information?
- Does it express a bias? If so, why?
- Is it possible that the reporters were given incorrect information?

5. Other sources—Newspapers, magazines, films, filmstrips, and recordings are sources children can use to secure information. They need to evaluate the sources to determine which are most valid. Children are encouraged to use a variety of resource materials. The resource materials should stimulate critical thinking, initiating questions such as the following.

- Does the author of the material express a point of view?
- Does the author use any methods of propaganda in the writing?
- Does the information vary from source to source?
- Is the author stating fact or opinion?

## Locating Information

Skills children need for locating information are:

1. Knowledge of available resources (as discussed in the preceding section).
2. Understanding of how the resource is organized—alphabetically, topically, and so on.
3. Ability to use the table of contents, which lists the major headings.
4. Ability to use the index, which cites a page number for each entry.
5. Knowledge of cross references, which indicate a related topic that may give additional information.
6. Ability to glean information from illustrations.
7. Ability to read maps, graphs, and charts.

## Outlining and Notetaking

Information is outlined to provide a skeleton of the important points. An outline is used in helping children organize their information; however, useless outlining of page after page of material for practice is a waste of time. Because an outline presents important information in a shortened and simplified form, children should start with the short form. The main points about a topic are called the main topics or main headings, and are designated by Roman numerals. Points about the topic that fall under the main headings are subtopics or subheadings, and are designated by capital letters. Details about the subtopics follow them and are designated by numbers, as in the following example:

I. Africa
   A. Geography
      1. Mountains
      2. Rainforests
      3. Rivers

Notetaking necessitates a decision regarding the purpose of the information. Before they start to take notes, children should be encouraged to ask themselves: (1) Am I attempting to entertain someone with the information? (2) Am I selecting information that I think an audience would not know? and (3) Am I selecting information I think everyone should know about the topic? After they have answered these questions, they can begin to select the appropriate information.

## Oral and Written Reports

Skills needed for oral and written reports can be developed through a wide variety of activities. These skills also can be identified as expressive skills, for the children express themselves in writing, speaking, or drawing. After research has been completed, the development of a method of sharing the information with the group becomes necessary. Criteria for the success of this method are: (1) Did the children gain knowledge from the reports? (2) Did they exhibit an interest in the report? The guidelines established for reporting include:

- Present the information in such a way that others will be interested in the topic.
- Be sure this information is accurate and easily understood.
- Don't obscure the information in gimmicks to develop interest.

The type of information that has been secured will determine, to a certain extent, the choice of presentation. Children should learn what type of presentation best communicates the information they have to report. The oral skills to be developed are:

1. To acquire poise and confidence in a group situation.
2. To speak with expression.
3. To acquire fluency in phrasing.
4. To speak clearly and slowly.
5. To express an idea so that it may be understood.
6. To adjust volume of voice to size of group.

## Panel Discussions

Organizing information for a panel discussion generally is better accomplished by intermediate-grade children, but variations of the panel can be presented by young children. For example, first- or second-grade children can prepare their part of the presentation in charts, with or without pictures they have drawn. If a child has difficulty in writing, the teacher can prepare a chart from the child's dictation or the children can use pictures and give information in their own words. Questions to be asked back and forth by the panel members are only beneficial if they are prepared in advance so the children know what to expect.

Intermediate-grade children need to be cautioned against merely reading their reports rather than discussing them. A time limit of two to three minutes for each discussant helps the children to learn to be concise and to select only the most pertinent information. To increase interest in their discussion, children will benefit from visual aids such as illustrations, transparencies, charts, graphs, or a short filmstrip. The following are points children should remember for any oral presentation.

1. Stick to the topic of your report.
2. Speak clearly and slowly enough to be heard by all.
3. Use inflections in your voice.
4. Maintain good eye contact with your audience.

## Debates

To be effective, debates should be utilized by intermediate-grade children. They are more capable of the extensive research needed to discover all the pros and cons of an issue. The issue selected for the debate should be one that provokes critical analysis and presents the possibility for taking a position. An example might be—Resolved: The United States Government should spend sufficient funds for research to continue its space probe to Mars; or, Resolved: The City Council should pass building safety codes that will protect the public. Rules should be established for the debate, with the time limits set for each presentation and rebuttal. The children should be cautioned about becoming too emotional over the debate. They should understand that a debate is won by presenting the most persuasive arguments for their side.

## Role Playing

A historical incident or an attempted solution to a problem can be role played. In this activity, the children can use their own language and ideas, based on their research, to depict some incident. Role playing the signing of the Declaration of Independence or peace treaty talks will help children to understand and to remember these events. Role playing gives children the opportunity to express emotions and to attempt to involve themselves in a situation. Children at any grade level can participate in this activity.

## TV or Radio Programs

Patterning an oral report after the format of a TV or radio program adds an element of interest. Some children may even add the commercials to make it realistic. Children who have difficulty with oral presentations are often less self-conscious when given the opportunity to pretend to be someone else or to hide behind a microphone.

Show formats such as "This Is Your Life" or "You Were There" are appropriate for historical incidents, while an interview-type format like the "Today Show" is good for factual and opinion reports. The former "Huntley-Brinkley" news format is enjoyed by children for factual reporting.

## Dramatic Presentations

Similar to role playing, but with more definite lines and costumes and props, skits and plays can be used by children to present oral reports. Once again, this activity increases the element of interest, and children can hide their self-consciousness behind a character in the play. An example of this type of activity might be a skit depicting a day in the life of a child in Mexico—showing the food, clothing, home, and customs. This information is much more easily remembered as a result of visual representation.

The lines for a dramatic presentation can be taped. Children can practice by taping and playing back the presentation until they are satisfied with the performance. Preparation of any oral report can be improved by the use of the tape recorder. Each child has the opportunity to hear his or her mistakes and improve the quality of his or her voice.

## Written Reports

Skills to be developed in the written reports are:

1. Organizing the information in a meaningful sequence.
2. Selecting the relevant information.
3. Using correct language, capitalization, and punctuation.

The information gathered by a committee or individual may be compiled into a written report when the teacher sees a need for increased skill in this area. The written report might be assembled in a scrapbook with illustrations or in a booklet form. Children can use a textbook format with a table of contents, chapter headings, glossary, and other elements. Reports such as these should be interesting, concise, written in the child's language, and available for all to read. A display of the reports can remain on the reading table until all have had the chance to read them. These reports can be used for reference when possible.

**Graphic Reports**

Committees or individuals can present their research information through graphic representations. For example, the preparation of a wall mural depicting methods of transportation may be more easily interpreted by children than a verbal description. Or the building of a model village may relate more to children about life in Peru than a dozen written reports. The child who is more adept at painting than writing or speaking can meet with success in this type of activity.

## SUMMARY

Social studies content may create problems in reading, but it also provides opportunities for children to put into use and improve those skills they have acquired in reading and language arts. If teachers implement similar techniques as those used in teaching children to read, some of the problems can be alleviated.

## NOTES

1. Roger Johnson and Ellen B. Vardian, "Reading Readability and the Social Studies," *The Reading Teacher* 26 (February 1973):483–488.
2. Thomas N. Turner, "Making the Social Studies Textbook a More Effective Tool for Less Able Readers," *Social Education* 40 (January 1976):40–41.
3. John D. McAulay, *Communities Around the World* (New York: W. H. Sadlier, 1971), p. 40.

## SELECTED REFERENCES

Bergeson, Clarence O. "Using Learning Resources in Social Studies Skill Development." *Social Education* 31 (March 1967):227.
Fraenkel, Jack R., ed. "Critique and Commentary/Is Teaching Reading a Responsibility of the Social Studies Teacher?" *Social Education* 42 (April 1978):312–317.

Lundstrum, John P., ed. "Improving Reading Skills." *Social Education* 42 (January 1978):8–31.

———. "Reading in the Social Studies: A Preliminary Analysis of Recent Research." *Social Education* 40 (January 1976):10–18.

O'Connor, John R. "Reading Skills in the Social Studies." *Social Education* 31 (February 1967):104.

Skeel, Dorothy J. *Developing Creative Ability*. South Holland, Ill.: H. Wilson, 1967.

———. *Developing Language Arts Skills*. South Holland, Ill.: H. Wilson, 1968.

Smith, James A. *Creative Teaching of the Social Studies*. Boston: Allyn & Bacon, 1967.

# 13
# Map and Globe Skills

"Where do you live?" "What is it near?" "How can I get there?" These are common questions asked by a person attempting to locate someone's house. Depending upon the location and the individual's ability in locational skills, he might answer by naming the place, expressing the distance from his present location to his home, expressing this distance in terms of the time required to go there; or, he might designate the location by readings of latitude and longitude to be more exact. With the increased speed of today's travel, the time involved in reaching one's destination has changed; however, many of the skills required to locate a place remain the same. Mass media, which includes a great number of unfamiliar places in its reporting, and the increased mobility of people, enhance the study of locational skills. Map reading requires the learning of a new language, which enables the individual to interpret map symbols. Six basic skills have been recognized as comprehensive for map reading and interpretation:

1. Ability to orient the map and note directions.
2. Ability to recognize the scale of a map and compute distances.
3. Ability to locate places on maps and globes by means of grid systems.
4. Ability to express relative locations.
5. Ability to read map symbols.
6. Ability to compare maps and to make inferences.[1]

Limited research has been completed to determine children's ability with map skills at varying grade levels. On the basis of child development studies, Bacon contends that young children learn to think geographically much sooner than they learn to think historically.[2] Rushdoony found that primary children were able to profit from instruction in map-reading skills recommended for fourth and fifth graders. He suggests that curriculums be revised to introduce map skills to children at an earlier level. He also found a high positive correlation between map-reading achievement and intelligence, reading achievement, and arithmetic achievement.[3]

Most social studies educators agree that effective instruction in map and globe skills is accomplished through developmental tasks and that this instruction should be conducted in the context of the study of a topic. Thus, the six basic skills will be developed in the primary and intermediate grades in the context of a suggested topic. In the following discussion of methods for teaching map skills, the six basic skills (listed above) will be indicated by the number to which they correspond in the list. In mastering these map skills, children will need to build upon a progression of learning experiences. These suggested activities are representative and are not intended to be the only ones developed at each grade level.

## SKILLS BY GRADE LEVELS

### Kindergarten

As the children study the family and home, they develop a map of the community, using blocks placed on butcher paper to represent the school and their homes (5). A trip outside the school on a sunny day enables the children to note the location of the sun when they arrive at school and when they leave. With this knowledge the children are able to place the sun on their maps as a directional guide (1). The children place blocks on the map to locate other outstanding buildings, such as the fire station, library, and places of worship relative to their homes (4). Beginning at the school, they count the number of blocks (in a city), kilometers, or miles (in a rural area) to their homes (2). The teacher draws the same map on a piece of paper representing their homes and other buildings with drawings (5). The children compare their block map with the teacher's map to locate their homes (6). The simple slate or physical-relief globe is then used to locate the placement of their homes in relation to the other areas of the world (3, 1, 5).

### First Grade

Young children are fascinated by the study of a culture different from their own, especially one they think is quite far away. Japan is an example of a culture that might be used in first grade. The children first locate Japan on a simple globe and realize that it is a group of islands (1, 5). The teacher uses a tub of water and a cardboard representation of the islands to help develop this concept (6). The children note the direction of Japan from their homes (1). In an attempt to determine the distance of Japan from the children's homes, they compute the time in days it would take to reach the islands by plane or boat (2). By using a floor map of the world with land masses and water indicated, they place a toy plane and boat on

# MAP AND GLOBE SKILLS

the map, and move them at their approximate speed of travel—one day of school for the plane and five days of school for the boat (1, 2, 3, 4, 5). Using a globe that has an attachment showing the division of day and night, they interpret the time differences (6, 5).

## Second Grade

Wall maps can be introduced at this level, but transition from the floor map to the wall map should be provided. During a study of community workers, children can make a large floor map using symbols to locate the buildings of the workers, such as the fire station and police station (1, 4, 5). The teacher should then draw to scale a smaller map of the area, hang it on the wall, and permit children to place buildings on the map (2, 3, 4, 5). Have the children locate their city or town on a simplified state map (1, 5, 6). Then refer them to a map of the United States to see where their state is located (1, 2, 3, 4, 5, 6).

## Third Grade

During a study of contrasting communities, children learn that people wear different clothes in different parts of the world. The relationship of this understanding to map interpretation is then presented. Pictures of people in typical dress for a particular time of year are placed on a map of the world that has a three-color key—water, lowlands, and mountains (1, 5). People are placed, for example, on the equator, on lowlands and mountains, on a desert area, near the North Pole, and in the children's own community. Climatic conditions are estimated from the type of clothes worn and the effect of location on the climate (2, 3, 5, 6). The effect of altitude on climate and the resulting type of clothing also is interpreted. A representative relief map of clay or flour and salt is made to relate water, lowland, and mountains to the three-color key (1, 5, 6).

## Fourth Grade

Beginning a study of their state, the children use a large sand table to prepare a model representing the physical features of their state such as mountains, valleys, lakes, rivers, and lowlands (1, 2, 3, 5, 6). As the study progresses, the children can locate on the map major cities, their own city or town, recreational areas, and major products of the state (1, 2, 3, 4, 5, 6). The products and characteristics of an area located in the same latitude with approximately the same land formation should be compared (1, 3, 5, 6).

## Fifth Grade

Fifth graders should use degrees of latitude and longitude for locating places. As children report daily news events from around the world, they should indicate the location of the event in degrees of latitude and longitude. The children can use individual desk maps to locate the places (1, 3, 4, 5). A world map with time zones designated is used to determine the time difference between the children's location and that of the event (1, 2, 3, 4, 5). The children interpret the map key representing physical features and relation of latitude to determine the land formation and climate of the news event's location (5, 6). The map key can also be used to interpret water formations or ocean currents that might be applicable to the event (5, 6).

## Sixth Grade

During a study of the United Nations, committees of children can select areas of the world where United Nations organizations are operating, such as UNICEF, peace-keeping troops, and the economic advisory committee. Reproduce maps of these areas with the opaque projector to ensure accuracy (1, 2, 3, 6). Reproduce physical features, using a five- or seven-color key (5, 6). These maps can be done on transparencies using overlays to represent political divisions, cities, physical features, products, and population (1, 2, 3, 4, 5, 6).

## OTHER SUGGESTED ACTIVITIES

Because children need many concrete experiences to help them understand the concepts of map reading and interpretation, activities that can be used with various topics are suggested for both the primary and intermediate grades.

## Primary Grades

Study the land formation around the school, observing any variations and vegetation. Build a model of the area, using clay or the sand table. Children in the upper-primary grades can refer to a physical map of the state to understand how the color key represents the land formation.

Plan a field trip to study local geographic features such as a river basin, rock formation, canyon, plateau, plain, or mountain. Observe them

# MAP AND GLOBE SKILLS

at different times of the year to note the effects of nature—the changing seasons, rain, wind, and snow.

Construct a globe, using a balloon as the base. Place strips of papier-mâché over the balloon. When it dries, the balloon can be broken, and the land formations and water can be painted on the papier-mâché.

Children who are planning trips should study road maps and physical relief maps to anticipate land formations before they start their journey. They can follow the road map during the trip and share their experiences with the other children after they return.

Obtain aerial photos of different land formations and compare them with the same location of a geophysical map.

## Intermediate Grades

Children should work with map construction frequently, especially when they are studying different areas of the world. Various materials can be used, including plasticene clay, sawdust mixture, flour and salt, and papier-mâché. Children should develop a color key to indicate elevations.

The teacher can make sure the students understand geographical terms such as "bay," "isthmus," "peninsula," and others by helping them to construct models of these physical features when they occur in the course of the study. Blank maps of the area under study are also helpful learning aids. As the study of an area progresses, each child can complete a map by drawing in the physical features, major cities, and other major aspects.

Children should be able to interpret many things from the information given on political and physical maps. When introducing a new area for study, but before any preliminary reading or introduction has been made, the teacher should ask the children to suggest as much information about the area as possible from interpreting the map. In a study of cities, children should suggest geographic reasons for the locations of the cities.

## PROBLEMS TO DETERMINE THE EXTENT OF CHILDREN'S SKILLS

As children begin to acquire skills in map reading and interpretation, they should be presented with problem situations that require them to use the skills they have learned. The following problem example might be presented to kindergarten or first-grade children after they have learned directions and know where the sun rises and sets. The picture on the following page is placed on a transparency.

## Question

If the sun is just rising, which way is the wind blowing?

This problem requires the children to think about the direction from which the sun rises and the resulting shadows. The bending of the tree indicates the direction of the wind.

As children learn to identify the types of products grown in different climatic and geographic regions, they should be able to describe conditions necessary for their growth. The teacher might present pictures of different types of vegetation and ask the children to name the type of climate and geographic conditions necessary for their growth.

The fact that the location rather than the physical appearance or natural resources of an area sometimes determines its importance offers an interesting problem for children to analyze. Some examples follow:

### Place "A"

This is a chain of islands that covers in all an area of about 6,400 square miles. Some small shrubs and mosses grow here, but there are no trees. The climate is very cold and foggy. The population survives largely through fishing....

### Place "B"

This is a rocky peninsula, which is largely a limestone "mountain" rising 1,400 feet above the water. It covers an area of about two square miles....

## Place "C"

This is an island of volcanic origin. It is about 65 miles long and 2 to 18 miles wide. It has an area of about 463 square miles. Its climate is hot and humid, and it is subject to a large number of wind storms each....[4]

After a discussion of possible reasons for the importance of these places, the teacher can reveal their names—the Aleutian Islands, Gibraltar, and Okinawa.

Many schools provide camping experiences for their students to enhance the in-class activities. These outdoor experiences provide excellent opportunities for students to try their mapping skills. They can be given an area of the campsite to map, including the locating of streams, hills, and trails. Students can learn to use a compass and their map skills for orienteering, which is "a competitive exercise in which participants find their way along a predetermined course using a map, compass, and perhaps a series of teacher-supplied clues. The objective is to find the shortest route around a series of control points."[5] Also, the opportunity to find the "buried treasure" adds excitement to a map activity. Teachers can design the treasure map to utilize the map skills they want children to practice, for example, "Walk ten paces east to the oak tree, then turn north, walking until you reach the river."

When older children have a good grasp of the color key on a map and knowledge of the various theories about building a city, the following problem as was suggested in Chapter Five can be presented:

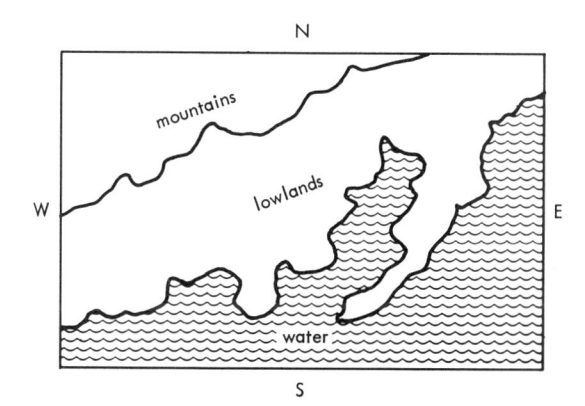

### Questions

If you were to pick the site for a city in this area, where would you build it? Why?

This map should be presented on a transparency, using a color key to distinguish the different physical features. The problem can be tackled individually or by the total class. The teacher may wish to add additional information about the natural resources, the winds, or other physical features. It should be noted that this also can be used as an excellent inquiry activity to initiate a study of cities.

## USING INTEREST CENTERS TO INCREASE SKILLS

There are numerous activities related to maps and globes that children can complete on their own without the aid of the teacher. By developing an interest center for them in one corner of the room, the children can participate in the activities during free time or while the teacher is working with other groups. There should be a globe and a variety of maps available in the area. The following are some examples of the type of activities to plan:

1. Clip out downtown street maps of two city areas such as Savannah, Georgia and Chattanooga, Tennessee. These two cities have quite different land-use patterns. Pose questions for the children to answer:
   What information can you find out about these cities? How are they alike? How are they different?
2. Clip from a map skill book the page which lists the geographic terms and the physical model that has examples of each type of land formation for them to match.
3. Find an enlarged physical features map of an area of the world such as Alaska and pose the question: How much information can you find about this area?
4. Supply a globe, a piece of string, and an air-age map with questions about the "great circle routes."
5. Provide a map with the degrees of latitude and longitude plainly marked. Have children locate certain places in the world by their degrees of latitude and longitude.
6. Find a clipping of a news event that has occurred in some other area of the world. Ask questions relative to the geographic factors of the area. Example: Are there any bodies of water nearby? What type of land forms are found there? On what continent is it located?

Map skill workbooks and old textbooks provide good sources for these activities as well as travel books, newspapers, and magazines.

MAP AND GLOBE SKILLS

## URBAN MAP SKILLS

Since there are large numbers of people living in urban areas and a corresponding number of urban problems, it is important that children acquire an understanding of the urban concept. What is a city? How can it be described? The following presents an accurate conception:

1. A substantial number of people (number);
2. Living in close proximity (density);
3. Over an extended period of time (stability); and
4. Engaging in a variety of economic activities (occupational diversity).[6]

Activities introduced to acquire this concept include categorizing communities according to size, classifying occupations by community size, and working with aerial maps of cities.

Children can construct land-use maps of one part of the city (probably their own areas) or select a few functions such as industrial and residential for mapping the entire city. Listed below is a land-use category system that may be used by the children for city land uses:

1. Single family residences.
2. Multiple family dwellings or apartments.
3. Commercial or business: retail, wholesale, and service.
4. Industrial, manufacturing, and railroads.
5. Public schools, government functions, parks, and places of worship.
6. Streets.
7. Vacant and unused lands.[7]

Problems that confront cities, from the building of a new highway to urban renewal, are presented in simulation materials such as Urban Planning and the MATCH kit, The City. The materials give children the opportunity to play the solutions to these problems.

## MAPS AND GLOBES

Every elementary classroom should contain a globe. In kindergarten and first grade, a simple globe of slate or one that shows only the outline of the continents should be used. The slate globe can be drawn with tempera or chalk and then washed or erased. Children should be permitted to manipulate the globe and to locate places such as their home and the United States. Reference to the globe by the teacher whenever feasible is important, for the children should form the habit of seeking it when the need arises.

Older children can use a more detailed globe—for example, the three- or five-color key of physical features can be used for the middle grades and a seven-color key for the intermediate grades. Use of a globe showing political boundaries with each country a different color has sometimes led children to believe that a country actually is the color shown on the globe. A globe that uses green for lowlands, brown for mountains, and blue for water might better orient children to globe usage.

Care should be exercised in the transition from globes to maps. The comparative size of Greenland is a good indicator of how shapes and sizes change from a globe to a map. Some map projections increase its size considerably, while others decrease the size. The teacher might have the children split a tennis ball or the peel of an orange and attempt to flatten it completely to help them to see what happens in the transition from a globe to a flat map.

Wall maps are generally not used before the end of second or third grade, depending upon the ability and background of the children. As indicated earlier, the first maps used should be homemade. Commercial maps should not contain too much detail to avoid confusing the children. They should be large enough to be read easily across the classroom. Every upper-grade classroom should have a physical-political map of the world, and, if money allows, physical-political maps of North America and other continents. Little use is made of separate physical and political maps, and the combination saves money.

A chart of geographical terms is a useful instructional tool for older children. This chart pictorially shows most of the geographic terms such as "isthmus," "harbor," "bay," and "plateau." These terms, however, should be taught as the need arises. They should not all be taught from the chart at one time.

The wall map of the world should be pulled down each day for ready reference. Games utilizing locational skills can be introduced during free play time—for example, a box with slips of paper containing places to be located might be kept by the map rack. Depending upon the grade level, various clues to the areas' locations can be added. Intermediate-grade children may use only the degrees of latitude and longitude for their reference.

To increase the children's understanding of the grid system, a simple demonstration can be completed. Place an "X" anywhere on the blackboard and have children tell exactly where it is located. Place several other "X's" on the board and give the same direction. Children soon realize that some additional reference points are needed. Draw horizontal lines several inches apart and number them. Problems still arise in determining the exact location until numbered vertical lines have been added. Children should readily associate this method with that used on maps and globes to increase accuracy in locating places.

Maps and globes can be purchased from a number of companies. The following list is representative of some of these companies. Catalogs can be secured upon request.

> George F. Cram Co., Inc., 730 E. Washington Street, Indianapolis, Indiana 46206
>
> Denoyer-Geppert Co., 5235 Ravenswood Avenue, Chicago, Illinois 60640
>
> C. S. Hammond and Company, Inc., Maplewood, New Jersey 07040
>
> Rand McNally and Company, P.O. Box 7800, Chicago, Illinois 60639

Map companies generally supply teachers with guides for instructional uses of their materials, and they also suggest lists of map and globe skills for each grade level.[8]

*National Geographic Magazine* supplies maps with each publication, but they usually contain too much detail for younger children. State chambers of commerce and embassies of foreign countries will provide maps of their areas. News magazines contain maps of areas where the news is happening. Weekly news maps with pictures of the events can be secured from *Time* magazine for a minimum charge.

## NOTES

1. *Skill Development in Social Studies,* 33rd Yearbook (Washington, D.C.: National Council for the Social Studies, 1963), p. 157.
2. *New Viewpoints in Geography,* 29th Yearbook (Washington, D.C.: National Council for the Social Studies, 1959), p. 150.
3. Haig A. Rushdoony, "Achievement in Map-Reading: An Experimental Study," *Elementary School Journal,* 64 (November 1963):74.
4. Jan O. M. Broek, *Geography: Its Scope and Spirit* (Columbus, Ohio: Charles E. Merrill, 1965), p. 90.
5. Michael Jacobson and Stuart Palonsky, "School Camping and Elementary Social Studies," *Social Education* 40 (January 1976):45.
6. Gary Manson and Carol J. Price, "Introducing Cities to Elementary School Children," *Journal of Geography* (May 1969): 296.
7. Fred A. Lampe and Orval C. Schaefer, Jr., "Land-Use Patterns in the City," *Journal of Geography* (May 1969):302.
8. Service Publication No. M44, Denoyer-Geppert Company, Chicago, Ill.

## SELECTED REFERENCES

Arnsdoff, Val. "Geographic Education: Principles and Practices in the Primary Grades." *Social Education* 31 (November 1967):612–614.

Bacon, Phillip, ed. *Focus on Geography*. 40th Yearbook. Washington, D.C.: National Council for the Social Studies, 1970.

Carpenter, Helen McCracken, ed. *Skill Development in Social Studies*. 33rd Yearbook. Washington, D.C.: National Council for the Social Studies, 1963.

Drummond, Dorothy W. "Developing Geography Concepts in the Intermediate Grades." *Social Education* 30 (December 1966):628–631.

Hanna, Paul R.; Sabaroff, Rose; and Davies, Gordon F. *Geography in the Teaching of Social Studies: Concepts and Skills*. Boston: Houghton Mifflin, 1966.

Kennamer, Lorin, Jr. "Geography in the Middle Grades." *Social Education* 31 (November 1967):615–617.

Larkin, James M., and White, Jane J. "The Learning Center in the Social Studies Classroom." *Social Education* 38 (November/December 1974):697–710.

Lee, John R., and Stampfer, Nathaniel. "Two Studies in Learning Geography: Implications for the Primary Grades." *Social Education* 30 (December 1966):627–628.

McAulay, John D. "Geography Understandings of the Primary Child." *Journal of Geography* 55 (April 1966):33–37.

———. "What Understandings Do Second-Grade Children Have of Time Relationships?" *Journal of Educational Research* 54 (1961):312–314.

Rushdoony, Haig A. "Achievement in Map-Reading: An Experimental Study." *Elementary School Journal* 64 (November 1963):70–75.

Stoltman, Joseph P. "Children's Conceptions of Space and Territorial Relationships." *Social Education* 41 (February 1977):142–145.

Wisniewski, Richard, ed. *Teaching About Life in the City*. 42nd Yearbook. Washington, D.C.: National Council for the Social Studies, 1972.

BIRTHDAY CHART
The Months of the
January
Enero
February
Fabrero
Marzo
July

# Part Five
# Utilization of Materials

A rich and inviting supply of materials is available for use in social studies instruction. Fresh new materials enhance the social studies. The textbooks are colorful and appealing to children, films and filmstrips can be found to supplement almost any study, children's trade books add a spark of interest, realia kits present an opportunity to see the artifacts of a country, simulated games permit active involvement, and the vast amount of free and inexpensive materials provide extensive background information.

Part Five discusses the selection and utilization of materials in elementary social studies with regard to, when feasible, the different methods of instruction.

# 14
# Utilization of Materials in the Social Studies

The following discussion of materials for use in the social studies includes children's trade books, games, programmed materials, cartoons, graphs and charts, textbooks, multimedia kits, films and filmstrips, and free and inexpensive materials. These materials are a representative but not exhaustive list of those available.

## CHILDREN'S TRADE BOOKS

Two types of children's books can be incorporated with social studies—informational books that are primarily concerned with facts, and fiction books that incorporate facts with hypothetical situations. May Hill Arbuthnot suggests that the following criteria be considered in selecting informational books:

1. *Scrupulous accuracy*—Children have a tendency to accept what is in the book and therefore care should be exercised to check the accuracy of the information presented.
2. *Convenient presentation*—The information should be organized in such a way that children can easily find what they are looking for.
3. *Clarity*—Little value will come from the information *unless* it is clearly stated for ease of understanding.
4. *Adequate treatment*—Sufficient information should be included to ensure understanding, but irrelevant details should not obscure the facts needed.
5. *Style*—An informational book should be interesting and as well written as possible.[1]

Informational books include titles such as Mable Pyne's *The Little Geography of the United States,* which uses picture maps and colorful illustrations. *Landmark Books* is a series that is concerned with the various periods of development in the United States. Genevieve Foster's *George Washington's World, Abraham Lincoln's World,* and *Augustus Caesar's World* take a horizontal look at history to help children understand the events taking place in other parts of the world throughout the lifetime of each of these men. Both the *American Heritage Series* and *American Adventure Series* are written about the lives and events of famous people in American history. *The Childhood of Famous Americans Series* contains about one hundred selections dealing with people such as Abraham Lincoln, Booker T. Washington, and Babe Ruth. These stories begin with the individual's childhood and end during his or her adult life. The *We Were There Series* emphasizes dramatic events in our history. Any of these books can be used in research activities by individuals or committees. Role playing and dramatic presentations are easily adapted from books about historical events or famous people.

*People and Places* by Margaret Mead discusses anthropological concepts of the similarities and differences among peoples of the world and offers suggestions that might solve humankind's problems so all may live together peacefully. *Why We Live Where We Like* by Eva Knox Evans presents geographical information about the United States and the interdependence of people. Her final chapter, "Your Own Home Town," encourages the readers to seek information about their own community.

For the child who has an aversion to geography and history, fiction books like Holling C. Holling's *Paddle-to-the-Sea* or *Tree in the Trail* should prove fascinating as well as educational. *Tree in the Trail* presents the history of our westward movement through the experiences of a cottonwood tree on the Santa Fe Trail. *Paddle-to-the-Sea* is the story of a small, carved canoe containing the figure of an Indian. The canoe is set afloat from the Upper Great Lakes to make its way to the sea. These books contain accurate geographical and historical material presented in a way that should interest children and motivate them to learn more about the topics under consideration.

Depicting the forces of change, Virginia Lee Burton's *The Little House* finds itself in a country setting until the growth of the surrounding area overwhelms it and a city grows up around it. Intended for young children, this book can be used in conjunction with a study of the local community.

Pat Hutchin's *Changes Changes* will help children understand the concept of change.

Children who read Eric Carle's *Have You Seen My Cat?* have a better understanding of multiethnicity.

Lois Lenski is another author who has described the lives of children in various parts of our country. *Strawberry Girl* and *Cotton in My Sack* were written about farm workers in Florida and Arkansas. Her *Prairie School* discusses the hard life of the Plains states.

Books about minority groups include *Striped Ice Cream* by Joan Lexan; *The Contender* by Walter Lipsyte; *A Ride on High* by Candida Palmer; *Lillie of Watts: A Birthday Discovery* by Mildred Pitts Walter; and *The Soul Brothers and Sister Lou* by Kristin Hunter. They are all stories about ghetto children's lives. *Candita's Choice* by Mina Lewiton is a book about the adjustment problems of a Puerto Rican child in New York City. *That Bad Carlos* and *The Spider Plant* discuss respectively a boy who is acquiring a bad reputation and family life. Stories about poverty are depicted in *My Name is Pablo, Maggie Rose, Her Birthday Christmas,* and *The Family Under the Bridge.*

Books about children from other lands such as May McNeer's *The Mexican Story,* which provides descriptions of accounts in the history of that country, or *Nine Days to Christmas,* which gives an account of the customs of a country, are useful when studying other cultures. Folktales of our own and other countries provide an excellent introduction to the study of other areas. Children are fascinated to learn why certain traditions have withstood the passing of time. Helen Huus's *Children's Books to Enrich the Social Studies* is an excellent resource. These children's books add a touch of interest and uniqueness to social studies that cannot be found in any other resource. Many other fine books too numerous to mention can be used readily in social studies. In addition, *Social Education* publishes a review of children's books to be used in the social studies.[2]

## SIMULATIONS AND GAMES

New materials have been developed for the social studies classroom. They are labeled "simulation," "simulation games," or just "games." Herman, in the *Encyclopedia of the Social Sciences,* defines simulation as a situation having human players and rules and outcomes that are sufficiently elaborate to require the use of calculators or computers. Games are more simplistic, more manual, and less amenable to computer analysis. Simulated games are situations in which the less sophisticated may "assume the roles of decision makers in a simulated (imitated) environment according to specified procedures or rules."[3]

No specific rules have been established for designing simulated games, but elements that might be involved in them are suggested.

1. Identification of objectives—What will be learned by the game?
2. Construction of a simplified model of the process or system that will best serve the objectives.

3. Identification of the various actors or teams so that the number would demonstrate the model effectively and also conform to classroom needs.
4. Provision of resources for the players to exchange in competition with other players.
5. Establishing rules or limits of permissible behavior during the game.
6. Identification of objectives or goals for the actors as they engage in trading resources.
7. Development of a scene or setting the stage for the beginning of play.[4]

The exciting aspect of simulation games is their involvement of the children, who actively participate in decision making, diplomatic maneuvers, or some other equally stimulating experience. Most children enjoy these simulation games and benefit educationally from their participation. Because there are no hard-and-fast rules for game design, teachers and students can produce their own games, utilizing the previously discussed elements. Four games that were developed by teachers for a sixth-grade classroom are: *Inflation*—simulates the inflation of a money system; *Production Line*—"demonstrates the greater efficiency of the production line as compared to the output of individual craftsmen";[5] *Landlocked Nations*—demonstrates "why nations through history have been willing to fight for control of narrow waterways";[6] and *Parent-Satellite Nations*—helps children gain insight into the development of a nation from a satellite to a power in its own right.

There are several commercially produced games for elementary school classrooms, but more are available at junior, senior, and adult levels. *Caribou Hunting* and *Seal Hunting*, elementary school games, are both board games in which students simulate some of the difficulties Eskimos experience in acquiring an adequate food supply.[7] *Democracy*[8] presents the processes of our government, while *Inter-Nation Simulation*[9] offers an international view. Within a frontier setting, *Powderhorn*[10] gives students the opportunity to pursue the meaning of democracy, the necessity for checks and balances in government, and an opportunity to see how it feels to be in a minority group. *Bafa Bafa: A Cross Culture Simulation*[11] explores the meaning of culture and contact among cultures. It examines how prejudice and stereotyping occur. *Import*[12] allows students to participate in the activities of six importing companies in various ports, expanding their understanding of international interdependence. *Starpower*[13] distributes wealth in the form of chips, which emphasizes the low mobility of low-income members of society. *Pollution*[14] and *Water Pollution*[15] emphasize ecology problems and permit children to make decisions about their solutions. *Inner-City Planning*[16] provides the opportunity for making decisions about the planning of a city. *Sunshine*,[17] specifically designed for junior high school children, can be adapted for the upper-elementary grades. This game presents some of the situations that can occur in the course of race relations in a city. *Ghetto*[18] is another that relates the conditions and problems of living within an inner-city area. *Consumer*[19] is designed to teach something about the problems and economics of installment buying. *Market*[20] aids children in the acquisition of the concepts of supply, demand, and prices. *Sierra Leone* and the *Sumerian Game* are both computer-based games in economics.[21] "The child makes decisions and enters his answers at the computer terminal"[22] and immediately receives a progress report.

"Proponents of simulation and games in social studies education claim that intuitive thinking is developed, learning is made entertaining and relevant to student life experiences. Emphasis is placed on developing analytical approaches and organizing concepts transferable to other problems."[23] Certainly more research is needed in this area, but teachers can experiment in their own classrooms to determine the success of games with their students. Do the games improve intuitive thinking? Are children more interested in learning? Do they learn as much? A review of research indicates that:

1. Simulation games do not appear to have any clear advantage in teaching content to students.
2. Games and simulations appear to have a positive influence on student attitudes.
3. Games and simulations appear to be influential in encouraging students to become more active in the learning process.[24]

One area that particularly needs exploring is that of the lasting effect of game playing on children. Does it change values? Does it increase competitiveness? What effect does the power to manipulate the lives of others assumed in a game have upon children? These are questions that require answers before the total effectiveness of games can be determined.

## PROGRAMMED MATERIAL

The objective of programmed material is to give the learner elements of a subject in sequential order. This material provides immediate feedback for the learner, who then knows whether the answer is correct. Many programmed materials require review before the learner can go on, if an incorrect answer is given. The success of achieving correct answers is expected to motivate the learner to continue the study.

Programmed materials are available in several forms—textbooks, teaching machines, and computers. In programmed textbooks, answers to questions appear either on another page or are covered by a flap on the same page. Teaching machines are found in a variety of forms such as the Cyclo Teacher of *Encyclopedia Britannica,* which hides the answer until the children move to the next question, or computer-based systems, which assess children's answers and present information for their next step.

The potential of programmed materials has not been realized, especially in the area of computerized instruction. The research completed to date has not determined what type of material is best presented by programming.

Few programmed materials have been produced for elementary school. Some examples of those in use are *Learning to Use a Globe Set I and II,* by Ewing and Seibel, which is a scrambled text to teach global concepts. A programmed text for teaching about maps is *Geography of the United States* by MacGraw and Williams. *An Introduction to American Government* by Rosenhack illustrates the separation of powers in our federal government. The latter two texts are for use in the upper-elementary grades.

## CARTOONS

Cartoons are best used to stimulate discussions, present a particular point of view, and provide an opportunity to interpret the opinion of others. Most cartoons use symbols that require previous experience to be understood. If children lack this experience, teachers should assist in the interpretation.

Criteria for selecting cartoons for instruction include:

- Does the cartoon present an idea quickly and effectively?
- Does it present an idea that would be difficult to introduce using a different approach?
- Will it be understood by the majority of the students without too much assistance?

Cartoons that might embarrass children of a certain race, religion, or national origin should be avoided unless the discussion to be initiated concerns prejudice or a controversial issue. Frequently, a cartoon expresses a view of a controversial issue better than most methods.

To enable all of the children in a class to see a cartoon at the same time, the teacher should make a transparency for the overhead projector or mount it for the opaque projector. Children should be encouraged to collect cartoons that provoke thought. These cartoons can be used in school for committee presentations or individual reports. Children delight in developing their own cartoons. This activity aids them in understanding the subtle use of symbols.

The following cartoons are examples that should effectively provoke discussion.

*"Filibuster or no filibuster, I don't want my secret recipes in the Congressional Record!"*

(SOURCE: Gurney Williams, ed., Look on the light side (Englewood Cliffs, N.J.: Prentice-Hall, 1957), reprinted from Look magazine.)

Discussion questions for the above cartoon can be: What idea is this first cartoon attempting to portray? What does this cartoon suggest happens during a filibuster in Congress?

UTILIZATION OF MATERIALS IN THE SOCIAL STUDIES     251

The next cartoon quickly presents an idea. The idea presented, however, is one that children might not readily perceive.

Many cartoons are too sophisticated for young children, but occasionally an appropriate one can be found. Also, the reluctant learner may be motivated about a topic by the use of cartoons where he or she would be otherwise uninterested.

"Boon to mankind, ha! One of these days it'll get loose and burn up the whole world."

(SOURCE: Gurney Williams, ed., Look on the light side (Englewood Cliffs, N.J.: Prentice-Hall, 1957), reprinted from Look magazine.)

## GRAPHS AND CHARTS

Just as cartoons can present certain ideas more effectively, graphs and charts can often be used to illustrate an idea or present information more readily than other methods. Children who have difficulty with reading may interpret a graph or chart successfully and acquire the concept that others read.

It is necessary to assist children in learning to read and interpret graphs and charts. Young children should start with picture graphs that are related to something familiar to them. An example is Figure 14.1, which uses stick figures to indicate the lunch count for the day.

Each child can readily perceive how he or she is represented on the graph. Children may wish to label the graph with their names to be sure that all are represented. Later, the teacher can explain that it is possible to represent several people with one figure, as shown in Figure 14.2. Bar graphs in the classroom can be used to represent the daily temperatures, as shown in Figure 14.3. After the children can interpret the bar graph, line graphs (illustrated by Figure 14.4) can be introduced using the same information as the bar graph for comparison and ease of understanding. Circle graphs, illustrated by Figure 14.5, are easily understood when they are used to show how a pie might be divided among the children.

Preparation of graphs using information related to classroom experiences during early primary grades will provide children with the understanding necessary to tackle the more abstract statistics presented in the middle and upper grades. Correct labeling of the graphs is vital, and emphasis should be placed on reading them accurately.

**Figure 14.1**   Room 10 Lunch Count

**Figure 14.2**   Room 10 Lunch Count

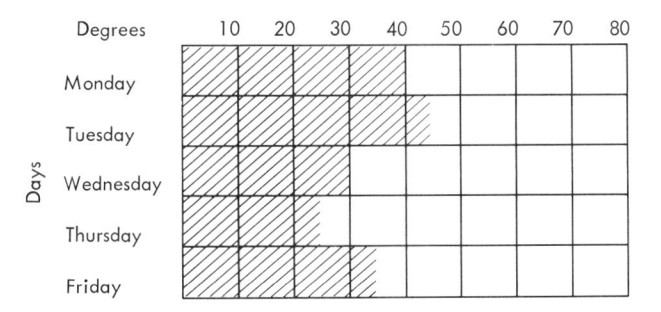

## UTILIZATION OF MATERIALS IN THE SOCIAL STUDIES

**Figure 14.3**   Daily Temperature (Bar Graph)

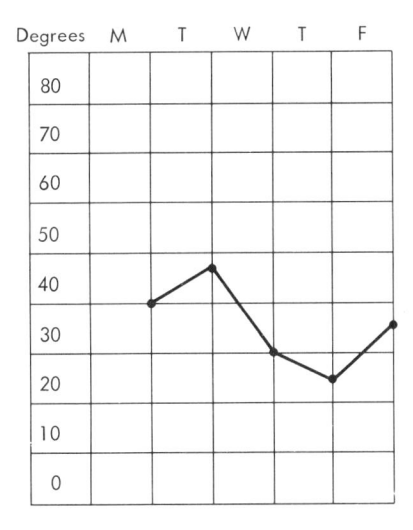

**Figure 14.4**   Daily Temperature (Line Graph)

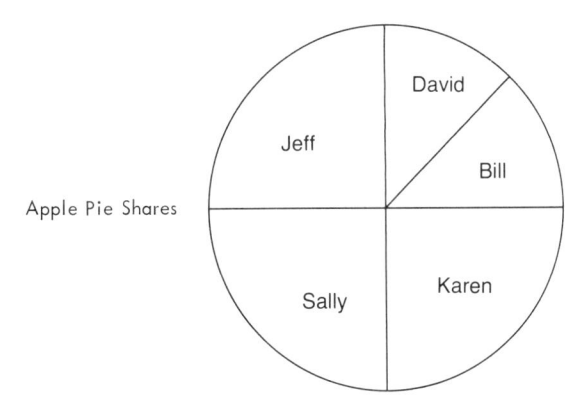

**Figure 14.5**   Apple Pie Shares

A variety of charts are found in every elementary classroom. Most children are introduced to school activities through the use of experience charts. Here, a mutual class experience is recorded, using the children's description for all to read. Charts also are developed to record the rules of a game, the directions for committee work, and the helpers for the week.

A chart with pictures (for example, one depicting the process of making paper from the cutting of a tree through the finished product) is called a flow chart. These charts aid in understanding the steps involved in a process. In the primary grades, children can be introduced to them by using the book *Pelle's New Suit,* which describes how Pelle obtains a new suit from the time he shears wool from the sheep until he picks up his suit at the tailor's shop. Young children can draw and interpret a flow chart of the process described in the book. More complicated processes such as drilling and refining oil can be understood by older children. Commercial flow charts are available on legislative processes such as "How a Bill Becomes a Law," or manufacturing processes such as "Milk from the Farm to You." Charts can be used for comparison—comparing the before and after, past and present, or another country's government with ours. A chart is described as a pictorial or line diagram of a topic.

## PICTURES

Pictures are an extremely valuable resource in social studies. They can be used to develop numerous skills such as observing, classifying, grouping, comparing, and contrasting and to introduce inquiry and problem-solving situations. Also, concepts that otherwise might be difficult to present may be done through pictures. Sources for pictures are extensive—including newspapers, magazines, posters, and slides and photographs that individuals have acquired through travels.

Commercial companies are now producing picture series that are valuable in that they often provide resources that are difficult for the individual teacher to acquire. Many sets of pictures have guide books with suggestions for presentations and a series of questions intended to provoke inquiry. *Discussion Pictures for Beginning Social Studies* by Harper & Row is an example of such a series. *Interaction of Man and His Environment* by Rand McNally provides sets of pictures for contrast and comparison. Pictures to promote role-playing situations are provided by *Words and Actions.*[25] *Cross Culture Study Prints*[26] is a set of thirty-one carefully selected photographs to uncover preconceptions and misconceptions about other lands and cultures.

# TEXTBOOKS

A prime source material for the social studies is the textbook. Frequently, it is the basis or guide for the organization of instruction in the classroom. For this reason, care should be exercised in selecting textbooks. The following criteria of selection are suggested:

1. Is the organization of the textbook easily followed?
2. Are the concepts presented in a manner that most students will be able to understand?
3. Are there sufficient illustrations, maps, charts, and graphs to increase the reader's understanding?
4. Does the text contain a table of contents, index, and sufficient appendices to aid the reader in locating information?
5. Are references listed where additional information can be secured, such as films, books, and records?
6. Is there a teacher's guide with suggestions concerning uses of the text in instruction?
7. Does the text contain a multiethnic presentation of topic?
8. Are the authors respected scholars from the social sciences and social studies education?

## Utilization

For too long, the textbook has been used by too many teachers as a crutch in teaching social studies. This practice is exemplified by the teacher who, whether unprepared for the lesson or lacking an understanding of teaching principles, has each student read a text paragraph orally and then discusses the concepts. The underachieving reader does not benefit from the oral reading, and the more capable reader is bored. Several other techniques would better utilize the resources of the text. A sample lesson plan follows:

*Topic:* Mexico.
*Objective:* To understand the culture of Mexico by acquiring knowledge of its historical development.
*Materials:* Textbook study guide and visual aids.
*Procedure: Group I, Underachievers*—Use a textbook that contains a physical-political map of Mexico, a historical map of early Spanish explorations, and a story of Cortez's capture of the Aztecs. Use realia of Mexico,

including a record of Spanish and Mexican Indian language, dolls dressed in native Mexican dress, pottery, and musical instruments.

1. Using the maps in the textbook, discuss the location of Mexico in relation to the United States and its geographical areas. Using the historical map, trace the routes of the Spanish explorers to Mexico.
2. Read the story of Cortez's explorations and conquest of the Aztecs to the children. Observe the realia of the country and discuss how the Spanish conquest influenced its culture.

*Group II, Average Achievers*—Have the children read silently the chapter on Spanish exploration and conquest in Mexico. Establish a purpose for the reading with the following study-guide questions.

1. Try to determine the reasons why Spanish explorers were interested in the New World, particularly Mexico.
2. Trace the route of Cortez in Mexico and discuss the type of problems the physical features and climate gave his men.
3. Why was Cortez able to defeat the Aztecs?

*Group III, Above Average Achievers*—Use the same study guide as above with these additional activities and questions.

1. Read another account of the Spanish conquest from a different resource and compare the two descriptions.
2. Are there any discrepancies in the accounts?
3. If so, why would this difference occur?
4. Discuss what you think Mexico would be like if the French or English had conquered the Aztecs.

In this sample lesson plan, all groups utilize the text, but each with a different level of abstraction.

The textbook can be used by committees for exploratory reading or research information. The suggested references included in the textbook provide excellent resources for extending research activities. The textbook also can be used for individual or group research in a problem-solving situation. Textbooks have been criticized because too many of the situations they present describe life in suburbia and fail to interest children who come from disadvantaged homes. Today, many textbook series are attempting to alleviate this problem.

Beginning teachers find the guide to the textbook invaluable for suggested teaching techniques, instructional activities, and additional resources. The danger in using the guide lies in the teacher's failure to adapt the use of the text and guide to the needs of the children in a particular classroom.

## MULTIMEDIA KITS

Media materials organized around a major topic have been assembled into kits for use in social studies instruction. These kits contain films, filmstrips, records, realia, written information, and a teacher's guide to instruction. International Communications Foundation[27] has assembled these kits for the study of other cultures. Many kits are available for countries such as Pakistan, Afghanistan, and Turkey, for which it often is difficult to find sufficient information at the children's level.

Examples of the materials available for Mexico are films of the life of the people, filmstrips on aspects of the culture, records of the language and stories, and realia including dolls dressed in the native dress, pieces of clothing, and musical instruments. Also included is the teacher's guide with background information and suggested teaching techniques for use of the materials.

As previously mentioned, MATCH[28] kits provide multimedia materials organized around a specific topic. Currently available are these: *The City, A House of Ancient Greece,* and *Japanese Family. Free to Be You and Me*[29] is a multimedia kit to explore sex stereotyping. *Children Everywhere*[30] examines the similarities and differences that exist among the children around the world.

The advantage in using such kits is the accessibility of materials —many of the items included would be rather difficult for teachers to obtain elsewhere. Because some children will learn more from handling realia than from viewing a filmstrip about the items, use of the different media helps meet individual differences in the classroom.

These kits can be used with several teaching methods. Individual or committee research can be organized around the materials for unit teaching or problem solving. Because disadvantaged children benefit from concrete materials, the kits can be used successfully with them. The kits also can be presented to the entire class as introduction to a new study or for enrichment. More of these kits will soon be available.[31]

## FILMS AND FILMSTRIPS

Films and filmstrips provide visual representations instead of the abstract representations provided by text descriptions. Both sources of information are important and must be carefully chosen. Criteria to be applied in the selection of every film or filmstrip include:

1. Is there continuity of content throughout the film or filmstrip?
2. Is the photography of good quality?

3. Is the sound of the film easily understood?
4. Will the presentation of the film or filmstrip contribute to the understanding of the topic under study?
5. Is the information presented accurate?
6. Can the information be understood by elementary school children?

Films and filmstrips should be selected on the basis of their best use. Does the film introduce a new topic effectively? Does it provide background information? Does it motivate interest in a topic? Would it be effective as a culmination to a study? Guides are available to aid teachers in selecting films and filmstrips.[32] *Booklist,* published by the American Library Association, gives reviews of the books, films, filmstrips, and multimedia kits that are provided.

## FREE AND INEXPENSIVE MATERIALS

The teacher can obtain an abundance of free or inexpensive materials which can aid considerably in social studies instruction. Travel agencies and transportation companies such as airlines, railways, and trucking industries supply teachers with posters and charts of places to visit and with booklets that explain the transportation systems. These packets may also have background information for the teacher. Chambers of commerce in cities and states and embassies of countries provide extensive information about their areas. They often include maps and colorful posters and regulations for travel in their areas.

A variety of manufacturing, publishing, packing, and insurance companies have educational materials that they supply to teachers upon request. Agencies of the United States government provide materials at a small charge. Several guides are available with information about securing these materials.[33]

Pictures and information from magazines and newspapers often add resources for the study of a topic. Teachers should start a file of these resources for use when needed. For easy accessibility, the file should be divided into possible topics of study. Slides, photographs, and postcards collected from the teacher's own travels also should be added to the resources.

## NOTES

1. May Hill Arbuthnot, *Children and Books* (Chicago: Scott, Foresman, 1964), pp. 565–566.
2. "Notable Children's Trade Books in the Field of Social Studies," *Social Education* 40 (April 1976):238.

3. *Simulation Games for the Social Studies Classroom* (New York: Foreign Policy Association, 1968), p. 9.
4. *Simulation Games,* p. 114.
5. Charles Christine and Dorothy Christine, "Four Simulation Games That Teach," *Grade Teacher* (October 1967):112. Reprinted from *Grade Teacher Magazine* by permission of the publishers. Copyright October 1967 by Teachers Publishing Corp.
6. Christine and Christine, "Four Simulation Games That Teach," p. 114.
7. Education Development Center, 15 Miflin Place, Cambridge, Mass. 02138.
8. Western Publishing Co., 850 3rd Ave., New York, N.Y. 10022.
9. Science Research Associates, 259 East Erie St., Chicago, Ill. 60611.
10. Western Behavioral Sciences Institute, 1150 Silverada, La Jolla, Calif.
11. Simile II, 218 Twelfth St., P.O. Box 910, Del Mar, Calif. 92014.
12. Ibid.
13. Ibid.
14. Educational Research Council of America, Houghton Mifflin Publishing Co., Boston, Mass.
15. Urban Systems, Inc., 1033 Mass. Avenue, Cambridge, Mass.
16. Macmillan Publishing Co., 100 A Brown St., Riverside, New Jersey 08075.
17. Interact, P.O. Box 262, Lakeside, Calif. 92040.
18. Western Publishing Co., New York, N.Y.
19. The Johns Hopkins University, Department of Social Relations, Baltimore, Md. 21218.
20. Industrial Relations Center, University of Chicago, Chicago, Ill.
21. Board of Cooperative Educational Services, Westchester County, Yorktown Heights, N.Y. 10598.
22. *Simulation Games for the Social Studies Classroom,* p. 21.
23. Leonard W. Ingraham, "Teachers, Computers, and Games: Innovations in the Social Studies," *Social Education* 31 (January 1967):53.
24. Donald R. Wentworth and Darrell R. Lewis, "A Review of Research on Instructional Games and Simulations in Social Studies Education," *Social Education* 37 (May 1972):432–440.
25. Fannie R. Shaftel and George Shaftel, *Words and Actions* (New York: Holt, Rinehart and Winston).
26. Cross-Culture Study Prints, Inter Culture Associates, Box 277, Thompson Place, Conn. 06277.
27. International Communications Foundation, 9033 Wilshire Boulevard, Beverly Hills, Calif.
28. The Children's Museum, Boston.
29. McGraw-Hill Book Co., New York, N.Y.
30. Educational Division, Learning Tree Filmstrips, 934 Peart St., P.O. Box 1590, Boulder, Co. 80302.
31. Educational Media Guide, The Educational Media Council, New York.
32. *Education Film Guide* (H. W. Wilson, 950 University Avenue, New York, N.Y. 10052).

33. Educators' Progress Service (Randolph, Wisconsin 53956) publishes *Educators' Guide to Free Films, Educators' Guide to Free Filmstrips, Educators' Guide to Free Social Studies Materials, Educators' Guide to Free Teaching Aids,* and *Educators' Index to Free Materials.*

## SELECTED REFERENCES

*Free and Inexpensive Learning Materials.* 18th ed. Nashville, Tenn.: George Peabody College for Teachers, 1976.

Gillespie, Judith. "Analyzing and Evaluating Classroom Games." *Social Education* 36 (January 1972):33–42.

Hogan, Arthur J. "Simulation: An Annotated Bibliography." *Social Education* 32 (March 1968):242–244.

Ingraham, Leonard W. "Teachers, Computers, and Games: Innovations in the Social Studies." *Social Education* 31 (January 1967):51–53.

Joyce, Bruce R. *New Strategies for Social Education.* Chicago: Science Research Associates, 1972.

Livingston, Samuel A., and Stroll, Clarice S. *Simulation Games: An Introduction for the Social Studies Teacher.* New York: Free Press, 1973.

"Notable Children's Trade Books in the Field of Social Studies." *Social Education* 40 (April 1976):238.

Walsh, Huber M. "Learning Resources for Individualizing Instruction." *Social Education* 31 (May 1967):413.

Wentworth, Donald R., and Lewis, Darrell R. "A Review of Research on Instructional Games and Simulations in Social Studies Education." *Social Education* 37 (May 1973):432–440.

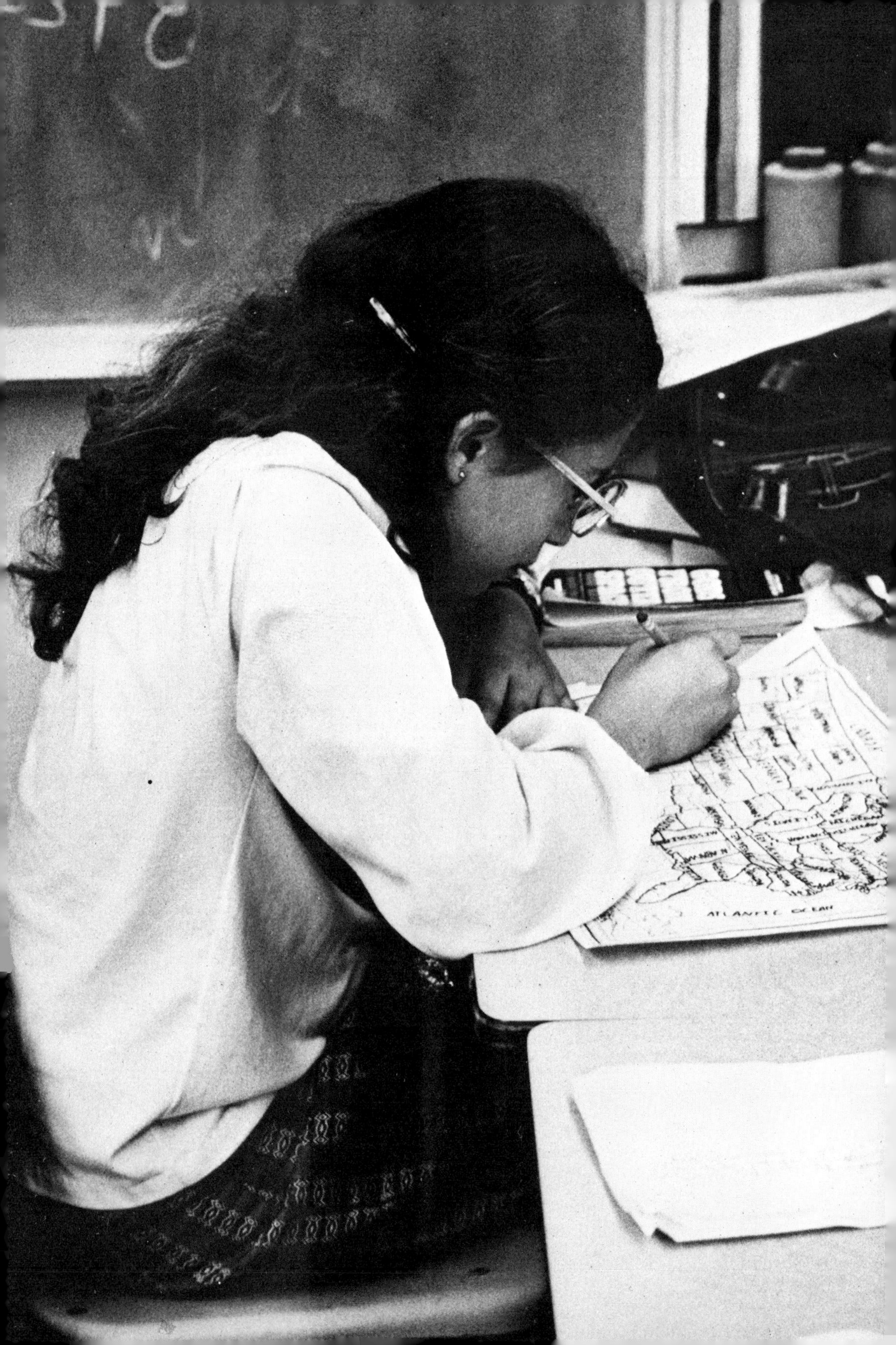
ATLANTIC OCEAN

# Part Six
# Evaluation

Was the program of instruction in social studies successful? Were the teaching techniques effective? Have the objectives of the social studies program been achieved? Have the children acquired skill in intuitive thinking, problem solving, and developing human relationships? These are some of the questions that teachers ask themselves about the outcomes of their social studies instruction. How can they determine the answers to these questions? What evaluation techniques are effective for different aspects of the program? Will the method of instruction affect the evaluation techniques?

Part Six discusses methods and techniques of evaluation used at the national, state, local, and classroom level.

# 15
# Evaluation of Social Studies Instruction

Evaluation of instruction at any level, whether classroom, local, state, or national is accomplished by measuring the extent to which the children have achieved the established objectives. The objectives state the expected outcomes of the instruction for the children. An appropriate technique of evaluation to determine if the objectives have been reached must be selected. The primary purpose of evaluation is to determine the progress achieved by the children, but it may also indicate a need to change the method of instruction or the materials utilized.

The focus of evaluation, however, might shift at the different levels—classroom, local, state, and national. The teachers in the classroom are concerned with each individual child's ability to achieve, while local, state, and national concerns are more global—how well do all the children achieve? The philosophy of education, whether humanistic or behavioral, will determine what objectives are established at each level. Different techniques of evaluation may therefore be used at each level.

**IN THE CLASSROOM**

Evaluation of instruction in the classroom should be continuous and should encompass all learning experiences. Teachers should ask themselves these questions as they plan learning experiences: How will this experience benefit the children? Have I taken into consideration the individual needs and abilities of the children? What objective or objectives will this experience achieve? Too often teachers are not certain what should be evaluated or what standards of evaluation should be used. Frequently there is confusion over evaluation and grading.

Evaluation is assessing the needs and abilities of the children—Bert is a shy nervous child, but capable, who learns best by visual means, while Rebecca is outgoing and an auditory learner. ("Visual learner" here refers to a child who must see things or words for maximum understanding, while "auditory learners" refer to children who hear things and verbalize to understand. There are some learners who are tactile, which means they need to touch things or trace the outlines of letters and words to learn them.) The teacher then uses the knowledge about the children to develop objectives for instruction and evaluates to determine if the objectives have been achieved and if the proper method of instruction and materials have been used. Grading is the assessment given to a child's achievement against the standard that has been established. If the objective states that the child should score 80 percent accuracy on a 100-item test of knowledge, and if he or she scores only 75, the grade would be a U or D dependent upon the grading system.

Teachers should establish goals for the social studies program for the entire year and then select weekly or daily learning experiences that will lead to the attainment of the overall goals. Obviously, evaluation is necessary throughout the teaching/learning process and may be accomplished for: (1) evaluation of a single learning experience; (2) evaluation of a group of experiences organized around a unit of study or problem-solving situation; and (3) longitudinal evaluation of the progress achieved over a period of time, whether a month, semester, or year.

At each point in the educational program, teachers establish objectives or goals based on the assessment of the needs and abilities of the children, provide learning experiences, and evaluate the extent to which the objectives have been achieved. The evaluation involves several facets—the proper assessment of the needs and abilities of the children, establishment of the objectives based on the needs, the success of the teaching technique, the materials utilized, and the attainment of the objectives. Figure 15.1 illustrates the process.

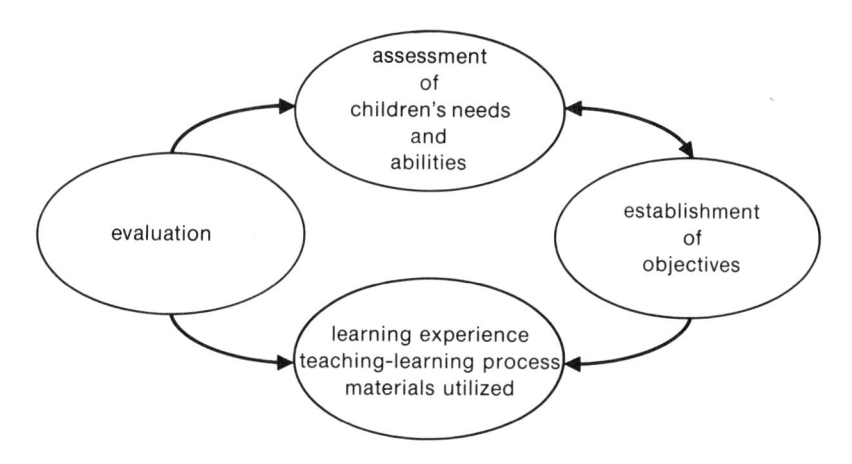

**Figure 15.1** Process of Evaluation

If objectives have been stated in behavioral or performance terms, the teacher can evaluate the learning experience more easily. An example (given in Chapter One) of a cognitive objective stated in behavioral terms is:

*To list at least one of the Mexican holidays that is different from those celebrated in the United States.*

This knowledge can be evaluated by an objective test item or an essay question. The teachers know exactly what they expect of the children.

An example of an affective objective in behavioral terms is:

*To value the contributions the many subcultures have made to our heritage and express an appreciation for them.*

Again, the teachers know exactly what is to be evaluated. They can observe the children at work and at play and note their comments concerning other cultures, or they can use a questionnaire to determine each child's attitudes.

Readily acknowledged is the difficulty of evaluating the affective domain. Obviously, a measurement of the knowledge or understanding gained through instruction can be more easily obtained (through objective or essay tests, discussions, and conferences) than can a measurement of the attitudes acquired or changed by the instruction. Successful evaluation, however, requires that multiple methods be used to complete the total picture of the achievement of the instruction. Observation, a checklist, and conferences may help the teacher to assess attitudes; an objective test reveals the amount of knowledge gained; and an essay test, group discussion, or conferences indicate the amount of understanding obtained. More difficult to assess may be the problem-solving and valuing skills of the individual. Each method contributes its data to complete the complicated task of evaluation.

## METHODS OF EVALUATION

### Observation

In the classroom, teachers use the method of observation most frequently to evaluate learning experiences and assess the needs and abilities of individual children. As they conduct a discussion, teachers observe the expressions on the children's faces. Are they interested? Which children are always ready with the answers? Are there shy children who never enter the discussion? Do the children appear to understand? Would another method of instruction be more effective? Are the materials effective? During committee participation, the teacher observes the children working together. Are they willing to share? Do all children participate in the decision making? Does the child understand what he or she values? Does he or she act upon his or her values? Does each child complete his or her work on time? Is the child a visual learner? Does Robert need more concrete experiences? Because it is often difficult to remember the answers to these questions for each child, teachers find it necessary to develop a record for reference. The most common method used is a checklist of the objectives of the learning experience on which the teacher records each child's success or failure in achieving the objectives. A sample checklist follows:

|  | Willing to Share | Listens to Others | Completes Work on Time | Expresses Opinion | Posesses Creative Ideas | Identifies Value Issues |
|---|---|---|---|---|---|---|
| 1. Kay | U | U | O | O | O | O |
| 2. Bill | O | S | S | U | U | U |
| 3. Rita | S | S | S | S | S | O |
| 4. Gay | O | O | O | O | O | S |

O  Outstanding
S  Satisfactory
U  Unsatisfactory

Another method of recording on a checklist involves keeping a separate sheet for each child, as shown in the following example.

Name    Gay             Grade      5
        Map Skills                 Social Skills

| Map Skills | | Social Skills | |
|---|---|---|---|
| Ability to interpret color key | ✓ | Gets along well with others | |
| Locates places readily | | Accepts responsibility | ✓ |
| Ability to compute distances | ✓ | Shares materials | |
| | | Supports value beliefs | ✓ |

Use of the checklist facilitates observation and makes it more systematic. The checklist provides the teacher with definite behaviors to observe and a valuable record for use in reporting the children's progress.

## Rating Scales

Rating scales are more effective when the teacher is attempting to pinpoint a child's performance on a scale ranging from excellent to poor. Also, scores from rating scales are more easily translated to letter grades if such grades are required by the school's evaluation system. The following is a sample rating scale that a teacher might use during an observation period.

*Objective:* The child participates effectively in committee activities.

| | Excellent 5 | Good 4 | Average 3 | Fair 2 | Poor 1 |
|---|---|---|---|---|---|
| 1. Contributes ideas to group goal. | | | | | |
| 2. Does share of the work. | | | | | |
| 3. Listens to the opinions of others. | | | | | |
| 4. Works well with all types of children. | | | | | |
| 5. Locates information. | | | | | |

## Anecdotal Records

Some teachers prefer to make specific notations about children's behavior. With this procedure, they record statements about how each child reacts to learning situations or responds to statements from peers and the teacher. An example:

> Stewart was quite disturbed by Kim's reference to colored people. He corrected her, but also showed hostility toward her during game time.

> Rita improves daily in her ability to understand the valuing process. She quickly identified the value issues in today's skit.

Truman is constantly verbalizing his answers during worktime.

This type record is particularly helpful when teachers are reporting pupil progress to parents through conferences or letters.

## Conferences

The opportunity to converse with a child on a one-to-one basis is often a revealing form of evaluation. Attitudes, understandings, needs, abilities, and interests may be assessed by this method. Certain guidelines should be followed while conducting an individual conference:

1. Identify the goal of the conference—for example, direct the conference toward learning about the child's attitude toward people of another culture.
2. Prepare questions and discuss them during the conference—for example, "If you were to take a trip anywhere in the world, where would you go?" "Why?"
3. Establish good rapport with the children as soon as possible—discuss some personal event, a game, an interest.
4. Listen carefully to what the child has to say and make notations about the child's answers after the completion of the conference.
5. Leave the conference with a word of encouragement to the child and a definite plan of action.

The children should be prepared for the conferences and have their own goals and questions in mind. Before the conference, they might ask themselves: Are there questions I want to ask? Do I understand what we are studying? Does the teacher have suggestions for the improvement of my work? Do I have any projects or research I want to complete? If children have a thorough understanding of the purpose of the conference, it will be more profitable for them and their teacher.

Individual conferences also can be used for oral testing. The child who has difficulty with reading or the child who has a mental block about tests can have the test administered in a conference situation. Also, diagnostic instruments can be administered.

Individual conferences are open to criticism, especially if the class is large, because of their time-consuming nature. However, five or ten minutes spent with an individual child is well worth the time in terms of the results. In addition to obtaining the intended evaluation, the teacher also will get to know the child and may be able to spot possible problem areas. Ten minutes in an individual conference could help solve a problem for a child that might otherwise go unnoticed. In the conference, the teacher also has the opportunity to guide the child toward self-evaluation with questions such as: Are you satisfied with your work? Do you think you could do better? What do you see as your problems? The number of individual conferences held will depend upon their success, their intended purpose, the children's reactions, and the teacher's schedule.

## Group Discussion

The total class or small groups such as a committee can evaluate a mutual experience. This type of session permits children to compare their group's performance with the performances of others and to assess their role in the total group process. In this situation, children should learn the role of constructive criticism. This example, of a group discussion following the presentation of an oral report by a committee of sixth graders, illustrates these values.

TEACHER: As we look at the guidelines for presenting an oral report, how well do you think Kim's group followed them?

JERRY: I didn't think the report was very good.

SANDY: Me, neither.

TEACHER: What is our first rule in evaluating someone else's work?

JERRY: Look for something that was well done and comment on that.

TEACHER: Yes, and if we criticize their work, what should we include?

SANDY: We should tell what was wrong and how it might be improved.

TEACHER: Right; shall we try again?

JUAN: The group used pictures to illustrate their talk, which made it easier to understand.

KATHY: Yes, and the art work was so beautiful.

MURPHY: Some of the members of the group did not speak out so we all could hear and that spoiled their report.

SID: If they had moved out in front of the table, it would have been easier to hear them.

In this example, the teacher quickly turned what might have been a useless evaluation session into positive constructive criticism.

In another group session, the children might evaluate the behavior and performance of the group on a field trip and the value of the trip. The teacher would ask for comments on general behavior and request that children refrain from pinpointing individual actions that might embarrass the children involved. In assessing the value of the field trip, the children compare what they learned with the goals that were previously established for the trip.

Group discussions can be conducted daily to evaluate topics such as groups working together, the effectiveness of materials utilized, or the children's understanding of a film, outside speaker, or a reading. Such discussion aids teachers in determining the effectiveness of a particular teaching technique. Through discussion and comparison of the work completed by individuals and groups, these sessions also lead the child toward introspection and evaluation of his or her own behavior and achievement.

## Problem-Solving and Valuing Skills

Different forms of evaluation are necessary with the introduction of the problem-solving-inquiry methods of teaching and the valuing process. The usual objectives or essay-type tests are not effective because the outcomes of the instruction are expected to be the process skills of identifying a problem, formulating hypotheses, testing hypotheses, drawing conclusions, forming generalizations, and applying generalizations to new situations. The teacher is not attempting to assess whether a child has acquired a certain value, but rather if the child can identify the value issues, clarify his or her values, and support them.

Problem situations can be presented to children in different forms. The following might be given to younger children and they would generate their own alternative solutions.

> The children in the poor neighborhood of a community wanted a playground. There was a vacant lot on their street owned by one of the businessmen in town. How could they get their playground?

An example of the problem with alternate solutions provided is:

> One of the boys in the second-grade class was poorly dressed and often came to school hungry. He would take food from the other children's lunch boxes. There was a cafeteria in the school, but the boy did not have enough money for lunch. What should the children do?

1. The children could take turns bringing lunch for the boy.
2. The children could tell the teacher the boy was taking the food.
3. The children could have their mothers put extra food in their lunch boxes.
4. The boy could work in the cafeteria to earn his lunch.
5. Other solution?

Older children can be confronted with more difficult problems such as these:

If a country is wealthy, has a high standard of living, sufficient natural resources, and a surplus of goods, should it help a country or countries that have starving people? If so, how can it help, and would there be any problems if it helped the country or countries? How much help should the wealthy country give the poorer country?

In addition to determining the extent of a child's problem-solving skills, it also is possible to assess the valuing process in the same manner. By asking children to indicate what value issues are involved in the problem and what value is most important to them, depending on the solution they choose, the teacher can determine to some extent whether children can identify value issues and support their own value positions. Any of the above problems will give such an opportunity, as well as the one that follows:

If a manufacturing company is seriously polluting a stream with its waste products and killing the fish that are usually caught by sportsmen, what should the local community do? The company has indicated it cannot withstand the cost of controlling the pollution and continue to operate at full capacity. Many of the people in the community work for the company and would lose their jobs if the company closed. On the other hand, the sportsmen bring tourist trade to the community. The community has discussed the possibility of forming an industrial park.

Here are some possible solutions for the community. Choose the one you think is best and give your reason for choosing it.

1. Share the expense for controlling the pollution with the manufacturing company.
2. Pass an ordinance that would force the company to control the pollution or close the factory.

3. Ignore the situation and lose the tourist trade.
4. Form a community corporation to develop an industrial park that would control polluting wastes for this company and encourage future companies to move into the area.
5. Suggest any other solutions you have.

Do you need further information before you can make a decision? If so, what information is needed?[1]

## Analyzing Questions

The thought patterns of children can be assessed to a certain extent through the types of questions they ask. The following dialogue was taped during an activity in which the teacher wrapped an article inside a package and the children were required to ask questions to find out what was in the box.

T: There is something in this box.

P: Can I feel it?

T: No. You have to try and figure out what is in this box by asking questions. You can't say, "Is it this? or Is it that?" You have to ask questions that will help you figure out what is in the box. The only kind of question that you can ask me would be the kind that I can answer with yes or no. Now here is a sample of the kind of question that you could ask. You could say, "Is it made of wood?" And I would say yes or no.

P: Is that little girl in there? (Remembering the first discussion)

T: No. Now remember that I said you have to ask the kind of questions that I can answer with a yes or no and you have to work toward finding out what is in the box.

P: Is it made out of wood? Is it made out of steel?

T: No.

P: Is it made out of rubber?

T: I will have to take back what I said. It is partly made out of wood.

P: Is it plastic?

T: No.

P: Does it have legs?

T: No.

P: Does it have wheels?

T: No.
P: Does it have a face?
T: No.
P: It's a picture and it is made out of paper.
T: No.
P: Is it a box?
P: Is it made out of leather?
T: No.
P: Is it a piece of fish?
P: Is it a doll?
T: No.
P: Is it made out of glass?
P: Is it red, white, and blue?
T: Part of it is red.
P: Is it black, green, and purple?
T: Part of it is purple.
P: Purple donkey.
P: Is it a little dress?
T: No.
P: Is it some animal?
T: Yes.
P: Is it different colors?
T: Yes.
P: Is it a painting she made for you?
P: We can't guess it.
T: Keep asking questions. You are asking is it this or is it that. Why don't you find out something about it?
P: How can we?
T: By asking questions.
P: Will you tell us one thing about it?
T: If you ask a couple of questions, I will let you shake the box.
P: Is it a house?
T: You are not asking questions about it. What do you know so far about it?
P: That it is of different colors and that it is made of wood.
T: It is part wood. That is right.

P: Is it the face of her?
T: No, it doesn't have anything to do with the little girl.
P: Is it a pitcher?
P: Is it a little bucket?
T: No, it doesn't have anything to do with the little girl. What do you know so far about it?
P: That it is different colors and it is part wood.
P: Where did you get it from?
T: It has to be a question that I can answer yes or no.
P: Can we shake it?
T: You can shake it but not too hard.
P: Is it a block?
T: No.
P: Is it puzzles?
T: No.
P: Is it cookies?
T: No.
P: Is it hammers and things?
P: Are you going to open it?
T: You are going to try and find out without my opening it.
P: Is it wooden blocks?
T: Remember I said it was only partly wood. What other kinds of questions can you ask about it to try and find out?
P: May I see what it is?
T: No. Ask some questions about it. We said it wasn't steel.
P: Is there any green in it?
P: Is there yellow?
T: Yes.
P: Do you know what it is?
T: Sure, I put it in there.
P: She got it from her house.
T: I said there was some red in it.
P: Some play apples, play bananas, and play grapes.
P: Different-colored rocks?
T: No.
P: What they eat out of?

P: OK, open it then.
T: You haven't asked good questions.
P: It is a statue.
P: You got it from home; what can it be?
T: What are you doing? Instead of asking questions about it, you are guessing. So think of some questions you can ask about it.
P: I don't never know any.
T: Can't think of any questions?
P: Nope. Not a single one.
P: What can you use it for?
P: Can you make a house with it?
T: What are some questions you can ask about what you can do with it?
P: Is it big?
T: Now, Lonnie is getting to some good questions. No, Lonnie, it is not.
P: Is it little? Is it middle-sized?
T: It is a little larger. . . .
P: Is it large?
T: No.
P: Is it soft?
T: No. That is a good question. So if it isn't soft—
P: It is hard.
P: Is it hairy?
T: No. Your questions are very good.
P: What kind of wood is it made out of?
P: A wood that is different colors and not the kind of wood that we have.
T: No, it is not pretty wood necessarily. Kind of plain wood.
P: It is made out of skin?
T: Can you think of any more questions? Now what do you know about it so far?
P: It is different colors and it is hard.
P: It is middle-sized.
T: Very good. How can you find out what we do with it?
P: What they work with, what they eat on.
P: What their floor is made of.

# EVALUATION OF SOCIAL STUDIES INSTRUCTION

T: I told you it didn't have anything to do with the little girl. You want to find out what you do with it. How would you find out what you do with it? What questions would you ask?

P: Does it take batteries—a motorcar?

P: Do they play with it?

T: Yes, you might call it that.

P: Is it round?

T: Yes.

P: Little round blocks?

T: The whole thing isn't round but part of it is round.

P: She said is it a scarecrow?

T: No. That is made out of part wood, isn't it? There is one thing that you haven't asked me about it.

P: Can you burn it?

T: No. The wood part of it you can burn but you wouldn't want to.

P: Could it be a clock? Is it striped?

T: There is one question you haven't asked me. You haven't asked me if you could eat it.

P: They are food.

P: Is it a sugarcane?

T: No, but it has sugar in it.

P: It is candy.

T: Yes, I'll give each one of you a piece.[2]

From the discussion it is apparent that some children have difficulty using the information that they have gathered and piecing it together. Their thought patterns are not well organized. Certain children can be identified as asking the better questions and interpreting the data acquired from the previous questions. It is obvious that these children need subsequent opportunities to ask questions to get information, as well as opportunities to interpret data that is already provided.

## Teacher-Made Objective Tests

The type of test teachers devise depends upon: (1) what they are attempting to evaluate and (2) their method of instruction. For example, the teacher who has presented purely factual information would not give an essay test that evaluates understanding. It is advantageous for teachers to prepare their own tests, for they can then base the test questions on the things they deem most valuable for evaluation.

Essay tests can present problem-solving situations, determine understanding, and assess attitudes. The reliability of scoring an essay test is questioned, however, and the time required to score such tests is listed as a disadvantage.

Objective tests can test a wider variety of topics and they are more easily scored, but they require more time in planning and writing than essay tests. The Educational Testing Service suggests the following steps in preparing an objective test:

*Step 1.* List the major topics covered in your particular teaching unit. This list should not exceed five.

*Step 2.* Indicate the number of items you want to devote to each topic.

*Step 3.* List under each topic the things you want students to know about, understand, or be able to do.

*Step 4.* Collect materials on which to base items (textual material—typed or read by teacher, pictorial material, music, or specimens to be examined).[3]

*Step 5.* Begin writing of the items for your test.

*Step 6.* Submit the items for review by another individual.

*Step 7.* Rewrite or replace defective items.

*Step 8.* Arrange the items into a test. May be arranged from easy to hard or by common subject matter.

*Step 9.* Prepare directions for the test.

*Step 10.* Prepare an answer key.[4]

Different test elements that can be included are: (1) completion, (2) alternative response, (3) multiple choice, (4) matching, and (5) rearrangement.

Questions for evaluation can be prepared on each level of the Taba model, moving from the information-type to interpretation and application. This then determines the extent to which children's thinking skills have developed and the extent to which they can apply the information they have learned. Some sample questions for the children to answer in written or oral form might be:

*Concept Formation*
Who were the first people to colonize New England?

*Interpretation*
Why did these people come to America?

*Application*
What might New England be like today if the Spanish had settled there first?

## Child Self-Evaluation

One of the goals of instruction in any subject area is that of self-evaluation. The children who can look at their progress objectively and discuss their strengths and weaknesses have achieved a valuable goal. Checklists based on the objectives of social studies are helpful, for they allow children to record their achievement. The process of asking questions about their activities aids children in self-evaluation. Examples of items for such checklists are:

1. Do I try to do my best work?
2. Do I look carefully at all sides of an issue?
3. Do I enjoy working with others?
4. Do I listen carefully to what others have to say?
5. Do I respect others who are different from me?

Another method of self-evaluation involves keeping a record of a series of experiences, for example, in a diary or log. As the children record descriptions of the activities, they should be encouraged to discuss their role and the degree to which they achieved the goal they had established. Children, too, need to realize that there are limitations to their abilities and that they should not set unrealistic goals for themselves.

## LOCAL EVALUATION

Evaluation of social studies instruction by the school district generally is accomplished through standardized achievement tests, evaluation by committees of teachers, and self-evaluation by individual teachers. Standardized tests are administered to determine the children's achievement as compared to the norm for selected groups across the nation. Care should be exercised in interpreting these tests, because children in a specific school may vary considerably in socioeconomic status, experiential background, and intelligence from the groups on which the norms are based. These test results should not be used to compare the teachers' competency nor the pupils' achievement from year to year. These tests do, however, indicate areas of instruction (for example, map-reading skills or sequential relationships) in which groups of children score low and therefore need additional instruction.

The *Sixth Mental Measurement Yearbook* provides information about the most recently published tests. This information includes a discussion of the test, price, and publisher. *Tests in Print* is another resource that briefly describes all tests available.

A selected list of standardized achievement tests for elementary school follows:

> *Sequential Tests of Educational Progress: Social Studies, 1063, Grades 4–6.* Cooperative Test Division, Educational Testing Service, Princeton, N.J.
>
> *Stanford Achievement Test: Intermediate and Advanced Social Studies, Grades 5–9* (New York: Harcourt Brace Jovanovich, 1954).
>
> *Metropolitan Achievement Tests: Social Studies, Grades 5–6* (New York: Harcourt Brace Jovanovich, 1964).

Committees of teachers selected across school and grade levels are frequently assigned the task of evaluating the social studies program for the school district. On the basis of the established objectives, they may develop evaluation forms to be used in observing classrooms. The observation forms may be completed by administrators or teacher members of the committee during a visit in the classroom. The disadvantage of this method of evaluation is the limited time available for observation in each classroom.

Formal models of evaluation have been developed that provide guidelines for districts to use in the collection of evaluation data. One example, supplied by Robert Stake, suggests a matrix of description and judgment with three main bodies of information: antecedents, transactions, and outcomes.[5]

Teacher self-evaluation forms also may be developed to be completed by individual teachers. This type of evaluation gives the teachers the opportunity to evaluate their programs of instruction in terms of the standards established by a school district. If such a self-evaluation form is not a part of the school-district evaluation, teachers may devise their own checklist.

More recently, evaluation has been attempted through the use of videotaping, interaction analysis, and team-teaching observation. Use of a portable videotape machine permits televising of a segment of the instruction conducted in the classroom. Preserving the experience on tape allows teachers to view the lesson later by themselves with a supervisor to determine its effectiveness.

Interaction analysis has been researched by numerous educators, including Marie Hughes, B. Othaniel Smith, Donald Medley and Harold Mitzel, John Withall, and Ned Flanders. Category systems have been developed to classify verbal interaction in the classroom. These systems consist of the establishment of basic categories for teacher talk, student talk, and silence to determine the amount and type of verbal interaction. Tape recordings of class sessions can be made for later categorization of the verbal interaction, or trained observers can use the category systems during live sessions. Most researchers emphasize that these systems are not directed toward evaluation per se, but rather toward the improvement of instruction. Their aim is to move away from teacher-talk-dominated instruction toward more verbal interaction from the students.

Team-teaching situations permit evaluation of instruction in group sessions by team members. As one member of the team is presenting a lesson, other team members can observe and analyze the results of the instruction. Close faculty cooperation is necessary to permit open discussion of the methods and techniques used during the teaching. Self-evaluation also can be accomplished by a team member as he or she observes another's teaching.

At the state level, the primary purpose for evaluation is to determine the extent of curriculum revision necessary, if any. The state of Oregon divided the state into ten regional districts for preevaluation before attempting any revision. California organized a Statewide Social Science Study Committee, which included classroom teachers and social science educators, to analyze the social studies curriculum of the state. The result was the abridgement of the new curriculum. Pennsylvania conducted an Educational Quality Assessment in which ten broad goals were selected.[6]

## NATIONAL EVALUATION

Evaluation of instructional programs has been undertaken at the national level in recent years. Different groups of teachers, scholars, and curriculum specialists from across the nation have been engaged to develop instruments of evaluation. The National Assessment of Educational Progress, a study funded by the United States government, states as its purpose "to find out what Americans know, believe, and are able to do. It is an attempt to find out about such attainments in most fields of study considered important in American schools; for example, reading, language arts, science, mathematics, social studies, citizenship, fine arts, and vocational education."[7] Notice that social studies and citizenship are to be assessed separately.

Before test items were written, the objectives of social studies education were developed. These objectives were formulated by a panel of scholars, teachers, and curriculum specialists and were submitted to a panel of citizens for approval. Five major objectives were established:

1. Within the limits of his maturity, a person competent in the area of social studies uses analytic, scientific procedures effectively.
2. A person competent in the area of social studies had knowledge relevant to the major ideas and concerns of social scientists.
3. He has a reasonable commitment to the values that sustain a free society.
4. He has curiosity about human affairs.
5. He is sensitive to creative-intuitive methods of explaining the condition.[8]

"On the basis of these objectives, a series of test items will be devised for varying age levels. Interviews, free response, and questionnaires will also be utilized. Data will be obtained for boys and girls, geographic regions, four age groups; 9, 13, 17 year-olds, and adults; urban, suburban, and rural, and two socioeconomic levels."[9] Concern was expressed that the evaluation would be used to compare school districts, schools, and teachers. But because the data will be compiled in categories as stated above, there will be no way to compare different school districts, schools, teachers, or children.

Reports of the findings are from the Citizenship and Social Studies Sections given in the 1969–70 and 1971–72 assessments. Some changes in the objectives were made before the next assessment. A sample of results from the 1969–70 assessment follows: Citizenship Goal D was "know the main structure and function of Government."[10] Forty-eight percent of the 9-year-olds, 81 percent of the 13-year-olds, and 90 percent of the 17-year-olds stated a reason for having a government.[11] Assessments will be made every five years.

A center for the Study of Evaluation, a Research and Development Center funded by the U.S. Office of Education and located at the University of California at Los Angeles, has been developing a very complete model for the whole process of evaluation.[12]

Evaluation of an educational program—whether at the national, state, local, or classroom level—is an attempt to determine what the instruction has accomplished. It cannot be completed, however, without goals or objectives as guideposts. Research has indicated that "evaluation is not really done well on any large scale; vague or ambiguous objectives contribute heavily to a lack of comprehensive evaluation; in most cases evaluation is regarded as being synonymous with grading and testing; and evaluation is not viewed as an integral part of instruction."[13] Thus, teachers must assess the needs and abilities of the children, identify that which is to be the result of their instruction, plan the learning experiences, expose the children to them, and then evaluate to determine the success of their programs.

## SUMMARY

In the beginning of this book, attention was drawn to the fact that children and teachers come to the classrooms with different needs, abilities, values, hopes, and aspirations. The success with which these needs and abilities are assessed and the hopes and aspirations met will be to some extent dependent upon the effectiveness of the evaluation process.

## NOTES

1. From Dorothy J. Skeel and Owen Hagen, *The Process of Curriculum Change* (Santa Monica, Calif.: Goodyear, 1971), pp. 81–83.
2. Dialogue from Dorothy J. Skeel, *Children of the Street: Teaching in the Inner City* (Santa Monica, Calif.: Goodyear, 1972), pp. 27–31.
3. Educational Testing Service, Cooperative Test Division, Princeton, N.J. *Making Your Own Tests*, p. 15.
4. ETS, *Making Your Own Tests*, pp. 1–7.
5. Dennis D. Gooler, "Evaluation and Change in the Social Studies," *Education Products Report* 3 (October 1969):6–13.
6. *Educational Quality Assessment*, Pennsylvania Department of Education, 1970.
7. Dana Kurfman, "A National Assessment of Social Studies Education," *Social Education* 31 (March 1967):210–211.
8. "A National Assessment of Social Studies Education," pp. 210–211.
9. Ibid., p. 209.
10. National Assessment of Educational Progress, *National Assessment Report 2: Citizenship, 1969–70*. Educational Commission of the States, Denver, 1972, p. 42.
11. *Citizenship Report 2, op. cit.* p. 43.
12. Irving Morrissett, "Accountability, Needs Assessment, and Social Studies," *Social Education* 37 (April 1973):271.
13. Joseph Decaroli, "What Research Says to the Classroom Teacher/Evaluation," *Social Education* 36 (April 1972):433.

## SELECTED REFERENCES

Berg, Harry, ed. *Evaluation in Social Studies.* 35th Yearbook. Washington, D.C.: National Council for the Social Studies, 1965.

Bloom, Benjamin S., ed. *Taxonomy of Educational Objectives: Cognitive Domain.* New York: David McKay, 1956.

Campbell, Vincent N., and Nichols, Daryl G. "National Assessment of Citizenship Education." *Social Education* 32 (March 1968):279.

Chase, W. Linwood, and John, Martha Tyler. *A Guide for the Elementary Social Studies Teacher.* 2d ed. Boston: Allyn & Bacon, 1972.

Dal Santo, John. "Guidelines for School Evaluation." *Clearing House* (November 1970):181–185.

Eulie, Joseph. "Meaningful Tests in Social Studies." *Clearing House* (February 1971):333–336.

Gooler, Dennis D. "Evaluation and Change in the Social Studies." *Education Products Report* 3 (October 1969):6–13.

Krathwohl, David R.; Bloom, Benjamin S.; and Mesia, Bertram B. *Taxonomy of Educational Objectives: Affective Domain.* New York: David McKay, 1964.

Kurfman, Dana, ed. *Developing Decision-Making Skills.* 47th Yearbook. Washington, D.C.: National Council for the Social Studies, 1977.

———. "A National Assessment of Social Studies Education." *Social Education* 31 (March 1967):209–211.

Michaelis, John U., ed. *Social Studies in Elementary Schools.* 32nd Yearbook. Washington, D.C.: National Council for the Social Studies, 1962.

Morrissett, Irving. "Accountability, Needs Assessment, and Social Studies." *Social Education* 38 (April 1973):271–279.

NCSS Examines Aspects of the National Assessment of Educational Progress. *Social Education* (May 1974):397–430.

# Appendix 1

**CRITERIA FOR EVALUATING TEXTBOOK MATERIALS**

Subject _____

Grade Level of Materials ____

Student's Name _____

Textbooks evaluated were: (a) _____

(b) _____

Ratings on the form should be for the textbook you choose as the better of the two. Put an * by that book title. Comments should indicate why you made that choice. Evaluate this book in terms of the following scale:

SCALE: 0–2 No or little extent
3–4 To some extent
5–6 Great extent

I. SUBJECT MATTER CONTENT

1. To what extent do the materials focus on the major concepts and/or big ideas?  0 1 2 3 4 5 6
Comments:

2. To what extent is the subject matter geared to a variety of interests, and the physical, mental, and social abilities of the students for which the materials are being considered?  0 1 2 3 4 5 6
Comments:

(SOURCE: Adapted from Indiana's 1974 Social Studies Adoption Evaluation Form.)

3. To what extent does the content of the textbooks—both the pictorial and written content—reflect the pluralistic, multiethnic nature of our society, both past and present?
Comments:

0 1 2 3 4 5 6

4. To what extent does the material depict both female and male members of various groups in society in situations which exhibit them unbiasedly in a wide variety of roles?
Comments:

0 1 2 3 4 5 6

5. To what extent is the role of the various religious and socioeconomic groups, both past and present, accurately and fairly presented?
Comments:

0 1 2 3 4 5 6

6. To what extent does the book tend to encourage a positive self-image for children of all ethnic groups?
Comments:

0 1 2 3 4 5 6

7. To what extent does the author stress the importance of rational thought in discovering and testing the validity of values: e.g.,
   a. supporting opinions with facts?
   b. defining the nature of the value conflict?
Comments:

0 1 2 3 4 5 6

8. To what extent do the books support the use   0  1  2  3  4  5  6
   of higher level questions?
   Comments:

9. Can the textbook function as a basis for   0  1  2  3  4  5  6
   decision making?
   Comments:

10. Does the textbook consistently relate the   0  1  2  3  4  5  6
    knowledge presented to the immediate concerns of the learner?
    Comments:

11. Does the textbook present a well-sequenced   0  1  2  3  4  5  6
    program of map and globe skills?
    Comments:

II. ORGANIZATION

1. To what extent can the teacher depart from   0  1  2  3  4  5  6
   the sequence of materials prescribed by the
   author without impairing the effectiveness
   of the materials?
   Comments:

2. To what extent are the materials arranged   0  1  2  3  4  5  6
   to clarify the scope and aims of individual
   lessons, units, and sections?
   Comments:

III. VOCABULARY AND READABILITY

    1. To what extent does the language of the materials accommodate the range of abilities and backgrounds of the students most likely to be using the materials?    0 1 2 3 4 5 6
Comments:

    2. To what extent do the materials provide suggested strategies for the range of reading abilities of the students most likely to be using the materials?    0 1 2 3 4 5 6
Comments:

IV. TEACHER'S EDITIONS

    1. To what extent does the Teacher's Edition combine reproductions of the pupil's page and lesson plans?    0 1 2 3 4 5 6
Comments:

    2. To what extent does the Teacher's Edition provide optional as well as specific instructional procedures and interesting activities?    0 1 2 3 4 5 6
Comments:

    3. To what extent is the Teacher's Edition clear in format and an effective guide for the instructional program?    0 1 2 3 4 5 6
Comments:

## V. TEACHING AIDS

1. To what extent do the book and materials have accompanying audio-visual aids, including records, filmstrips, film, tapes, laboratory kits, and skill cards?   0 1 2 3 4 5 6
Comments:

2. To what extent are testing materials available?   0 1 2 3 4 5 6

3. To what extent are the appendices and bibliography adequate in terms of scope and content?   0 1 2 3 4 5 6

## VI. PHYSICAL MAKE-UP

1. To what extent does the format of the materials attract and hold a child's interest?   0 1 2 3 4 5 6

2. To what extent are the books substantial with durable bindings?   0 1 2 3 4 5 6

3. To what extent are the printing, graphics, and visuals suitable for the grade level being considered?   0 1 2 3 4 5 6
Comments:

# Appendix 2

## EVALUATION OF TEACHING AIDS

Name of teaching aid being considered _____
Name of manufacturer _____
Address of manufacturer _____
Type of product (i.e., manipulative materials, film, slides, game, etc.) _____
Discipline(s) in which the product might be used _____
Cost _____  Grade levels _____
Designed to foster concepts \_\_\_, skills \_\_\_, attitude \_\_\_

I   Instructions: List the rating you wish to make for each criterion: 3-excellent, 2-good, 1-fair, 0-not useful. Add all the ratings and determine the overall rating by using the following scale:
    33-42 excellent: highly recommended for purchase and use
    23-32 good: recommended for purchase and use
    13-22 fair: not recommended for purchase and use
    0-12 not useful: not considered useful

## CRITERIA

\_\_\_ 1. Approach suggested for use of the aid
\_\_\_ 2. Concept, skill, and/or attitude development
\_\_\_ 3. Extent of provisions for individual differences
\_\_\_ 4. Can be used by children individually \_\_\_ or in small groups \_\_\_ (Check one.)
\_\_\_ 5. Interest appeal to students (Do you think the product can be used in a way students will find interesting?
\_\_\_ 6. Can be used frequently during the year
\_\_\_ 7. Can be used for more than one grade level
\_\_\_ 8. Made of durable materials
\_\_\_ 9. Easily stored
\_\_\_ 10. Practicality
\_\_\_ 11. Learning device vs. busywork
\_\_\_ 12. Expectations of teacher for demonstration
\_\_\_ 13. Commercial product vs. teacher-made product (If a similar aid were made by the teacher, would utility and attractiveness diminish?)
\_\_\_ 14. Appropriate level of difficulty of content or format for intended age level

\_\_\_ Total points \_\_\_ Rating of the aid

II  Respond briefly to the following questions.

1. What concepts, skills, and/or attitudes are the product likely to foster?

2. Are the objectives cited in (1) above appropriate for the elementary-school curriculum?

3. Does this material lend itself to the integration of at least two areas among science, social studies, mathematics, and health? Explain.

4. What aspect of the product will make students interested?

5. Compare the quality of the product with the cost to determine the desirability of purchase.

Additional Comments:

# Photo Credits

*Page*

| | |
|---|---|
| xvi | Cary Wolinsky, Stock, Boston |
| 68 | Marshall Licht, The Stockmarket, L.A. |
| 160 | Frank Siteman, Stock, Boston |
| 194 | Owen Franken, Stock, Boston |
| 242 | Cary Wolinsky, Stock, Boston |
| 262 | Marshall Licht, The Stockmarket, L.A. |

Cover photo by Cary Wolinsky, Stock, Boston.

# Index

Activities
  culminating, 126–127
  individual and group, 124
  initiation, 121
  inquiry, 99–110
  integrating, 125
  map and globe, 230–237
  multicultural, 150ff
Anthropology
  concepts, 30, 34
  definition, 30
  importance, 34
  method of inquiry, 30, 34
  perspective, 31–33
Arnsdoff, Val, 240
Attitudes
  definition, 11
  measurement, 12
Ausubel, D. P., 111, 112

Bacon, Phillip, 36, 229, 240
Bailey, Wilfred, 56
Bandwagon technique, 168–169
Banks, James A., 15, 66, 158
Baptiste, H. Prentice, 153, 158, 159
Baptiste, Mira, 153, 158, 159
Barth, James L., 14, 15
Becker, James, 192
Behavioral objectives
  attitudes and values, 11–12
  definition, 9–10
  knowledge, 10
  skills, 13–14
Bereiter, Carl, 140, 157
Berg, Harry, 284
Bernstein, Jean, 208
Berryman, Charles, 175
Beyer, Barry K., 36, 66, 86, 112
Bloom, Benjamin, 111, 284
Borton, Terry, 216
Broek, Jan O. M., 36, 239
Brubaker, Dale L., 15, 112
Bruner, Jerome, 41, 70, 85, 86, 88, 111, 112

Career Development Curriculum, 58
Carpenter, Helen McCracken, 197, 240
Cartoons, 249
Cartwright, William H., 37
Castillo, Gloria A., 216
Chase, Larry, 215
Chase, W. Linwood, 15, 175, 284
Checklist, 267
Children
  description, 2, 3
Children's interests, 117–119
  directing, 119
Children's trade books
  criteria for selection, 244
  fiction, 245–246
  informational, 245
Classroom atmosphere, 4, 5, 94, 117, 141, 184
Classrooms
  description, 4, 5
Clements, H. Millard, 111
Committee work
  description, 209
  organization, 210
  teacher-pupil planning, 210
Communication skills
  debate, 225
  oral and written reports, 224
  panel discussions, 224
  reading, 217
  role playing, 225
Concept
  definition, 17–18
  extending, 79, 84–85
  interdisciplinary, 72
  introducing, 79–84
  multidisciplinary, 72, 74–76
  teaching, 70ff
Conceptual framework, 18, 73ff
Conditions of change, 39ff
Controversial issues, 169
  economic 171–172
  environmental, 173–175
  political, 172–173

Controversial issues (continued)
  social, 170–171
Cox, Benjamin, 112
Crabtree, Charlotte, 55
Crowder, William, 175
Crystal, Josie, 158
Crump, Claudia, 158
Current affairs activities, 164
  bulletin boards, 164
  class newspaper, 165
  news reporting, 165
  objectives, 163
  reading newspapers, 166
  role playing, 166
Curriculum development
  decision making, 63–64
  historical perspective, 39–42
  local conditions, 42
  national agencies and projects, 55–63
  program planning, 63–64
  sample program, 45–49
  state requirements and guidelines, 50–54
Curriculum projects
  Career Development, 58
  Development of a Sequential Curriculum in Anthropology for Grades 1–7, 56
  Family of Man, 56
  Global perspectives, 58
  Intergroup Relations Curriculum, 56
  MACOS, 58
  MATCH, 58
  Rights and responsibilities, 56
  Social Science Laboratory Units, 56
  Taba program, 59–63

Davison, Susan, 66
DeCaroli, Joseph G., 113, 283
Deutsch, Martin, 64
Dewey, John, 111
Dunfee, Maxine, 111, 158

Easton, David, 36
Economics
  concepts, 26, 34
  definition, 26

Economics (continued)
  importance, 34
  issues, 171–172
  method of inquiry, 27, 34
  perspective, 27, 28
Educational goals, 8, 44, 63–65
Educational Testing Service, 278
Elkins, Deborah, 16
Ellis, Arthur K., 15, 112, 113
Emotionalized words, 168–169
Engleman, Siegfried, 140, 157
Environmental factors, 42, 136ff
Environmental issues, 20ff, 173ff
Evaluation
  analyzing questions, 273–277
  anecdotal records, 268
  checklists, 267
  classroom, 264–266
  conferences, 269
  group discussions, 270
  local evaluation, 279
  national assessment, 281–282
  problem solving, 271
  rating scales, 268
  self-evaluation, 279
  standardized tests, 280
  teacher-made tests, 277
  valuing, 271–272
Experiential background, 42, 136ff
Exploratory questioning, 121

Fair, Jean, 111, 112
Fielder, William R., 111
Ford, G. W., 86, 87
Fox, Robert, 56, 66, 98, 111
Fraenkel, Jack R., 87, 208, 227
Friedlander, Bernard Z., 111, 112

Gagné, Robert M., 15, 83, 86
Games, 246–248
Gay, Geneva, 158
Geography
  concepts, 21, 34
  definition, 21
  importance, 34
  method of inquiry, 21, 34
  perspective, 22, 23
Gibson, John S., 56, 64
Giese, James, 158
Gillespie, Judith, 260

# INDEX

Gillespie, Margaret C., 15
Global education, 66
Global perspective
  activities, 188–190
  curriculum materials, 180–183
  implementation, 183–187
  objectives, 178–179
  problems, 187–188
Goldmark, Bernice, 112
Grambs, Jean Dresden, 158
Grant, Gloria, 158
Graphs, 251–254
Gratz, Pauline, 175
Gronlund, Norman E., 15
Gross, Norman, 66

Hagen, Owen, 283
Hanna, Lavonne, 135
Hanna, Paul, 39, 86, 240
Hansen, lorraine Sundal, 66
Herman, Wayne L., Jr., 15
Hill, Wilhelmina, 135
History
  concepts, 19, 34
  definition, 19, 20, 21
  importance, 19, 34
  method of inquiry, 34
Hoffman, Alan J., 66
Hopkins, Lee, 135
Howitt, Lillian, 175
Huus, Helen, 220

Individual activities, 124
Inductive reasoning, 88
Initiation
  problem solving, 99
  unit, 121ff
Inn, Agnes M., 86
Inquiry, 88ff
  activities, 99ff
  model, 98
  objectives, 97
Integrating activities, 125
Interdisciplinary
  definition, 71, 72
  program, 76ff
Interest inventory, 119
Intergroup Relations Curriculum, 56, 64
Introduction, 1–68
Investigating Man's World, 74ff

Jarolimek, John, 15, 66, 135, 176
John, Martha Tyler, 15, 175, 284
Johnston, Montgomery, 36, 37
Joint Council on Economic Education, 55
Joyce, Bruce R., 15, 70, 86, 87, 135, 260

Kenworthy, Leonard, 15, 190
Kneller, George F., 15
Knowledge
  definition, 10
  evaluation, 266
Kohlberg, Lawrence, 199–200, 207
Krathwohl, David, 111, 284
Kurfman, Dana, 283, 284

La Benne, Wallace D., 216
Law related education, 58
Lee, John R., 15, 55, 240
Lesser, Gerald, 157
Lippitt, Ronald, 56, 66, 98, 111
Lohman, John, 112
Lundstrum, John P., 228

MacDonald, Gordon J. F., 36
Mackey, James, 208
MACOS, 58–59
McAulay, John D., 16, 135, 218, 227, 240
McCune, Shirley, 66
McNamara, Robert S., 190
Mager, Robert F., 9, 15
Magic Circle, 212–215
Mallen, John T., 16
Map skills
  globes, 237
  grade level, 230–232
  intermediate, 233
  primary, 232–233
  problems, 233–236
  urban, 237
Martin, Richard S., 36
Martorella, Peter, 15, 87
Massialas, Byron, 112
MATCH, 58, 257
Materials, 244–260
  cartoons, 249
  children's trade books, 244

Materials (continued)
　films and filmstrips, 257
　free and inexpensive, 256
　games, 246
　graphs and charts, 251–254
　multimedia, 257
　pictures, 254
　programmed, 248
　simulation, 246–248
　textbooks, 255
Mathews, Martha, 66
Metcalf, Lawrence, 208
Methodology, 69–159
　concept, 70ff
　inquiry, 88ff
　multicultural, 136ff
　unit, 114ff
Michaelis, John U., 15, 36, 37, 55, 114, 134, 176, 284
Miller, John P., 216
Miller, Rueben G., 36
Moncrief, Lewis M., 36
Moore, Virginia D., 36, 87
Morris, Donald, 191
Morrissett, Irving, 87, 283, 284
Muessig, Raymond H., 37, 66
Multicultural education, 136–159
　culturally disadvantaged, 136–152
　ethnic and racial minority, 152
　physically and mentally handicapped, 155–156
　sex stereotyping, 156–157
Multidisciplinary
　definition, 72, 73
　program, 74ff
Multimedia, 257

Name calling, 168–169
National assessment, 283
National Council for Geographic Education, 55
National Council for the Social Studies, 55
Newspaper
　class, 165, 167
　reading, 166

Objectives
　behavioral, 9–14
　current affairs, 163
　global education, 178–179

Objectives (continued)
　multicultural education, 136
　problem solving, 97ff
　unit, 115–116
Oldham, Sally, 191

Palomares, Uvaldo, 192
Passow, A. Harry, 157
Pasternak, Michael, 158
Pelto, Pertti J., 36
Philosophy, 33
Plain-folks technique, 168–169
Political science
　concepts, 23, 34,
　definition, 23
　importance, 34
　method of inquiry, 23, 34
　perspective, 24, 25
Problem solving, 88ff
Preston, Ralph C., 15
Price, Roy, 55, 87
Project Social Studies, 55–57
Propaganda techniques, 168–169
Psychology, 33
Pugno, Lawrence, 86, 87

Questioning
　definition, 89
　levels, 90–94
　strategies, 90–94

Ragan, William B., 16, 135
Raths, Louis, 200, 208
Reading
　group, 220
　questioning, 218–219
　vocabulary, 219
Reference materials, 221
　locating information, 223
　outlining and notetaking, 223
Remy, R. C., 192
Reflective thinking, 88
Resource unit, 114ff
Rice, Marion, 56
Riessman, Frank, 140, 157
Rogers, Vincent R., 37
Rokeach, Milton, 15, 201
Role playing
　current affairs, 166
　inquiry, 103ff

# INDEX

Role playing (continued)
 multicultural, 150
 values, 206
Rose, Sanford, 36
Rosen, Bernard, 208
Ryan, Frank, 16, 112
Ryan, Thomas F., 66
Rushdoony, Haig A., 240

Sagl, Helen, 111
Schaible, Lucille, 56
Schwab, Joseph, 70, 86, 87, 111, 113
Seif, Elliott, 16
Self-evaluation, 279
Shaftel, Fannie, 111, 112, 151, 158
Shermis, S. Samuel, 14, 15
Shirts, Gary, 191
Simon, Lawrence H., 15
Simon, Sidney, 200, 201, 208
Simulation, 246–248
Skeel, Dorothy J., 113, 135, 158, 159, 191, 208, 228, 283
Skills
 communication, 217ff
 interpersonal, 209–215
 map and globe, 229
 valuing, 199–208
Smith, James A., 228
Social sciences
 anthropology, 30ff
 concepts, 17–19
 definition, 17
 economics, 26ff
 geography, 21ff
 history, 19ff
 philosophy, 33
 psychology, 33
 sociology, 29ff
Social Science Laboratory Units, 56
Social studies
 attitudes, 11
 definition, 5–8
 knowledge, 10
 objectives, developing, 8
 instructional, 9
 skills, 13
 understanding, 10
 values, 11, 12
Sociology
 concepts, 29, 34
 definition, 29
 importance, 34

Sociology (continued)
 method of inquiry, 29, 34
 perspective, 29, 30
Sourauf, Frank J., 36
Sterling, Ronald E., 112, 191
Standardized tests, 280
Stodolsky, Susan, 157
Suchman, Richard, 113

Taba, Hilda, 16, 66, 82, 85, 87, 111
Tabachnick, B. Robert, 111
Teacher-made tests, 277ff
Teacher-pupil planning, 122
Teachers
 description, 3, 4
Tennyson, W. Wesley, 66
Textbooks
 criteria, 255
 reading, 217
 utilization, 255ff
Thomas, John L., 87
Thompson, A. Gray, 15
Torney, Judith V., 191
Turner, Thomas, 227

Unit development
 advantages and disadvantages, 134
 conditions of classroom, 117
 culminating activities, 126–127
 directing children's interests, 119
 evaluation, 127
 initiation, 121
 objectives, 115–116
 organization, 114
 role of children, 117
 role of teacher, 116
 sample unit, 127–137
 selection, 117
 teacher/pupil planning, 122
Unruh, Glenys, 158

Valuing
 cognitive-developmental, 199
 evaluation, 271–272
 values analysis, 203
 values clarification, 200

Walsh, Huber M., 260
Ward, Barbara, 176

Ward, Paul, 36
Watson, Richard L., Jr., 37
Webster, Staten W., 16, 157
Welton, David, 16
Wentworth, Donald, 260
Williams, Jo Watts, 15
Williams, Marianne E. T., 208

Wisconsin State Department of Public Instruction, 36, 50–54, 64
Wisniewski, Richard, 159, 240
Womack, James G., 87
Wood, Jayne Millar, 177, 191

Zacharias, Jerrold R., 41